NEW

BEGINNINGS

by

Graysen Morgen

2022

New Beginnings © 2022 Graysen Morgen
Triplicity Publishing, LLC

ISBN-13: 978-1-970042-19-1
ISBN-10: 1-970042-19-2

This is a work of fiction. Names, characters, places, and incidents are the product of the author's imagination and are used fictitiously. Any resemblance to actual persons, living or dead, business establishments, events of any kind, or locales is entirely coincidental.

Printed in the United States of America
First Edition – 2022
Cover Design: Triplicity Publishing, LLC
Interior Design: Triplicity Publishing, LLC
Editor: Megan Brady - Triplicity Publishing, LLC

Also by Graysen Morgen

Boone Creek (Law & Order Series: book 1)

Castor Valley (Law & Order Series: book 2)

Never Let Go (Never Series: book 1)

Never Quit (Never Series: book 2)

Bridesmaid of Honor (Bridal Series: book 1)

Brides (Bridal Series: book 2)

Mommies (Bridal Series: book 3)

Crossed Reins

Real Love

Playing the Game

Mission Compromised

Meant to Be

Coming Home

Crashing Waves

Cypress Lake

Falling Snow

Fast Pitch

Fate vs. Destiny

In Love, at War

Just Me

Love, Loss, Revenge

Natural Instinct

Secluded Heart

Submerged

Special thanks to my editor, Megan Brady.
Muchas gracias!

For my son.
B'fhéidir go bhfeicfimid go léir an domhan trí do shúile.

Prologue

BANG! POP! BANG…BANG!

"Damn it!" a strong female voice yelled. She took a few deep breaths, trying to calm her racing heart. "I hate the 4th of July," she grumbled. "I hate being home on the 4th of July," she added, pulling the pillow over her head as another round of fireworks popped. "I hate being home," she sighed, tossing the bedding away. She swung her feet to the side, placing them on the soft carpet, then she stood up and walked out of the room.

The full bathroom at the end of the hall seemed smaller than it had when she was a kid. Looking at the tattoos littering her muscled arms in the mirror, she realized it was probably because she was a lot bigger than she had been at ten years old. She ran her hand through her short blonde hair. It was a tad longer on top than the closely cropped, faux hawk style she usually wore it in. "I need a trim," she mumbled to the grass-colored eyes staring back at her. She splashed cold water onto her face, and dried it on the nearby towel, before walking back to the room.

She glanced around as she replaced her pajama shorts with a pair of well-worn jeans. Pictures and awards from Village High School Rugby Team and Moore County Rugby Club adorned one wall. An Army: *Be All You Can Be* poster was on another. Looking over at the full-size bed with a blue camouflage patterned comforter, she shoved her hands into her front pockets and walked back out of the room.

"I knew those fireworks would wake you," Patty Malloy stated, hearing footsteps coming down the stairs. "John and Barbara have their grandkids all week," she added, glancing up from the magazine she was reading in time to see her daughter enter the room, looking slightly disheveled. "I should've warned you when you said you were coming here for the weekend."

"It's fine." *They did a lot more than wake me.*

"Do you want me to make you something?" Patty asked.

"No. I need to get back to my apartment," her daughter replied, returning with a glass of water. She'd driven up to spend some time with her mother before deploying again soon.

Patty stared at her only child, trying to read what was on her mind. Then again, she wasn't sure she wanted to know. Tristan Cecile Malloy was so much like her father. They both had the same demeanor and good looks that turned heads. Except, Tristan had been blessed with her mother's blonde hair, instead of her father's brown locks. Having grown up as a rugby player, Tristan also had her father's strong build. Even at thirty-one years old, she was ripped like a twenty-year-old competitive CrossFit athlete. But her hours in the gym were no longer for sport. Instead, she'd kept herself in top form for the last thirteen years because of the Army and the grueling duties that came with being in Special Forces.

No, Patty definitely didn't want to know what her daughter was thinking about. She couldn't imagine what it was like to deploy for weeks or months at a time to the middle of a war zone, then come home for a couple of weeks…only to go right back again. Her daughter didn't talk about what she did or the things she saw…and Patty never asked.

Tristan's life had fallen apart when her father had passed away at the beginning of her senior year of high school. She was captain of the school rugby team, a rugby club champion, and on track to be the valedictorian for her class. Donald Malloy was killed in a car accident when a pile up happened on the interstate. He was Tristan's world and vice versa. Her grades slipped and she was nearly kicked off the rugby team. Her mother and her coach encouraged her to keep playing because her father would've wanted her to, but when the college letters came in, she tossed them in the trash. Patty was shocked when Tristan came home one afternoon, two weeks before graduation, and stated she'd joined the Army. She thought it was a phase that Tristan would grow out of when her four years were up, but here she was thirteen years later. Not only was she still in the Army, but she had thrown her heart and soul into it, just like she'd done with rugby, and had become a well-respected commissioned officer in her battalion. She worked hard physically and mentally and demanded the same from the team of soldiers she led.

*

Tristan checked her phone when she sat down on the couch. There was one missed call with a voicemail. She recognized the number as being from the base, so she listened to the message.

Captain Tristan Malloy, your deployment has been changed. Please contact your Company Liaison for details and further instruction.

"Shit," she mumbled, hanging up and dialing a phone number. The liaison line rang twice before a voicemail message picked up.

"Charlie Company, SFODD421B. You are moving out at nineteen hundred. Report to your commanding officer or team leader by fifteen hundred."

Tristan ended the call and checked the black, military grade watch on her left wrist. It was already eleven hundred.

"Everything okay?" Patty asked.

"Yeah. Our deployment got moved up. I need to get over to the base."

"You're leaving earlier? I thought you had another week or two."

"Things changed, I guess. We're leaving tonight."

Patty sighed. She hated the Army. "Well, let me rearrange my schedule."

"You don't have to see me off every time I leave," Tristan said, smiling at her mother. She was beautiful, and the epitome of sophistication with long, slightly graying, blonde strands that bounced along her shoulders, high cheek bones, and a pronounced nose. Patty never went outside unkempt, and certainly never left her house without being properly dressed. She reminded Tristan of a Diane Keaton and Jane Fonda, meshed together.

"You're my only child. I'll do as I please. Besides, I'm driving over anyway to meet Gretchen and help her with Caleb's wedding reception. The table assignments are a downright mess."

"Alright. I'll head over to my apartment now and pack my deployment bag. Want to meet at Louie's in two hours?" It sounded like a dump and looked it on the outside, but inside, Louie's was one of the finest dining

4

restaurants in Fayetteville, North Carolina, and close to the base and Tristan's apartment.

"That's fine. Get a table for three if you get there before I do. Gretchen has been in a tizzy over this wedding. She'll probably need a drink when we're finished."

Tristan laughed. Her mother was hardest on the people she was closest too, and her sister Gretchen was no exception.

Chapter 1

Tristan faced the mirror, dressed in her Army Combat Uniform. The mixture of muted green, light beige, and dark brown camouflage made her eyes look darker than their natural grass color. Out of habit, she pressed down on all the embroidered patches called tabs, which clung to her uniform with military grade Velcro. Her rank insignia tab, consisting of two wide parallel bars, was in the center of her chest. Malloy, her last name, and Army, for her branch of service, were both on her upper chest. Her left shoulder sleeve insignia was for her unit; a shield-shaped flash with red stitching, and two curved tabs were above it; one with: Special Forces and the other with: Ranger. A subdued American flag was on her right shoulder sleeve insignia. Both her rank and American flag tabs also had infrared in them, allowing her to be identified as friendly in case of an attack at night.

"Here we go," she said to the eyes staring back at her as she closed her jacket and slipped the green beret on her head. The distinct black and red insignia patch of her unit was front and center on the beret and her rank was pinned in the middle of it.

*

The prop noise of the C27 Spartan plane buzzed in Tristan's ears over the AirPods that played music from the playlist on her phone. After a brief stop at a base in Texas to pick up some cargo, they were finally on their way to

South America. With the extra cargo towards the rear, Tristan had an unobstructed view across the plane to where her team was seated along the wall. Her eyes traced the outline of each one of them.

Sergeant First Class Oliver Nigel was the communications expert, and navigator when needed. His Hispanic heritage gave him naturally tan skin and dark hair that he wore in a traditional 'high and tight' military cut. He was the one who tried too hard but was also the prankster.

Next to him was Sergeant Dana Perry, the team medic, and only other female. She had slightly longer than shoulder-length strawberry blonde hair that she kept in a tight bun at the back of her head. She wasn't solid muscle like Tristan, but she was strong for her petite size. She gave the boys hell if they needed it and took no shit from them either.

One of two weapons specialists, Staff Sergeant Steven Hoffman, was on the other side of her. He was the team's demolitions expert. His deep brown hair was also high and tight. He was the high-strung personality in the group, always challenging the others to compete with him at something, but Nigel was the one who usually volunteered.

Next to him was Sergeant Anthony Tucker, the engineer. He was extremely smart and could build anything using next to nothing. He had milk chocolate colored skin and black hair that was buzzed as short as you get it without being bald. He was often the one to get between Nigel and Hoffman when one of their competitions got out of hand, so they called him the peacekeeper.

The last man on their team, Chief Warrant Officer 2 Michael Fowler, was sitting right beside Tristan. He was a sharpshooter with a rifle, and her second in command. He had mousy brown hair that was short on the sides with it long enough on top to run his fingers through, and he had the pale skin of a Wisconsin native. He was quiet and reserved, choosing to sit back and watch what went on around him.

Noticing Tristan looking around at everyone, Fowler plucked the right earbud free and leaned closer. "Is there a reason we deployed six hours early?" he asked, slightly yelling so she could hear him over the engines.

Tristan glanced sideways at him and nodded. "It's the Army. They do whatever they feel like doing," was all she said before taking her AirPod and shoving it back in place. She knew a little more than that, but now wasn't the time and place to brief her team. They'd been part of an anti-terrorist operation in South America for a little over a year to stop a drug trafficker and arms dealer who was funding terrorist organizations and supplying them with weapons. The US Army was quietly working out of a joint military base in Colombia. All their missions were planned, executed, and commanded from that base. It didn't compare to being in Baghdad, which was where she was stationed prior, but it was a war zone all the same.

Domingo Torres had been running his drug cartel for the better part of two decades, starting small and building his organization through the continent and into North America. When the South and North American governments came together to try and eliminate him once and for all, a plan was set in motion. The US Army began running covert operations, gathering intel, and cutting off supplies to the cartel a little at a time under the cover of joint military training exercises.

Army 4th Special Forces Group, 2nd Battalion, Charlie Company was stationed in North Carolina and generally deployed all over on special forces operations that would last anywhere from a few weeks to six months, then they'd go back home and wait to go out again. Tristan led the Special Forces Operational Detachment Delta: Bravo Team, and in the fourteen months they'd been part of the operation, they'd been on countless missions around South America, all commanded from the joint base in Colombia. She was never sure where they were headed until they touched down and she was briefed on the mission.

*

When the plane began losing altitude, Tristan opened her eyes, pulled the AirPods from her ears, and tucked them in her rucksack. The rest of the team followed suit, stowing their personal belongings as they moved closer and closer to the ground.

Once the plane touched down and taxied to the destination, they unbuckled their belts and waited to disembark behind the cargo after the rear door was lowered. A man dressed in the same type of combat uniform was waiting for them. Instead of a beret, he wore the more traditional patrol cap. The cluster leaf of his officer rank was embroidered in the center of the front of the cap and his last name was embroidered in black across the back. Tristan brought her team to attention, and everyone saluted him.

"Welcome back to Colombia," Major Roland Irving said, returning their salute. He was their commanding officer while in Colombia and second in charge altogether, while Lieutenant Colonel Kurt Powers commanded the entire operation. "Lt. Col. Powers is waiting for us in the command center. Leave your bags outside. Your team can head over to the barracks when you're finished," he added before turning and walking away.

Tristan fell instep slightly behind him on the left, with her team following in a line behind them as they walked across the flight line and entered the building near the three hangars. The command center covered the entire second floor. This was where the colonel's office was located, as well as the ready room where all the missions were planned, and the comms room where the missions were commanded. Tristan took the stairs two at a time. They'd been deployed to the same base for special ops missions so many times in the last fourteen months, she knew her way around like the back of her hand.

"Bravo Team, welcome back," Lt. Col. Powers stated as he walked out of his office. "Everyone's in the ready room."

Tristan walked inside with her team and filled up the only available seats in the small room. Lt. Col. Powers stepped in behind them and took his place at the front of the room. While he shuffled papers and spoke briefly to Maj. Irving, Tristan looked around. Most everyone in the room was a familiar face, except for three people in the back. Before she could get a good look, the colonel began speaking.

"Good afternoon, everyone. Let me start by welcoming the newest airborne members of our operation: Chief Warrant Officer 3 Courtney Hewitt, Chief Warrant Officer 2 John Maguire, and Sergeant Howie Smith. They are the air crew of an MH-60 Black Hawk, and better known as the Outlaws. They'll be the mission transportation for Third Squad, Bravo Team," Lt. Col. Powers said, looking at Tristan, before readdressing the room.

"Alright. Let's bring everyone up to speed on the latest operation. First Squad - Alpha Team, you'll be meeting with an informant near El Tambo. It's about an hour and a half from here through the mountains. You depart at 0700. Third Squad - Bravo Team, you'll be wheels up with the Outlaws at 0730. You're heading to Mataje on a recon mission. It's on the boarder of Colombia and Venezuela. Second Squad - Charlie Team, you're sitting this one out. Any questions?"

"Alpha Team, at the ready, Sir," their team leader, Captain Judd Dewey, said with a cocky grin towards Tristan.

"Bravo Team, at the ready, Sir," Tristan replied without looking over at him. The two teams had been back and forth on missions since the operation began and had also worked together in Iraq. Judd Dewey and Tristan Malloy were about as friendly as a cat and a dog, but if one needed the other, their job was to be there because that's what soldiers did, especially the green berets.

"Outlaws are ready to kick the tires and light the fires, sir," Chief Hewitt stated.

"Hooah!" he said, using the Army's battle cry, before leaving the room.

As soon as the colonel was gone, Maj. Irving stepped to the front. "You heard the colonel. Everyone, rendezvous with your commander for squad specific instructions. We'll gear up and meet in the hangar at 0630 for the sendoff. Dismissed."

"Well, they wasted no time," Fowler said, standing with Tristan. "I don't see why we had to get here six hours earlier than scheduled though."

She shrugged and mumbled, "I'd rather be here, anyway."

"Excuse me, Captain Malloy?" a female voice stated.

Tristan spun around. The woman standing a few feet away was dressed in the same uniform, but with a maroon beret, which she was holding in her hand. Her Chief Warrant Officer 3 rank was in the center of her chest, a single bar with three black squares. Chocolate brown hair was braided and twisted into a bun behind her head, and matching eyes stared intensely at Tristan. She looked young. Way too young to be an Army helicopter pilot.

"I'm Courtney Hewitt. This is my co-pilot John Maguire and our crew chief, Howie Smith."

Tristan nodded, eyeing both men. Maguire looked like an out of place farm boy with dirty blonde hair, and Smith just looked like a boy in general. She wondered if he was even old enough to drink.

"Is this your first time down here?" Tristan asked, pulling her eyes back to Chief Hewitt.

The woman nodded. "Don't let that fool you. We'll get you where you need to go."

"I don't doubt it. Otherwise, you wouldn't be flying with Special Forces," Tristan stated. "I was referring more to the locals than the terrain. Do any of you speak Spanish?"

Chief Hewitt looked at her crew and everyone shook their heads.

"I suggest you learn some. It'll come in handy when trying to decide who's a friendly and who isn't."

"Noted," Chief Hewitt said with a slight nod.

"If you'll excuse me, I need to catch up to my squad and go claim a rack."

"We actually don't have traditional racks in shared barracks."

"I know. I've lost count of how many times I've been here in the last fourteen months," Tristan replied, walking away.

*

Tristan had been back in Colombia for less than three hours, but it already felt like she'd never left. Nothing had changed since she was deployed there for a multitude of missions only a couple of weeks earlier, except their helo crew. She knew who the Outlaws were. They were one of the highly trained helicopter squadrons fielding attack, transport, and recon helos for special operations, and other classified uses whenever and wherever the Army needed them. However, she didn't know anything about Chief Hewitt. She wasn't sure she even wanted to know. She had enough on her mind with the upcoming mission and keeping her team safe. There was no room for the added worry of a cocky, hotshot young pilot.

The barracks on base were made of old buildings that had been partitioned into small private rooms, allowing the soldiers to at least have some space to themselves, even if it was closet sized. The community bathrooms were separated by gender, and with only about fifty soldiers on their side of the joint base, the women rarely ran into each other, and the men weren't waiting in line daily to brush their teeth or take a shower. The base was one of the oldest in the country, and the Colombian government was only utilizing half of the space. It worked out perfectly for the joint operation. Once the US Army arrived, several upgrades were made to the communications systems, but not much else.

Lieutenant Colonel Powers' Task Force was a full operation. However, it was no bigger than a platoon. It consisted of two Special Forces Operational Detachment Delta squads, both from the 2nd Battalion in the 4th Special Forces Group, and an airborne squadron from a different unit altogether. Each squad gathered intel and did recon, but they also took out targets, when necessary, and almost always...quietly. First Squad was on the ground in Colombia, driving Humvees through the roughest of streets known for gang banging and drug slinging. Second Squad was all airborne and spent their days and nights flying planes and helos all over the continent, tracking the cartel through the air, and taking out targets when necessary. Third Squad was sent all over the continent to lily pads by helo, which are small, mostly remote areas where they gather intel or do recon missions and take out targets quietly. Tristan's team was the Third Squad. The lieutenant colonel also had an Intelligence Detachment. They were the brains of the operation and had their own squads performing different tasks. Each squad in the operation was commanded by a captain. Maj. Irving managed all the captains and was Lt. Col. Powers' second in command.

After changing from her beret to her patrol cap, Tristan left the barracks and headed towards one of the small barren buildings. *Canteen* was roughly painted over the door. It was originally a storage building that had been turned into a rec room with two pool tables, a couple of dart boards, and a TV. Not long after, a makeshift bar was built inside with a handful of ratty old stools placed in front of it. Eventually, a beverage cooler and two beer taps appeared underneath the bar, and three food vending machines lined the back wall near the restroom.

By the time Tristan had started getting deployed to the base, it had become a functioning bar that was tended mostly by privates and a few corporals who were stationed there as part of grounds maintenance, and their sergeant managed the bars operation. Most deployment bases did not serve alcohol, but the Colombian government had provided them with plenty of beer and coffee, so they made use of it.

"Our fearless leader has arrived!"

Tristan looked over to see Nigel, her team's communications specialist waving her over as she removed her cap and went inside. He was standing near one of the pool tables with the stick in his hand, and obviously locked up in a losing game with Hoffman, one of their weapons specialists.

"Nope," she said, shaking her head as she walked back to the vending machines and shoved a few bills in. Two bags of Doritos dropped to the bottom. She hadn't eaten since brunch with her mother and aunt, and the cubed steak they were serving in the dining facility, also known as DFAC or the chow hall, hadn't look all that appealing. She grabbed the bags and quickly tore one open as she walked over to the bar and plopped down on an empty stool. "Jackson, you're still here?" she said, looking at the young corporal working behind the bar.

He nodded. "Can I get you anything, Captain?"

"Bottled water."

A few seconds later, he placed an ice-cold water in front of her. "These came in on the supply shipment today. Until then, we only had about a case and a half left."

"I came in on that plane, too," she said, munching on her chips.

The corporal nodded and placed a napkin on the bar next to Tristan. She looked over to see Chief Hewitt sitting beside her.

"Do you mind sharing? You grabbed the last of the Cool Ranch."

Tristan sighed inwardly and slightly shook her head. "You can buy them for the dollar I spent getting them."

"They're fifty cents a bag," Hewitt laughed.

"I don't have change for a dollar, so it'll cost you the whole thing," Tristan replied seriously.

"You really don't like me, do you?"

"I'd have to know you to like you," Tristan said, getting up from the stool. She grabbed her chips and water, then walked out of the building.

"Is she always a hard ass?" Chief Hewitt muttered, looking at the young guy behind the bar.

"She's a captain. Aren't they all?" He smiled, then stiffened. "No offense to you, of course."

"None taken. I'm only a chief warrant officer, not a captain." She laughed and stuck her hand out. "Courtney Hewitt. It's nice to meet you."

"Mason Jackson," he replied, shaking her hand. "You must be new."

"What gave it away?" She grinned.

"Picking a battle with Captain Malloy."

"Do you know her well?"

"Not really. She's as tough as nails, though."

"How long has she been here?"

"I'm not sure, but it's been quite a bit. Anyway, can I get you a drink?"

"I'm good. Thank you."

"You make friends with everyone," Maguire said, sitting down beside her.

"Not everyone," she muttered to herself.

*

Courtney Hewitt was a third generation Army helicopter pilot. Her grandfather had flown Hueys in medevac missions in Vietnam, and her father had flown Apaches in attack missions during Desert Storm. Both were career men, and both survived their wars. When she'd told them she'd changed her mind about college and decided to join the Army, they weren't happy with her. 'It's a hard life,' they'd both said. She didn't care. All she wanted to do was fly. She'd grown up listening to all their stories. It was her turn. Dropping both of their names on her application to Warrant Officer Flight School had given her a slight leg up on the competition and she was accepted on a fast-track program that was geared towards recruited high school graduates.

Fast forward seven years, and here she was, flying for Airborne Special Forces and deployed on a covert operation with an Army terrorist task force made of Special Forces Delta Units in South America. For the last two years she'd been flying missions all over Afghanistan. The change of scenery was nice, but she knew the deployment would have challenges of its own, namely the varying terrain and instrument flying in the cover of darkness.

Challenge accepted, she'd thought the day she received the news she was shipping out of the desert. It didn't much matter where she was going if it was somewhere new. Her crew had been just as excited.

Sergeant Howie Smith was new to the Outlaws and had only been part of her crew for eight months before the deployment transfer. He'd replaced their former sergeant after he was diagnosed with Lyme Disease which sent him home with a medical discharge from the Army. She and Maguire had been flying together for three years and trusted each other like no other. On the ground, they were like brother and sister, ribbing each other every chance they got. In the air, they were like twins with the same mind, who finished each other's sentences. She couldn't have asked for a better co-pilot.

Chapter 2

Tristan stood in the hangar with the rest of her team, gearing up for the mission. They were all dressed in their ACU cargo pants and combat boots, but they wore Army Combat Shirts instead of the normal t-shirt and jacket that went with their uniform. The front and back torso of the shirt was tan, and the camouflage pattern of their uniform was across the shoulders and down the sleeves. This allowed them to be much cooler in the hotter climates. The right shoulder sleeve had her name and rank insignia, and her left shoulder sleeve had the American Flag and her unit insignia, all in subdued colors that blended with the uniform camo, and both sleeves also had infrared tabs.

Like everyone else, she pulled on her tactical vest that was fitted with ceramic plated body armor and was the same camo as the rest of her uniform. The name tape with her last name was on the front right chest and her rank insignia was in a small square in the center, similar to the way it looked on her uniform jacket. The vest also had infrared tabs on the front and back. Three of the pouches on her vest had extra magazines for her rifle and handgun, each of the others had her radio, a map of their mission location with coordinates and the surrounding terrain, a small first-aid kit, a laser marker for aerial support, an LED flashlight, a handgun, and two protein bars.

Once she had her vest in place, she fastened the waistband and side protection modules. Then, she grabbed her combat helmet, also in the same camo pattern, with her last name written in black across the bottom in the back.

She clipped the chin strap to her vest, then pulled her matching gloves on. Her M4 rifle was already checked, loaded, and re-checked.

"Third Squad," Maj. Irving called, stepping over to Tristan. "Chief Hewitt has been instructed to land one click from the site location. You are to go in on foot, gather as much intel as you can, and return to the helo. If you see anyone, do not engage. This is supposed to be a lily pad, but it hasn't been in use in several years. We want to know if anyone is using it, and what for."

"Yes, sir," she replied. As soon as he walked away, she relayed the details to her team.

"Hey, turd squad, don't get into trouble. We'll be too far away to come rescue you," Capt. Dewey called, grinning at Tristan. She simply shot him a bird and headed out of the hangar towards the waiting helo with her team.

"He's a dick," Fowler stated.

"Yep," she muttered. The Alpha team Humvee drove away as she pulled her helmet on and secured the strap under her chin.

*

The Army Aircrew Combat Uniform looked like the ACU that everyone else around the base wore with a zippered jacket and cargo pants that had their insignia patches and tabs on it. However, their uniforms protected against flash fires. Their vests, called Air Warriors, did not contain the plated body armor everyone referred to as chicken plates. Instead, they had pouches and pockets full of necessary items and survival gear that a pilot would need on a mission, including a handgun and extra rounds, an electronic oxygen delivery system, a radio, and an electronic data manager with a GPS and enhanced situational awareness. Their flight helmets had integrated radios, detachable night vision goggles, communication ear plugs, and a visor.

"Here they come," Maguire said as he and Courtney went over their preflight inspection.

She signed the bottom of the clipboard and slid the pen into the slot on the front of her vest, all without looking up. "Let Howie handle them," she mumbled as she walked around to her side of the helo and opened the door. As the crew chief, it was his job anyhow. Once she was situated in her seat, she began strapping in. Four large, color display screens lined the dash, two in front of each pilot; one with a GPS map that tracked them, and one with all their digital gauges. An array of buttons and switches was on the console between them, along with two more smaller screens.

"You ready?" he asked, getting in beside her.

"As always," she replied with a smile, as she started turning on the switches. "Systems."

"Check," Maguire replied.

"Flight Instruments."

"Check."

Fuel Systems."

"Check."

Once they were finished, she radioed command. "Eagle, Outlaw One. You copy?" she radioed.

"Copy, Outlaw One. You are clear for wheels up. Have a safe flight."

"Roger that," she replied, looking over at her co-pilot.

"Rock and roll," Courtney and Maguire said together as they fist bumped. Then, they started the engines.

Nothing compared to the feeling of her right hand on the cyclic stick that came out from under her seat and was positioned between her legs, her left hand on the collective lever on the left side of her seat, and her feet on the torque pedals. With one last look and a nod to Maguire, she pulled up on the collective lever and the helo gently lifted off the ground, straight up into the air. The morning sun had risen, painting the sky in an array of orange and purple hues. She reached up to slide the visor down on her helmet before pushing the cyclic lever forward and left, then she pushed the left torque pedal down, causing the helo to bank left and head off in the direction of their mission. Flying at their cruising speed of 142 knots, or the equivalent of 163MPH, put them on the ground in just over an hour.

As soon as the base was out of sight, Courtney glanced up at the small mirror that allowed her to see everything behind her. If she turned her head slightly to the right, she'd see the back of Howie in the jump seat behind Maguire, facing the right rear door with his M4 rifle in his hands against his chest. They weren't expecting hostiles, but if they encountered them, he'd be ready. His job was to manage everyone in the helo, maintain the service of the helo, and protect the helo at all costs.

With her eyes forward, Courtney glanced from the screens in front of her to the fishbowl windows all around the front of the helo, giving her an extensive view of the mountain range below as they flew over it. The base they were using was hidden in a flat spot in the middle of the mountains, allowing them to stay hidden from everyone around them, including the cartel.

*

Tristan listened to the pilots' occasional chatter back forth with each other, and with the base, along with everyone else. Their radios were all on the same channel. The pilots had the option of going to a private channel to talk to each other, but they'd chosen to stay on the main channel for the duration of the flight. She'd mostly ignored them unless they were giving updates on the flight. She was sitting in the middle of the helo in the most protected space. Her weapons specialist, Staff Sgt. Hoffman, was in the left jump seat, manning the door across from the helo crew chief. The engineer, Sgt. Tucker, was on her left. Her second in command and other weapons specialist, CW2 Fowler, was on her right, leaving the medic, Sgt. Perry, and communications specialist, Sgt. 1st Class Nigel, behind them. She had a full view of the cockpit, as well as views out the windows on both sides of the helo.

Her adrenaline level rose, giving her the natural high of a war junkie. It was an eight-ball made of anxiousness, tension, fearlessness, and eagerness…mixed with the excitement of the unknown. It was the buzzing feeling a soldier got just before he or she breeched the enemy's door, rappelled, or fast-roped out of a helo and into his backyard. The tiny hairs on the back of her neck stood up like static electricity. They were close to their drop point; she could feel it in her veins. It was time.

"Bravo Team at the ready," she said into her radio.

"Hooah!" they answered.

*

Courtney held the cyclic centered to stop the momentum of the helo and pressed down on the collective lever to begin lowering their altitude until they touched down softly.

"Like butter," Maguire said, flipping some of the switches as they powered down the machine.

Courtney grinned like a Cheshire cat. "Eagle, Outlaw One. We're on the ground."

"Copy," command replied.

Tristan motioned for her team to get out of the helo. "Eagle, Bravo One. We are Oscar Mike," she radioed, letting command know they were on the move. They quickly formed two lines of three people with her in the front of the left row and Fowler in the back of the right row. Everyone had their rifles aimed as they moved together, covering the twenty-five yards between the helo and the building.

Howie hopped out of the helo and kept watch with his rifle against his shoulder.

Courtney and Maguire had nothing do except sit and wait. These missions were the worst. She had the adrenaline rush of flying into a new place in what could still be a hot zone, and then she had to sit and calmly wait for the ground team to do their job. Then, she'd fly them back to base. Granted, it was better than getting shot at, but she still craved the rush of flying with her hair on fire, dipping the helo so her crew chief could take a shot at the person on the ground, chaffing their belly with bullets.

"How do you like it so far?" Maguire asked.

"What? South America? Or the new deployment orders?"

"Either. Both." He shrugged.

"It's growing on me. The terrain is sketchy as hell. So, there's that."

He laughed.

"How's it going out there?" she radioed, checking on Howie.

"Nothing in site but a stray cat, Chief."

"Roger."

"Outlaw One, we have hostiles twenty klicks out, heading your direction," Command radioed.

"Copy," she replied.

*

Tristan's team entered the building and split their lines into two separate teams as they went in, clearing each of the four rooms of the building. Tristan's team worked their way through the east, checking two rooms while Fowler's went to the other two on the west side. There wasn't much in the dilapidated, concrete structure. A few desks and tables had been ransacked and turned over. Magazines and newspapers littered the floor. The kitchen was even cleaned out.

"There's nothing here," Fowler said, when they met up in the middle.

"Yeah," she replied, tilting her head slightly when she noticed the blocks of the wall were uneven behind him. She stepped around him and raised her leg, kicking her foot hard into what looked like a concrete wall. The plaster busted as her foot went straight through it.

"Son of a bitch! A hidden room!" Fowler yelled. He quickly helped Tristan bust through.

Three computer servers were on a standing desk, all still up and running.

"You about ready to wrap up the package with a nice little bow, Bravo One? We have heat coming our way," Courtney radioed.

"Five minutes," Tristan replied as she and her team rushed to disconnect and pack up the hard drives from the units.

"Negative. Hostiles are ten klicks and moving in fast. We are wheels up in one minute," Courtney stated.

Tristan ignored her as they continued packing the equipment, but she kept her eyes on the seconds as they ticked down on her watch. She could hear the helo engines starting.

Fowler stuffed the last of the drives into his rucksack and the team rushed out of the room.

"Bravo One! What's your position?" Courtney demanded.

"Outlaw One, the hostiles are five klicks and closing on your south side," Command radioed.

"Wheels up!" Tristan yelled as they all rushed out of the building, loaded themselves and their bags of equipment quickly into the helo and slammed the doors shut.

Courtney pulled the collective lever and lifted them off the ground, before pushing the cyclic forward to send them soaring off, away from the hostile's direction. "That was cutting it a little close, don't you think?"

"I thought you guys were Outlaws. A pickup truck full of drug thugs shouldn't scare you, Chief," she radioed back.

Maguire glanced at Courtney but didn't say anything.

"The handful of thugs weren't the problem, Captain. We're combat trained, and always at the ready."

Maguire switched the radio to their private channel. "Are you trying to get into a pissing contest with her? She's going to win. We're not ground pounders!"

"She pissed me off. If I say we're leaving, then we're leaving. End of story," she grumbled. "The last thing we need is a damn fire fight!"

"I agree. But we have to work with them for the next however many weeks or months. We should probably give it a mission or three before we start threatening to leave them behind."

Courtney laughed. "You know me too well."

*

As soon as the helo landed and powered down, Maj. Irving was waiting for them outside of the open hangar. The communications squad grabbed all the computer hard drives and raced back inside like ants on a mission.

"We debrief in five," he said.

"Yes, sir," everyone replied, saluting him before he went back inside.

Maguire began walking around the helo to do his post flight inspection as Tristan and her team went into the hangar to remove their gear and store it in their lockers. She removed her helmet, then unfastened her tactical vest. The tan shirt she had underneath it was wet, but the wicking material would cool down and dry once her vest was gone.

"Captain, you got a minute?" Courtney said, leaning against the wall behind her. The rest of Tristan's team and Courtney's air crew had already left.

Tristan was hot, sweaty, tired, and hungry. The last thing she wanted to do was deal with a cocky young pilot. "Sure," she replied.

Courtney watched Tristan's muscles flex in her arms as she removed her vest and placed it in her locker. The combat shirt she was wearing hugged her upper body, revealing the broad shoulders and narrow waist of her well-built physique. A wet line of sweat ran down the center of her back between her shoulder blades.

"You wanted something," Tristan said, turning around to face her with questioning shamrock green eyes.

Courtney's mouth watered and her nipples hardened. "Uh…it was…nothing important. We need to get to the debrief."

Tristan raised a brow and shrugged before walking out of the locker room.

Courtney smacked the back of her head against the lockers. "Pull it together. You're salivating like a horny teenager," she muttered to herself before leaving.

Chapter 3

After a lifting session in the makeshift gym, which basically had equipment made of whatever the soldiers could scrape together on base, Tristan showered and dressed in her Army PT gear, which was the only thing they were allowed to wear on base outside of their uniforms: a black t-shirt with Army written across the front in gold, and a pair of black gym shorts with Army on the bottom left in gold. She slipped her feet into sneakers with ankle socks and put on a ballcap with Army written on the front. It was only two in the afternoon, but it was the weekend, and everyone was off. It was also the end to her team's first week back in Colombia.

She shoved her wallet into her pocket and headed towards the *Canteen* to get a drink and maybe hustle one of the wet-behind-the-ears rookie soldiers at a game of pool, something she was well known for around base. Most of the newbies were warned not to play with her, but each time they were young and cocky and threw their money down on the table. If they were dumb enough to do it, she was smart enough to take their cash.

*

Courtney was sitting on one of the stools, nursing a beer when the door opened. Her head turned as Tristan stepped inside, removing her hat. Her blonde hair was fashionably styled in a faux hawk, but the first thing Courtney noticed was the full sleeve tattoos jutting out from under her short shirt sleeves and covering both arms in a mixture of color and grayscale. She seemingly ignored Courtney as she stepped up to other end of the bar and ordered a beer.

"How was the gym?" Fowler asked, walking over to her after making his shot at one of the pool tables.

"Hot as hell. The A/C isn't working," she said, taking a long swig of her beer.

"I thought one of the Joes from maintenance squad fixed it the last time we were here?" he replied, referring to a junior enlisted soldier.

"It hasn't worked at all for the ten days I've been here," Courtney said.

They both turned to look at her, almost as if they didn't know she was even in the room.

Tristan caught sight of the woman at the end of the bar wearing a black tank top with Army written across the front in gold. The distinct silver beads of her dog tag chain contrasted against her tan skin as it ran down her chest and disappeared above her hidden cleavage. Chocolate colored hair hung down in front of both shoulders in subtle waves, and matching brown eyes stared fixated on the beer bottle label she was slowing peeling. Tristan didn't have time to react or think about reacting when the bar door opened and Judd Dewey stepped inside, tossing a football up and catching it.

"Hey, turd squad! You all want to get beat at a real game?" he said with a cocky grin.

"Oh, for God's sake," Fowler muttered, shaking his head.

"I just took a shower. Maybe some other time," Tristan replied, finishing her beer.

"Come on. You can shower again. Or…is it really about your cute tennis shoes. Don't want to mess them up, do you?"

Tristan shook her head. "Fifty a head."

"What?!"

"You heard me."

"And so did I," Courtney said, raising a brow. Gambling on base was against the ethics code.

Tristan glanced at her. "Push-ups…Chief." She glanced back at Dewey and grinned as she slid her empty bottle back across the bar before getting up. Fowler followed suit as they walked out of the bar.

Dewey went out behind them. "Deal," he said, "But we get the ball first." He stuck his hand out, waiting for confirmation.

Tristan nodded and squeezed his palm. As soon as Dewey was out of earshot, she turned to Fowler. "Go round up the team."

*

Courtney was about to order another beer and put some quarters in the juke box when Howie walked into the bar. He took one look at her and did a quick about face. Curious as to what was going on, she shoved her money back into the pocket of her shorts and walked out of the bar. A little more than a handful of enlisted soldiers were walking out towards the hangars, and Howie was one of them.

Once she reached the other side of the hangars, she saw the group of soldiers in the thick grassy area across from the flight line and the runway. She shook her head and walked over. The football game had indeed begun, and a quarter of the base was on the sideline watching. It was Sunday, so no one was on duty except for the MPs and security. Even the commanding officers were tucked away somewhere other than their offices.

Tristan had traded her t-shirt for a gray tank top with Army written in black on the front, and her hat was back on her head, but backwards. Courtney quickly noticed her tattoos went all the way up over her shoulders and connected across the top of her back. The rest of Bravo Team and all of Alpha Team were out in the grass with her, forming a six-on-six game. Tarmac cones they'd obviously removed from the runway, were opposite each other, marking their end zones.

A few of the Joes had left the bar with beer bottles they were chugging as they cheered loudly. Courtney shook her head in disbelief. She looked around, hoping to see another officer in the mix, but the crowd shuffled to see a particular play and she wound up directly on the sideline. Her eyes found Tristan instantly as she dropped back to sling a pass through the air just before one of Alpha Team rushed in to grab her. She narrowly escaped his tagging hands as she released the ball. Courtney watched it sail all the way to the other end and directly into the hands of Sgt. Tucker, the engineer on her team.

"Touchdown!" someone yelled.

Courtney had grown up watching football with the men in her family, so she was familiar with the game. "Who's winning?" she asked the young soldier next to her. With everyone in PT gear, no one knew ranks. In that moment, they were all just people enjoying a Sunday afternoon.

"Bravo by two touchdowns!" he replied without taking his eyes off the game. "Bravo Team Leader is a former rugby player. She's going to wipe their asses clean!"

"I take it you're not a fan of Alpha, then?"

"Capt. Malloy saved my life three years ago in Iraq."

"What happened?"

"I was on a routine supply run with two other guys when a little kid ran up to the truck. I was green as goose shit and on my first deployment. I slowed to say hi to him and the little fucker tossed a grenade. It went under the truck and exploded, rendering us immobile. We immediately took on heavy fire. Her team came in on a helo a few klicks away and extracted us. I was shot in the leg, but it was through and through and healed easily."

"Does she know you're here…on this base?"

"Nah. There's no need to drudge up all of that old shit. We've all moved on from the Devil's Desert."

"Yeah, I know what you mean. I was in Afghanistan."

He nodded and started yelling again. "She faked them with a quarterback sneak!"

Courtney turned her eyes back to the game as Tristan ran past two of the Alpha Team players and through the touchdown cones.

*

"This is it. Last play of the game. There's only five minutes left," Tristan said, checking the watch on her wrist. "There's no way they'll get the ball from us and score two touchdowns."

"Give me the ball," Perry said. "I'm the last person they'll expect," she added.

Tristan looked at her team medic. Her strawberry-colored hair was soaked to the skin, but the grin on her face said it all. They were having a great time beating the team who constantly razzed them. "Okay," she agreed. "Can you catch it if I put it in your hands?"

"Yep. I used to do this with my brothers in the backyard and those little shits played tackle, not tag."

Tristan laughed.

"Let's go turd squad!" Dewey yelled.

Tristan turned around and stuck her middle finger up at him. "Alright, let's end this shit!" she yelled to her team before breaking their huddle. She glanced at the soldiers on the side as she walked to the line. She froze when her eyes landed on Courtney. A pair of very nice, tan legs jutted out from under the shorts her tank top was tucked into, and a few strands of her hair were plastered to her forehead with the sweat. One of her brows was raised with a smirk on her face, and her arms were crossed at her chest, covering the curves of her breasts.

Tristan grinned and took her position on the line, centered behind two of her team members, with the ball in her hand. "Hike!" she yelled and dropped back. She scrambled to the right, pump-faking the ball. Then, quickly threw it towards the left sideline where Perry was all alone. She caught it easily and began running towards the cones, crossing through them before anyone could catch up to her.

"Son of a bitch!" Dewey growled.

"Game over bitches," Hoffman said with a big smile on his face. He was the team's demolitions expert, as well as a weapons sergeant.

Both teams traded giving each other the middle finger and a few other choice words as Dewey walked up to Tristan.

"You got lucky," he muttered.

"Chief Hewitt's in the crowd," she stated as he reached for his pocket to hand her the money they'd bet.

"I'll catch up with you in the barracks in an hour," he said, sticking his hand out to her.

"Sounds good," she replied.

*

Everyone began dispersing as the two teams started walking away. Tristan's blonde hair was dark at the edges from being wet with sweat and droplets covered her temples and sides of her neck. As Courtney caught up to her, she noticed her muscled body was even more prominent in the tank top. She had no doubt that Tristan could hold her own against any male soldier at that base quite easily.

"What are you going to do with your fifty bucks?" she said.

Tristan stopped and turned around. "No money changed hands. It was all in good fun."

"Uh huh," Courtney muttered.

"I have thirteen years of service under my belt. I've worked my ass off my entire career to get to where I am. Do you think I'd really throw it away for fifty bucks?" Tristan stated.

Courtney watched a bead of sweat run from her temple, down the side of her face. The skin of her cheek looked baby soft. She remembered a dimple forming on one side when she'd grinned at her in the bar. She had a youthful appearance up close, surrounded by the hard edges of a well-trained soldier. Courtney suddenly wondered how old she was. With thirteen years of service, that would put her in her early thirties more than likely, but she looked much closer to Courtney's twenty-six years.

"I'm not here to ruin careers," Courtney finally said, forcing herself to peel her eyes away. "But I'm not going to ruin mine in the process either," she added.

"Good to know." Tristan nodded. Courtney was very easy on the eyes, but she was also currently under the same command, and Tristan certainly didn't need, nor want, to get tangled in that spider web of red tape.

Chapter 4

Two days after the infamous football game, Tristan found herself sitting in the ready room listening to Maj. Irving go over the newest recon mission that was set to take place in less than forty-eight hours, and in Venezuela, where they weren't exactly welcomed. The lieutenant colonel had already given an overall mission statement on what he wanted to accomplish. It was the major's job to form the plan of execution. It sounded simple: fly in, rappel down a mountain to an abandoned warehouse, gather intel, climb back up the mountain, fly back to base. However, it was anything but *simple*.

"He wants us to do the drop here," Courtney said when he walked out of the room, leaving Bravo team and the Outlaws to work out the fine details. She was pointing to a spot on the map. "The building is down here in this region."

"It seems reasonable," Maguire replied.

Tristan sat in the second row of chairs, tossing Whoppers into her mouth from the box she'd pulled from her pocket.

"Hit me," Fowler said.

She tossed one over and he caught it with his mouth. The rest of her team sat quietly, waiting for the two pilots to finish drawing lines and marking points on the map. They knew their team leader well enough to know not to pay attention to what was happening in the front of the room.

"It's not going to work," Tristan finally said with a sigh as she stood and tossed her empty candy box in the trash.

"What?" Courtney questioned, her voice thick with irritation.

"This doodle you have here. It's not going to work."

"Excuse me?" Maguire said.

"I'm telling you both that this plan will not work."

"What makes you so sure?" he said sarcastically.

"No offense to either of you. I know you know how to read the terrain on a map, but...have either of you ever rappelled down the side of a mountain in the dark? Or tried to climb back up? And with forty plus pounds of gear?" She motioned for her team to join her at the map. "It's too steep to go in or out right here," she said, drawing a big X through their drop point.

"What do you suggest?" Courtney asked.

"You're going to have to drop us over here," Tristan said, circling a completely different part of the mountain. "We'll rappel down. It's only about a hundred-foot right drop. The warehouse is a klick away, over here." She placed another circle on the map. "We'll have to double back in this direction, about two klicks," she added, pointing opposite from the drop circle she'd drawn. "And rendezvous with you here for pick up," she continued, adding another circle. "The terrain isn't steep. We'll be able to climb back up using this switchback and pop a flare in the landing zone."

"This leaves us in the air," Courtney stated.

"Correct. There's no reason for you to be on the ground where you can be ambushed," Tristan replied.

"What about your team? You won't have any source of backup."

"If we needed backup, we wouldn't be the team assigned to this mission," Tristan said.

"That sounds pretty cocky to me," Maguire muttered under his breath.

"Listen, I'm not trying to undermine anyone. We're obviously all good at what we do. My point is, we are green berets. We are literally trained to do this and have been doing it as a team for years. Besides, the warehouse is supposed to be deserted."

"Not to get in the middle of the Papa Charlie, but I agree with Capt. Malloy," Howie stated, using the slang for pissing contest. "It makes sense with the terrain to not let ourselves be exposed. If we came under fire, they wouldn't be able to get right back to us no matter where we were. And, if they came under fire, I'd be the only one going in anyhow. You two can't leave the bird."

"We're going with Capt. Malloy's plan," Courtney said. "End of discussion."

"Hooah!" everyone said together.

*

Later the same evening, Courtney walked into The *Canteen*. Tristan was at one of the pool tables, dressed in PT gear similar to what she'd worn a few days ago. Courtney was unfamiliar with what appeared to be a logo as one of her tattoos and curiosity got the best of her. Plus, she'd heard the rumor about Tristan being the base pool shark. "I've got the winner," she said, setting a pair of quarters down on the side of the table, which was what someone did to claim a game since it cost fifty cents to clear the balls and start a new game.

Tristan was laid over the table, about to sink the eight ball. She slowly brought her eyes up Courtney's body until they met the brown ones staring back at her. "I'm actually heading out after this."

Courtney raised a brow and grinned. "What's wrong? Scared of a little competition?"

Tristan smiled and shook her head. "No. Not at all. I just didn't want to embarrass you."

"We'll see who embarrasses who, Captain," Courtney said with a little arrogance in her voice.

"Roger that," Tristan replied, sinking the eight ball easily. She avoided Courtney's penetrating eyes as she put the quarters in, retrieved the balls from the side of the table, and began placing the balls in the triangle.

"Do you want to break?" Courtney asked as she added chalk to the cue stick Tristan had just used.

"After you," Tristan said as her eyes held Courtney's.

Courtney winked slowly at her, then she lined her stick up and slammed the white cue ball hard into the triangle of colored balls. The crack of the balls smashing together resonated through the small bar. Two solid color balls went into pockets right away. "Excuse me," she said, sliding up next to Tristan to take her first shot, which sunk into a side pocket. Then, she leaned down over the table, seemingly going for a harder to reach corner pocket shot. Tight gray shorts hugged the small curves of her ass just above lean, tan legs. Her long brown hair fell over her shoulder, resting on the table as she bent further down. She slowly pulled the stick back and tapped the cue ball with just enough pressure. It rolled into another solid ball, sending it into the corner pocket easily.

Tristan's mouth went dry, and heat burned her core. She felt like she was back in the desert and suddenly wished she'd gotten a beer as she shoved her hands into her shorts pockets and took a step back from the table. The slight move in her peripheral vision caused Courtney to hit the cue ball off center and miss her shot. Tristan reached out for the stick, finally happy to have something to concentrate on other than Courtney. Their eyes locked and hands brushed together as she grabbed the stick. Just as quickly, Courtney retreated from the table and Tristan began lining up her shots. One by one she sunk the striped balls until there were only two left on the table. Courtney was out of sight and briefly out of mind, allowing her to be in her element...until she slid the cue stick back to make a shot and heard a loud throat clearing. She looked over her shoulder to see Courtney behind her with crossed arms and a raised brow. Tristan's eyes ran down her body, finally landing on the stick pointed directly between her legs. With a sly grin, she pulled the stick back even further and thrust it into the cue ball, all without taking her eyes off Courtney. The white ball hit a striped one, sending it directly into the side pocket.

With her last striped ball in an awkward spot between two solids, she'd have to do a trick shot. Tristan walked around the table, eyeing all the angles. Seeing one she liked, she set herself up, bent down over the table and pulled the stick back.

"Nervous yet?" Courtney whispered, allowing her breath to tickle Tristan's ear.

Tristan froze her shot and turned her head slightly, nearly putting her lips against Courtney's. "I don't get nervous," she murmured.

"Hey, Cap! It's closing time," the young soldier behind the bar called.

"I guess we'll have to finish this another time," Courtney said, backing away with her eyes fixated on Tristan's.

Tristan's brow raised suggestively.

Courtney grinned and walked away, leaving her standing at the table, still holding the cue stick.

Chapter 5

"You look tired."

"I'm fine, Mother," Tristan said, smiling at the camera lens on the computer monitor. "In fact, I slept in today. We're going out on a night mission in a few hours."

"Hold on a minute, someone's at the door."

Tristan shook her head. Her mother returned a minute later. "Who was it?"

"I don't know. Some lady asking for your father. She looked like a salesman of some sort. He's been gone for over fourteen years. You'd think they would update their systems."

"Yep. Anyway, how are things going with the wedding?"

"Oh, my word, don't get me started on that cluster of a mess," her mother said, shaking her head.

Another soldier popped his head in, looking to see if the computer was available. "Listen, I gotta go. I'll call you again as soon as I can," she said before ending the call. "It's all yours," she said to the other soldier, pulling her patrol cap out of her pocket as she exited the room and made her way out of the building.

*

Tristan pulled her tactical vest down over her head and fastened the straps. The watch on her wrist read 19:50. The sky was dark with the first sign of stars beginning to appear. She checked all her pockets and pouches, making sure she had everything she needed for the mission before pulling her gloves on and grabbing her rifle and helmet.

"Do you really think this place is going to be derelict?" Perry said, while checking the last of her gear a few feet away.

Tristan shrugged. They were the only two in the locker room, but she never truly showed all her cards to her team. They fed off her emotions, so it was best to hold them close. "I have to go with what they tell us and trust the intel is right. You've been doing this long enough to know it's a roll of the dice."

Perry nodded in agreement before they walked out together. The rest of the team was already out in the hangar, and Courtney's air crew was on the flight line, doing their preflight check.

*

"I heard things got a little heated at the pool table the other night," Maguire said.

Courtney raised a brow. "Explain heated."

"Apparently, you ran everyone out of there and taught Capt. Malloy how to play pool."

"Ha!" she laughed. "It wasn't quite like that." *But yeah, it was definitely heated.*

"I'm good to go," he said, signing the bottom of his preflight sheet.

"Me too. Howie, are you about ready?"

"Affirmative, Chief."

Courtney watched Bravo Team smack their Kevlar helmets together inside the hangar like a group high-five, before putting them on as they walked out onto the flight line. Her eyes scanned the group for their fearless leader.

However, covered in all their gear and wielding a rifle, she couldn't tell them apart, aside from their height, until Tristan gave her last minute instruction and waved for everyone to get into the helo.

Once everyone was situated, she and Maguire went through their flight checklist, then fist bumped and began pushing the buttons and flipping the switches to start the engines. "Eagle, Outlaw One. You copy?" she radioed.

"Affirmative, Outlaw One. You're clear for wheels up. Have a safe flight."

"Copy," she replied, giving a last look around before grabbing the controls and lifting the bird into the air, and heading towards the programmed route. She was an excellent instrument flyer, but preferred daylight flights using visual aids. "Welcome aboard, Bravo Team. We are scheduled for a two-hour flight this evening. Unfortunately, there will be no cabin service. Sit back, relax, and enjoy the inflight entertainment," she radioed in her best flight attendant voice.

Tristan shook her head. Maguire and Howie both laughed.

*

The radio stayed mostly silent for the duration of the flight, except for the occasional back and forth between the pilots as they checked and rechecked their instruments. The two-hour duration went by quickly and before Tristan knew it, they were on the ground.

"Eagle, Bravo One. We are Oscar Mike," she radioed.

"Copy."

Tristan's team set their ropes and began rappelling over the side of the mountain cliff. It took less than a minute for each member to reach the bottom. Once they were on the ground, she radioed for Howie to retrieve their ropes.

"Outlaw One, what is your position?" Command radioed.

"Flying high and standing by. Over," Courtney replied as they lifted off and disappeared.

Tristan pulled her night vision goggles down, along with the rest of the team, then split them into their usual formation. "We're going in together. This place is too big to split up," she said into her radio.

"Roger," Fowler replied, changing his position to bring up the rear of the group.

The side door was unlocked, so Tristan quietly slid it open. The first thing she saw was a staircase, and then a long corridor behind it. "We'll work our way up," she whispered into the radio as she headed down the hall and through the double doors on the end. The room opened into a massive space with several large crates. "Clear the room," she said, motioning for the team to split into two groups. She went left with Nigel and Hoffman, and Fowler went right with Perry and Tucker. Each team checked every nook and cranny as they worked their way around stacks of crates and an array of tools, including three large welders.

"What the hell are they doing?" Hoffman questioned once they came back together and removed their night vision.

Each of them had the flashlights attached to their rifles turned on, lighting everything up as they began opening the crates.

"They're full of parts," Tristan said. "Nigel, get your camera out. Take as many still shots as you can. Hoffman, you and Tucker get the rest of these crates open but do it carefully. We don't know what is in them. Whoever is working here, hasn't been gone long. There are cigarette butts on the ground over here," she pointed.

"He could be upstairs," Fowler said.

"Take Perry with you and do it quietly. We need to get the hell out of here," she said.

"Roger," he replied, double-timing it out of the room with his night vision back over his eyes and Perry hot on his heels.

Tristan walked over to the other crates once they were opened. Nigel stood next to her, filming the contents. "Looks like a bunch of sheet metal," she muttered. "Alright. Get them closed back up. We need to make it look like we weren't here and get the hell out. Fowler, how's it looking up there?"

"Nothing but an office with a bunch of schematics all over the walls. We took pictures. On the way back down now."

"Roger."

As soon as they came off the staircase and entered the main room where the rest of the team was, they heard someone yelling.

"¡Oiga! Hey!" two men yelled, rushing towards them from a door on the other side while firing guns.

"Eagle, Bravo One. We've got company," Tristan radioed as everyone took cover.

"Get rid of them, Bravo One." Command radioed back.

"Roger that," she replied. "Fowler, you and Tucker take the left side. I'm going to flank you with Hoffman. Nigel, you and Perry stay here. There's no telling how many more of them there are, and if they heard the gunshots, they'll be coming in hot."

"Copy," they both said, taking cover behind one of the large crates.

*

While listening to radio and trying to make out what was going on with the fire fight, Courtney circled the warehouse twice from about five miles out and did not see any hostiles moving towards the location.

"I'm going to set us down. We have to get them out of there," she said.

"Where?"

"Between the mountain and the warehouse. You saw it on the map, it's flat terrain and there's a full klick between them," she replied, watching her instruments.

"This is going to be hairier than their crazy plan," Maguire said as he constantly checked the instruments on the dash.

"Bravo One, Outlaw One. We're putting the bird in the nest. Copy?" she radioed, letting them know she was putting the bird on the ground nearby for extraction.

"Negative, Outlaw One. We'll be at the rendezvous point in ten mikes."

"Bravo One, it's not your call to make. We'll be in the nest in three mikes," Courtney radioed back as she slowly brought the helo in overhead, careful of her surroundings with both eyes on the dashboard instruments as they began to lower until they touched the ground. The side door opened, and Howie jumped out, ready to assist Bravo Team if needed, but to also protect the helo if hostiles appeared. "Bravo One, Outlaw One. Bird is in the nest."

"That was nuts. Let's hope getting out of here is just as easy," Maguire said, shaking his head.

*

Tristan shook her head. This was the last thing she needed. She had to get her team out of that building now. She quickly spun around, crawling on her stomach under a table full of tools. Once she was in position, she moved her rifle carefully, waiting for the man to come into sight. As soon as he did, she squeezed the trigger, shooting him right between the eyes. Blood splattered out the back of his head as he fell back. "One down," she radioed. "Fowler, what's your position?"

"East of the entrance door," he radioed.

The sound of the helicopter became louder as it approached. Tristan was about to double back when she heard the pop of a rifle from her team.

"Two is down," Hoffman said.

"Eagle, Bravo One. Two hostiles are down," she radioed as Nigel took identification pictures of both men since neither had a wallet.

"Bravo One, this is Eagle Command. Have you cleared the scene?" the lieutenant colonel said.

"Affirmative, sir," Tristan replied, surprised to hear him on the radio. Then, she turned to her team. "Let's get the fuck out of here."

They came out single file and ran to the helo sitting a hundred yards away with the rotors still spinning. Howie was outside, waiting to lay down cover fire as they crossed the distance and jumped into the waiting helo.

"Eagle, Outlaw One. We've retrieved the package and are Oscar Mike," she radioed as she grabbed the controls and carefully navigated the space between the mountain and the building as they lifted off and flew away. "Piece of cake," she said over the private channel, grinning at Maguire as she pointed them towards the base.

He simply nodded.

"Your ass puckered a little bit...didn't it?"

"I'm not gonna lie," he said.

Chapter 6

When the helo touched down, Tristan slammed the side door open and dismissed her team. She was so angry she ignored both pilots as she stormed off towards the open hangar. Command had already said they would debrief in the morning, so she had nowhere to go except the locker room to dump her gear, then to her barracks.

Once she was inside the locker room, she tossed her helmet into her locker, then began loosening her vest. She heard the door open but didn't bother looking to see who it was as she pulled the vest over her head and stowed it in the locker. Then, she pulled her shirt free of her pants and tossed it in the bin to be laundered before pulling a tan t-shirt on.

"You know your team left the flight line without being dismissed," Courtney said from a few feet away as she removed her own gear.

"Do you really not realize what you did?" Tristan said, spinning around to face her. Courtney had taken her hair down and removed her jacket, leaving her in the same tan t-shirt and camo pants. "Landing that helo right there could have easily gotten us all killed, or worse, stuck in a country where we have no leg to stand on. So, excuse me if I was a little too pissed off to wait for the major."

"There were no hostiles in the area," Courtney replied, her brown eyes staring back at Tristan as her heart began to thump in her chest.

"What if there had been? They could've easily been hiding and ambushed you!" Tristan said, raising her voice.

"We had it under control. There were only two hostiles. If we can't handle two people, then we don't need to be in special forces!"

"I *do* know how to do my job, and that was to get your team *and* get them out! You were under fire!" Courtney yelled.

"*That's* what we are trained for! It's literally our job! You transport us in and out, not decide what we do and how we do it!" Tristan spat, clenching her teeth.

"I was in command of the helo. It was my call to make. I understand you outrank me, and you're the leader of that ground team, but if it has to do with the helo, I'm in command."

"Seriously. You're going to pull that shit on me?" Tristan shook her head.

"What's your problem with me? I risked my own life and the lives of my crew to go in there and get you and your team out. A simple thank you would've been ideal, but you attack me instead. What's really going on here?"

Tristan moved closer, leaving just over a foot between them. "I don't like people who can't decide who they want to be," she stated.

"I know who I am and what I want."

"Could've fooled me," Tristan huffed, shaking her head.

Courtney grabbed a fistful of the front of her t-shirt and snatched her closer. Tristan's mouth crashed into hers in a heated kiss full of lips, teeth, and tongues, that sent her head back against the lockers. Her heart pounded in her chest, sending blood directly to her belly like a pool of lava. She let go of Tristan's shirt and ran her hand up into her short hair.

Both of Tristan's hands were flat against the lockers on either side of Courtney's head and there was just enough space between their bodies to see light. The suddenness of the kiss had taken her off guard, but she quickly recovered her brain cells before they'd disappeared below her waist, and stepped back, pulling her mouth away from Courtney's.

The two women stared at each other with questioning eyes and heaving chests.

"We can't do this," Tristan finally said, taking another step back to put more space between them.

"We're both officers, and we're not in the same battalion command," Courtney replied, moving closer.

"Those lines are a little blurry, don't you think?"

"I see them just fine," she whispered.

The muscles of Tristan's core began to tighten, and the fabric of her underwear became increasingly wet between her legs. She couldn't ever remember wanting someone so badly and wanting to smack them at the same time. The throbbing ache between her legs won over her shouting brain and she gave in, putting her hands on Courtney's cheeks and pressing her back up against the lockers as their lips devoured one another once more.

Courtney's hands went directly to her waist, pulling Tristan's t-shirt free and sliding her palms up the rippled muscles of her damp torso until they cupped her breasts through her sports bra. She rubbed her thumbs over erect nipples, enticing a hiss from Tristan's mouth as she softly pinched them through the thin fabric.

Tristan's hands left Courtney's face and found their way under her shirt. Her lips broke free of the breathtaking kiss as she pulled the sports bra up and bent her head, taking one breast into her mouth. Courtney's hands quickly moved from under Tristan's shirt to the top of her shoulders. One palm reached up, grabbing a handful of her short hair, seemingly holding her mouth in position. Tristan licked and sucked the nipple between her lips while her hands worked the enclosure of her pants open.

A loud bang sounded outside the door just as Tristan's hand slipped under the waistband of Courtney's underwear. Both women jumped apart with their hearts beating nearly out of their chests. Tristan's shirt tail was out, but she was fully covered. Courtney rushed to adjust her bra, pull her shirt down, and close her pants. She finished and spun around in time to see the door across from them opening.

"Captain? Chief?" the young private startled, fumbling with the mop and bucket as he tried to salute.

Courtney chanced a look in Tristan's direction. Their eyes locked in a split second, and everything came flooding back to her. She swore she could still feel Tristan's hot wet mouth on her breast. She cleared her throat to keep from letting any other sound escape.

"At ease, soldier. We were just leaving," Tristan said, seeing the glaze in Courtney's eyes. She turned to face him. "It's all yours. Let's go, Chief. We have an early morning."

Courtney followed her out into the hangar that was now closed with the helo tucked inside.

Tristan sighed, shaking her head.

"Are we good?" Courtney asked, her demeanor changing drastically once they were out in the open.

"Squared away," Tristan answered, meaning they were fine, and everything was good, before they each headed off in opposite directions as if nothing had happened. "Debrief ought to be loads of fun," she muttered to herself. *Damnit all to Hell.*

*

Courtney wanted a shower, but what she needed was sleep...and release. Her body was still wound up from Tristan's hands and mouth on her, but her brain was in overdrive as it replayed the mission. With nothing else to do, she pulled a tank top on over her bare breasts, and a pair of soft cotton shorts on over her bikini briefs, both with ARMY written on them. She lay on her rack in her private room in the barracks and set her watch alarm to go off just after dawn so she could go for a run to clear the fog from her head and start the day fresh before the debrief. As she closed her eyes, she willed herself to drift off to sleep, but all she kept seeing was Tristan's green eyes. "This is going to be a very long deployment," she sighed.

*

"I was expecting an ass chewing this morning after last night's debacle," Fowler said as he rounded the corner. Tristan was beside him and the rest of the team was behind them, forming two lines as they jogged in formation around the base. Working out was the only thing to do on the base, besides going to the *Canteen*. With their rigorous missions and heavy gear, it made sense to always stay in good physical condition. They sometimes paired up when they went to the gym, but they usually ran together as a team.

"Nah. They were more interested in the intel we brought back," Tristan replied.

"Oh, look. Here comes the turd squad," Judd Dewey called as he and a couple of his soldiers stepped out of the *Canteen*. "How's that homemade PT course working out for you? I heard you had to be rescued."

"Maybe if you *ran* a PT course, those little chicken legs of yours wouldn't let you down when you played tag football," Fowler yelled back. "Must be nice riding around in a Humvee all day. Let us know when you actually get your boots dirty."

"Why? Are you gonna clean them?" Dewey's second in command said, evoking laughter from his team.

"Just remember who they'll send in to rescue you when you guys need it," Tristan yelled as they passed by. "It won't be an overzealous pilot."

"Is that what we're calling it?" Fowler asked as they kept running out of earshot of the Alpha Team.

"That's how I labeled it in my debrief." She shrugged.

"Ouch."

"It's true. She didn't need to land that damn helo where and how she did it. We had the situation under control and were on our way out. We had an agreed upon rendezvous point for extraction. She chose to go completely off mission."

"I agree," he replied. "It's still good to know she's a badass and has our six. It took balls to land like that in the dark on terrain she'd never seen before."

She nodded. He certainly wasn't wrong. Courtney was a damn good pilot. Tristan wondered if she was more annoyed by the fact that Courtney flew like she had no fear, or the fact that she boldly swooped in to help them out, no questions asked; something no other helo pilot had done before. After their tryst in the locker room, she began to question if that was just who Courtney was, or if she acted because of her interest in Tristan.

*

Courtney was happy to have the debrief over with. Capt. Warren had pulled her aside, asking whether or not she deemed it necessary to fly in and land like she did without knowing the full extent of what was going on inside the warehouse. She'd looked him straight in the eye and said she'd do it again in a heartbeat. As an Airborne pilot, her job was to get those soldiers where they needed to go and get them hauled back out at all costs. He told her to never lose her instincts because they made her a phenomenal pilot, but to wait for command to make the call next time, meaning wait for him to tell her what to do. She politely saluted and went on her way, all the while thinking he'd never stepped foot off a base since he graduated from OCS. He reminded her of the junior officer pricks she'd met when she first started out. *Maybe one day he'll grow into his boots.*

Since she was still in the command center, she headed down to the computer room and dialed her parent's number. She hadn't spoken to them since she'd arrived, and having come straight from Afghanistan, they had no idea where she even was.

"Mom!" she said as soon as her mother appeared on the screen.

"Oh, my gosh! Is it really you?" her mother asked, excited to see her.

"I'm sorry it's been a hot minute. My unit was heading for garrison duty and got redeployed instead," she said.

"Wow. So, no rest for the wicked," her mother laughed, knowing how headstrong her daughter was. "Where are you now?"

"I can't disclose, but I'm not in Afghanistan anymore."

"That's good to hear. I just sent you a care package a few days ago. I hope it finds you."

"It will, as long as you sent it to my garrison base. They'll know how to get it to me," Courtney said. "Where's dad?"

"He's out playing golf." her mother shook her head. "He's going to be mad he missed you."

"I'll call back again in a few days. I just had some free time and wanted to give you an update. This isn't a full deployment. We'll be rotating in and out, so I'll let you know when I'm back state side."

"Oh, that's great. We'd love to see you!"

"Me too. Take care, Mom. My love to you and dad," she said before ending the call. She missed her parents, but she loved what she was doing. Plus, they understood. Her mother was a military wife for the twenty-five years her father had served and had grown up a military child. Simply put, it was in their blood. Everyone knew how the system operated.

Chapter 7

Not knowing what to do about the situation with Courtney and avoiding her were two very different things, but Tristan handled them both the same. It was easier to keep to herself, choosing to go to the gym and right back to her room…which she'd been doing for the last few days, until her team was scheduled for another mission.

She dressed in her uniform with the combat shirt, subconsciously checking the tapes and insignia on both shoulder sleeves before tying her boots and blousing her pants. She grabbed her crisp patrol cap off the bed and held it in her hand as she shut the door and walked down the hall.

"You ever get sick of it?" Perry questioned as they exited the barracks together and pulled their caps on.

"You mean the last minute, scarcely detailed missions that nearly get us killed in the middle of God knows where and for something that is usually of no value?"

Perry chuckled.

"Sure. I wouldn't be human if I didn't. But is there something else I'd rather be doing…" She paused for a second. "I guess if there was, I would've been out by now." She shrugged.

"Yeah, me too." She nodded.

The rest of the team was in the locker room checking their pockets and pouches when they walked in and began doing much of the same. It was early evening, but still dark enough to be called a night mission. Tristan's eyes scanned the lockers a few feet away from hers. If she closed her eyes, she swore she'd see Courtney standing there. She shook her head, willing her brain to get back on track. She was headed out on a mission and needed the focus of a clear head. She pulled her vest down onto her shoulders and fastened the straps while she waited for everyone to finish gearing up. Then, she turned off the lights so they could check their night vision and the flashlights on their rifles. After confirmation from everyone, she flipped the lights back on and opened the door to head out into the hangar.

The helo sat out on the flight line with both pilots already inside. Howie, their crew chief was standing to the side, waiting for the Bravo Team. It was his job to be the last person into the helo, assuring everyone was accounted for.

"Bravo Team. Anytime, anywhere!" the team yelled as they smacked their helmets together in a salute to their battalion company for good luck.

*

Courtney watched from afar as she went through her flight information. She hadn't seen Tristan at all in the last few days. She'd been in and out of the meetings while the new mission was being put together, but she'd still been around the usual places. The base certainly wasn't big enough to lose anyone.

"Cargo is squared away," Howie called over the radio as he slammed the door shut and got into his jump seat.

"Copy," she replied, as she went down the flight checklist with Maguire.

"Rock and roll," they said together as they fist bumped.

"Outlaw One, Eagle. You copy?" Command radioed.

"Lima Charlie," she replied, meaning loud and clear.

"You are cleared for wheels up. Have a safe flight," they radioed.

"Roger that."

She gave one last look at the dash instruments before starting the engines and lifting the bird into the air.

"Bravo Team, we'll be touching down at your destination in approximately one hour. Sit back, relax, enjoy your flight, and as always, we thank you for flying with the Outlaws. Hooah!" Courtney said across the radio.

Maguire smiled and shook his head.

*

Tristan ignored the pilots and listened to the staccato sound of the rotor blades chopping the air instead. Her mind was on the mission. It was like any other they'd been on, and none of them were the same. They were all classified as reconnaissance, but some were intel sweeps, some were meetings with informants, and some were all out gun battles. Tristan never knew what they were walking into. She often wondered if the brass who sat behind screens all day, cooking up these missions, had ever set foot in actual foreign soil outside the walls of a military base.

Either way, she knew what her team had to do. An informant had given Alpha Team a location to check out. He said the cartel used safe houses all over South America and often moved from one to the other. He had information proving they'd been at this particular one in Venezuela within the past month. This mission was an intel sweep of one of the houses. Tristan had already gone over the different possible scenarios with her team. With the tiny bit of information command had given her, she really wasn't sure if they were about to startle the hell out of a local family, knock on the cartel's front door, find a vacant home full of rats, or get ambushed like baited prey.

*

"Bravo One, we are fifteen klicks and closing on the drop zone," Courtney radioed.

"Copy," Tristan replied. It was the first time they'd said anything directly to each other since the incident in the locker room.

A few minutes later, the helo touched down and Bravo Team jumped out. Within seconds they were running away on foot as the helo went back into the air. These were the missions Courtney wasn't a fan of. She never knew what would happen when she dropped a team off in the dark. She didn't have a connection to their IR tabs like command, so she had no way of knowing where they were until they marked an extraction zone or popped smoke, depending on what time of day it was. The only thing she could do was listen to the radio chatter.

"This is where the fun begins," Maguire said as they flew up to an altitude high enough to not be noticed, but also maintain a holding pattern within about a ten-to-fifteen-mile radius of the purposed extraction point in case they were needed in a hurry or had to lay down cover fire.

"Yep," she replied, checking, and double checking her instruments. "Let's hope we don't have to land this baby in the driveway this time."

He laughed. "That would definitely wake the neighborhood."

Luckily, the house was on the outskirts of one of the smaller cities and didn't have any direct neighbors for anyone to come in contact with.

*

Tristan's team had a little less than a two-mile hike on a slightly uphill slope through the woods, skirting a dirt road that supposedly led to a clearing where the house was located according to the cartoon map the command center had given them. The sky was dark with barely a sliver of a moon. The weight of her vest rested more on her hips than her shoulders, but she still felt the additional forty pounds on her legs as she trudged through the thick woods. Beads of sweat wet her hair line and ran down the middle of her back. In all her time spent in South America, she still hadn't gotten used to the tropical, humid climate. She literally felt like she was wet all the time. It was worse than the heat and humidity of North Carolina.

As she was checking the GPS and her handmade map, she heard rustling and then a screeching sound. She froze and held her fist up for the team to stop in place as she began scanning the woods through her night vision goggles.

"What the hell was that?" Nigel whispered.

"Probably a crocodile," Hoffman muttered.

"Shut up, both of you. We're nowhere near the Amazon," Tristan grumbled as she flipped her goggles up on her helmet and pulled her thermal imaging camera from one of her vest pockets. She began scanning the woods all around them through the monocular. There were no heat signatures on the ground, but she did pick up several birds up on the trees and one thing that seemed to be moving from tree to tree. The distinct small size and curled tail made her shake her head and put the camera away.

"I see it. Looks like it's coming this way," she said in a low, serious tone. "It's going to eat you guys alive if you don't get moving."

"What is it?" Perry questioned.

"A monkey," Tristan laughed. "Way up in the damn trees." She shook her head. "Get squared away and keep moving. The clearing should be just up here." She pulled her night vision goggles back down and started walking.

Within a couple of minutes, the clearing came into view. The dirt road had led directly to the dimly lit house in the middle.

"Someone's there," Hoffman whispered.

"Everybody down," Tristan replied, bringing her team to a squatted stop about fifty yards from the house. It looked like a dilapidated farmhouse in the middle of nowhere when she lifted her night vision goggles. "Fowler and Tucker, take the right flank. See if you can see anything on the other side."

"Copy," they both replied and headed off together through the cover of the thick woods to check the other side of the dwelling.

"Nigel and Perry, stay here. Hoffman, you're with me," Tristan said as she pulled her night vision goggles back down and put her rifle to her shoulder.

Hoffman crouched down behind her as they slowly moved closer to the tree line. She used hand signals and kept the radio silent as they crept closer and closer to the house, until they were literally up against it, squatting under a window. She flipped her night vision goggles up. "Watch my six," she whispered as she inched up until she could look through the closed window. A thin curtain covered the glass, but she could easily see through it, searching for any signs of life. She cringed slightly as a rat scurried across the floor.

She crouched back down. "Bravo Two, you copy?"

"Lima Charlie," Fowler replied. "We are unable to see anything."

"Copy. The only thing I saw was a rat."

"I think it's empty," he said.

"We won't know unless we go in there. Command, Bravo One. We've reached Tango Five with signs of potential occupancy, but no visual confirmation. Commencing with breach. Over."

"Copy, Bravo One."

"Roger that," she replied. "Perry and Nigel, move towards the front of the house. Hoffman and I will meet you there. Fowler, you and Tucker go in through the back door. Wait for my count."

"Copy," everyone said as they began to move into position.

*

"I hate this part," Courtney said, using their private channel as they continued their holding pattern.

"You can't be a pilot and a ground pounder," Maguire replied, causing her to laugh.

"I'd definitely rather be a pilot. I mean listening to everything as it's happening. It's like an eerie movie, but instead of black and white on the TV, it's over the radio, which is even worse because it allows your imagination to run wild."

"When you put it that way..." He shrugged and switched the radio back over.

"Outlaw One, Command. You copy?"

"Lima Charlie," she radioed back.

"Bravo One has breached Tango Five. Standby for the extraction call."

"Roger that."

*

Tristan and her team walked through the house with their rifles aimed, ready to put a hole in anything that moved. However, they found nothing but empty beer bottles, cigar and cigarette butts, and trash. Whoever had been staying there was long gone. The team poked around but found nothing except for a piece of paper with the name *Juan Ortega* written on it. He was Domingo's right-hand man and the second in command of the cartel. Tucker took a few pictures of the paper, as well as the sparsely furnished rooms of the small house with trash lying all around.

"This place is giving me the creeps," Hoffman said as a rat ran by him. He quickly trained his rifle on the rodent, zeroing in on him with the sight.

Perry shook her head as she watched him.

The sound of a car engine got their attention. "We've got company!" Nigel yelled, seeing the headlights coming directly towards the house.

"Everyone out the back! Double-time into the woods! Go! Go! Go!" Tristan shouted.

Fowler led the way out of the house with the rest of the team hot on his heels in a single file line with Tristan at the rear. Once they were outside, they broke off, running parallel to each other to move faster. Tristan pulled the door closed carefully and sprinted behind them.

By the time the two men were walking through the front door, Tristan's team was already squatted down ten yards inside the wood line and completely out of sight.

"Bravo One, Command. Status?"

"Oscar Mike," she radioed, letting them know they were out of the house and on the move.

"Copy, Bravo One."

Tristan checked her watch. "Outlaw One, Bravo One. You copy?"

"Lima Charlie," Courtney answered.

"We are less than two klicks due south of Zulu Two. ETA for extraction, ten mikes. Over," Tristan radioed, putting the GPS away as she half walked and half jogged, leading the team at a steady pace through the dense forest, all the while keeping the edge of the dirt road fifteen yards out to her right.

"Copy, Bravo One. En route. ETA to Zulu Two, ten mikes."

*

The helo arrived overhead just as Tristan's team exited the tree line of an open field with a ratty old soccer goal at one end. The grass was high, giving the impression it hadn't been played on in quite some time. She didn't think about what may or may not be living in that grass as she sprinted towards the waiting helo with her team.

Once everyone was inside, Howie slammed the door closed and Courtney pulled the collective lever up, lifting them off the ground. She pushed the cyclic to the left, causing the helo to bank in that direction before straightening out and continuing a forward path towards the mountain range that separated Venezuela and Colombia.

"Command, Outlaw One. Oscar Mike with the package in tow. Over."

"Copy, Outlaw One."

With nothing else to do, Tristan leaned her head back against the jump seat and stared ahead. She was in the middle of the row, essentially in the center of the helo, and had a full view of the pilots. The world outside the windows was pitch black, leaving her nothing to look at except Courtney, under the helmet and heavy camo, as she maneuvered the helo with soft movements and steady hands. She thought about the paper they'd found with Ortega's name on it but had no idea what it meant. Military Intelligence wasn't her forte, because if it had been, she certainly wouldn't be sitting there in that helo sweating her ass off. That she was certain of. However, it still made her wonder what significance it was, if any. She even thought about home…something she rarely did to begin with, and never on a mission. At that point, she wanted to think of anything other than what was really on her mind. What were she and Courtney going to say to each other? Was it a mistake? Or a prelude to more? She wasn't even sure what she wanted it to be; if it *could* even be anything. She was a commissioned officer, but Courtney was a warrant officer. Generally speaking, they could be together if they were in different commands or units, which in essence they were, but their current deployment to the special task force, put them together under the same command. They had different commanding officers. She was under Maj. Irving and Courtney was under Capt. Warren, who commanded the second squad, airborne group of plane and helo pilots. However, they were all currently under Lt. Col.

Powers' command. Any way she looked at the lines, they were blurred. The last thing she needed to do was cross them. She would most certainly be in more trouble, and Courtney could potentially risk losing her flight wings. Was it worth it? They barely knew each other.

"Outlaw One, we have you on radar. You are clear to set the bird in the nest," Command said, bringing Tristan out of the mental fog she'd gotten stuck in.

"Roger that," Courtney replied as she flew closer to the flight line and began lowering the helo in front of hangar two, where it was usually stored.

"Bravo Team, we'll debrief in the ready room at 0800 hours," Maj. Irving said as soon as they were out of the helo. "Dismissed."

Tristan's team saluted him before walking away. "Everyone in DFAC by 0700," she said, telling them meeting in the dining building where they ate their meals.

"Roger," they all replied.

Once they were in the hangar, their helmets quickly came off, and by the time they were in the locker room, everyone was starting to peel out of their tactical vests. Perry, Nigel, and Tucker also carried rucks, or backpacks with extra needed equipment for their specialty on top of their tactical vests, so they were happy to get the additional weight off their backs.

As soon as she had her gear stowed, Tristan pulled her patrol cap from her locker and headed out of the room. She needed a shower and she wanted something to eat. DFAC was closed for the night, so she had to settle on whatever snacks she had lying around in her barracks room from the care package her mother had sent a week earlier.

Chapter 8

The sun began directing its hot rays down onto the base at first light. Tristan had trekked enough the night before, so she'd opted out of her morning run before breakfast and the mission debrief, which had lasted two hours.

When the meeting ended, the lieutenant colonel left the room, but Maj. Irving had remained behind. He was the only one in the room with Bravo Team.

"Pack your bags, Bravo Team. You're going stateside," Maj. Irving said. "Wheels up at 1300."

Tristan's jaw dropped. They'd been in theater less than a month, and their shortest deployment thus far had been six weeks, and most had been eight.

"I know this is a need-to-know basis but *is* there something we need to know?" she asked, looking at him.

"No," he answered, shaking his head. "You guys were supposed to be on leave for an additional ten days when we called you back to handle these last three missions. We're sending you back to finish your leave and report to garrison until your next deployment as usual."

"Yes, sir," she said. When he left the room, she looked around at her team. "You heard him. Pack up and be on the flight line at 1230. Dismissed."

Everyone got up and went their separate ways. Tristan headed towards the personnel office to pick up her team's garrison orders. Then, she went to her barracks room and neatly packed her uniforms, PT gear, and toiletries into her deployment bag, along with a few personal items. As she sat on the side of her rack, she felt her shoulders slump. She'd been doing this a long time, so she knew how to handle the deployment cycle of emotions and the mental stress it caused for both the soldier and his or her family. She actually loved her job and looked forward to being in other countries around the world, so it was quite the opposite for her each time her team went home.

She'd been best friends with her father since the day she was born, and when she lost him, she lost a piece of herself…but she'd somehow found it in the Army. Seeing her mother and spending extra time together was always nice, and they'd gotten much closer over the years, but they were nothing like most mothers and daughters. Plus, she was very single and lived the life of a soldier. There was no girlfriend or wife to come home to or children waiting to climb all over her. She got her love and camaraderie from her team and the other soldiers around her.

By the time she finished allowing herself to go through the withdrawal stage and close her deployment bag, she only had an hour and a half left before she needed to be on the flight line. She quickly headed over to the locker room to pack her gear. The first thing she did was empty all her ammo cartridges and check her rifle and handgun to make sure there were no rounds in the chamber. It was against regulations to fly with open rounds on a transport, unless you were an MP or had special circumstances. Once she'd finished with that task, she went about stowing her gear in her deployment bag. Her head popped up when she heard the door open behind her.

"Why didn't you tell me you were going home?" Courtney asked.

"I just found out a couple hours ago. Besides, it's not like we're…"

"Friends?" Courtney finished for her.

Tristan looked at her. "I don't know. What did you want me to do? Take you into an abandoned building and have sex?"

Courtney grinned and shrugged. "I'm not saying I would've stopped it."

Tristan shook her head. "Are you trying to get thrown out of the Army?"

"No. I'm trying to tell you I like you."

"It'll never work. The brass would never go for it."

"We're not even in the same battalion. Commissioned Officers and Warrant Officers date all the time."

"We're currently under the same CO for this deployment," Tristan stated, stuffing her helmet into her deployment bag on top of her tactical vest.

"You're leaving, so unless you've been re-deployed, you're going back in garrison, wherever the hell that is."

"East coast, and I'll be back. My team has been deploying in and out of here for a little over a year. If anything, you won't be here when I get back," she said, zipping the bag closed.

"We'll be here for a while. We finished up a long stint in Afghanistan, and this seemed like a nice cozy place to put us after we were in hell."

"I know the feeling. We were in Iraq before here. This place is a cake walk…most days."

Courtney nodded in agreement.

"I should go," Tristan said, keeping her eyes locked on the chocolate brown ones staring back at her.

"Have a safe flight," Courtney said.

Tristan's eyes moved to her mouth as her lips parted. Her mouth watered at the thought of kissing her.

"Get going, Captain. I'll be here when you get back," Courtney said with a smile and a playful wink.

*

For the first time in her military career, Tristan wished the C-12 transport plane had windows she could see out as they raced down the runway and lifted into the air. She'd never cared to look back from a place she was leaving...until now. With an inaudible sigh and barely noticeable shake of her head, she put her AirPods in and left Colombia behind.

*

With Bravo Team gone, Courtney's helo crew was temporarily reassigned in second squad and tasked with flying recon missions tracking vehicles crossing the border into Panama, which was like several missions they'd had in Afghanistan, plus pursuing speed boats coming and going from Colombia.

"I guess it beats twiddling our thumbs until they return," Maguire said as they walked out of the ready room.

"And here I thought we'd just sit around playing pool and darts." She shrugged.

He laughed.

They sometimes went weeks without a mission on their last deployment and would literally volunteer for supply runs or other mundane flights for the hell of it just to log hours. Then, other weeks they'd be flying so much, they were barely able to fit sleeping and eating into their days. So far, deploying to Colombia as a part of the task force was proving to be pretty good.

*

The four-hour flight was coming to an end when Tristan pulled her AirPods from her ears and stuffed them and her dead iPod into her pocket. As she glanced around, she noticed Hoffman was asleep; Perry was reading a book; Fowler and Nigel were playing Texas Hold'em with a ratty old deck that she knew was missing at least four or five cards; and Tucker had his headphones on with his eyes closed. Her mind drifted back to the base as she stretched her stiff muscles. She couldn't figure out why she couldn't get Courtney Hewitt out of her head. They'd made out, but never had sex. The *what if* kept replaying in the back of her mind. "It's not going to happen," she mumbled to herself, just before the plane touched down.

Chapter 9

Tristan's apartment was only about two miles from the base, and it was the first place she went when her team was dismissed after the flight and formally put on leave for the next ten days. She replied to her mother's voicemail with a text saying she was home but wasn't coming over until the next day. All she wanted to do in that moment was take a shower, eat a hot meal, and relax on her couch. The last thing she expected was a knock on the door. She'd removed her jacket and boots but was still wearing her camo pants and tan t-shirt as she walked over, peeping through the tiny hole. A well-dressed woman with mocha-colored skin and long dark hair pulled up in a bun, was standing on the doorstep. The folder in her hand made her look like a salesperson. Tristan was about to walk away when the woman rapped her knuckles on the door once more.

Oh, for crying out loud. Tristan sighed and pulled the door open. "I'm not interested in what you're selling. Honestly, I'm not trying to be a jerk. I just got home from deployment an hour ago and all I want to do is relax."

"I assure you, I'm not selling anything," the woman said. "I'm looking for Tristan Malloy."

"That would be me."

"Tristan Cecile Malloy, daughter of Donald Arthur Malloy?"

"Yeah…" Tristan muttered slowly in surprise. "Who did you say you were?"

"I didn't. My name is Janice Brown. I work for the State of North Carolina. May I come in?"

Tristan pulled the door open further and stepped back. Her rucksack and deployment bags were both on the floor in the living room. Ms. Brown stepped around them and tucked her knee length skirt on the sides as she took a seat on the couch. Her black heels crossed at her ankles in a very professional and practiced manor.

"Would you mind showing me your ID?"

Tristan eyed her for a second. "My father died thirteen years ago. So, I'm not—"

"I'm aware, Ms. Malloy."

"It's Captain, actually," Tristan corrected as she pulled her military ID from her bag and handed it to the woman. She remained on her feet because this was where she felt the most steady and comfortable, and this woman made her nervous.

Ms. Brown looked at the ID, then up at her before handing it back and opening the folder in her lap. "Do you know who Katie Adams is?"

"Never heard of her," Tristan replied, shaking her head.

"She recently passed, and the State of North Carolina is trying to locate her next of kin."

"I'm sorry, but I have no idea who she is. And why did you mention my father?"

"I believe you may be Ms. Adams' half-sister. Donald Malloy was on her birth certificate as her father."

"What?" Tristan took a step back like she'd been slapped across the face. "There's no way. He was married to my mother from a year before I was born until the day he died. How old was this person?"

"Katie Adams was twenty-two."

Tristan shook her head. "You must have the wrong person. Where is her mother? She should be able to clear this up."

"Unfortunately, she's deceased as well. She passed away from injuries in a car accident a year and a half ago."

Tristan ran her hand through her hair and took a few steps. She knew her father. He was her best friend. Her parents were happy. There was absolutely no way he fathered another child.

"There's more," Ms. Brown stated. "Katie Adams left behind a son who is currently in the state foster care system until I can locate her next of kin to hopefully take custody of him."

Tristan stopped pacing the floor. "She had a kid?"

"Yes. That would make him your nephew, if in fact she is your sister."

"Holy shit," Tristan muttered. "I'm sorry," she apologized, looking over at the woman.

"No problem. I understand this is a lot to take in."

"I really don't believe you have the right person."

"We can actually clear everything up pretty easily if you submit to a DNA test. It'll take the lab a few weeks to get the results back, and of course, I can't do anything until then, but at that point we will know for sure and be able to move forward accordingly."

Tristan nodded. "How do I do that?"

Ms. Brown went into the folder and pulled a business card that was paper clipped to the first page. She then handed it to her. "This is the lab name, phone number, and address."

"Is that her?" Tristan said, looking at the little bit of page she could see as she took the card.

"Yes," she replied, handing her the page. The photo at the top was of a young woman with curly, light red hair. She was very thin and very pale. Her eyes were light blue and sunken in, and her smile was almost crooked. Tristan had a feeling in another time, she would've been pretty.

"Was she sick?" Tristan asked, handing the page back to her.

"She was an addict and died of an overdose," Ms. Brown replied, sticking it back into the folder.

"Oh, my God." Tristan's shoulders slumped and her heart sank. "Do you have a picture of her son?"

"Yes, but he's a minor. I can't show it to you until I know for sure you are his next of kin."

"Okay. How old is he? Can you tell me that at least?"

"Five."

"Oh…" Tristan said in surprise.

"Again, once we have the results, I'll be able to go over everything in much more detail with you."

"I understand."

The woman stood and held out her hand. "It was nice meeting you, Captain Malloy. Thank you for your service. I apologize for interrupting your return home and being the bearer of such overwhelming news."

"It's okay," Tristan said, shaking her hand before walking her to the door. Once it was closed, she sunk down to the floor with her head in her hands. "This can't be," she whispered.

*

Patty Malloy was dressed in a short sleeve blouse with a thick necklace that looked like it was made of stones, and a pair of slacks. Her blonde hair hung around her shoulders with her gray strands starting to show a little more here and there. She pulled the door open with a big smile. "I thought you were coming out tomorrow?" she said, hugging her daughter.

Tristan shoved her keys into her pocket. She was still wearing her tan t-shirt but had changed from the cargo pants of her uniform to an old pair of jeans. "Change of plans," she said, closing the door before following her mother into the living room.

"I'm supposed to meet Maryanne Townsend for an early dinner. Had I known you were coming, I would've made other arrangements."

"Who is Katie Adams?"

"That name doesn't sound familiar."

"A state social worker showed up at my apartment today," Tristan said, watching the color drain from her mother's face.

"I told that woman not to bother you with this mess," she grumbled shaking her head.

"Mess?" Tristan tried not to raise her voice. "I would think this is a hell of a lot more than a mess! Did dad really have an affair and father another child?"

Patty sighed. "Sit down, Honey."

Chapter 10

Courtney stepped out of the hangar with all her gear on and pushed a pair of aviator sunglasses onto her face as she looked up at the clear sky. Tristan had been gone for two days and the base seemed oddly quiet without her team around.

"Rain's gone if that's what you're looking for," Judd Dewey said when she turned towards the Humvee parked just outside of the hangar where he was standing.

She nodded, but never said anything to him. She knew just from watching his interaction with Tristan that he was a pompous ass. The last thing she wanted to do was give him reason to speak to her.

"Chief, Jezebel is ready to rock and roll," Howie said, climbing out of the side door of the helo, saluting her and Maguire as he came up behind her.

"That's what I like to hear," she replied with a smile. "Wheels up in ten."

"Roger that."

She grabbed her pre-flight inspection sheet and began walking around the helo as Maguire did the same.

They were scheduled for a routine reconnaissance flight, tracking vehicles that were driving through the mountain range between Colombia and Venezuela. It truly didn't matter to Courtney. They could be flying pigs from one farm to another, as long as she was in the air and at the controls.

Once she was strapped into her seat, Courtney flipped the switch for the radio. "Command, Outlaw One. You copy?"

"Lima Charlie, Outlaw One. You are clear for wheels up. Have a safe flight."

She and Maguire fist bumped. "Rock and roll!"

*

"Your father worked very hard to climb the ladder with Carolina Electric, and when he became a junior executive, he was given a secretary. I remember him coming home and ranting about how they had just hired someone off the street and threw her into the position. I don't believe she did her job well in the beginning. But your father being the kind and generous person he was, took it upon himself to teach her how to do the job. Fast forward a year later, he comes home from work one night and says he has something to tell me. You were about eight at the time and begging us to let you play flag football."

"I remember that. You said absolutely not. Football is not for little girls," Tristan muttered. "Then, the next morning at breakfast you told me we were going to tryouts after school, so I better eat all my breakfast." She shook her head and ran her hand through her hair. That was the turning point in her life. The day she joined that team, was the day she knew she was nothing like the other girls at school. She was rough and tough and fit right in with a group of scrawny little boys, often leading by example when she made game-winning plays. Even at that young age she loved being on the field, running around, catching, and kicking the ball, and chasing down other players. She also loved tackling, but that wasn't allowed in flag football. Although, it didn't stop her from doing it anyway every now and then. She looked back at her mother as a tear slid down her cheek. "That was the night he told you, wasn't it?"

Patty nodded. "He said it was only one time, the night of the company Christmas party. I wasn't with him that year because you had gotten Chicken Pox. I was too scared to leave you with a sitter because I thought you were going to scratch your skin off." She shrugged. "Anyway, she told him she was pregnant, and it was his. He swore it wasn't because he was protected. I told him I wanted a divorce that very same night. He sat on his knees crying, begging me not to go through with it. He kept saying the baby wasn't his. When I asked what if it was, he said he didn't care. You and I were his family. She moved to another department, then left the company before the baby was born."

Tristan sat across from her mother with her head in her hands. "Did he know about her?" she asked without looking up because she already knew the answer. The man who was her whole world was nothing more than an adulterer and a deadbeat father.

"Yes. The woman sent him a Christmas card to the office with a picture of her. He came home and showed it to me. The little girl looked like his baby pictures, red hair, and all. He couldn't deny her any more than he could deny you. He sent the mother a ten-thousand-dollar check and a letter stating he wanted no part of the child's life. If she cashed the check, she agreed that he would remain anonymous," Patty sighed. "That woman and her child didn't come up again until he died ten years later."

"How could he just push her out of his life like that? She was his child!" Tristan spat as she wiped a few more stinging tears from her cheek. She wasn't much of a crier at all, but her emotions were on overload.

"Honey, he'd made a grave mistake and the thought of losing you and I outweighed a bastard child with a woman he got drunk and slept with. That's how he put to me. However, he knew a lot more than he was letting on because he named her in his will."

"What?"

"I nearly fell over when his attorney said ten-thousand-dollars was to go to this woman to put towards her daughter's college fund. That was the last I'd heard of either of them until the day that social worker showed up at the door. I'm sorry she died, but I want nothing to do with any of it."

"Are you serious?" Tristan shook her head in disbelief. Her sorrow had quickly turned to resentment. "I just..." She took a deep breath before she said words her mother had never heard her say. "I don't understand how he knew about her but tossed her to the side with a check like a bill he'd just paid. How could he do that? What about me? She was my sister! How did you let me go on with my life knowing I had another part of him out there? Especially after he died! You're as monstrous as he was!"

"Tristan, they were trash. He would've lost his job if it had ever come out that he'd slept with an employee. We handled things the way we needed to handle them."

"With money," she sneered.

"She didn't have to take it. In fact, she could've taken him to court and ruined all our lives, but she didn't."

"No, she probably wanted nothing to do with him. Instead, she raised her daughter on a poor, single mother's salary." She shook her head once more. "She died of an overdose. Did you know that, Mother? My sister...she was an addict. And she was twenty-two years old. Her son was born when she was only seventeen. Her mother passed before she turned twenty-one. Her life was way harder than I could have ever imagined my life being, and it didn't have to be that way. I hate him for what he did to her. And I'm sorely disappointed in you for keeping this from me. I'm an adult. I've been one for a long time now. You could've told me."

"Tristan, I don't understand why you are so upset. Honey, it was in the past. There was no need to dredge all of that up. You idolized your father. If you had known the truth, you would've hated him then instead of now."

"I would have found my sister and helped her! Maybe…she'd still be alive."

"Your father never did take a DNA test as far as I know, but he could've hidden it from me. I found school pictures of the girl in an old chest he kept in his closet. The woman must've continued sending them. I honestly don't know much of anything, Tristan. The day he sent the letter with the check, and she cashed it, was the last time they were spoken of in our home. I don't know how much contact he had with them or if he ever met her. I have no idea. All I do know is, they are all dead and gone. It's in the past where it belongs."

"I'm not dumping that little boy to the curb like my father did to his mother. I have an appointment in the morning to take a DNA test."

"Oh, my god, Tristan. That's the last thing you need to do. What does it matter? He's in foster care, he'll get adopted to a good home. It's best to not get involved. He's not our problem."

"Are you kidding me? If she really was my sister, then he's my flesh and blood!"

"So, are you going to leave the Army and become a parent all of a sudden?"

"I don't know what I'm going to do, but I'm certainly not going to pretend he doesn't exist!" She slammed her hands on her knees and stood up. "Mother, I love you, but I need to go get some air."

"Where are you going? Are you coming back?" Patty questioned.

"I need to be alone for a while," Tristan replied before walking out the door.

*

"It's a clear day with a blue sky and nothing between us and the mountains below," Maguire said on their private channel. "What a waste of time. I mean, don't get me wrong, I love flying, but we've passed over this region three times now. There aren't even roads down there. It's just a small trail."

"And a truck," Courtney replied before switching back to the main channel as she pushed the cyclic stick to the right and banked the helo into a sweeping turn to follow the vehicle. "Eagle, Outlaw One. We have a bogey in site, heading east along the trail. We are in pursuit, over," she radioed.

"Copy, Outlaw One. Remain in pursuit until border crossing."

"Roger that."

Maguire pulled a pair of high-powered binoculars to his eyes to get a better look at the vehicle and possibly the driver while Courtney flew the helo. The small truck cut through mountain switchbacks and used over-invasive maneuvers to try and lose them, but Courtney was too good of a pilot to let that happen. "He's gone off the trail!" he said.

"He's going to come out over here," she said, banking the helo to the right.

Sure enough, the truck popped out of the tree line and back onto the narrow trail. Courtney moved in behind him, making sure to keep the helo well above the treetops. When the truck turned once more, heading into a flatter part of the mountain, Maguire noticed the person in the passenger seat hanging out of the window. Before he could get a better look at the person, he saw the muzzle flash of the automatic rifle he was holding.

"They're shooting at us!" he yelled.

"Eagle, Outlaw One. We're taking fire three klicks from the border. Permission to engage. Over," she radioed as she banked left, then right again, trying to avoid the rounds coming at them. The helo was essentially too high up to do damage, but she wasn't taking her chances.

"Outlaw One, permission granted. Repeat. Engage the enemy. Copy?"

"Lima Charlie," she replied. "Howie, get on the gun and blow that truck off the side of the mountain when I bank right," she said.

"Roger that!" He moved from his jump seat to the gun and swung the side door of the helo open. He pressed the trigger, lighting the vehicle up with a string of bullets in rapid succession as the helo banked, putting the truck right into his line of sight.

Suddenly, the truck swerved and went over a cliff and tumbled down the side. Courtney couldn't land the helo anywhere near the area, and she didn't have a ground team aboard anyhow. She quickly radioed the coordinates to command as she hovered over the wreck, waiting for signs of life. After a few minutes, she pushed the cyclic to the left and flew away.

*

Tristan's blacked out Jeep Wrangler pulled through the iron gates of the cemetery and came to a stop in front of a row of large marble headstones. She cut the engine and got out. The sun was still in the sky, but its rays were starting to slowly fade. She didn't have long before the gates would close and lock for the night.

She walked over, stopping in front of one of the stones with *Donald A. Malloy* etched across the front with the words *Loving Husband and Father* below his birth and death dates. "Loving my ass," she sneered as she read it. "I found out about my sister today. If I said I hated you for doing this to mom, that would be an understatement. I thought the sun shined out of your ass. It turns out, you're just as much of a piece of shit as the next deadbeat dad." She paused and looked around, silently wondering where her sister was buried. "She's dead you know. The life you left for her was broken. It consumed her in ways you would've never understood. I guess that's why I can't even look at my own mother. She knew all along, and she just let you write a check and push this kid out of your life. She should've told you to own up to what you'd done and be a goddamn man! I work with soldiers every day who have more balls than you ever did and they're just boys! Most of them can't even legally drink!" she growled. "And to top it all off, your grandson is living in a foster home because he has no family! You could've prevented all of this...all the lives you ruined, if you'd just been faithful to your fucking wife, you piece of shit! You're right where you belong!" She spit on his headstone and walked away.

Chapter 11

A mix of songs from several different movie soundtracks blasted through the one AirPod Courtney kept in her ear as she ran laps around the base. Sweat soaked her hairline and ran down her cheeks to her neck. She wasn't a daily runner, but she tried to get in close to ten miles a week, give or take depending on her mission schedule. She also wasn't much of a weightlifter either, but she gave it enough effort to stay in great physical condition because her job depended on it. When she'd started high school, she was built like a popsicle stick. She knew she wanted to fly like her father and grandfather, and after joining the ROTC program, she realized she'd never make it through boot camp, so she made it her mission to get stronger and more physically fit overall. When she turned eighteen, she enlisted in the Army under the DEP (Delayed Enlistment Program) allowing her to graduate high school two months later. She reported for active duty soon after, left for boot camp, then to WOFTS (Warrant Officer Flight Training School), and she never looked back.

The pilot of a C12 Huron that had just taken off for a routine scouting mission, dipped his wing at her as he lifted into the air. She was jogging along the outskirts of the flight line, completely out of the way, but not out of site. She gave him a salute as she kept running. The 'boys' hadn't exactly accepted her at first, but she was feisty and proved right away that she could fly just as good as the select few, and a lot better than the rest. It wasn't long before she was accepted as one of them.

Once she'd finished her run, Courtney showered and went over to the communications building. It was her day off, so she was dressed in PT gear. The few soldiers and officers she ran into said hello as she made her way to the small room with five laptop computers set up in cubicles. She sat down at an open one and plugged her wired earbuds into the side of the computer before clicking on the program that would allow to her video call.

"Court? Is that you?" her father said when he answered. "Hold on...Shelly, I can't get the damn video to come on. I think it's Courtney calling."

Courtney shook her head laughed. "Dad...yes, it's me."

"Ah...there she is!" he said, smiling at the woman filling the phone screen. "How's it going, Kiddo?"

"Not bad," she answered. "Are you with Pop?"

"Yeah, he's here. Hold on," her father said, walking through the house with the phone.

"Hi, Dear!" her mother said.

"Hey, Mom! Miss you!"

"Here he is," her father said, handing the phone to his dad.

"What am I doing, Jimmy?" the older man said as he adjusted the glasses sliding down the end of his nose.

"Just talk, Dad. It's Courtney. She's on deployment."

"Hi, Pop! Happy birthday!" Courtney said loudly.

"Oh...It's Courtney!" the old man said. "Hey, Kid! How's it going out there?"

"Good. Everything's good." She smiled. "How are things back there?"

"Your old man is cooking steaks on the grill."

She laughed. "How old are you now, Pop?"

"Eighty. Can you believe it? I can't hear worth a damn without these things in my ears. Wear your ear protection, Kid. I was lucky to have a helmet on my head at all back when I was in the air. You young guns have it made these days with the all the bells and whistles."

"Yes, sir." Courtney laughed and shook her head. She missed her family. They were a little quirky, but she loved them just the same.

"Have you been flying much?" her father asked, taking the phone from his dad before he went into a tirade about his time in Vietnam.

"About every three days, mostly recon," she answered.

"Those are days that drag on forever," he said, recalling his own military days on deployment.

"Yes," she agreed. "Give my love to everyone."

"Will do," he said. "Stay safe and watch your six."

"Roger that," she replied before the call ended.

*

Tristan sat in her Jeep, parked outside of the clinic she was directed to by Janice Brown, the state social worker. They'd been open for close to an hour, and although she hadn't needed an appointment, she'd arrived early anyhow. She just couldn't seem to get out of her vehicle. She knew without a doubt that Katie Adams was her sister, but as soon as she took the DNA test, it became official. Everything she knew of her father was a sham. The pedestal she'd held him on would collapse deservedly, crumbling his memory in a cloud of dust, and the displeasure she felt towards her mother would surely turn to disgust.

"The longer you sit here, the longer you'll have to wait for the results," she sighed, then tossed her ball cap onto the passenger seat and got out.

No one was in the waiting area when she walked inside and signed in on the sheet full of stickered lines at the desk. Before she could turn around and take a seat, the frosted glass slid open, and the receptionist pulled the sticker with her name on it.

"You're here for DNA testing?"

Tristan nodded. "Oh, wait. I have a case number I'm supposed to give you," she said, pulling the piece of paper from her pocket and handing it to the woman.

"Great. We'll call you back in a few minutes," the woman replied, taking the paper, and closing the glass window.

Tristan took a seat across from the door. She contemplated reading one of the magazines on the table beside her chair, but Cosmopolitan and Women's Weekly were definitely not at the top of her reading list. She stared out the window at the passing cars instead, until the side door opened and a nurse in light pink scrubs appeared. She was young, with a bubbly personality and flashy smile.

"Ms. Malloy?" she asked.

"Yes, that's me," Tristan replied, standing up.

"My brother is in the Army, too," she said, reading her chart as she led Tristan down the hall and into a small room. "He's stationed in California."

"Oh, really. What's his MOS?"

"Um…I'm not sure what that is."

"What does he do in the Army?"

"He's a mechanic of some sort. He calls himself the low man on the totem pole," she laughed. "He's only been in about a year and a half."

Tristan nodded, watching as she went into a cabinet and pulled out a sterile package, which she then tore open. A pair of latex gloves, a rather large Q-tip, a plastic tube with a lid, and a small Ziploc style bag, were the contents. The nurse pulled the gloves on and grabbed the Q-tip.

"Are you ready?" she asked, looking at Tristan. "It doesn't hurt, I'm just going to rub this on the inside of your cheeks."

"Sounds easy," Tristan replied, opening her mouth.

The nurse swabbed all around inside of her mouth, then stuck the Q-tip into the plastic tube and closed the lid. She attached a sticker with Tristan's name and the case number to the tube before putting the tube in the bag, sealing it closed, and adding another sticker to the outside of it.

"Ok, you're free to go."

"That's it? No blood or anything?"

"Nope." She smiled. "Just saliva."

Tristan nodded. "Tell your brother to hang in there. Without those low men, the totem pole wouldn't be standing," she said before leaving.

*

With ten days left in her leave and a three to five week wait for test results, Tristan knew she needed to get her head straight before she deployed again. She packed her large rucksack as soon as she got home, making sure to put enough provisions inside for a week, plus a few changes of clothing, small camp cooking supplies, toiletries, a few other odds and ends like her foldable fly-fishing rod, a fly reel, and a small case full of flies. She clipped her sleeping bag to the top of the bag and her one-person tent to the bottom. Then, she dressed in a pair of cargo shorts, a breathable shirt, a pair of dessert boots she had from her deployment in Afghanistan, and a ball cap with ARMY written on it. The last thing she grabbed before leaving her apartment was her hiking map of the Uwharrie National Forest.

*

The mature forest was cooler than the urban areas surrounding it, which wasn't saying much for the late summer heat and humidity. Tristan wiped beads of sweat from her forehead and kept trudging along the trail until she heard the soothing sound of the running stream coming off the river. She checked the map and took the next switchback marked on her path. The rarely used path led to a clearing alongside the clear water. She dropped her rucksack and set her tent up near the firepit circle made of river stones. She unpacked the rest of her gear and looked up at the sun. From its position, she knew it would begin to set in just a few hours, leaving her with little time to catch, clean, and cook her dinner. A brown trout swam around the rocks a few feet away. She watched it scurry as she stuck her hands in and splashed the cool water on her face.

The zippered pouch of flies Tristan had brought with her were passed down from her grandfather. They'd spent many weekends hiking, camping, and fishing together. She'd spent countless hours watching, learning, and practicing the finesse of fly fishing until she could cast a fly nearly as good as he could. She let her mind wander back to those treasured memories as she tied a wooly bugger fly to the line of her pole and tossed it out onto the top of the water. This was the one place she felt calm and at peace. A place where she could let go of the challenges she faced and demons she carried every day from her line of work. Hiking in, breathing the fresh air, and fishing the stream was a form of meditation for her. It gave her a semblance of balance and allowed her to come back out with a clear head and a clean slate, both of which she needed now more than ever with the proverbial bomb that had dropped into her lap.

After making the fly land and take off a handful of times, a brown trout snatched it off the surface. She pulled the free line in her hand hard enough to set the hook in its lip. Then, she began reeling it back towards her. The tip of her pole bent over and shook around as the fish tried to escape. With only a few feet of line left to reel, she bent down and plucked the nicely sized fish from the cool stream.

Chapter 12

Courtney walked into the bar wearing the same PT gear as everyone else. Her hair was down around her shoulders, giving a much more feminine impression than the stuffy, unisex uniform she wore daily. Several heads turned as she stepped up to the bar and ordered a light beer.

"Hey Chief, you wanna join our game?" Judd called.

She turned around with a raised brow.

"We're not gambling. It's just a friendly game...mostly for bragging rights," he said.

"What do you think?" she asked, looking at the corporal who had just served her.

"You missed Capt. Malloy wipe the floor with him at the pool table earlier, so I'm sure his ego is already deflated," he said with a shrug.

"Wait. What? Capt. Malloy is back?"

"Yeah, I believe her team got back yesterday."

Courtney chugged the rest of beer and tossed a five-dollar bill on the counter.

"Aren't you joining us?" Judd called as she headed for the door.

"Maybe next time," she replied as she left. Her mind was racing in ten different directions, but they all led to one location and that was where she headed.

*

Being back in Colombia was better than being at home where Tristan was stuck inside a whirlwind of emotions.

The short hiking trip had cleared her head enough for her to see past the anger, but she still had questions she'd never get the answers to, and she'd have to live with that. She spent most of her remaining time in the gym or on base doing various things. When the time came to redeploy, she left without speaking to her mother...something she'd never done during her entire time in the service.

Once she'd landed on foreign soil, the weight of home lifted off her shoulders. She had learned years ago to separate herself from home every time she deployed, and this time around, she was more than happy to let go. Since she'd been back, she did everything she could to stay busy. She'd changed the batteries in her equipment, cleaned her guns, repacked her gear, ran a few miles and kicked Judd's ass at pool...and it had only been twenty-nine hours.

She was lying half propped up in her rack, finally looking at some down time as she turned the page in the thriller she was reading, when she heard a faint knock at her door. Their barracks rooms were single occupancy, but still only about the size of a dorm room. She had a rack the size of a twin bed with a table beside it, and a footlocker on the other side of the room that had a makeshift closet above it. Her uniforms hung neatly in a row across the short bar at the top. Her patrol cap and green beret were both hanging on hooks in the wall, and her boots were on the floor under them. Her automatic rifle was leaning against the wall close by, near the table. Out of instinct, she'd reached for it when she heard the knock. She stood, wrapping her fingers around the barrel, ready to throw it up on her shoulder with her other hand on the trigger as a soft knock sounded once more. She tilted her head curiously as she held onto the gun. If it were someone from her team on the other side of the wooden door, they wouldn't purposely try to be quiet. If the base was under attack several different alarms would've sounded, so she knew it wasn't that.

"Who is it?" she asked.

"When were you going to tell me you were back?" Courtney sighed as she leaned her back against the door.

Tristan set her rifle against the wall beside the door and let go of it. "You shouldn't be here."

"There are a lot of things I shouldn't be doing," Courtney muttered. She stepped forward and turned around when she heard the lock click. "Tell me to go," she whispered when the door opened.

"I can't," Tristan murmured, grabbing the front of Courtney's shirt, and pulling her inside.

The door closed behind them as their mouths came together in a ferocious kiss. Courtney ran her hands up the front of Tristan's body, tugging on the short hair on top of her head as Tristan broke the kiss and moved her mouth down to Courtney's neck. Her hands slid under the t-shirt covering Courtney's torso, easily pulling the shirt up with them as they moved to caress her breasts. Neither woman could get enough of the other. Their bodies rocked together with their hips grinding, searching for more contact. Tristan unhooked Courtney's bra and snatched it and her shirt up over her head, tossing them to the floor as she buried her face in her breasts. Courtney moaned as Tristan's mouth and tongue assuaged her hard nipples. She barely had time to kick her shoes off as Tristan bent down, picking her up. She wrapped her legs around her waist and her arms around her shoulders, kissing her fervently as Tristan walked over to her bed, lying Courtney down on her back. Then she sat back on her knees and removed her own shirt, tossing it back behind her before bringing her naked torso down to Courtney's.

Wetness pooled between Courtney's legs as Tristan's nipples grazed hers. Her chest heaved with every ragged breath as they traded kisses fueled by thrusting tongues and gentle bites. Suddenly, she rolled Tristan to her back, careful not to throw them to the floor in the process, then she leaned back on her knees and grabbed the waistband of her jogger pants and pulled them down. Tristan lifted her hips, allowing Courtney to finish undressing her. She was already so far gone; it wouldn't take much for Courtney to finish her. She lost sight of Courtney through her heavy-lidded eyes as she knelt, burying her mouth between Tristan's legs.

Tristan swallowed a cry in her throat as Courtney's warm, velvety tongue licked and sucked her throbbing wet clit. She reached for her head, tangling her hand in the long hair spread over her thigh while her other hand grasped at the bedding beneath her. Her hips rose to meet every pass of the tongue driving her wild. She gasped and moaned as Courtney slid two fingers inside of her, matching the thrusts with her tongue. Tristan had never had another woman take control in the bedroom and it had been close to a year since she was intimate with anyone. Her senses were wildly heightened to a level beyond comprehension. She grabbed the pillow, biting down with it over her mouth to keep her from screaming as the powerful orgasm tore through her body like a savage beast, ripping her in half on its way out.

"Oh my god," she gasped, panting for air, begging her body to breathe before she passed out. Her mouth was dry, and her numb legs were tingling down to her toes.

Courtney wiped her mouth and hand on the bed and grinned before moving back up Tristan's naked body, settling herself in a straddling position on top of her. She leaned down, kissing her softly. "I should go before the calvary comes rushing to see what's going on with their beloved captain," she said with a grin. Tristan tried to protest, but she quieted her with a finger against her lips before climbing off her and covering her bare torso with the t-shirt Tristan had been wearing when she'd arrived.

"This isn't over," Tristan said, sitting up in the bed, still completely nude.

"Not by a long shot," Courtney replied with a grin as she pulled the door open and stepped into the hall.

Tristan put her head in her hands. "What in the hell just happened?" she whispered to the empty room as she shook her head.

Chapter 13

"I hope you're all well rested and ready to hit the ground running, Bravo Team," the colonel said as he stood at the front of the room.

"Yes, sir," Tristan replied. They'd been back for three days and were starting to get a little restless.

He drew a circle on the map with a red marker. "This outpost is being used as a fueling station and needs to cease to exist. If we cut them off here, we stop them from crossing the mountain range. At least in this direction for now. Outlaw One will fly you to a drop point two klicks away." He added a blue X. "You'll set a demo charge, extinguishing the site and anyone using it, then double-time it to the extraction point three and a half klicks to the east."

"Sir, won't that put us over the border?" Tristan asked.

"Yes. Do you have a problem with that, captain?" he questioned.

"Alpha Team is at the ready, sir," Judd chimed in.

Tristan rolled her head over her right shoulder in time to see him smiling like a Cheshire cat. "Bravo Team is locked, loaded, and ready to kick ass and take names, Sir," she replied.

"Outlaw One will be at the extraction point," Courtney said. "You get your team there. We'll do the rest."

"Alright. It seems we have that all cleared up. Alpha Team, you'll be heading to recon and potentially destroy another post they've been using. You need to be available to back up Bravo if things go south and vice versa. You'll be about fifty klicks apart, but on two different sides of the mountain and in two very different countries. Be careful...all of you."

"Hooah!" the group replied, standing as he left the room.

"You all heard the colonel. Dismissed," Maj. Irving said.

"Don't get captured, turd squad," Judd muttered as he passed by.

"Don't get lost," Tristan replied.

"He's a dickwad," Hoffman grumbled.

"Yep," she said in agreement as her eyes zoomed in on Courtney, who was in the back with her flight crew. She turned back around to see Maj. Irving walking up to her and her team.

"Be on the flight line at 2100," he said. "Make sure you're ready to fast-rope from the helo. You need to be out quick to keep the noise down. There are no settlements in the area, but you never know who is in ear shot."

"Yes, sir," they replied together.

"I'll catch up with you guys," Tristan said when she saw Courtney break from her crew. She quickly caught up with her in the stairwell. "Are we good?" she said, heading down the stairs behind her.

Courtney stopped and spun around. "Why wouldn't we be?"

"I just..."

"We're good, Captain." Courtney smiled.

"Roger that," Tristan whispered as she watched her walk away. "I hope you know what you're doing," she said aloud to herself.

*

The tryst with Courtney outweighed the pressure of Tristan's family situation tenfold. Thoughts of her cheating father and lying mother had been replaced almost instantaneously, and despite the reason being possibly unethical and perhaps career ending, she found it welcoming.

"You okay? You seem a little out of sorts," Perry said as she readied her gear next to Tristan. They were in the locker room of the main hangar where all their gear and the flight crew's gear was stored.

"Hmm…yeah. Fine. Just going over the mission in my head." She forced a thin smile at her team's medic as she checked and rechecked the pockets and pouches of her tactical vest before pulling it over her head. Her attention turned to Courtney as she and her crew headed out to the flightline.

Perry watched her line of sight. "I can't figure her out. She's pretty, and obviously good at her job. The boys think she's the greatest thing since sliced bread." She shook her head. "What about you?"

"She can fly a bird. That's all I care about," Tristan answered nonchalantly as she secured the straps of her vest and grabbed her rifle.

*

Courtney finished her preflight checklist and high-fived Maguire as they passed by each other. "What do you think, Howie?" she said, patting him on the back.

"Good to go, Chief."

"That's what I like to hear," she said with a smile.

"Here come the children," Maguire muttered, looking at Bravo team heading their way as he opened his cockpit door.

Courtney laughed and walked around the front of the helo to climb in. She was buckling her belts when Bravo team shuffled in with all their gear. "We're wheels up in two," she radioed over the channel they were connected to.

"Copy," Tristan replied.

Maguire turned the switch to change the receiver to their private channel. "Are we kissing their asses now?"

"Just trying to be cordial, that's all. There's no need in ruffling feathers or getting into a pissing contest." She shrugged and began going down their pre-take-off checklist.

"Outlaw One, Eagle. You copy?" command radioed.

"Lima Charlie," Courtney replied, watching the gauges as she and Maguire began starting the helos two engines.

"You are cleared for take-off."

"Roger that," Courtney answered before commencing with their ritual of fist bumping and yelling, "Rock and roll!"

*

The helo lifted off the ground and banked right, cutting through the midnight sky like a warm knife through butter. Tristan could see out the side windows, as well as the front, but there was nothing to look at. The forest full of trees was somewhere below and the sliver of a moon was somewhere above. Other than that, it was complete darkness lit up by the LED screens on both sides of the dash and backlighting of the instrument panel in the center.

She was more than prepared for the mission, but adrenaline coursed through her veins anyhow. Her decision to skip dinner was starting to haunt her as her stomach growled, but the meatloaf and mashed potatoes didn't sit well with her the last time it was served, and she wasn't taking any chances. The drop destination was still forty minutes out, so she pulled a protein bar from one of her vest pockets and tore it open. The scent of strawberries and cream tickled her nose as she bit down, eating half the bar in one bite. She didn't have to worry about sharing. She'd taught her team how to pack survival provisions early on. They each had a water canteen, chlorine tablets, enough MREs and protein snacks to last up to five days, and toilet paper. The females also had sanitary supplies because despite what the calendar said, the time of month could rear its ugly head at any moment.

*

"Ladies and gentlemen, we are approaching your destination. Please prepare to jump out of a perfectly good helo at your own risk in T minus ten minutes," Courtney radioed.

Tristan shook her head before putting her hand in the air with one finger up and spinning her wrist around, giving the signal to prepare to fast-rope down. Fowler went to the left side of the helo with Tucker and Perry. Tristan went to the right with Hoffman and Nigel. Everyone grabbed a black rope with both hands and sat on the edge of the floor with their legs dangling over as the helo doors opened. Courtney brought the helo to the exact coordinates and lowered down to a hovering position.

"Bravo team, you are clear to drop," she radioed. "I'll see you at the extraction point."

"Roger that," Tristan replied, then gave the call for everyone to go over the side and slide quickly down the ropes.

Within seconds they were on the ground, releasing the ropes. The helo reeled the lines back in and flew away, leaving them in the middle of nowhere in complete darkness.

"We had to do this on a nearly moonless night," Hoffman grumbled. "I can't see shit."

"Everyone, go to night vision," Tristan said, pulling the GPS from her vest pocket. "The rendezvous point is two klicks to the east. We're going to skirt the edge of this goat trail," she said, referring to the dirt road. "Nigel, you have the nav."

"Copy that," he replied, attaching his GPS to his forearm so he could easily see the map and their heading.

Tristan kept her rifle at the ready like everyone else with the rifle butt to her shoulder and her finger just off the trigger as they traversed the uneven terrain of the road along the side of the mountain. Anytime they heard a noise, they backed into the tree line and squatted down, but so far had seen nothing.

"RP is 100 yards out," Nigel radioed.

"Everyone, watch your six. We have no idea if any hostiles are around. Our orders are to fireball the building and get the hell out of here," Tristan said. "Fowler, you take the left flank, covering Hoffman. Once he sets the charges, move your asses double time. Tucker, I want you to skirt around to the high ground up there. Take out anyone who doesn't light up with an IR tab. Nigel, you and Perry stay in the tree line. Be prepared to cover Hoffman and Fowler. I'll be off to the right side, ready to go in if shit goes sideways."

"Copy that," everyone stated and headed off.

Tristan's pulse rate rose from the adrenaline coursing through her veins. She'd done this a thousand times, and each time the variables changed, but the outcome was always the same: complete the mission and get home. She trusted her team, but there was nothing more unpredictable than the enemy.

"Tucker, hit me with the play by play," she said. He had the vantage point up on the hill, watching everyone moving into position through his rifle scope.

"Hoffman is dropping off the hot pockets," he said, watching Hoffman stick the clay bar charges to the side of the building. "Hold on, we're about to have company," he added, moving the scope up towards the road. Headlights were bobbing in the distance and moving closer.

"I see it," she said. "Fowler, Hoffman, get out of there. That truck will be on you in two minutes!"

"The clay won't stick to the side of the building," Hoffman said.

"Toss it onto the roof!" she radioed back. "Tucker, keep an eye on the building door. I'm going in on the right flank. Perry, beat your feet and get on my six."

"Copy," she replied, running over.

Three men came out of the building as the truck pulled up with only one occupant. The driver got out and they all exchanged words.

"Hot pockets are in the oven and ready to heat up," Hoffman said.

"Hold your position," Tristan whispered. "Tucker, do you have eyes on all five guys?"

"One is walking the perimeter. Fowler, he's going to be on you in five...four...three...two..."

Fowler shot the guy between the eyes as he rounded the corner. The rest of the men heard the shot and sprang into action. Tristan and Perry rushed in from the opposite side, shooting three of the men. The last one went into the building and locked the door. Tristan heard him shouting, more than likely on the radio, calling for help.

"We have to get the fuck out of here!" Tristan radioed. "Everyone in the truck...now! Tucker, we'll get you at the base of the hill. Nigel, move your ass!"

Fowler was behind the wheel with Tristan in the passenger side of the tiny, two-seater pickup. Perry and Hoffman dove into the back. It took three tries to get the truck going, then another two to get it into gear.

"Get this piece of shit moving, Fowler!"

"I'm trying! I'm trying!" he yelled, finally getting it into gear. He popped the clutch, and the truck took off, sputtering down the dirt road.

"Cook the pockets!" Tristan shouted as the truck slowed enough for Tucker to dive into the back. Hoffman pressed the button, and the charges went off, blowing a huge orange ball into the sky as the building exploded. The truck jerked all around the rough road as it sputtered along at full speed.

"Perry, get on the radio with command. Find out where Alpha is. Nigel, navigate us to the extraction point," Tristan said as she scanned the terrain in front of them with her night vision goggles.

"We're heading in the wrong direction," Nigel stated. "The extraction was three and half klicks east. We're almost five klicks south at this point."

"Son of a bitch," Tristan muttered.

"Um…we can't turn around now!" Hoffman yelled as headlights appeared in the distance, followed by the faint sound of gunfire.

Fowler quickly turned the truck's lights out. They were riding along the side of the mountain with literally nowhere to go but straight ahead.

"Keep it to the floor. I don't care if we Dukes of Hazzard this piece of shit. That's an order!" Tristan said to him. "Perry…where the hell are we with the extraction?"

"Command is trying to patch me directly to the helo, but they're not responding."

"Forget the helo. We need to find Alpha. They were supposed to be within backup range."

"Copy that!"

The headlights were slowly gaining on them, but still too far away for the shots they were firing to do any damage. The only luck Bravo Team had going their way, was the chasing truck obviously didn't have any RPGs, or they would've fired them off by now.

"Bravo, this is Alpha One. What's your position? Over."

"Alpha, Bravo Three. We are fifteen klicks from our RP and moving south."

"Bravo, we are twenty-five klicks to the north of your RP."

"Son of a bitch!" Tristan growled as shots began to ping off the back of the truck.

*

Courtney banked the helo to make a slightly wider circle. They'd lost radio communication with Bravo team not long after dropping them and were told to remain in a semi holding pattern five klicks from the extraction point, which was where they had been for the last half hour.

"How long was this supposed to take?" Courtney questioned, mostly to herself.

"I don't know. I've never been a ground pounder. I assume command will radio us when they are ready for extraction."

"Eagle, Outlaw One. Do you have an ETA on extraction?" she radioed.

"Standby, Outlaw One. Bravo is under fire. We are currently trying to rendezvous them with Alpha for extraction."

"Eagle, we can be at the drop point in two minutes. Permission to extract them ourselves?"

"Negative, Outlaw One. Bravo is Oscar Mike. Standby."

"Damnit," she grumbled. "I knew we shouldn't have gone so far away, especially after losing radio communication with them."

"If Alpha is closer, they can get them. They're already on the ground."

Courtney was worried about Tristan, but she couldn't let that worry turn into fear. Tristan was well trained, as was she. And her training was specialized in these types of situations. She was about to radio again, demanding that they be sent in for extraction, when the radio crackled to life.

"Outlaw One, Alpha is unable to extract. Please reroute to the new coordinates we just sent you. Two vehicles are traveling southbound. Bravo is the lead vehicle. Repeat: Bravo is the lead vehicle, and they are taking on heavy fire from the chase vehicle."

"Roger that," Courtney replied and quickly spun the helo around, heading off in the direction of the updated coordinates as quickly as possible. In her mind, they couldn't get there fast enough, despite the helo's top speed being quick enough to put them at the RP within minutes.

From two miles out, Courtney saw the orange fireball light up the night. Her heart sank. Seconds later, the red brake lights from a vehicle came into sight off and on in the distance like tiny glowing and bouncing blobs. "I'm pretty sure that's a vehicle moving down there," she said. Then, she pulled her night vision goggles down. "It's definitely a truck and they're riding with their lights out."

"Bravo, this Outlaw One. You copy?" Courtney radioed, silently praying they were on the road and not over the side of the cliff in the fireball.

*

Fowler swerved from side to side, trying any type of evasive maneuver to keep the strafing of bullets from hitting anyone inside the truck. Perry, Nigel, Tucker, and Hoffman were all in the supine position on their backs, blindly sticking their guns up and returning fire. Tristan was crouched in the passenger seat with her rifle out the window, also returning fire.

"Can't this piece of shit go any faster?!" she growled.

"It's buried to the floor!"

There was no use in asking Nigel for an alternate route to try and lose the truck. It was less than fifty yards from them and would easily follow whichever way they went.

"Everyone, grab a grenade. We're going to pull the pins and toss them on my count. One of them has to hit this fucking truck!" She grabbed a grenade from her vest. "We pull the pin on two and throw on three. Ready?"

"Roger!"

"One, two, three!" she yelled, tossing the grenade as hard as she could at the truck behind them. Suddenly all five grenades blasted at the same time. The truck swerved and flipped over, bouncing down the side of the mountain as it burst into flames. "Holy shit!" she screamed. "We did it! We got the motherfuckers!"

"Should I stop?" Fowler asked.

"No! Keep going. There could more of them. Just keep the lights off and drive." She took a deep breath to slow her racing heart. "Is everyone okay back there?"

They all answered back. Surprisingly, they'd made it without anyone getting hit by the array of bullets.

"Eagle, Bravo One. Do you copy?" she radioed. When she got nothing in return, she tried again. Then, one more time.

"There's a helo in the distance," Hoffman radioed.

"That has to be Outlaw," Tristan said. "Perry, see if you can raise them on the radio. I've lost control with command."

"Roger that," she replied, pulling the higher frequency radio from Nigel's ruck, and turning it on. She tried three different channels with no response. Then, she flipped to the fourth known channel and heard Outlaw radioing for them before she could say anything.

"Lima Charlie, Outlaw! This is Bravo Four. Boy, are we glad to hear your voice!" she radioed back before handing the radio up to Tristan.

"Likewise, Bravo Four. What's your location?" she asked.

Tristan relayed their coordinates, which matched with the helo overhead. Then, she had Fowler flash the lights three times.

"We have eyes on you, Bravo," Courtney radioed. "I don't see anything but mountains. I'm going to have to put it down on the road using the instruments."

"Are you good with that?" Maguire asked, after switching to their private channel.

"If I wasn't, I wouldn't be doing it," she replied, then switched back over. "Bravo One, we're going to set down a hundred yards ahead of you in the road."

It was risky, but Tristan knew there wasn't much of a choice. They were in the middle of a mountain range, in the middle of a nearly moonless night. "Stop here. When the helo is on the ground, we'll drive closer. Hoffman, you and Tucker get out and help their crew chief keep a look out. Perry and Nigel, you get in the helo. Fowler, you and I will send this truck over the side. Everyone copy?"

"Roger," they all said.

"Outlaw One, we're pulling back here. You're clear to set it down. We'll come to you."

"Roger that!" Courtney replied as she began scanning the ground with her night vision goggles for the flattest spot she could find. Then, she worked the controls, slowing lowering the helo until the skids hit the dirt. Howie slid the side door open and jumped out, flashing a light so they knew it was all clear before taking position to guard the aircraft.

Fowler drove the truck quickly towards the helo, then skidded to a stop. Everyone jumped out the back, following their orders while Fowler and Tristan put the truck in neutral and began pushing it towards the edge of the road. He tossed a grenade inside before they shoved the truck over the side of the cliff. The bottom was only about fifty yards away, but the grenade went off halfway down, exploding the truck into a fireball as it tumbled.

Chapter 14

The debriefing lasted four hours, pushing everyone into the early hours of the next day, before they were finally dismissed. Tristan's team had to sit and listen to Judd explain why they weren't in position to come to their assistance when called upon, and instead halfway back to the base after completing the mission they'd been sent on. They were told by command to return to base, but Tristan wasn't buying it. Anger fueled her hungry, exhausted body and was the only thing keeping her awake at that moment. She'd dismissed her own team after a few quick words expressing her gratitude and pride towards their actions, and was waiting alone in the stairwell when Judd walked in.

"Where the fuck was your team?" she demanded, pushing off the wall.

"You heard me in the meeting. We were told to go back to the base," he said.

"You think this is a game, walking around calling us stupid names and making snide comments! My team could've died out there tonight!" she growled and turned to walk away.

"You're tired, get some rack time," he said.

Tristan spun around so fast, he jerked back towards the wall thinking she was going to hit him. The look on his face made her laugh. She shook her head and left him standing there against the wall.

Too amped up to sleep, Tristan headed towards the hangar to store the gear she was still wearing. Once inside, she removed her patrol cap and stowed it back in the pocket she kept it in before heading over to the locker room. Courtney was standing inside when she pulled the door open.

"What are you still doing here?" she asked, setting her helmet down on the bench while she opened her locker.

"The same thing you're doing," Courtney answered. She'd been in there for a few minutes, talking with her crew members before Tristan's team came and went, leaving her alone with her thoughts as she finished her flight log and stowed her gear.

Tristan removed her tactical vest and shoved it into the locker under the shelf her helmet was sitting on. She removed the insignia tapes from both arms of her long-sleeved combat shirt and unzipped the ¼ zipper before pulling it over her head and tossing it in the laundry bin. This left her in the tan T-shirt she wore underneath. She had the option of putting her ACU jacket on, or another combat shirt, but she chose neither as she slammed the door closed. Technically, she was still in uniform from the waist down and it was against regulations to wear a partial uniform at any time. You were required to be in full uniform, or PT gear when deployed, unless you were in your barracks room.

"You're out of regs," Courtney stated as Tristan turned to leave the room.

She stopped walking and turned around. "Are you going to report me…Chief?" she said with a raised brow.

Courtney's eyes locked with hers.

"There's no one around. I've been up for almost twenty-four hours and spent the last four hours explaining in detail how my team and I narrowly avoided the bullets strafing at our heads. So, forgive me for not giving a shit about regs right now."

"Easy," Courtney said softly. "I'm not the enemy here. As soon as I heard your team was under attack, I demanded the location. Command wasn't telling me, so I had already started heading towards your last known RP without authorization. When they finally gave me the coordinates, I got to you as quickly as I could." She shook her head and sighed. "You can walk out of here naked for all I care. I'm just glad you're okay."

Tristan crossed the room and pinned her to the lockers with a searing kiss. Her hands worked to unzip the ACU jacket Courtney was wearing, then moved to the belt and closure of her pants. Once they were open, she pulled them down low on her hips, allowing enough room for her hand to slip inside.

Courtney wrapped her arms around Tristan's neck, holding her close as their lips and tongues devoured one another. Her gut tensed and wetness dripped between her legs as Tristan's fingers slipped beneath her panties.

Tristan's mouth moved from Courtney's lips to her neck. "Tell me to stop," she whispered, grazing her teeth over the edge of her ear as her fingers inched lower. Her free hand was under Courtney's shirt with her palm flat against the smooth skin of her back.

"No..." Courtney panted as her hips moved involuntarily.

Tristan's fingers moved within the folds, circling her clit a few times before sliding softly inside of her. Courtney gasped and smacked her head back against the metal lockers. Her heart pounded wildly in her chest and her breath heaved with every stroke. She moaned in protest as Tristan's fingers slid out and circled her throbbing clit.

Tristan dragged her mouth along the pulse vein in Courtney's neck, then back up to her lips, assuaging her with another long, languid kiss as she pushed her fingers back inside. Courtney's legs opened wider, nearly ripping her pants as the smoldering muscles deep inside of her tightened around Tristan's fingers, squeezing them in place as she thrust down hard. A guttural whimper escaped her lips as she shuddered against Tristan.

Once her breathing evened out, Tristan delicately pulled her fingers free and rubbed them along Courtney's torso under her T-shirt to the bottom of her bra. Their eyes met before Tristan backed away and sighed.

"What's wrong?" Courtney asked as she closed her pants and zipped her jacket back up since she was still in full uniform.

"We shouldn't be doing this, for starters."

"We're both consenting adults. Plus, we're pretty good at it." Courtney half smiled.

Tristan shook her head. "I'm serious."

"Are you married?"

"What? No. I certainly wouldn't have done anything with you if I were. I'm not a piece of shit," she growled.

"Whoa. Why are you angry?"

Tristan ran her clean hand through her short hair. "I'm sorry. I'm just tired and frustrated." She looked over at Courtney. "I don't want to hurt you, but a relationship and everything that goes with it just isn't what I need or want right now."

"I never said I wanted anything. What's happened between us happened because we're attracted to each other. We don't have to label anything or make any promises."

Tristan nodded.

*

Courtney wasn't privy to the closed-door discussions about what had happened. All she knew was everyone had been eerily quiet for the past two days. The entire base had been grounded until the internal investigation was over. With nothing else to do, she went for a short jog and wound up at the helo hangar. The last person she expected to run into when she walked inside, was sitting on a bench, cleaning her gun.

"Fancy meeting you here," Courtney said as she grabbed the clipboard and began scanning the helo maintenance log.

"Yeah, well there's not much to do since those who are higher up the food chain than I am, are busy trying to untie this cluster with Alpha team." She shrugged.

"You don't think they purposely turned back…do you?"

"I don't know what to believe anymore," Tristan replied, thinking back to the deep lies she uncovered about her family. As far as she was concerned, everyone was capable of lying to save their own ass. She finally looked up, catching a glimpse of Courtney in a pair of black shorts and an Army green tank top. Her hair was pulled back in a ponytail and a pair of aviator sunglasses were up on her head. She looked young. Too young to be doing what they'd been doing.

"What?" Courtney said, seeing the questioning look in her eyes.

"How old are you?"

Courtney laughed. "That's an odd thing to ask."

Tristan shrugged.

119

"Twenty-six."

Tristan nodded.

"How old did you think I was?"

"You look about nineteen at the moment."

Courtney chuckled. "Thanks...I think." Her face scrunched into an awkward smile.

Tristan shrugged once more as she began putting her freshly cleaned rifle back together.

"Do you have any siblings?" Courtney asked nonchalantly as she went back to the log.

"No. Yes...I don't know. It's complicated." Tristan shook her head. "I thought we weren't doing this."

"Doing what?" she called over her shoulder.

"Having a relationship. Getting to know more about each other."

Courtney sighed. "You started it."

"Well, I don't want to finish it," Tristan said as she grabbed her rifle and headed towards the door.

"I've been looking all over for you," Fowler said as he rushed into the hangar, almost knocking directly into her.

"Slow down. What's wrong?"

"Everything okay?" Courtney asked.

"Chief," he said with a nod in her direction. "You might want to hear this, too."

Courtney set the clipboard down and walked over to them.

"The investigation is over. We've been called into a mandatory meeting in one hour, along with Alpha team."

"This ought to be good," Tristan mumbled.

"I need to see if we were called back as well. Excuse me," Courtney said, stepping around them.

Fowler noticed Tristan watching her walk away.

"Anything I need to know about?" he said.

"Nah, just chitchatting during off hours," Tristan muttered as they headed off in the opposite direction.

*

Tristan sat in full uniform in the front row of the conference room, along with the rest of her team. Alpha team was directly behind them in the second row, and Maj. Irving, Capt. Warren, and the captain of the comms center were all sitting up front to the side of the podium as Lt. Col. Powers led the meeting.

"What happen two days ago was the biggest cluster fuck I have ever been privy to, and I was in Desert Storm, Desert Shield, Kosovo for a half second, and Iraqi Freedom. The short of it is, we fucked up in the command center. Alpha Team got the blame and Bravo Team was nearly turned into Swiss Cheese."

He shook his head before continuing. "The long of it is, a direct order was miscommunicated, sort of like the game of telephone. By the time it got down to the low men on the totem pole, or the end of the phone line, the order had not only done a complete 360, but it had also gone several miles off course. Upon further investigation, we have concluded that Alpha Team was following an order from their direct command and by no means intentionally left their position as backup for Bravo Team. Also, we discovered Helo 12, crewed by the Outlaws, was struck with technical difficulties and lost communication with Bravo Team for nearly the entire duration of the mission. This morning, affirmative action was taken to see to it that a simple fuck up of this magnitude never happens again under my command. Also, I received word from General

Thorpe that the members of Bravo Team will receive the Army Valorous Unit Award for their extraordinary heroism while in action against an armed enemy. You all have already been awarded this decoration, so you'll be given an oak leaf cluster to signal the number of subsequent times. Now, if there are no questions, I'm going to cut you loose so we can get back to the reason we were all sent here in the first place."

Everyone stood at attention as he left the room.

"Bravo Team, you'll receive your commendations at a formal ceremony during your next garrison," Maj. Irving stated. "Dismissed."

"Well, isn't that some shit. Another leaf to wear on a ribbon once in a fucking blue moon," Hoffman grumbled. "How about a hazard pay bonus?"

"Stand down, soldier. You know how this works. They fucked up so they give us more pretty decorations to make up for it. At the end of the day, you guys keep re-enlisting and I keep adding more service time, so it's our faults. Take the rest of the day off to regroup. I'm sure we'll be back on mission sooner rather than later," Tristan said.

Fowler patted her on the back before walking off with the rest of them. She went back into the building and headed for the computer room referred to as the call center and sat down behind a laptop. It took her less than thirty seconds to login and a minute later, her mother's face filled the screen.

"Tristan!" she gasped, holding her hand to her chest. "I was beginning to worry. You deployed again without saying goodbye. You've never done that."

"Things didn't exactly go so well the last time I was home, so…"

"I knew you would take it extremely hard, which was why I never wanted you to know in the first place. You idolized your father and now you hate the man."

"Mother, I didn't call you to talk about all of that."

"Oh...Is everything okay there?"

"I'm good." She nodded. "Getting another commendation actually."

"Oh my! That's wonderful. What is this one for?"

"Surviving."

"Excuse me?"

"My unit came under attack a couple of days ago. We got ourselves out of it without harm, so we're getting a heroism award called the Valorous Unit Award. This is my fourth time getting it, so I'll just get another tiny bronze cluster leaf to pin to the actual ribbon that only comes out during ceremonies or other formal dress events."

"Honey, I don't know why you do it. Why not come home and—"

"Have a regular job?" Tristan shook her head. "Because I'm in the Army, Mother. This is what I do. This *is* my job."

"Either way, you know I'm very proud of you and thankful you didn't get hurt. I worry so much about you."

"I know. I'll be fine. I should get going though. The signal is horrible, so I need to let someone else get on here while it's working."

"Okay. All my love."

Tristan waved just before the screen went black.

Chapter 15

"Hand me a crescent wrench," Courtney said, blindly reaching for the tool. She was up on top of the helo with the engine housing open. When the metal tool touched her palm, she grasped it and pulled, but the tool didn't release. "What the hell, Howie!" she grumbled, turning her head.

Tristan was standing on the ground, holding the other end of the tool. She looked freshly showered and comfortable in her PT gear. Courtney's chest tightened, squeezing the air from her lungs. She hadn't seen Tristan since the investigation ended two days earlier.

Tristan's eyes held Courtney's. It didn't matter that she was in uniform and probably on duty. She hadn't bothered looking around the hangar to see if anyone was nearby.

"Where's your uniform?" Courtney said, when Tristan finally let go of the wrench.

"On the floor of my barracks room."

"What?" Courtney muttered, sliding the engine cowling back into place and tightening it with the wrench.

"You heard me."

Courtney's throat was dry, and her knees knocked together as she climbed down. "Aren't you supposed to be working?"

Tristan shook her head. "Aren't you done for the day?"

Courtney checked her watch, surprised to see the time. "Yeah, about two hours ago."

"Then, why the hell are you still here?"

Because if I'm not flying, I'm going stir crazy and when I have time to sit and think, all I want to do is feel your hands on me. She turned around and began putting the tools away. "I lost track of time," she lied.

"I was about to go get a drink...but I can think of a few things I'd rather do instead," Tristan said, following her.

"Oh, yeah?" Courtney questioned as she closed the toolbox and turned around.

Tristan placed her hands on Courtney's waist, as she backed her up against the heavy metal box. "Yeah," she whispered before claiming her lips in a searing kiss.

Courtney ran her hands up the front of Tristan's torso, kneading her breasts before sliding up higher, pushing against Tristan to break the kiss, and put some space between them. "As much as I want this right now, I'm still in uniform." She smiled.

"I can easily help you out of it."

"I know you can." Courtney grinned, shaking her head. "Are you going to the *Canteen*?"

"What else do you have in mind?"

Courtney grabbed a fistful of t-shirt and pulled Tristan back to her mouth for another lustful kiss that left them both breathless.

"I thought you were in uniform...Chief?" Tristan teased as she began lowering the zipper of Courtney's uniform jacket.

"You make me crazy," Courtney sighed, pushing her hand away.

"You make me wet," Tristan whispered, kissing her hard before stepping back. She turned and walked away before Courtney could gather any of the thoughts racing through her mind, long enough to say something.

*

Tristan sipped from her mug of beer, then she set it down and cleared four balls from the table in only three shots.

"Son of a bitch," one of Judd Dewey's team members grumbled. He was the chief warrant officer, and Judd's second in command.

"I told you not to taunt her," Fowler said, shaking his head sarcastically. This was their third game and so far, Tristan had schooled him every time. The pool was up to a hundred dollars because after the second twenty-five-dollar game, the young guy had taunted her with double or nothing. Of course, Tristan had said yes.

"I'm going to beat you," he snapped, grabbing his cue stick, and lining up for his shot.

"Might cost all of your paycheck," Fowler laughed.

The young guy ignored him as he made the shot, sinking one ball, but missed horribly on the second. Tristan only had two more balls on the table, plus the eight ball. She set her empty glass down and made three fast, but calculated shots, ending the game.

"Damn it!" the young guy yelled as he reached into his pocket. He pulled out two fifty-dollar bills and laid them on the table. "This isn't over," he complained as he started walking away.

"I look forward to next time!" she called, turning around to watch him scurry over to his friends at the dart board as she put the money in her pocket and left the bar. As she walked back to her barracks room, she thought about Courtney and was slightly disappointed that she hadn't seen her after their encounter in the hangar.

*

Tristan said hello to a few fellow soldiers when she entered the barracks building, then made her way down the hall. The first thing she noticed when she stepped inside her room was the clothing folded nicely in a small pile on her footlocker. She immediately turned to see Courtney lying in her bed under the covers. She pursed her lips and kicked her shoes off.

"So, we're breaking and entering now?"

Courtney raised a brow and smirked wickedly. "As if gambling on base is any better? How much of that guy's money did you take, anyhow?"

"A hundred bucks," Tristan laughed. "How did you know?"

"I went in there looking for you. I left during the second game when it looked like you might be a while."

"So, you decided to sneak in here and wait for me?"

"You left me no choice."

"No, I left you in the hangar, wet and wanting me."

"Exactly!"

Tristan shrugged. "You let the uniform get in the way."

"There's no uniform in the way now," Courtney said, lifting the covers to show her fully nude body.

Tristan's mouth watered and wetness instantly soaked the crotch of her underwear. She kept her breathing even as she pulled her t-shirt over her head, grabbing her sports bra with it. She flung them on the floor before pushing her shorts and wet underwear down to her ankles. She stepped out of the clothing and flipped it onto the top of the pile before crawling on the bed on top of her.

Courtney quickly rolled Tristan to her back and straddled her. "Do you know how badly I want you?"

"Why don't you show me?"

Courtney bit her own lip between her teeth, then leaned down, biting Tristan's bottom lip before moving to her breasts. Tristan inhaled the rosewater scent of her shampoo and conditioner as Courtney's long, chestnut hair fanned over her shoulder and the side of her arm. The feeling of Courtney's hot, wet mouth sucking her nipples drove Tristan wild. She moaned as warm wetness coated the sheet beneath her. Courtney snaked one hand along the center of Tristan's torso. Reaching down between them, she slipped her fingers through the silky folds, massaging Tristan's clit in languid circles.

With Courtney straddling her, Tristan had very little leverage, but her hips still rose each time Courtney's fingers dipped lower, pleading for them to enter her on every pass. Sensing her need, Courtney moved down, replacing her fingers with her mouth on Tristan's clit as she pushed two fingers easily inside of her.

Tristan still wasn't used to surrendering control to another woman in bed, but Courtney had a way of taking what she wanted and leaving Tristan sated and speechless in the process, forgetting all about any sexual encounters she'd had before her...and Tristan loved every minute of it.

As her body finally succumbed to the woman between her legs, Tristan bit back the guttural moan that threatened to escape her mouth as she gasped and writhed under her. When she calmed, Courtney moved back up, straddling her once more as she locked eyes with Tristan and licked her lips seductively slow.

Tristan sat up, claiming Courtney's mouth in an insatiable kiss as her hands slid along the smooth skin of her back, from the top of her ass all the way up under her long, wavy hair and back again. Without breaking the kiss, she kept one hand on her back and moved the other to one breast, caressing it while rubbing her thumb over the hard nipple jutting out. Courtney's wetness coated her skin where their lower bodies connected when she thrust her hips back and forth.

Tristan wrapped her arms around Courtney and broke their succulent kiss long enough to roll her to her back, before devouring her mouth once more. She kept one hand slightly under Courtney and moved the other down between her legs, sliding her fingers through the wetness in teasing passes over her opening and around her clit before sliding inside. She took her time, slipping her fingers deep inside, then almost all the way out in gentle strokes.

Courtney wrapped her legs around Tristan, using her as leverage as her hips rose to meet each agonizingly slow thrust. She felt like every nerve in her body was alive with electricity and she was in no hurry for the euphoric sensation to end. She pulled her mouth free from the kiss, taking one raspy breath after another with her lips against Tristan's ear and the side of her neck while her hands ran up and down her back, reveling in the soft skin covering the corded muscles in her shoulders and along her spine.

Tristan placed delicate kisses along Courtney's neck and the top of her shoulder to her collarbone before lifting just enough to lock eyes with her. She'd never connected with a lover the way she had with Courtney. The visceral passion shared between them scared the hell out of her and thrilled her all the same. Her chest tightened as she watched Courtney's heavy-lidded eyes and gasping breath when the rolling waves of pleasure descended upon her, slowly building to a peak as they released one after the other.

Courtney thrust her hips into Tristan with quivering thighs, squeezing her inner muscles tightly around the fingers deep inside as the tidal wave finally consumed her. She sunk her teeth into Tristan's shoulder to keep from screaming out in pleasure as she held on for as long as she could, riding the wave until her body could take no more. Suddenly, her sweaty, rigid body collapsed like a wet noodle underneath Tristan.

When Tristan eased her hand free and rolled to the side, Courtney turned towards her and placed her hand in the center of her chest as her mouth curled into a smile. "We should commit a court-martial felony more often," she teased.

Tristan laughed and shook her head. "You're such a bad girl."

"Being bad can be oh so good."

"I definitely agree."

Courtney sat up and swung her legs to the floor. "Seriously, I should go before someone catches me in here."

Tristan ran her hand down her naked back. Courtney closed her eyes for a second and briefly thought about staying the night, but there was no way she could explain being in the wrong barracks first thing in the morning. She ran her hand through her hair, pushing it back over her shoulder before standing and moving to put her clothes back on. Tristan stayed on her side with her head propped up by her arm, watching intently.

Once she was fully dressed, Courtney went to the door, but looked over at her before pulling it open. "To be continued?"

"Looking forward to it," Tristan replied. As soon as the door closed, she flopped to her back and sighed. She needed to be up in a few hours because her team was running through a fully dressed readiness drill. She wasn't privy to the conversations behind closed doors, but she'd been doing this long enough to know something big was coming. The readiness drill had been ordered by the colonel himself, and multiple teams were involved. She checked the time on the wristwatch lying on the nightstand. "Fuck," she muttered, noting she had to be up, dressed in full gear, and at the ready in three hours.

Chapter 16

"You're looking a little sluggish," Fowler said, bumping shoulders with Tristan. "Maybe it had something to do with last night."

"I'm fine. I had one beer and played a few games of pool," she replied, pulling her ruck straps a little tighter. They were standing on the flight line, preparing for inspection while wearing every piece of gear they owned.

"Looks more like you didn't get any sleep," he added.

"Are you implying something, Chief Fowler?" she snapped.

"No. Not at all," he said, shaking his head.

"Malloy, front and center!" Maj. Irving called.

Shit. She squared her shoulders and walked over to where he was standing, stopping directly in front of him. "Yes, sir?" The first thing that went through her mind was someone saw Courtney leaving her barracks room. The second thing was someone snitched about the pool table gambling.

*

Courtney walked over to her helo, which was sitting outside of the hangar, facing the flight line. Her crew was scheduled for a routine maintenance flight in two hours. Howie was already doing his pre-flight checklist. She opened her cockpit door and climbed inside to sit in her pilot seat and go over her flight log. It was the end of the month and it needed to be turned in. Once she was finished, she'd get started on her own pre-flight checklist and then go get geared up for the flight. As she sat there, her eyes panned down the flight line to where Tristan and Judd Dewey's teams were lined up wearing their full gear. She cocked her head when she realized it was Tristan standing in front of the captain, in what looked like a verbal ass-chewing.

"Everything okay?" Maguire asked as he opened his door.

"Huh…yeah," she muttered, pulling her eyes back to her log.

He watched her for a long minute. "Looks like the grunts are on the major's bad side this morning," he said, shaking his head.

"Mmmhmm," she mumbled.

"You like her…don't you?"

"Who? What?" she said, finally looking at him with a confused expression. She hadn't paid any attention to what he was saying. She ignored his mumbling as she continued working.

"That can't be good," he said.

She sighed in frustration and turned her head. "No…that definitely isn't good," she whispered. "I'll be back. Wheels up in thirty minutes," she added, checking her watch. She forced herself not to look over again as she walked into the hangar.

*

"You were supposed to be briefed later today, but since your squad seems to be a little keyed up this morning, I'll go ahead and give you the good news," Maj. Irving said. "Bravo Team has been reassigned to garrison. You're all getting your commendation and a weekend of R&R. Wheels up at 1400."

"Roger that," she replied.

"Now, get back in line and stop interrupting formation."

"Yes, sir." She did an about face and retook her position.

"Alright, ladies," Maj. Irving started. "As you know, Alpha and Bravo have both been cleared to get back in the field. The cartel is on the move. We can't afford another snafu. Let me rephrase that, we will NOT have another snafu. Are we clear?"

"Yes, sir!" the group answered together.

"I'm counting on all of you to put the last mission behind you and move forward. You are all green berets in the United States Army. It doesn't get any more badass."

"Hooah!" everyone shouted.

"Teams, your CO's have your orders. Dismissed."

Everyone saluted, then broke from formation.

"Differences behind us?" Judd said, walking up to her.

Tristan looked him square in the eyes. "We *have* always and *will* always have your six, but if you ever forget about ours again…" she trailed off, gripping her jaw.

"I was obeying orders. What would you have me do?" he spat.

"Are you really going to go there," she growled through her clamped teeth as she stepped into his space with clenched fists. "Only a pussy or a traitor leaves his brothers behind…orders or not. So, which one are you?"

"Capt. Malloy, let's go," Fowler said, squishing between them and casually pushing her back. "We have a mission to prepare for," he added.

Tristan relaxed her hands and took a deep breath as she and Fowler walked away. She glanced over at the helo, her eyes searching for the pilot.

"What was that all about back there?"

"I'm sorry," she said, looking at him.

"There's nothing to apologize for. That condescending asshole needs to be put in his place. Just…maybe, not on the flightline next time." He grinned.

She laughed.

"I seriously thought you were going to hit him."

"He would've had to hit me first. I've never in my life started a fight, but I'll damn sure finish one."

"You had all of Bravo at your six. You always do, and you always will. The guys respect the hell out of you, me included."

"Thanks. It won't happen again. I said my peace. He knows where I stand. He'll either man up and do his damn job, or he'll let his predispositions ruin his career." She shrugged. "Come on, we're headed stateside to get our commendation."

"Seriously?"

"Yeah, we leave this afternoon. Go inform the team."

"Alpha isn't going with us, are they?"

"Honestly, I have no idea," she said before they parted ways. Tristan went into the locker room, and he kept going in search of the rest of the team. As soon as she was behind closed doors, Tristan sat on the bench and put her head in her hands. When she heard the door open, she jumped to her feet.

"Hey," Courtney said softly. "It's just us." She moved closer, willing herself not to place her hand on Tristan's cheek. They were both in uniform and if they were caught doing anything physical, it wouldn't end well. "Is everything okay?"

"Yeah. All good."

"It didn't look okay out on the flightline."

Tristan sighed.

"You can talk to me."

"There's nothing to say. I'm a little keyed up about our new mission."

"Enough to go toe to toe with Capt. Dewey?"

"He had a problem, and I was giving him an answer. Nothing less, nothing more."

Courtney nodded, but she didn't believe her. In part, she couldn't blame Tristan. Courtney was a lower rank, and their physical relationship was already taboo as it was. If she knew details about certain issues she wasn't privy to, Tristan could be held accountable. Courtney respected her, and whatever it was between them, enough to not put her in that position. She finally gave into temptation and lifted her hand to Tristan's cheek.

"You're breaking the rules, Chief."

"I know," she whispered, leaning in, and pressing her lips softly to Tristan's, before pulling away.

Tristan grinned. "I'm turning you into a bad girl."

"Uh huh," Courtney laughed.

"I like it."

"I'm sure you do." Courtney smiled and shook her head before they parted ways.

*

Tristan licked her lips, trying to taste any remnants of Courtney as she walked away from the hangars and entered the main building to meet with her commanding officer about their garrison assignment. Then, she needed to put on her full ACU and prepare to depart the base. She usually called her mother when she was headed home, but all her thoughts were on the paperwork she knew was sitting in her mailbox. She'd done her best to push her home life aside for the past month but knowing she would be home later that evening...it seemed to all come flooding back.

*

"Outlaw One, hold your current position. We have a bird taking off on runway two. You will be clear to land on pad three once he has cleared your airspace," the tower radioed.

"Copy," Courtney replied, watching the C12 Huron take off in the distance.

"I wonder when we'll get assigned to garrison and get a chance to go home," Maguire mumbled.

"Hopefully, sooner rather than later," she said.

"Outlaw One. You are cleared to land on pad three."

"Copy that."

Courtney brought the helo in, landing softly in the space before shutting the engines down. They'd been in the air most of the day, first on a maintenance flight, then a recon flight after that. She unbuckled her belts and flung her door open before taking another few minutes to fill in her new flight log for the month.

"I don't know about you, but a cold beer is calling my name," Maguire said.

"I second that!" Howie said.

"You in?" he asked, looking at Courtney.

"Definitely." She smiled. "I'm going to change to my PT gear. I'll see you in about thirty."

"Copy that."

Courtney was the last person to leave the helo. One of the maintenance corporals came over with the tug and pulled the bird back into the hangar. She saluted and headed off towards the locker room to stow her gear. As soon as she finished, she went to her barracks room and changed into a black t-shirt and shorts with Army written on them. She thought of Tristan, wondering how the rest of her day panned out as she pulled her long, wavy hair out of the tightly twisted bun and ran a brush through it. Then, she slipped her feet into a pair of sneakers to let them breathe a little after being laced up in combat boots all day and headed out the door.

*

Howie and Maguire were already sitting at the bar, each with a longneck in his hand, when Courtney walked in.

"Gentlemen," she smiled in their direction. "Corporal, I'll have what they're having."

"Copy that, ma'am," he replied, grabbing a light beer from the cooler, twisting the cap off before placing it in front of her.

Courtney leaned her back against the bar and took a long swallow.

"She's not here," Maguire whispered. "In fact, none of her team is."

"Who are you referring to?" she questioned, as if she didn't know.

He raised a brow.

"Hewitt, you up for a game?" Judd asked.

She laughed. "The last one didn't hurt bad enough?"

"Anyone can beat me once. But can you do it twice?"

"I've seen Capt. Malloy wipe the table with you quite a few times. Besides, you know gambling is against regs."

"There's no money changing hands. It's just a friendly game. Besides, Malloy and her team are stateside."

"What do you mean?"

"They're getting commendation medals and flew home for the ceremony."

She chugged her beer and set the bottle on the bar as a swirl of confusion, anger, and disappointment ran through her head. "I'm in. You rack 'em," she said, finally settling on anger.

Chapter 17

The P.O. box Tristan used for her mail was overflowing with an abundance of junk mail, all of which she tossed in the nearby trashcan as she flipped through the stack. Her gut tightened and her lungs quit inhaling when her fingers grazed the envelope from the State of North Carolina Children and Families. She wanted to know what was written on the papers inside more than anything, but the base post office wasn't the best place to get the biggest news of your life.

"Malloy?" a male soldier said as he walked up to her.

Tristan turned around and cocked her head to the side like a confused dog as she tried to remember how she knew the man, especially since he hadn't addressed her by her rank and he was enlisted. Beckett was stitched on his name tape, the sergeant first class rank was on the tab in the center of his chest, and a black Military Police band was around his upper arm.

"My apologies, Captain," he said, popping to attention. "It's been a long time. You might not remember me," he said. "I'm Rex Beckett."

Suddenly, her days in bootcamp came flooding back to her. "T-Rex!" she exclaimed, pulling him into a hug. "Man, it's been years!"

"Yeah," he laughed. "It looks like you're doing well," he added, noticing her special forces tab and rank.

"Not too bad. I'm a Special Operations Detachment Leader."

"Wow. That's great. I never pegged you for an officer back in boot."

She chuckled and shook her head. "Yeah, me either. I was a ranger for six years and when I made platoon sergeant, I decided to go to OCS and move over to special forces. Anyway, what about you? Have you been an MP all of these years?"

"Yes and no. I was active duty for eight years as an MP, but I've been in the reserves for the last five. I didn't re-sign, so I'm out in about four more months. I'm an officer for Fayetteville PD."

"Awesome. I'm still active duty. I just landed not too long ago. I'm actually on leave from deployment."

"Cool. Did you ever get married and have kids?"

"No. You?"

"I've been married for three years. My wife and I have a baby on the way. Hence my leaving the service for good. Once I'm done, we're moving up to Michigan where her family is. I'm getting off the streets and going to work as a law enforcement academy instructor up there."

"Awesome. I'll probably be here until the Army kicks me out," she laughed. "Maybe I'll be a stuffy old general someday."

He chuckled. "I'll let you get going. I know you said you're on leave."

"Yeah. It was good seeing you though. Take care."

"You, too."

As she walked away, Tristan smiled at the memories of all the grueling days they spent together. A lot of sweat, blood, and tears were shed, but they made it out and went on to do bigger and better things. Her smile faded when she remembered the crucial envelope she held in her hand. She quickly folded it in half and stuffed it in her pocket before pulling her green beret onto her head as she exited the building.

The short ride to her apartment took less than five minutes. As soon as she walked in, Tristan tossed her deployment bag to the floor and pulled her jacket and beret off. She didn't bother with the rest of her uniform as she sat down on the couch and tore the envelope open. Her eyes scanned over several words and numbers she didn't understand until she read: Conclusive DNA Match. She dropped the papers on the coffee table and leaned back against the cushions. That was it. With a simple piece of paper and three little words, she had a dead sister and an orphaned nephew.

"Son of a bitch," she sighed. During the entire process Tristan was never fully sure which way she'd wanted the cards to fall. She already knew her father had stepped out on her mother. He'd admitted it. And now, the question of whether he'd fathered another child was answered. She had a sister she never got to know, and subsequently, wouldn't get to mourn...and both of her parents were to blame.

She sighed once more, then got up and walked into the kitchen and pulled open the drawer her cell phone was in. Whenever she deployed, she always left it behind. It took a second for the device to boot up, but once it did, she had twenty voicemails and three hundred emails. She couldn't care less about the emails, which she knew were all junk. Instead, she shuffled through the voicemails. The two from her mother were from when she was home last and deployed again without saying goodbye. She quickly deleted those without listening to them. The next dozen were telemarketing calls, all of which she sent straight to the trash. The last of the remaining voicemails were from the state social worker. To save herself some time, she listened to the latest one.

"Ms. Malloy, this is Janice Brown again. I assume you have received and reviewed the DNA test results. You are a match to the child in question. I know this may not have been the results you were hoping for. However, please return my call as soon as possible. I have some paperwork I need you to sign so that the child can be put on the adoption list. You are biologically his next of kin and will need to sign over your legal guardianship rights. Again, please call me as soon as possible. Thank you."

Tristan pressed the call button and leaned back against the counter as it rang.

"This is Janice," a female voice answered.

"Ms. Brown, this is Tristan Malloy."

"Oh! Ms. Malloy, I've been trying to reach you."

"I apologize for calling so late, and not getting back to you before now. I was deployed. I arrived home a little bit ago on a short leave."

"I understand. I assume you've either heard my voicemails or received the results in the mail by now."

"Both, actually."

"Good. So," she sighed, pausing.

Tristan heard the shuffling of papers and typing of keys on a computer.

"Okay, here it is," Janice said, talking to herself. "Sorry about that, I had to locate his case file. Loki's foster family has shown some interest in adopting him. Since you are his biological next of kin, you automatically get legal guardianship. Once you sign the papers, the court will relinquish your rights, thus allowing him to be adopted."

"Wait...did you say his name was Loki?"

"Yes, ma'am. Loki Adams. No middle name on the birth certificate."

Tristan chuckled. "Loki, from Marvel Universe and the comics."

"Um...I'm not sure," Janice replied, looking for reference in his file.

"Can I meet him?"

"Yes, of course. Are you sure you want to do that? It may confuse him as to who you are. The George's, his foster family, have had a rough time with him and believe their church is helping to get through to him."

"Yes. I want to meet him. Tomorrow, if possible," Tristan said, sounding more matter-of-factly.

"Uh...I'll have to check with the foster family. We usually like to give a few days' notice."

"I'm only here for a short time on leave."

"Okay. Let me give them a call, and I will get back to you."

"Wonderful." Tristan ended the call and went into her room to take a quick shower and change into civilian clothes.

It was already almost nine o'clock when she got out, but she had a voicemail from Janice saying she would pick Loki up from his foster home in the morning and meet her at ten a.m. at a local park in Fayetteville, about twenty minutes from her apartment near the base. She knew she would barely sleep and decided someone else needed to be up all night, too. So, she pressed the call button for her mother's number on her phone as she sat on the couch and put her feet up on the table.

"My father has a grandson, and I'm going to meet him in the morning," she said as soon as her mother answered.

"What? Tristan...are you home?"

"I got home a little while ago. Did you not hear what I said?"

Her mother sighed. "Honey, I wish you would leave that mess alone."

"I took the DNA test. She really was dad's daughter, and now he has a grandson sitting in a foster home."

"Just let him be, Tristan. He doesn't know you, and your father's dead and gone anyhow."

Tristan shook her head. "I'm meeting him in the morning. I thought you should know. Also, I texted you the information for my team's commendation ceremony in case you wanted to attend. Have a good night." She ended the call and tossed her phone on the table.

*

Heavy rain pelting the windows should've helped Tristan sleep, but her brain simply wouldn't shut down. Seeing Rex had brought back old memories that seemed like a lifetime ago. She was just a kid when she entered bootcamp; a star athlete in her hometown who had never had a drop of alcohol, done anything more physical than kissing, and certainly never held a gun. The Army had aged her more than she realized in the last thirteen years.

She was happy to see Rex doing well. Their bootcamp platoon had been a tightknit group of mostly males, with Tristan and three others as the only females. Rex had stood up to the few males in the group who felt like the girls didn't belong and they became fast friends. By the end of the ten weeks, she proved she was not only as good as the boys, but better when she graduated at the top of the class.

When she finally exited memory lane, her thoughts shifted to Loki. She wondered what he looked like. Did they share a resemblance? Was he told who she was? She remembered the social worker saying he was five. She tried to remember when she was five but couldn't recall anything. What would they talk about? Could a five-year-old hold a conversation? Obviously, his mother had been a Marvel fan if she named her son after one of the characters. She wondered if he liked Marvel Universe. She was more of a Captain America fan. Maybe they could talk about that. The empty questions kept coming as she finally drifted off to sleep.

*

"You seemed like you were on a mission last night," Maguire said, bumping into Courtney in the hangar.

She gave him an odd look, then shrugged her shoulders. "I needed to blow off some steam. What better way than wiping the table with that asshole in front of his team?"

Maguire laughed. "Remind me never to get on your bad side."

She grinned. "That's probably a good idea."

"Attention!" Howie exclaimed from the other side of the hangar when he saw the colonel walk in.

"At ease. I'm not here to bust any balls," he said. "Hewitt, I was wondering if I could go up with you today."

"Sure...uh...yes, sir," she said clearing her throat.

"Great. Wheels up at twelve hundred."

Everyone watched him walk out of the hangar and proceed down the flight line.

"What the hell was that about?" Maguire muttered.

"No idea," she replied, slightly in shock. She hadn't had a superior officer flying with her at the controls since she was in flight school. She could fly a Blackhawk with her eyes closed, so she wasn't worried about that. She was more nervous about the conversation they would have. *There's no way he knows.*

"Did you hear me?" Maguire said, smacking her with his clipboard.

"Huh? What?"

"I said, here's your chance to show him how much of a badass you are."

She forced a smile and checked her watch. It was only nine o'clock. *These are going to be the three longest hours of my life.* The first person she thought of was Tristan. *Damn it.*

Chapter 18

Tristan parked her Jeep in one of the multiple open spaces and took a deep breath when she climbed out. Families meandered close to the play equipment. She looked around, finally spotting the social worker on a bench nearby. A small boy was sitting beside her. She shoved her hands into the front pockets of her jeans and started walking.

"Captain Malloy, it's nice of you to join us," Janice said as Tristan moved closer. "Loki, this is my friend Tristan. She came here to meet you."

The little boy turned his head, looking in Tristan's direction. "I don't care. I want to go play!" he yelled.

"We will in a minute, but first, we are going to be nice and say hi," Janice replied.

"Hi," Tristan said, taking a seat on the opposite side of him. She held her hand out. "It's very nice to meet you."

He simply stared at her with a scowl on his face. His mousy brown hair stuck out in all directions, obviously in need of a trim, but the first thing she truly noticed were his eyes. They were the same shamrock green that she shared with her father and his father. She choked back a sob.

"Loki, why don't you tell her about school?" Janice encouraged.

"I hate school," he grumbled, crossing his arms. "I want to go play, damnit!"

Tristan gasped at his use of foul language.

"I'm sorry. We're still dealing with aggression and use of bad words."

Tristan nodded. She had never spent any time around children, but she stood up and held her hand out. "Would you like to go show me around?" she said, glancing over at the playground, then back at him.

"Fine," he said, hopping off the bench and avoiding her hand as he walked towards the equipment.

Tristan tagged along, following his lead as they climbed through a set of twisted metal bars, then headed over to a different area.

"What's your favorite color? Mine used to be green, but I wear it so much, I think I'm shifting towards blue," she said.

"I don't care."

"Do you like baseball or football?"

"No, damnit," he muttered, walking away to climb up a spiderweb style rope, then slide down a slide.

She waited for him to come down, then she followed him once more.

"Fuck this!" he yelled.

"Oh!" Janice exclaimed running over to him. "Loki, we do not use that word!" she stated sternly.

"I've been told worse," Tristan said, walking over to her.

Janice shook her head. "He's so out of control," she sighed. "From what I've gathered, his grandmother was his caretaker. When she passed, he was pretty much on his own. His mother left him alone quite a bit."

"How old was he when his grandmother passed?"

"Three, maybe four. I'd have to check the file."

Tristan nodded.

"The Georges have had a terrible time getting through to him. Two of their four children were fostered and adopted, so they are familiar with the process, but he has a lot more baggage than they've dealt with in the past. They took him out of the public school he was in and put him in the private school run by their church to help give him some guidance."

"And you think that's what he needs...church?" Tristan questioned.

"He needs time, to be honest. His brain is trying to understand mourning and loss, but it's coming out as aggression and anger. He needs to be in therapy...for several reasons. We're working on getting him into the state program. Unfortunately, it takes months."

"What about the private sector?"

"He's in foster care, so he has to go through the state."

"What happens if that family adopts him?"

"They will become his parents, so it will be up to them to decide what to do."

Tristan sighed. Her heart sank for the small child as she watched him complain as he walked around the playable art pieces. He looked lost and lonely, two things a child should never experience.

"I have the court papers with me, if you'd like to go ahead and sign them," Janice said, pulling her from the sadness that had engulfed her.

Tristan glanced at her, then her eyes went right back to Loki. "Give me a minute," she replied, before walking over to him.

"What do you want?" he muttered as he climbed onto a swing.

"Loki, do you like the Georges? Are they nice to you?"

"I hate them."

"What about your brothers and sisters? Are they nice?"

"I don't have brothers and sisters."

"Do you like living there with all of them?"

"What do you care!" he yelled.

"Because, if you don't like it, or they are not nice…you can maybe come spend some time with me and see if you like that better."

"How many kids are at your house?"

"None. It's just me."

"I don't want to go there. I want to go home!" he yelled again.

"The George's house is your home," Janice said, walking over when she heard Loki start yelling.

"No, it's not!"

"Loki!" she shouted when he ran away to another section of the play park.

"I want him to stay with me. I have something to do on base in the morning, then I'm off for a few days before returning to my deployment. I'd like him to spend the weekend with me in my home. I'll bring him back on Monday."

"Ms. Malloy, are you thinking of taking custody of him?" Janice asked with a bit of shock on her face.

"I don't know. But I am his family, and he deserves to know who I am and who his family is. When I return him on Monday, you'll have my decision."

"I'm not sure that's a good idea. He's established a relationship with the Georges, and…"

"I am his only next of kin, making me his legal guardian. Correct?"

"Technically, he is a ward of the state, but yes, you do have legal rights."

"Give me an address to pick him up. I'll get him tomorrow afternoon."

"As you can see, he is quite the handful. Are you prepared for that?"

"I am an Army Special Forces Captain who has led a team of soldiers into the armpit of Hell and back. I'm pretty sure I can handle an angry, mouthy five-year-old." *Or at least I hope so.*

"Okay," Janice exhaled. "I'll text you the address of his foster family. What time should they expect you?"

Tristan thought for a second. The commendation ceremony was at ten a.m., then there would be a luncheon afterwards. "I'll be there at thirteen hundred." She shook her head. "Uh…one o'clock."

Janice made a note in her phone as they walked over to Loki together.

"Loki, do you like my friend, Tristan?" Janice asked.

He shrugged and crossed his arms.

"She's going to come get you tomorrow, and you're going to spend a few days with her at her house."

"No!"

"Loki, we're going to have fun. I promise," Tristan said.

"I want my mama and my Gigi!"

Janice sighed. "We've talked about this. Your mom and Gigi are in Heaven with the angels."

"I want to go to Heaven with the angels, too!"

"Honey, you can't do that. They are gone and you are still here."

"You suck!" he shouted and went to run off. Tristan grabbed him on instinct and held him close as he thrashed around.

"Loki, it's okay. I'm not going to hurt you or ever let anyone else hurt you, I promise," she whispered to him. After a few seconds, he calmed down and she set him back on his feet. She squatted down to be at his eye-level. "We have the same eyes. Did you know that?"

"No," he mumbled.

"My dad and his dad had these eyes. I bet your mama had them, too."

"I don't remember," he said sadly.

"That's okay." She looked up at Janice, and then back at him. "I need to say goodbye, but I will see you tomorrow. Make sure you pack your favorite things, okay?"

He nodded and sighed.

Tristan stood back up. "One o'clock," she said, before turning and walking away.

*

Lt. Col. Powers looked quite a bit different wearing his flight gear. He returned Courtney's salute before they both climbed into the cockpit from either side of the helo. "You're in command. I'm your co-pilot," he said as he began buckling in.

"Yes, sir," she replied as she finished her belts and began running down the preflight checklist. "Eagle, this is Outlaw One. We are standing by."

"Copy, Outlaw One. You are clear for takeoff."

"Roger that." She started the engines and grabbed the controls, easily lifting the helo off the ground. "Our flight path for today will take us over the mountain range towards the coast to the west, and back," she said, informing the colonel.

"Copy that," he replied, looking out at the sky in front of them.

Courtney felt her nerves leave as soon as she was settled in her seat. It didn't matter who was sitting next to her once she had the controls in her hands. Her mission for the flight was surveillance of the path coming out of the mountains and along the coast, looking for anything suspicious, like cargo trucks moving product. The main information they learned early on about the Domingo Torres Cartel: they didn't use mules, and they always moved their product in large shipments.

Courtney zeroed in on a fruit truck chugging along the path below them. She took the helo down a little and to the side. "Howie, can you get a visual of the cargo?" she asked.

"Negative. It's covered with a canvas tarp."

"Eagle, Outlaw One. We are in sight of a vehicle moving cargo west along the mountain pass. Four klicks from Jaji. Over."

"Copy, Outlaw One. Do you have a visual on the package?"

"Negative. It's a fruit truck, but it's not hauling fruit. Over."

"Copy. Alpha Team is Oscar Mike. Continue with the mission."

"Roger that," she radioed and pushed the cyclic stick to the left and flew away from the mountain road.

"What would you have done if they had pulled the tarp off a 50 cal?" Lt. Col. Powers asked.

Puckered my ass! "Protocol is not to engage, Sir. However, if they had shot at us, Howie…uh…Sgt. Smith, would've returned fire, disabling the vehicle, Sir."

"And held your breath." He smiled.

"That's a given, Sir." She grinned.

"You know, Hewitt. I flew with your old man in Kuwait."

"You did, Sir?"

"Yeah. I was a green as goose shit new officer and part of his Apache squadron, back then. In fact, I commanded the mission that retrieved him and his crew when they were shot down. If I remember correctly, no one was hurt."

"Correct, Sir. He talks about flying over there quite a bit, but never mentions the crash."

"He was a damn good pilot. When they were hit, he was able to fly the badly damaged bird out of town and set her down in the lake. The soft landing saved his crew. The Iraqi's had no idea where the helo landed. By the time they'd arrived in the area to search for it, it had sunk. His crew hid out in the woods overnight and were rescued the next morning," he paused for a minute as he recalled that night. "Things like that stick with you. Anyway, you are most definitely his kid. You fly just like him."

"Thank you, Sir."

"I assume he's still alive."

"Yes, sir. Living the retired life these days." She smiled.

He laughed.

Chapter 19

Tristan stood on the flightline of her garrison base, dressed in her Army Service Uniform, which was her most formal uniform. The jacket was dark blue with a single row of four large gold buttons down the front. The shoulder boards on each of her shoulders had the bars for her rank. The gold piping around the wrist part of the sleeves had a green stripe in the middle for special forces, and her right sleeve had eight small stripes for her time overseas. The gold special forces badge was on both sides of her collar with US in gold above it on each side. Three and a half rows of colorful ribbons were up on her left chest. Her last name was on her right chest, opposite her ribbons, with her unit awards above it. The rest of her uniform consisted of lighter blue pants with a gold braid down the side, a white dress shirt with a black neck tab, shiny black dress shoes, and her green beret with her rank bars in the center of the crest.

Her team members were in a line beside her, dressed in the same uniform, but she and Fowler were the only officers. The rest were enlisted, so their ranks and unit insignia were worn differently. The men also wore neckties instead of the neck tabs the females had on.

Col. Curtis Baker, the commanding officer of the base, stood at the podium in front of the family members and other soldiers who attended the ceremony, also wearing what was more commonly known as the dress blue uniform, or Class A.

Tristan scanned the small crowd. She recognized the family members of her team, along with some of the other base staff who were in attendance. Her eyes paused briefly when she saw her mother.

"Good morning," he started. "We are here today to award these soldiers of the 4th Special Forces Group, 2nd Battalion, Charlie Company, Bravo Team with the Valorous Unit Award for their extraordinary heroism in action against an armed enemy." He glanced over at the soldiers standing at attention to the side, and slightly behind him. "Each of you have already received this award, so today you will be given an oak leaf cluster to attach to your unit ribbon."

He proceeded by calling out each of their names as his executive officer, Maj. Anthony Marcus, presented them with a bronze oak leaf, and shook their hands. However, the colonel stopped before calling out Tristan's name.

"Capt. Tristan Malloy, the commander of this team, also had actions that went above the meritorious degree for the Valorous Unit Award, and thus, the United States Army has awarded her with the Silver Star for exceptional valor in leading her team and completing their mission while engaged in action against an enemy of the United States," he said, flipping the velvet box open to show the ribbon and subsequent medal. "Capt. Malloy," he called, waiting for her to step up to him. She saluted, along with the major. He returned the gesture before handing her the box. She returned to her position in line with her team, standing at attention.

"This concludes today's ceremony. You are all encouraged to remain for the congratulatory luncheon, which will be served at the tables inside the hangar in just a few minutes. Thank you," he said. As everyone clapped,

157

he turned around and shook each of their hands and walked away.

"First of all, congratulations to our Silver Star team leader," Fowler said, shaking her hand.

Everyone congratulated her behind him.

"It was a team effort. If we hadn't worked together, they would've pinned these commendations to the top of our caskets today," she said.

"Yes, but without your leadership, none of us would be here," Nigel replied.

"Damn right!" Hoffman added.

"Okay, okay." Tristan smiled and held up her hands. "Let's go visit with our families and enjoy the weekend. We are wheels up Monday morning."

"Roger that!" the team exclaimed.

Everyone in the room came up to Tristan to congratulate her, including the dozen or so officers who had attended the ceremony. Getting the silver star was a huge commendation, and something she never thought she'd get. She was still slightly in shock as she smiled and shook hands.

"Thank you for inviting me to see this," her mother said. "It's been a while since I saw you all dressed up. That seems like quite a big deal," she said, looking at the medal in the box.

"It's the third highest honor in the Army. It doesn't get handed out. It's earned," Tristan said.

Her mother nodded. "I'm proud of you. I don't know what it is you actually do, but you must be very good at it."

"I'd like to think so. I'm still alive, aren't I?" Tristan muttered. She hated this strained relationship with her mother. They'd always been able to talk about almost anything. Her mother had two hang ups: her being gay, and her continuing to stay in the Army. The two things that literally were her life. Tristan had learned over the years to steer clear of conversations involving either, but after learning about the dark family secret, she just didn't care anymore. "Are you going to ask?"

"About what?"

Tristan shook her head. "He has dad's eyes. The same eyes grandpa and I also share with him."

Her mother shook her head. "I don't want to hear about him."

"Well, don't bother calling me this weekend, then. I'm picking him up this afternoon."

"Tristan—"

"Mother…I'm not doing this with you, and certainly not here."

"Hello. You must be Mrs. Malloy," Col. Baker said, stepping up to them.

Tristan popped to attention.

"At ease, Captain," he said with a smile.

"Colonel, this is my mother, Patricia Malloy."

"You must be very proud. She's an outstanding leader."

"Yes," her mother replied with a thin smile.

"Will you be joining us for lunch?"

"Unfortunately, no. I have some business to attend to."

He smiled and nodded before turning to walk away.

"I'm leaving Monday to rejoin my command," she said to her mother once he was gone.

"I really wish you wouldn't waste time with this nonsense. Sign the papers and let someone adopt him."

"I'm not cold-hearted like you and my father."

Patty Malloy gasped like a shocked southern woman in a soap opera. Then, she turned and walked away. Tristan walked over to the buffet table to fix herself a small plate of food, seemingly uncaring of her mother's sudden departure.

"What was that about?" Fowler muttered, sliding up beside her to shovel some mashed potatoes onto his plate.

"We don't see eye to eye on a family matter."

"Gotcha."

*

Tristan made sure to speak to the family members of her team, all of whom congratulated her, before leaving the base. She went straight to her apartment to change into a pair of jeans and a t-shirt. Then, made the drive out to the address Janice had given her. The fact that she'd just been awarded a silver star took a backseat to the ball of nerves forming in her gut when she thought about her weekend with Loki. She had no idea what she was going to do, she just knew she wanted to be near him. "What does a five-year-old like? Will he want to watch TV? What do kids even eat?" she questioned. "Maybe this is a bad decision," she sighed, pulling off at the exit. "There's no turning back now, Malloy. You're a Special Forces Captain with a Silver Star in the United States Army. Surely you can handle two nights with a five-year-old," she muttered to herself when the GPS led her into a neighborhood.

"Captain Malloy," Janice greeted when Tristan parked her Jeep along the curb and got out.

Tristan smiled and nodded in her direction.

"Are you sure you want to do this?"

"If I didn't want to, I wouldn't be here. You act like he's a mental patient or a convicted felon. He's just a little boy who's had everything taken away from him."

"Okay," Janice sighed. "The Georges are expecting us."

Tristan pushed her sunglasses up into the fauxhawk of her blonde hair and followed behind her as they walked up the driveway.

The front door swung open, and a man appeared before Janice could knock. He looked to be about mid 50's with a few extra pounds in his mid-section, and a sprinkle of gray in his brown hair. His dark blue slacks and pin-striped, white oxford shirt made him look like a businessman. Tristan suddenly wondered what he did for a living.

Janice held her hand out. He politely shook it as his eyes raked over Tristan like a foot on hot coals. "This is Loki's aunt, Tristan Malloy. This is Thomas George, Loki's foster father."

"It's nice to meet you," Tristan said.

"Yes, you as well," he replied as if he were forced to say it.

Suddenly, a bubbly woman appeared. She was wearing a floral print dress with flats and light make-up. The soft wrinkles in her brow indicated she was probably close in age to the man.

"Karen," the man said, "this is Loki's aunt, Kristen."

"Tristan," she corrected.

The woman tried to cover her gasp by clearing her throat as she took in Tristan.

"Is Loki ready to go?" Janice asked, breaking the awkwardness.

"Oh…uh, yes. Please, come in. I'll go get him," Karen said.

Tristan followed them inside. She looked around, unsurprised at the crosses and art with religious quotes on the walls. Tom was telling Janice about how Loki was doing now that he was going to the private school at their church. He made sure to go on and on about how Jesus was helping the young man expel his demons.

How the fuck do these people become foster parents? Tristan questioned, shaking her head. "May I see his room?" she asked, hoping it would help her figure out what the kid liked.

"It's down the hall on the right," Tom said.

Tristan was barely out of the living room and into the hallway when she heard Karen's voice.

"Come on, Jonah. You will be back very soon. Remember to pray to Jesus like Pastor Michael showed you."

Tristan cocked her head to the side like a confused dog as she took another step and peered into the room. Karen was bending down in front of Loki, and he wasn't interested in what she was saying to him.

"His name is Loki," Tristan stated, walking into the room.

"Yes. Jonah is going to be his new name when we adopt him. We're trying to get him used to it."

"Is he ready to go?"

"Yes. Grab your bag, son. Remember what Pastor Michael told you."

Tristan grabbed his bag and his hand and left the room. Janice's brows shot up when she saw Tristan walking with the boy and his stuff. Karen came rushing out behind them.

"We're ready. Is there anything else I need to do?" Tristan asked, looking only at Janice.

"Uh…no."

"What time will you have him back on Sunday? We go to church at nine," Karen said.

"He won't be back until Monday morning."

"What…we have church…he has to be there…and he has school…" Karen went on and on like a puppet about to explode because the screws were coming loose.

"It will be okay if he is a little bit late for school on Monday," Janice said, looking at Tristan.

"What time does school start?" Tristan asked.

"Promptly at 8:30 a.m.," Tom said, as if that were a big deal.

"Mrs. Brown, please text me the address. I'll have him there at 0900," Tristan replied, then she opened the door and ushered him out.

"Are we really going to your house?" he asked as they walked down the driveway.

"Yes."

"Why?"

"I'll explain when we get there," she said, opening the door and tossing his bag on the back seat.

"This is your car?"

"Yep."

"Cool!"

She helped him get in and get his seatbelt on. Then, she went around to get in. Janice was walking down the driveway when she started the vehicle and drove away without ever looking at the two people staring daggers at her from the windows.

"I want to sit up front," he grumbled.

"You're too short, bud."

163

"I'm not a bud."

"I'm sorry. You're not a Jonah either. Your name is Loki. Bud is short for buddy, sort like friend. I'll just call you Loki. How about that?" Tristan said as she changed gears and got onto the highway.

He kept silent so she went on. "It's about a two-hour drive to my house. What kind of music do you like?"

He stared out the window.

She pulled over and turned around to look at him. "Let's start off differently. My name is Tristan. I like fishing and camping, and I don't want to hear the word Jesus all weekend. It's your turn."

"What is fishing and camping?"

"You have a lot to learn." She grinned. "I'll tell you all about it."

He nodded. "I don't want to hear Jesus, too."

She smiled. *At least we're on that same page.*

*

The rest of the drive back to her house, Tristan explained all about fishing and camping, then alternated songs on the radio. When they finally arrived, she asked Loki what he wanted to do as they got his bag out and walked into her apartment.

He didn't answer as he plopped down on the couch, then got up and walked around, looking at the pictures on the wall. They ranged from her parents to her rugby days in high school, and throughout her career in the Army.

"Is that you?"

"Yes." She smiled. "I'm in the Army."

"Badass," he whispered.

"I have one big rule, no bad words in my house."

He rolled his eyes.

"Maybe we can eat some popcorn and watch a movie later. Do you like movies?"

He shrugged.

Okay, kid. You need to cooperate somewhat. "How about I tell you who I am? We can start there."

He stared at her awkwardly.

Tristan opened the cabinet at the bottom of the coffee table and pulled out a photo album. Then, she sat down on the couch and patted the spot next to her as she opened the book. Loki walked over to the couch but left a lot of room between them when he sat down.

"This man was my father, Donald Malloy. Most people knew him simply as Don. He was a great dad and a good man." She pointed to the opposite page. "This was his father and my grandfather, Arthur Malloy. He was a pistol and smart as a whip. He's the one who taught me to fish and camp."

"Why are you showing me these people?"

"Because…they're your family, too," she sighed.

"No, they're not."

"Yes." She nodded.

"My father had another child. She was your mother and my sister. That makes him your grandpa, and that man, your great grandpa. It also means that I'm your aunt. We are your real family."

"No! You're lying! I don't know you!"

"It's okay. I know this is a lot."

"Get away from me!" he screamed.

"Loki…" She blew out a deep breath. "I promise, I will never lie to you."

"Leave me alone!" he yelled and took off running through the apartment. There were only two places to go, her room and the spare room that she'd set up for him, so she just let him go.

"This is going to be a lot harder than I thought," she sighed, turning on the TV as she kicked her feet up onto the table. She checked the messages on her phone and scrolled through the guide for cartoons. Once she found something she hoped he would be remotely interested in, she turned the volume up.

About ten minutes later, Loki emerged with wet cheeks and plopped down on the adjacent recliner. "You're not my family," he muttered.

"Yes, I am. I will not lie to you."

He ignored her as he watched SpongeBob on the TV.

"Do you like pizza?" she asked, already placing a delivery order on her phone.

He nodded.

"Do you like pepperoni and mushrooms?"

"Yuck!"

"Okay, so no mushrooms?"

"No peckeroni."

"It's called pepperoni."

"Whatever," he muttered.

She finished placing the order then went into the kitchen. "I have water, milk, and lemonade. Would you like something to drink?"

"Coke."

"I just said, I have water, milk, and lemonade."

"I don't want that shit!"

Tristan took a deep breath and walked back into the living room. She grabbed the remote and turned the TV off as she sat down on the table in front of him.

"Turn it back on now!"

"Loki, I'm not going to tolerate this behavior. I am not going to hurt you. I am your real family."

He turned away.

She grabbed her phone and snapped a picture of his face, then took a selfie and used an app to put them side by side. "Do you see this? Look, we have the same eyes. Just like the two men in those pictures. We all have the same eyes because we are family, Loki. I'm trying to help you, but I can't if you don't let me."

He glanced at the picture when she zoomed in to show him.

"My mama and my Gigi were my family. They're gone!"

"I know. My dad and my grandpa are gone, too. It sucks, but we are still here, and we have each other." *I want to hug you so badly. Somehow, I know that's what you really need, but it's too soon.*

"I don't know you."

"It takes time. I don't know you either, but I want to." She stood up. "The pizza will be here soon. Now, what would you like to drink?"

"Lemonade," he huffed.

Chapter 20

Tristan was never home, so she only had basic cable and nothing streaming. However, she did have a DVD player and a pile of movies thanks to her mother's care packages from over the years. She went into the closet and ripped the box open. "There has to be something in here he can watch," she mumbled to herself. "Aha!" she exclaimed, grabbing the first Ironman movie. It was still one of her favorites, along with Captain America...and Captain Marvel, for obvious reasons.

"Do you know who Ironman is?" she asked, putting the disc into the DVD player.

"Nope."

"He's super cool. How about Captain America?"

"Nope."

"We can watch that one tomorrow," she said, plopping down on the couch with the remote in her hand. The empty pizza box was still lying on the small dining table, the contents having been devoured by the two of them.

Tristan pretty much knew every line in the movie, having seen it a dozen times, but it was very different seeing Loki watch it for the first time. He fidgeted a little through the dull parts, but once Tony Stark became Ironman, Loki was on the edge of his seat. She smiled, hoping somewhere deep inside she was getting through and connecting with him, even if it was only a little at a time.

By the time the movie ended, Tristan was half asleep and Loki wasn't far behind. She showed him to the spare room, where his bag was sitting on the bed.

"Can you get your pajamas on by yourself?"

"I'm not a baby!"

"Okay. Calm down. There's no need to be so aggressive. You know something, you are the only kid I have ever spent time with, so I'm learning, too."

"What's aggressive?"

"Mad, mean, angry," she answered. "The bathroom is right here next to this room. I put nightlights in all the rooms and the hall, so you can find your way around. Make sure you brush your teeth, okay?"

"I hate brushing my teeth."

"Well, if you don't brush them, they will fall out." She shrugged.

"I know they fall out," he pulled his lip back and showed her where he'd already lost a tooth that was growing in. "They grow back."

She laughed. "That only happens one time. If they fall out again, they're gone forever."

"No, they're not. You're lying."

She sighed. "Loki, I said I would never lie to you." She grabbed her phone and pulled up a picture of someone with a lot of missing teeth. "See, they don't grow back. The ones that are falling out right now are called baby teeth. Then, your big teeth grow in. If you lose your big teeth, you will look like this forever."

"That's gross!"

"Well, brush your teeth!"

He grumbled a few times but went into the bathroom with his toothbrush anyhow.

I'll take the small wins wherever I can get them, she thought as she went into her own room and changed into an Army tank top and comfortable cotton shorts. When she turned around, he was standing there. She swallowed her surprise. "How long have you been standing there?"

"Long enough to see your purple underwear."

"Great," she muttered. *Glad I don't go commando.* "When someone is in the bathroom or their bedroom, you should always knock. It's not polite to just walk in."

He shrugged.

"Did you need help with something?"

"The toothpaste is broke."

"What?"

"I just told you!"

"Let me see what's going on." She stepped around him and went into the bathroom. His toothbrush was lying on the counter next to a half empty tube of toothpaste. "Here," she said, handing him his toothbrush. Then, she squeezed the tube of paste from the bottom, sliding the contents to the top and out the hole onto his brush. "There you go."

She waited outside the door for him to finish and use the toilet. Then, she walked into the bedroom with him and pulled the comforter back. "Loki, do you have accidents in the bed at night?"

"No. I'm five, not a baby."

"Okay, just checking. It's ok if you do. I just wanted to know if I needed to put something on the bed just in case."

"Karen makes me sleep in special sheets, too."

"I'm not going to do that. I trust you. I hope eventually, you will trust me, too. Remember, I'm right across the hall if you need me. Nothing in here will get you or hurt you."

"I'm not scared."

"Okay then, goodnight." She turned the big light off but left the door open when she walked out.

*

Tristan was sitting at the bar in the kitchen, sipping a cup of coffee when Loki walked out of his room and into the bathroom. He was still in his pajamas with his hair sticking out in all directions.

"Do you like pancakes?" she asked when he meandered into the kitchen.

"Yeah," he mumbled, plopping down on the stool next to her.

She got up and tossed some frozen pancakes into the microwave. "I searched through the cabinet and found some chocolate powder I didn't know I had, so I made you chocolate milk," she called over her shoulder. When she turned around, he was already chugging the glass. She smiled and shook her head. "Do you want syrup?"

"Duh!"

"Excuse me? The correct answer would be, 'Yes, please. Thank you.' However, I'll settle for a simple yes."

"Fine. Yes," he huffed.

"That's better," she replied as she set the plate in front of him. "Would you like me to help you cut them?"

He rolled his eyes as he said, "Yes."

*

171

After breakfast, they both brushed their teeth and changed into t-shirts and shorts before going into the living room to watch TV. She was surprised he'd chosen to sit on the couch instead of the recliner which was further away.

"I have a bunch of movies for you to choose from. We can't watch them all today, but we have tomorrow, too," she said, showing him the array of Marvel movies on the table.

"Is this all we are going to do?" he asked.

I would love to take you to a lot of places, but I can't risk you running off. "Yeah, I figured we'd just hang out and spend time together. Is that okay with you?"

"What about church and bible study and—"

"I don't do any of that," she said, cutting him off.

His eyes opened a little wider as he looked at her.

"Do you want to go to church?"

"No! I hate church!"

"It's not nice to say you hate things. How about saying, you don't like it?"

"I don't like church," he huffed.

She smiled. "Me either. But some people do, and that's okay. Everyone is entitled to their differences. It would be a boring world if we were all the same. We'd be like robots," she said as she pretended to move like a stiff robot.

He laughed, then changed to a more serious tone. "What do I really call you?"

"Well, I'm your aunt. So, Aunt Tristan, or just Tristan. You decide."

"They make me call them Momma Karen and Daddy Tom," he said as he looked through the movies. "And they won't stop calling me Jonah! That's not my name!"

"Hey," she said softly. "Calm down. I'm not going to make you call me something you don't want to or call you by a different name. I like Loki. In fact, in a few of those movies, there is a character named Loki. I'm pretty sure that is where your mom must've gotten your name. I bet she was a Marvel fan, too."

He nodded. "Can we watch that one, then?"

"The one with Loki?"

"Yeah, sure. Let's start with this one, though," she said, pointing to Captain America. "Then, you'll know who everyone is."

"Okay," he muttered, sitting back on the couch, keeping his distance from her.

"Can I ask you something?" she said.

He looked over at her and shrugged.

"Do you like Mr. and Mrs. George?"

He shook his head.

"Do you want them to become your mom and dad?"

"No!"

Tristan could see this line of questioning was going down the wrong path, so she opened the DVD case and pulled the disc out. "Let's start the movie," she said, hoping to put a smile back on his face.

*

By the end of Sunday, Loki was sitting on the couch beside Tristan. When their last movie for the day ended, she turned to him.

"We have to get up early so you can go to school."

"I don't want to go back! I hate it there!"

"What have I told you about the word hate?"

He huffed. "I don't like it there."

173

"Do they hurt you?"

"No."

"Okay, can you tell me what you don't like?"

"Everything!" he shouted, then covered his face with his hands.

Tristan knew he was crying, and her heart broke for him. "Can I give you a hug?" she asked softly.

He turned into her and for the first time in her life, she felt a powerful instinct to protect, almost like a wild animal with a den full of babies. She wrapped her arms around him and breathed in his scent. In that very moment, she knew her answer. When he finally pulled away, she helped him wipe away the tears.

"Loki, I am your family. What's in here," she said, pointing to his chest. "Is the same in here. No matter where you are. The Georges want you to live with them and be their son." He started to get angry, but she put her hand on his cheek. "You don't have to do that. You can live with me...and be my son. You won't have to call me mom, but I will be just like a mom to you. And your name will always be Loki. I've already told you, I promise I will not lie to you, no matter what. How do you feel about that?"

He shrugged. "I like it here with you."

"Okay. Let's get ready for bed and go to sleep. We can talk about it again in the morning."

Chapter 21

Loki wasn't thrilled about going back to the George's, but his anger went out the window when Tristan walked out of her bedroom dressed in her ACU the next morning. The look on his face was a mix of surprise, excitement, and adoration. He'd asked a hundred questions about everything on the uniform before they could even leave the house. She was glad she wasn't in her dress uniform; they would've certainly been late. Just before she loaded him into the Jeep, she gave him a picture of herself. She was in her same ACU and standing on a base in Iraq. A Blackhawk was in the background behind her, and a smile was on her face. He tucked it into his pocket.

When she pulled into the parking lot for the church school, Loki wasn't happy at all, but he latched on, giving her a tight hug when she walked him to the door. The administrator turned her nose up at Tristan and took his hand. Tristan waved as he turned around to look at her when they started down the hall. She wasn't back in her Jeep when she felt a tear slide down her cheek. *Damnit.* She removed her beret and slid into the driver's seat.

*

Courtney had spent all of Saturday and Sunday grounded due to bad weather. She was keyed up and there were only two ways to expel the energy; one of them being flying. She'd thought about Tristan more times than she cared to admit. As much as she wanted to be angry with her for not telling her she was going on leave, or getting a commendation for the fiasco, all she could think about was seeing her when she returned.

The heavy rains had kept the base quiet all weekend. She'd spent most of her time in her barracks room, only venturing out to eat at the chow hall. She'd even avoided the *Canteen*, which had become a staple for the off hours of her non-flight days.

By Monday morning, the rain had been replaced by sunshine that had quickly dried everything back out. She hadn't been scheduled to fly, but she'd made a special request to go up anyhow. Her CO approved it and gave her crew an open window for a couple of hours. She used the time to practice training maneuvers like coming in hot to pick up a ground team, or leaving hot, which meant they were under fire. Howie kept his unloaded rifle pointed at the ground as his harness kept him from falling out of the open door.

After three passes through the area they used for training, she set the bird back on the ground. Being in the air had eased some of her pent-up energy, but it hadn't taken her mind off Tristan. She checked her wristwatch, wondering if she'd returned.

*

The buzz of the plane's engines had just about lulled Tristan to sleep as the conversation she'd had with Janice on the way to the base replayed in her head.

"Are you sure you want to do this? One weekend fails in comparison to taking him on full time as a parent. I'm sure we can work something out with the Georges for you

to still visit him if you allow them to adopt him," Janice had said.

"You have my final answer. I'm not signing the papers. I want full legal custody of him. I'm going to raise him as my son, and keep him where he belongs, with his actual family. Let me know what I need to do to move forward," she'd replied.

"You'll need to appear in front of a family court judge to plead your case, which basically means tell him what you just told me. After that, he'll sign the papers and you'll become Loki's legal parent. You'll need to fill out a packet of paperwork to file for the court hearing."

"I'm about to board a plan to get back to my deployment unit. When do these papers need to be filed?"

"As soon as possible to get the ball rolling. You can do it electronically since you are deployed. The court will accept it."

"I'll text you my email address. One last question, do I need an attorney?"

"I'll get the paperwork ready and emailed to you within the next couple of days, hopefully. And no, there's not a need for legal services. I'll handle everything for you and let you know as soon as we have a court date."

"Okay, I check my email every other day."

"Great. I'll be in touch," Janice had said before ending the call.

Tristan hadn't bothered calling her mother. She wasn't ready for the reaction she was going to have. Going through with all of this could literally drive a wedge so far between her and her mother, they could possibly never speak again. That was something she simply wasn't ready to face.

When the C12 finally touched down, Tristan awoke with a start after having finally fallen asleep.

"You okay?" Fowler questioned.

"Never better," she stated matter-of-factly. She stood, arching her back as she stretched, then tossed her ruck over her shoulder.

He smacked her on the back and fell instep behind her as they exited down the back ramp. Everyone put their berets on, then dropped their rucks and formed a line at attention.

"Welcome back, Bravo team. Hopefully, you're all rested and ready to go. We'll convene in the ready room at 0800. Fall out," Maj. Irving said, dismissing the group for the night.

Tristan grabbed her ruck, tossing it over her shoulder. "This is one night I'm actually excited to see that lumpy old rack," she muttered as they started walking towards the barracks.

Fowler laughed.

"Anyone up for the *Canteen*?" Hoffman called.

"No. You're all adults. I'm not going to babysit you. Just be in the ready room bright-eyed and bushy-tailed at 0800," Tristan stated.

"Hooah!" they all replied.

*

Courtney was clearing the table against a cocky soldier who'd spent more time flirting with her than playing pool when half of Bravo Team walked into the *Canteen*. Her hand literally let go of the cue, causing it to smack the floor with a loud thud. When she didn't see anyone else come in behind them, she turned back towards the guy she was playing against. "I'm going to call it a night. Looks like you win this one by default," she said before leaving the bar without another word.

She followed the path towards the barracks buildings, careful to stay in the shadow of the lights so no one noticed who she was and where she was going. Arriving quickly at building D, she pulled the door open and stepped inside, quietly walking down the hallway to the door she'd become familiar with. She wrapped her knuckles on it softly, hoping not to wake or alert anyone else.

The door cracked open, and a sleepy Tristan poked her head out. She was dressed in a tank top and shorts, most likely with nothing under them. Courtney's mouth watered.

"What are you doing here?" Tristan whispered.

"Do you want me to go?" Courtney murmured.

Tristan nodded for her to come inside. The scent of her rosewater shampoo and conditioner tickled Tristan's nose and went straight to her gut.

"Why didn't you tell me you were going on leave to get a commendation for the fuck up that nearly got all of you killed?"

Tristan shook her head. "Courtney, we're not..." She sighed.

"I get it. We're just fuck buddies." Courtney ran her hand through her hair, pushing it back over her shoulder. "I agreed to no relationship. I know that. But you could've at least told me about the commendation."

Tristan didn't say anything.

179

"You look like you haven't slept in three days. What's really going on with you?" Courtney questioned, moving closer.

Tristan grabbed her hand before it could touch her cheek. She knew she wouldn't be able to do what she needed to do if Courtney touched her. "I can't...*we*...can't keep doing this." She let go of her and took a step back. "I can't risk losing my career, my future retirement...things have changed. I'm sorry."

"Are you serious? What's changed?"

"My life," Tristan said.

"This is crazy." Courtney shook her head in disbelief.

"You said it yourself. No relationship. It was just sex, right? We got what we wanted from each other."

"Tristan..."

"Let it go."

Courtney threw her hands up in the air. "Don't I have a say in this?"

"The entire barracks is going to have a say if you keep raising your voice," Tristan muttered.

Courtney turned around and stormed out of the room as quietly as possible when all she wanted to do was slam the door. She ran down the hall and exited the building before the tears started to fall. "Damnit," she growled, wiping the streaks from her face. "What the hell happened? Why the fuck won't she talk to me?" She thought of going back to the *Canteen* but getting drunk was the last thing she needed to do. Instead, she headed in the opposite direction and went to her own barracks building.

*

Tristan leaned her forehead against the door, listening to Courtney's steps fade as she ran away. "Fuck," she mumbled, turning around, and sliding down the door until her butt was on the floor. She pulled her knees to her chest and let the tears fall. She cried for the lost little boy she left behind, and her own heart, which she'd just shattered to pieces. She knew it was the right thing to do. Sleeping together was already bordering on insubordination. If they were found out, they could both lose everything, and she'd worked too hard to allow something that stupid to end her career. Beyond that, she had Loki to think about. He needed every ounce of her attention and every drop of her heart. She knew the second he wrapped his little arms around her that she was going to make him her whole world and give him all her love, no matter what.

Chapter 22

Tristan's team was sitting in the ready room, awaiting the details of their next mission, when Lt. Col. Powers walked into the room.

"First, let me congratulate Third Squad, Bravo Team on receiving the Valorous Unit Award. As well as Capt. Malloy on receiving the Silver Star," the colonel said.

Everyone gave a brief round of applause.

"Moving on from the accolades, we have business to get down to," he continued as Maj. Irving flipped the switch to dim the lights. The screen at the front of the room lit up with mountainous terrain and a large body of water. She'd been all over the area enough times to know that was Lake Maracaibo…in Venezuela.

"I'm sure you're all familiar with the lake. That's not your mission," Maj. Irving said, pressing a button to zoom the picture in. A squiggly line zig-zagged it's way to the lake. "This…is the Catatumbo River. We believe the cartel is using it to move product into the lake, and subsequently, the Gulf of Venezuela and the Caribbean from there. Our satellite imagery shows a structure here," he said, circling a point in yellow. "We believe this is where they've moved to after we cut out all of their routes out of Colombia, but we need to be certain. Outlaw One is going to drop you over here." He drew a red X. "It's about twenty klicks, give or take. This is a STANO mission. You'll have four days to get to the building, gather as much intel as you can, and get to the extraction point without anyone ever knowing you were there. Outlaw One will be waiting at the extraction, but our window is short. We need to know what is going on in that building, and how they are moving product down river. Your only backup is two hours away on the other side of the border. Wheels up tomorrow at 1800. We'll brief once more between now and then to finalize the location, drop and extraction points."

"Yes, sir," Bravo Team said together.

The Outlaws, who's CO was also Capt. Warren, sat quietly in the back of the room. They'd already been briefed the day before and were now finding out exactly what the mission was.

"Outlaws, Bravo. Any questions?" Maj. Irving asked.

"How long is the extraction window?" Courtney questioned.

"Thirty minutes, give or take five," he replied. "Bravo will either be in place, or they won't."

"What do we do if they're not there and we time out?"

"They'll be spending another night on the ground in enemy territory. Let's all try to make sure that doesn't happen."

"Yes, sir," everyone said together.

"Any other questions?"

Everyone kept silent.

"Dismissed."

"Hooah!" the group yelled as they stood and saluted.

The major returned the salute, then looked directly at Tristan. "Ghosts leave no trace."

"Roger that," she replied as her spine stiffened.

Everyone began filing out of the room, but Tristan walked over to Maj. Irving.

"May I have a word with you, Sir?" she asked.

"If it's non-mission related, it'll have to wait. I have another meeting to get to."

She shook her head as she watched him walk away.

"Something I can help you with, Malloy?" Lt. Col. Powers asked.

"I had a non-mission related question, but it can wait."

"What is it?"

"How does leave work for a new parent?"

"Well, the Army has primary and secondary parental leave for new birth mothers and fathers. Primary caregivers are given six weeks and secondary are given 21 days. The same rules apply for adoption and same-sex couples."

She nodded, then noticed him eyeing her suspiciously.

"I'm not pregnant, Sir. I assure you."

"Is this for one of your team members, then?"

"Sir, I recently found out my dad fathered another child years ago. I was notified by the state when she died of an overdose. My deceased father was on her birth certificate. Anyway, she had a child. He's in foster care now, but because I am his next of kin, I was supposed to sign away my rights so he could be adopted. I've decided to keep my rights and raise him as my child."

"I see." He nodded and pursed his lips for a second. "First of all, I commend you for taking on such a task. Second, I apologize for your loss. I, too, know what it's like to lose someone to drugs." He paused for a second. "As for leave, if you become a new parent of any kind, whether through childbirth or adoption, you have a right to take parental leave. I assume you will be the primary caregiver."

"Yes."

"Do you know when this will all take place?"

"No, sir. I'm waiting for the case worker to email me the paperwork to sign. After that, we'll get a hearing date to go in front of the judge and make it official."

"I see." He nodded. "Maj. Irving will sign off on immediate primary caregiver leave when the custody hearing is scheduled."

"Thank you, sir. I apologize for the poor timing."

"Nonsense. You're doing a good thing, Malloy."

*

Bravo Team was in the hangar, readying their gear when Tristan walked in.

"Where did you go?" Fowler asked.

"I had a brief word with the colonel," she said. "Are we all good here?"

He nodded. "ORM. Man, we haven't done one of these in a hot minute."

"Yeah, I was thinking the same thing," she said, sitting down on the bench to ready her own gear. Overnight Reconnaissance Missions were one of the hardest tasks they ever took on as special forces because they were always deep in enemy territory with little to no way out. If you succeeded, you moved the needle quite a bit for your side, but if you didn't, it turned into an all-out war zone, and you were in the center of it. She looked over at the rest of the team. "Listen up, go do something to clear your mind today, because we all need to be focused tomorrow. No alcohol after dark, though. Dismissed."

"Copy that!" they replied before scurrying off.

"What about you? You've seemed a little out of focus since we left North Carolina," Fowler said.

"I'm squared away." She smiled.

"I'll catch up with you later," he said, noticing Courtney enter the hangar.

As soon as they were alone, Courtney walked over and sat down where Tristan was packing her gear.

"Silver Star…Congratulations. That's a pretty big deal."

"Thanks," Tristan muttered.

"Are you married?"

"What?" Tristan said, pausing her hands and looking up at her. "No."

Courtney stared at her. "I just…I guess I don't understand."

"I've never lied to you," Tristan sighed. "I have a lot of personal stuff going on, and this thing between you and I, it doesn't fit."

"Wow. We couldn't keep our hands off each other, then you go home for a weekend and suddenly we don't fit?"

"I'm sorry. That didn't come out right."

"Nothing to be sorry about. Like you said, it was just sex, right?" Courtney threw her hands up and shrugged.

Tristan opened her mouth to speak, but Courtney had already walked away. "Damnit," she mumbled as she blew out a frustrating breath. After a long minute, she went back to packing her ruck. She needed to make sure she had everything she could possibly need for four days and three nights on the ground in enemy territory, plus make sure the pack wasn't too heavy for the long hike in from the drop and back out to the extraction.

*

As darkness enveloped the sun, Tristan thought about going into the *Canteen* to check on her team, but they were all adults. Besides, running into Courtney, who would possibly be in there, was the last thing she wanted. Instead, she'd handwritten a letter to her mother.

Mother,

I've written this letter so many times in my career, it's become second nature. At one point, I stopped writing a new one and just relied on one generic version to leave behind when I went a on mission. But this time...my life is quite a bit different. So, here goes.

If you're reading this, I'm wearing my dress uniform with all my medals and merits displayed proudly on my chest, and I'm lying in a pine box. I chose this life for myself, and when it ended, I was at peace with my decision. My life was good. I was happy. Don't dwell on the loss of me. Life's too short. Dad's death should've taught you that.

I'm gone. You can't bring me back. But...my life wasn't just me in the end. You didn't know this, and forgive me for not telling you, but you were about to have a grandson. I was in the process of moving forward with my legal rights to Loki. He was going to be my son. I know how you felt about the situation, but it was my decision. It took a lot less than forty-eight hours for me to fall in love with that little boy. He deserves the world. I'm sorry I couldn't be the one to give it to him. Please give him the photo album in my house with all the pictures of me, dad, and grandpa in it over the years.

One last thing, there's a woman, Chief Warrant Officer 3 Courtney Hewitt. Give her my Silver Star medal.

Also, tell her about Loki...the entire story. She deserves to know why I ended things.

-Capt. Tristan C. Malloy, US Army

As soon as she was finished, she folded the paper and shoved it under her pillow. This was the same place they all left their notes to be sent back home if they were killed. She hated every moment of writing the morbid letter, but she had to do it. "Please don't ever let this have to be sent home," she prayed allowed.

*

The next morning, Courtney went up to the ready room to watch film on drop and extraction points. Both would be done under the cover of darkness, so she'd be flying on her instruments, but it still helped to get a visual of where she would be. The last person she expected to see when she walked in was Tristan, along with her team.

"What are you doing here?" she said sounding surprised as she looked directly at Tristan.

"I have a mission to prepare for," Tristan stated.

"When will you be finished? I, too, have a mission to prep," Courtney replied, checking her watch.

"I don't know." Tristan shrugged.

"Did it not *fit* your schedule yesterday?" Courtney said, agitation oozing from her voice.

"As a matter of fact, no. Everything didn't *fit* where I expected it to, so I made some adjustments, Chief."

Courtney and Tristan stood a few feet apart, eyeing each other like a pair of raging bulls about to attack one another.

"We'll be out of here by 1200," Tristan stated.

"Roger that," Courtney replied.

As soon as Courtney left the room, Tristan tossed the dry erase marker she'd been holding, as hard as she could across the room. It bounced off the wall with a thud and landed on the floor. *God damnit!* She tried to hide her emotions from her team, but they were all over the place. She was so angry with Courtney, she wanted to smash a chair into the wall instead of a marker, but that anger only fueled the fire burning in her belly, making her crave Courtney like a starving wild animal about to pounce on its prey. She rubbed her temples with both hands to keep from slamming her fists into the table. She hated hurting her, but she had no idea how to balance her home life and deployment...not anymore. Everything was changing so quickly; she could hardly keep up. It was easier to let Courtney go, than to fall in love with her and then face the uphill battle she was sure the Army would throw at them. She just wished Courtney would understand.

She finally brought her hands together in a praying position at her mouth as she blew out a long sigh. Her eyes met Fowler's in an unspoken understanding. He nodded and cleared his throat.

"Let's take five everyone. Grab a water, hit the latrine, stretch your legs, whatever," he said.

Once everyone left the room, Tristan slumped down in one of the chairs. Her chest ached and her head throbbed.

"Want to talk about it?" he said, sitting down beside her.

Surprised he'd stayed, she straightened her posture quickly.

"It's just you and me. We've been to the trenches of Hell and back together. I'm not going to hold anything against you."

"There's not really anything *to* talk about," she muttered.

"Love is brutal, man." Fowler patted her on the shoulder and shook his head.

"What?" Tristan laughed.

"I'm not one to give relationship advice, but…"

"You've been married for five years," she chuckled.

"Exactly. Getting there wasn't easy!"

"There's no relationship to give advice for anyway."

"We're your brothers and sisters. There's no need to hide from us. We've watched this thing blossom and grow between you and Chief Hewitt for months."

"You know I don't lie, Fowler. Believe me when I say there is no relationship…at least, not anymore."

"That was blatantly obvious. I thought you two were going to either rip each other's heads or clothes off. I couldn't tell which one."

Tristan laughed. "You got all of that out of a thirty second conversation?"

He grinned. "I know. I'm pretty good."

"Get the fuck out of here and find our team. We have work to do. I don't want to be here when she comes back in 90 minutes," she laughed, checking her watch.

*

Feeling like her head was going to explode, Courtney turned off the projector screen and left the ready room. She and her crew had spent the last three hours going over their drop and extraction zones until they were droopy eyed.

She'd pushed the morning conversation with Tristan as far to the back of her mind as she could. She had a job to do, and she needed a clear head to do it.

On her way downstairs, she passed by the computer room where four small cubicles held laptops for the soldiers to communicate with home at their leisure, barring the shotty internet service.

She put in the number for her parents and waited as the tiny dots chased each other in a row while the call was sent across the airwaves. She was about to end transmission when it finally connected.

"Courtney? Is that you? Hold on!"

"Mom?"

"I can't turn this damn thing on..."

"Hello?" Courtney laughed. "Mom, it's me! Don't hang up!"

Suddenly, the black picture disappeared, and her parents filled the screen.

"Courtney!" they both said cheerfully.

"Mom, you almost hung up on me," Courtney laughed.

"I can't figure out this damn new computer your father got," she said, shaking her head. "I'm so glad you called, though! I miss you."

"I miss you guys, too."

"How's it going out there, Kiddo?" her dad asked.

"I'm good."

"You look tired, honey. You should take leave and come home for a bit," her mother said.

"Yeah...maybe," she sighed. "Anyway, things are going well. I don't have a lot of time. I just wanted to say hi, see your faces, and hear your voices."

"Fly safe, Kiddo!"

"Love you!" her mother said.
"Love you, both!"

*

Tristan stood off to the side, avoiding another run in as she watched the door of the computer room for Courtney to exit. Once she was gone, Tristan went inside the room, catching the faint scent of rosewater wafting in the air where Courtney had just passed. She shook her head and blew out a frustrating breath as she sat down and logged into her email.

After scrolling through the constantly increasing mass of junk mail, she saw something from North Carolina Child Services and clicked on it. A short message from Janice opened, with the paperwork attached. She clicked on the file and began going through the pages. The first page was just her basic personal information. The second page had the actual court docket with her full name, along with Loki's name. The third page had the court order for a new birth certificate. Again, Tristan's full name was listed as the parent. However, Loki's name changed from Loki Adams to Loki Adams Malloy, which was how Tristan had told Janice she wanted it to be, with his former surname as his middle name. A smile spread across her face as she read his name. *Loki Malloy. I like it. I hope he does, too.*

Once she got to the end, she went back and electronically signed everything. Then, saved it and attached it to a reply email back to Janice.

Ms. Brown,

I have read through and signed everything. Please let me know as soon as we have a court date. I've already informed my commanding officer and will be taking extended leave at that point. I'll be out of reach for the next five days, so if there is any correspondence during that time, expect me to get back to you afterwards.

Thank you,
Capt. Tristan C. Malloy

As soon as she was done, she hit send. Then, she waited a few minutes and checked to make sure it had been delivered before signing out of her email. "It can't get any more official than that," she said to herself as she got up from the chair and left the room.

Chapter 23

"What the hell is taking so long?" Courtney muttered as she went over her flight log. She was already sitting in the pilot seat of the helo out on the flightline. Maguire was next to her, and Howie was outside waiting for Bravo Team to board. The traditional sendoff had happened thirty minutes earlier, yet the heavily geared ground team still hadn't boarded the helo.

"It looks like some kind of infantry mating ritual," Maguire muttered, watching them through his side window.

"They need to get a damn move on," she huffed.

"I take it we're no longer chummy with Bravo Team?" Maguire said.

"I'm just ready to get in the air. We have a long flight and short drop window," she replied.

"The children are Oscar Mike," Howie called.

"Copy," she said, as she began the call out with Maguire to check the gauges and started the engines.

*

"Bravo Team never backs down! We're here to kick ass and take names!" Tristan yelled, lifting her team up before they headed out. "Let's go ghost these motherfuckers!"

"Hooah!" everyone yelled as they all high-fived.

The rotor blades were already spinning around as Tristan jumped into the helo with her team. "Thanks for waiting for us," she said into the radio once she was buckled into her seat.

"We don't set the time constraints for wheels up," Courtney replied, then switched to the main channel. "Eagle, Outlaw One. Package is loaded."

"Copy, Outlaw One. You are clear for takeoff. Safe flying," Command radioed.

"Roger that." She lifted the bird into the air and banked right, disappearing into the night sky.

*

Tristan had chosen a different seat than she normally rode in simply because she didn't want to look forward and see Courtney during the entire flight. Instead, she stared out the side window of the helo and was able to only see Maguire when she glanced forward every now and then. Her mind was no longer on Courtney and the muddy water between them, nor was it on Loki and her decision to raise him. Instead, she was focused on the mission like a hawk zeroed in on prey. Her entire team was hyped up and ready for action, which was a good thing. They'd need the energy from the adrenaline rush for their two-and-a-half-hour hike through the dense forest. This was going to be only their second ORM since being deployed in Colombia. However, they'd done several while on other deployments. Tristan was fully confident in every member of her team. Everyone knew what to do and how to do it.

*

"Bravo One, we're five mikes from the drop zone," Courtney radioed as she flew over the tops of the forest trees.

"Copy," Tristan replied.

"This is going to be a little hair-raising," Maguire said, looking out at the near moonless sky.

"Nah, you'll be fine. Just squeeze your cheeks together and watch me do all the work," Courtney teased, keeping her eyes on the instruments and screens in front of her.

He laughed and shook his head as he looked through the windshield and side window with his night vision goggles.

Once they were into position, Courtney lowered the helo as much as possible, then kept it in a hover as both side doors opened. Bravo Team was already attached to the lines and ready to go.

Tristan looked down with her night vision goggles lowered on her helmet. "Bravo Team, prepare to drop in three…two…one…Go!"

Every member of the team fast-roped down at the same time. Fowler, Nigel, and Tucker went from the right side of the helo, while Tristan, Perry, and Hoffman went from the left. As soon as they were on the ground, they let go of the ropes.

"Bravo is free and clear," Tristan radioed, letting everyone know they were on the ground.

"Copy that," Courtney replied. Then, she pulled up on the collective lever and pushed the cyclic to the right, sending the helo flying off in the darkness.

*

Once the bird was out of sight, Tristan pulled her GPS and map from her vest pocket. "We're here," she said, pointing on the map while Tucker held a light over it. "We need to be here." She moved her finger up the map. "Everyone knows the route. We went over it a hundred times. Stay together in a cluster formation. It'll take us about two and a half hours to reach our post. We'll still have plenty of night left, so we'll eat, sleep, and prepare for morning."

"Hooah!" everyone replied.

"We have ghost orders. You all know what to do. We act quietly and leave no trace."

"Roger that," the group said together.

She put her map and GPS away, relying on the compass attached to her arm to keep them going in the general direction. It was Nigel's job as the comms and nav sergeant to make sure they stayed on the plotted GPS course and followed the path outlined on the map. The two of them stayed together in the front. Perry and Tucker were in the middle, and Hoffman and Fowler brought up the rear as they double-timed through the woods.

*

Courtney landed the helo perfectly on the space marked Pad 2. She and Maguire shut the engines down and removed their helmets before they began unbuckling their belts. She swung her door open, kicked her left foot out, and went to work logging the flight. She tried not to think about Tristan, or the fact that she'd just left her in the middle of nowhere, behind enemy lines, and wouldn't be returning for four days. She couldn't let the mission dwell on her, no matter who was involved. She'd never done it before, and certainly didn't need to start now. She had to keep a clear head and stay on point.

Once she was finished with her log, she grabbed her helmet and exited the helo as if she'd just finished a regular training flight. Maguire walked beside her as they entered the hangar and headed towards the locker room to store their gear.

"Are we ever going to talk about the elephant in the room or monkey on your back?" he asked.

Courtney set her helmet on the shelf in her locker and hung her flight vest on the special hooks beneath it.

"I'm not the brass. You can talk to me," he added.

She slammed the metal door closed. "John, I promise you, there's honestly nothing to talk about," she said, using his first name, which she never did, as she turned to look at him. They'd known each other for the better part of five years and had been flying together for most of them. She was his best man when he got married.

"At least...not anymore," she added with a sighed. She was tired and wanted nothing more than to hit the rack. "Be at the ready. We could be called out at any time."

"Roger that," he replied, nodding in agreement before she walked out of the locker room.

*

The cool night air felt good on Tristan's heated skin beneath the sleeves and pants of her uniform. Every breath filled her lungs, oxygenating her muscles as she continued walking briskly through the dense woods with 45lbs of gear on. She used her compass to maintain her heading, and every five minutes, Nigel checked the GPS and the map, ensuring they were on the right path.

The team was about halfway to their checkpoint when Tristan pulled a Payday candy bar from her pocket and began munching down. Everyone else began pulling snacks from their pockets and drinking from their canteens.

"What else do you have stashed in there?" Nigel said.

"Why? You got something to trade?" she asked, taking another bite of the chewy caramel and peanuts.

"Umm…" he pondered for a second. "I have a couple of granola bars and fruit and grain bars."

"Nope," she said as she kept trudging. Once she'd finished her snack, she wadded up the wrapping and stuffed it into one of her pockets. Then, she took a swig of water from her canteen.

Nigel shook his head.

When the team was finally in reach of their checkpoint an hour later, she brought them to a halt. "Let's make camp here for the night. We'll hike the last half mile before first light," she said.

"Amen," Hoffman sighed, removing his ruck.

Everyone except Tristan, dropped their gear and pulled out the MRE contents they'd packed. She kept watch while they ate and drank, replenishing their bodies from the exhausting hike. As soon as the first person was finished, they switched places and she sat down. The MRE contents she pulled from her ruck were spaghetti with meat sauce, a chocolate chip muffin top, Italian breadsticks, cheddar cheese spread, dried fruit, and chocolate/hazelnut protein drink powder. She went to work using the flameless ration heater, which was a bag with a water activated heating element. She put her spaghetti pack inside against the element, then added some water before closing the bag. While she waited for it to steam and heat up, she spread the cheese onto the breadsticks and ate them. Then, without giving care as to how it tasted, she ate her entrée. Once she was finished, she tucked the protein shake mix, beverage bag and muffin top back inside her ruck. Then, she squished the trash from everything else together into a small ball and put it in one of the outside pockets of her ruck. She finished with a minty fresh piece of gum to clean her teeth.

"Everyone put your ghillie on. It'll help keep you warm, but also keep us hidden for the night. We'll rotate in three-hour shifts. Tucker and I will go first. Then, Fowler and Perry, followed by Nigel and Hoffman."

"Roger that," they all said as they pulled their ghillie suits from their rucks and put them on over the uniforms and tactical vests they were already wearing, making everyone look like foliage on the ground. Then, they put their rucks together and put a ghillie cape over them, making them look almost like a bush.

*

Tristan and Tucker sat on the ground, opposite each other with their backs against trees, each scanning the woods through night vision googles and a thermal imaging monocular while holding a rifle in their lap. The rest of the team was fast asleep on the ground. In the last two and a half hours, she'd seen a few stray animals sniffing around, but nothing with a heat signature larger than a small dog. As she fought to keep her eyes open, she let her mind slip briefly to Courtney. She hated the way things had turned sour between them. That hadn't been her intention at all. As she tried not to think too long about it, she wondered how Loki was doing. Surely, Janice had received the email with the paperwork and had started the process.

"I could use one of those energy drinks right about now," Tucker said.

"They're disgusting and remind me of sugary camel piss, but I'd drink one with you," she radioed back as the thoughts running through her head faded away.

He laughed. "These off the grid missions make me miss the tiniest of creature comforts back home. You know what I mean?"

"Like a toothbrush?" she asked.

"Exactly."

She chuckled. "Come on. You get Fowler, I'll wake Perry. I'm ready to go to sleep."

Chapter 24

Courtney wanted to chug a cold beer with the guys and forget all about ever laying eyes on Tristan Malloy. Instead, she lay in her bed, staring at the ceiling, wondering what was happening two hours away on the other side of the border, and hoping she didn't get an emergency callout to go extract the Bravo Team because that meant Tristan was in trouble. "Where did it all go wrong?" she whispered to herself. "What the hell happened when she went home?"

*

Maguire found Courtney sitting on top of the helo, watching the sun rise when he walked out of the hangar. "Couldn't resist this beautiful sight?" he asked, climbing up beside her.

"More like couldn't sleep," she sighed. "What are you doing up this early?"

"I promised to call my sister. She's getting induced this morning." He looked at his watch. "I should be an uncle at some point."

"Awesome. Girl or boy?"

"A surprise, actually."

She nodded. "I could never do that. I'd have to know as soon as possible, or it would drive me crazy."

He laughed.

"So, what about you and Miranda? Any kids on the horizon?"

"Kids?" he squeaked. "We've barely been married two years."

"And?"

He shrugged. "She wants to start trying."

"I hear that's the fun part."

"My luck, she'll be fertile Myrtle and get pregnant right away."

She laughed.

"I don't want to wait too long and be too old to do things with my kids, but I also don't want to miss their lives because we're literally never home."

"Yeah." She nodded.

"What about you? Have you thought of having kids?"

She pulled her Rayban's from her pocket and slipped them on to cover her eyes from the brightness of the sun as the orange ball grew brighter, casting everything in an orange glow.

"I'm about as far removed from that scenario as possible, right now," she chuckled. "But I don't know. If it's in the cards, then yeah. I think I'd be a kickass mom."

"Somehow, I don't doubt it," he replied.

"Attention!" Howie yelled, scaring both Courtney and Maguire. They slid off the helo, barely landing on their feet as they popped to attention and saluted.

Capt. Warren was standing a few feet away with his arms crossed. "Is this how we await orders, now?" he asked.

"No, sir," they replied together.

"We were having a conversation about the extraction while the sun rose, Sir," Courtney lied.

He shook his head and returned their salute. "At ease."

They moved to parade rest with their hands behind their backs.

"We have more important matters than the two of you lounging on the helo," he sighed. "Alpha Team has been positioned in a mock distraction point. We're going to run the scenario during the day, so that if it happens at night, you'll have an idea of the terrain."

"Roger that," they both said.

"Wheels up in one hour," he added.

She watched him walk away before turning around.

Howie stared at her like a deer in headlights.

"Care to explain?" she grumbled.

"I was walking through the hangar towards the helo when I saw him off to the side. I yelled attention when I realized he was looking at the two of you up on top of the bird."

She shook her head and rolled her eyes.

"I'm sorry, Chief."

"It's not your fault, Howie. We weren't even supposed to report for another half hour. He just has his panties in a wad," she said. "Come on. We need to gear up. You heard him. We're playing with Alpha Team today."

"This ought to be fun," he said.

"Yep. Can't wait," she replied sarcastically.

*

An hour before the sun rose in the sky, Bravo Team was in position, twenty yards from the edge of the woods across from the abandoned-looking warehouse building and hiding under the cover of the thick brush in the woods. "Okay, boys and girl. You know the drill. STANO procedures," Tristan said, indicating the mission: Surveillance, Target Acquisition, and Night Observation.

"We have fifteen minutes to get our equipment up and running."

"Roger that," the team replied as they each went to work on a separate task.

Tucker went deeper into the woods and returned with a pile of limbs, which he used to fashion a blind to hide the camera equipment Fowler was setting up to monitor the doors and parking lot. Then, he worked on getting the microdrone into the air and operating it, while Tristan guided him using the binoculars and live picture from the drone camera.

Perry helped Hoffman set up a perimeter around the area they were in, using razor thin trip wire and more brush to cover their location. Then, she went back to help operate the camera equipment. He stayed behind to be the eyes and ears for the team, prepared to snipe shoot anyone trying to sneak up behind them.

Nigel worked on establishing communication with the base, ensuring they could contact each other on the radio and send and receive live feed imaging.

"Eagle, Bravo One. Do you copy?" Tristan radioed.

"Lima Charlie, Bravo One."

She gave Nigel a thumbs up. "Commencing with live-feed. Over."

"Copy."

The drone, known to the team as Killer Bee, was perched on the edge of the top of the building, in perfect position to video the vehicles and everyone who got out of them. It was small enough to completely fit in the palm of your hand and could be controlled from up to five miles away. The cameras had long-range, hi-def lenses. They were trained on the doors, taking pictures of everyone who entered and exited. So far, only one vehicle had appeared with a single male occupant. He'd gone directly into the building with his head tucked down. There was about a two-minute delay on the live feed, but the massive tree coverage made the signal go in and out every few minutes.

"Bravo One, standby."

"Copy," she radioed. "This is where the fun starts," she said, shaking her head.

Nigel laughed. "No kidding. All of this fancy equipment, now watch it not work."

"Don't jinx us. I'll offer you up to the major for latrine duty."

"Copy that," he whispered.

"Bravo, Eagle One. We are receiving transmission."

"Copy," she replied.

"Alright folks, we are live with command," she radioed to her team. "Let's get what we came for without another snafu."

"Roger that," everyone replied.

*

Courtney lifted the helo off the ground and flew into position a mile past the edge of the base where Alpha Team was simulating Bravo Team in distress and awaiting extraction. It was broad daylight, so she used both visual aids and her instrument screens as she moved into position. Maguire was next to her in the co-pilot seat, but she did everything unassisted.

"Holding position," she radioed.

Alpha Team clipped the carabiners to their harnesses and were lifted into the helo. Then, they were lowered back down to do it again in a more difficult area for her to get into and keep a hover.

Every time the radio crackled to life, she expected to hear Tristan's voice, but it was Judd Dewey instead. Nothing felt right during the entire session. Dewey was nothing like Tristan and Alpha Team failed in comparison to Bravo. They were all highly trained and very good at what they did, but there was an unmistakable difference between the two groups of soldiers. Courtney wondered if she was simply being biased because of Tristan.

"Chief Hewitt, do you copy?"

She cleared her throat. "Lima Charlie," she replied, kicking herself for having lost focus, even if only for a second.

"You're cleared for landing on Pad 2," Command said.

"Roger that," she replied.

"Are you good?" Maguire asked on their private channel.

"Squared away," she answered.

*

Several hours went by before the sun had finally set. Tristan had ordered her team to nap in shifts during the day so they would be able to stay awake for the night observation. No other occupants had arrived at the building during the day, and she was sure the night would be quite a bit different.

"Make sure the drone camera is in night mode," she radioed to Tucker.

"Copy," he replied.

"Same goes for you two with the long-range cameras and video," she said, looking at Perry and Fowler.

"Already done," he replied.

She gave a quick thumbs up and radioed Hoffman. "Bravo Five, do you copy?"

"Lima Charlie."

"You have our six."

"Roger that."

She had no idea exactly where he was, as it was his job to keep moving every few minutes, searching around for anyone coming remotely close to where they were located. At times, he could be behind them, or even directly in front of them. She was in the dark until he radioed his hourly updates.

"Bravo One, three vehicles approaching," Hoffman radioed.

"Copy," she replied. "Here we go."

The team watched as first a truck, then a car, followed by an SUV, pulled into the small parking lot. Six men got out of the truck and SUV, then four more from the car.

"Eagle-, we have 10 new hostiles on site."

"Copy, Bravo One. Standby."

"Of course," she muttered to herself, then radioed, "WILCO," meaning she would comply.

"How long is their delay?" Nigel asked.

"I have no idea. I guess we're about to find out." She watched the live video feed coming from the drone, as well as the long-range cameras. The men from the SUV were well-dressed, but the rest of them looked more like local laborers. They stood outside no more than half a minute, before filing inside. "Tucker, we need to see inside that building," she said.

"Roger that," he replied as he began repositioning the drone.

Suddenly, the door swung open and one of the guys stepped outside with an automatic rifle slung over his shoulder. Killer Bee flew right over his head and landed on top of the building. Tristan held her breath as the man glanced around, obviously hearing the buzzing noise, before shrugging and lighting a cigarette.

"Damnit, that was too close!" she grumbled softly as her heart pounded in her chest. "Tucker, take a second to get squared away. We need to find an open window, or at least one with clean glass."

"Roger," he replied, redirecting the drone to fly around to the opposite side of the building. The windows were either dirty or boarded up in the old building, so he repositioned the drone back on the roof by the front door.

"Bravo One," Perry radioed. "One hostile Oscar Mike." She zoomed her camera in to take perfect pictures of his face.

Tristan watched through her night vision goggles as the well-dressed man got into a car and sped away.

"Eagle-, incoming transmission. Standing by for confirmation."

"Copy."

While they waited, Tristan instructed Tucker to fly the drone around to the back of the building. A dilapidated dock jutted out of the river behind it, with ink colored water lapping softly against the bulkhead. The roll up back door began to open, and Tucker quickly flew the drone up to the roof, perching it with a bird's eye view of the dock.

"Eagle, Bravo One. You copy?"

"Lima Charlie," Command replied.

"Still standing by for confirmation," she radioed.

"Negative incoming."

"Damnit," she whispered. "Live-feed receiving?"

"Negative," Command radioed once more. "Remain in position."

"Roger," she replied.

"This is the cartel's full operation, isn't it?" Fowler asked.

"Looks like it to me, but the brass is dead in the water until the pictures and video go through."

He shook his head.

"Even if it is, our mission is STANO. We don't have engagement orders," she stated. "Once they know exactly who is in there and what they're doing, we will be far removed."

"Airstrike?"

"Maybe, but I think they're going to let the Colombian forces end this shit."

"We do all the work, and they take all the credit," he muttered.

"We're not here to start a war. Our deployment here was to work with the Colombian government and assist the local forces. We've done just that. We chased this son of a bitch all the way out of the country."

"I know," he replied.

Suddenly, the drone fell off the roof and crashed to the ground.

"Fuck," Tristan spat. All she saw before the feed went black was boots a few feet away. "Bravo, prepare to engage," she said to her team. "Eagle, Bravo One. Killer Bee is down in the hot zone, standby for retrieval," she radioed.

Chapter 25

"What do you mean?" Courtney said, rushing towards the ready room. She'd been woken from a dead sleep in the middle of the night by an alarm in her room, indicating her crew had been activated.

"Bravo must be in trouble," Maguire said, swallowing a yawn.

She tried not to think the worst as she pulled the door open to the command center.

Capt. Warren was waiting for them outside the ready room as they skidded to a stop and saluted. He quickly returned the salute and ushered them inside.

"Bravo is in trouble near the checkpoint here," he said, marking a red X. "Which is two and a half hours on foot from the extraction point out here," he added, marking a yellow circle. "We need you in the air and heading towards the original extraction point. We'll be able to direct you to a more precise location for extraction—"

"Stand down," Maj. Irving said, walking into the room.

Everyone had popped to attention when he'd entered, and quickly sat back down.

"You've been deactivated," he added, turning off the projector. "False alarm. Bravo Team is clear. You're dismissed."

Courtney and her crew saluted before leaving the room. "What the hell was that all about?"

"No idea," Maguire replied, finally letting the yawn take control.

"Have you not been to bed yet?" she asked, looking at him suspiciously.

"It was a girl. I found out earlier when I called my wife, and I finally got through to my sister right before the alarm went off."

The rest of their day had gone so off kilter, she'd forgotten all about that morning. "Wow. Congratulations, Uncle! And on Halloween, too!" she said, patting him on the upper arm.

"Yeah, congrats. That's awesome!" Howie added.

"Thanks." He smiled. "She's precious and so tiny. I've never seen anything so small. They dressed her in a little skeleton outfit with pink bones."

"Aww. What did they name her?" Courtney asked.

"Isobel Johnnie, after myself and my father, whose name is also John. They plan to call her Belle."

"Aww, that's adorable. She doesn't look like you, does she?" she teased.

Howie burst out laughing.

"I'm only kidding," Courtney chuckled.

"Uh huh," he muttered with a grin as they all headed into the locker room to remove their gear.

*

"Hoffman, take Perry and swing out wide. Come up behind the building to the west," Tristan said. "You'll be our direct cover from that side. Tucker and I are going in for the drone. We'll come up on the east side of the building. Fowler and Nigel, you both stay here." She pulled Fowler aside. "If this thing goes sideways, light this place up like a fucking roman candle."

"Roger that," he said.

Hoffman and Perry took off through the woods, moving northwest before cutting across the street and sliding up behind the buildings that lined the riverbank. Tristan and Tucker headed off towards the other side of the warehouse where a small patch of trees separated it from another row of old abandoned structures. She hadn't seen any cameras on the building, but she couldn't be a hundred percent sure. She and Tucker used hand signals as they reached the edge of the tree line and crossed the street. She knew they only had one shot. With the back door of the building open, anyone could come out at any time. The only thing they had going for them was it was a nearly moonless night. Together, they flattened themselves against the side of the building as they inched towards the rear and turned the corner.

"Two hostiles outside the backdoor on the west side," Hoffman whispered into the radio.

Tristan tapped Tucker on the shoulder, telling him he was clear to move.

The drone was on the ground in a dark area two feet past the building and just off to the side of the open door. It was upside down when Tucker reached it. He quickly grabbed it and hurried off into the small patch of trees, dropping to his belly for cover once he was clear. Tristan had tried to go behind him, but one of the men must've heard his footsteps.

"Hostile Oscar Mike!" Hoffman said as he moved his rifle to his shoulder, watching the man through the scope. He and Perry were both on their belly's.

Tristan balled herself up against the building. The darkness made her look like a small bush as she sat completely still, holding her breath. She watched the man through the covering over her face as he walked around, glancing out at the cluster of trees. She had her rifle tightly against her chest, but she wasn't in position to move it to her shoulder if she needed to take a shot. If he noticed her, she'd have to use a close combat move. She slowly pulled her knife from her pocket, careful not to let the Velcro closure make any noise as he continued looking around. She was hidden in plain sight because of the dark sky and shadow of the building she was up against, but if he continued walking, he'd run right into her. *Come on, motherfucker. Any closer and I'm going to shove this blade through your throat.*

"Carlos! Come on!" Tristan heard another man say in a thick Spanish accent.

The man a few feet from her shrugged and went back inside. Tristan jumped up and ran as fast as she could over to the trees. She dove to her belly and watched through her rifle scope. None of the men noticed because they were busy dollying crates around inside.

"What are they moving?" Hoffman questioned from his position on the opposite side.

"I can't tell. The crates are closed," Tristan replied. "Fowler, do you copy?"

"Lima Charlie," he answered.

"We have KB."

"Roger that."

"Tucker, status report?"

"DOA. Three broken rotors, and I only have two with me."

"Fuck," she grumbled. "Perry and Hoffman, head back to square one."

"Copy," Perry and Hoffman both replied.

She kept a watchful eye through the scope of her rifle for a few minutes, recording to memory everything she saw. Then, they backtracked across the road and scurried to base camp. She immediately got on the radio to command. "Eagle, Bravo One. Copy?"

"Lima Charlie. Extraction on standby."

"Negative Extraction. Situation Umbrella Charlie," she radioed, letting them know everything was under control.

"Copy. Negative extraction. Status on KB?"

"Retrieved. DOA."

"Copy. Charlie Mike," Command radioed, telling her to stay on mission.

"Roger that," Tristan replied before tossing the mic on top of the radio pack and flopping down on her butt as she sighed. "Talk about a nightmare on Halloween."

"No fucking kidding," Fowler muttered.

*

Courtney laced her sneakers and pulled her hair back into a ponytail. She stretched her legs and back muscles, then left her barracks building into a light jog. Cher's *Turn Back Time* played on the AirPod stuffed into one of her hears. She laughed softly, but it made her wonder, if she really could turn back time, would she change anything? "Great sex and a broken heart. Isn't that what every girl wants?" she muttered to herself as she continued running. When she turned to pass the hangars and run along the flightline, the sun was rising over the mountains in the distance. She stopped to watch it and thought of Tristan, wondering where she was and if she was watching the same sun light up a new day. She'd dropped her team in the middle of nowhere and had no idea where they were headed from that point. She wasn't privy to the confidential information regarding the mission. Her job was to drop them off and pick them up…no matter where or how, and she was damn good at it. Until this deployment, she'd never thought about the soldiers she'd left in the middle of a war zone or extracted from the armpit of Hell while bullets riddled her helo. She'd learned early on to leave her feelings behind when she deployed. They all did. It was something the Army engrained in them as kids going through the various schools that built them into the soldiers they were today.

"Why did you let me fall for you?" she whispered, wiping a tear before she took off running again, this time with the sun to her back.

*

Tristan's team spent the next day watching the warehouse, but no one went in or out. They couldn't risk being seen, so no one ventured over to watch the back of the building and the waterline. The drone battery had died sometime in the early hours before the sunrise, sending Tucker and Hoffman back to base camp with the rest of the team. Their mission had gone completely awry, but she hoped the video had worked long enough to record the open warehouse door and waterline, as well as the faces of the men. That was the main objective. They'd been in the country for over a year and had yet to lay eyes on Domingo Torres himself. They'd always seemed to be one or two steps behind.

"Want to trade?" Fowler said, as he opened the packet of his MRE labeled chicken burrito bowl.

"Nope," she replied, munching down on the pepperoni pizza slice from her MRE. "We need to break camp in about an hour," she added, checking her watch. "That'll give us three hours to get to the extraction zone."

"Roger that."

*

"Shake and bake, baby!" Courtney and Maguire said, smacking their helmets together as they walked out of the hangar and climbed into the helo. She pulled her shoulder belt straps tight and started flipping switches and checking gauges.

"Eagle, Outlaw One. You copy?" she radioed once she was ready to go.

"Lima Charlie, Outlaw One. You are cleared for takeoff."

"Roger that," she replied. "Let's go give Bravo a ride home," she said over the crew radio as she lifted the helo off the ground and headed towards the coordinates for the extraction point. She was glad she'd finally fallen asleep during the day because she had a feeling it was going to be a long night. She followed the screens in front, checking the altimeter, speed, radar, and direction over and over as she controlled the cyclic and collective lever with her hands and the rotor pedals with her feet.

*

Tristan's team was three-quarters of the way to the extraction zone when it started pouring rain. Their ghillie suits provided some water resistance, but they'd been removed and packed away before starting out on the two and a half hour, uphill hike. They each had a rain poncho, but it would just hinder their movement, and they didn't

217

have time to stop anyhow. The rain was slowing them down and if they missed the extraction window, they'd have to stay out there another twenty-four hours.

"I have a feeling this was the reason the window was so short," Fowler said.

"Yeah, looks like the brass missed the boat on this one," Hoffman muttered.

"Clearly," Nigel added.

"I'm pretty sure my ruck just gained ten pounds," Tucker said.

"Let's go, Bravo. Beat your feet. We only have 5 klicks to go!" Tristan yelled as the rain pelted her face and blurred her vision.

"Hooah!" they yelled.

The forest dirt under their feet had quickly turned to mud, making them trudge even harder. The entire team was tired, hungry, wet, and getting colder by the minute because of the lower temperatures of the night air. The last thing Tristan wanted to do was spend another night on the ground...especially the muddy, wet ground.

*

"Eagle, Outlaw One. Copy?"

"Lima Charlie, Outlaw One."

"Can we get a weather update? Our radar is showing a storm covering the extraction zone. We're currently ten mikes out. Over."

"Copy. Standby."

"We're flying right into a damn storm. That's why the extraction window was so short. They knew this shit was coming," Maguire grumbled.

"Yeah, well, there's not much we can do about it now. We're here, and I'm sure Bravo is down there shivering like wet rats waiting for cheese to fall out of the sky in the shape of a helo," she said.

Howie laughed.

"Outlaw One, our radar is showing the storm ten miles to the west of the zone. You should be clear for the extraction window," Command replied.

"It's pitch black out here. I'm flying on instruments only and our radar is showing us about to fly right into a massive storm," she radioed back.

"Outlaw One, copy. We're just receiving confirmation from Bravo. They are in the zone, and the weather is class two."

"Roger that. Switching channels." She quickly changed to the channel Bravo was supposed to be on. "Bravo One, Outlaw One. You copy?" she radioed.

She waited a minute, then radioed again as rain pelted the helo and wind blew it from side to side. *Come on.* She fought to stay on course as she flew around the zone awaiting radio confirmation. With the weather this bad, she was going to need Bravo to find a location, pop flares, and vector her in. "Bravo One, Outlaw One. Do you copy?" she said again.

"Lima Charlie, Outlaw One!" Tristan replied.

"Do you have a visual on our location?" Courtney asked. "We're in the soup up here."

"Negative."

"Bravo, we need flares and a vector call, over."

"Roger that. Standby."

*

"The helo needs a vector zone. They're in zero visibility. Let's go, Bravo!" Tristan yelled.

The team began searching for a space large enough for the helo to land, pick them up, and take off without hitting any trees.

"I thought command had a zone planned out," Fowler replied.

"This is it," she said.

Everyone worked together to map out an area. Thankfully, they were able to see through the rain with their night vision goggles enough to find each other in the only flat plain of the landing zone. Each of them popped a flare, marking the edges of the field. Then, Tristan ran to the center and popped another one for the helo to use as a guide.

"Hoffman, you stay on the south side. I can barely see the flares," Tristan said. "Outlaw One, extraction zone is a go."

"Roger that."

Tristan did her best to call out the distances to what she could see as the helo flew into position and began to lower down.

*

"There's no way we can land in this," Maguire said, clenching his jaw as Courtney fought to keep the helo in a hover.

"We're going to have to," she said.

"Outlaw One, Bravo one. Abort. These conditions are no good," Tristan radioed.

"Bravo One, negative. We are cleared for extraction."

Tristan had finally had enough. "You can't hover long enough in this mess to winch each of us up one at a time! If you land, you risk getting stuck, or crashing! It's no good. Abort mission!"

Suddenly, the helo dropped down, hovering a few feet off the ground with the side door open. Howie jumped out and helped all of Bravo Team climb inside before the helo lifted back up. Tristan was fuming from Courtney disobeying her command to leave them. Everyone shuffled to a seat as the helo bounced all around, swaying in the wind and rain as Courtney fought to get them through the horrendous storm. Tristan hadn't bothered changing the channel on her radio so she could talk to the pilot on the private channel. She was too afraid of what she might say to her.

"That was crazy," Maguire said on the private channel. "We shouldn't have done that."

"Would you rather risk leaving them out there to die?" she questioned before changing back to the channel with command. "Eagle, package has been retrieved. En route to the nest. Over."

"Copy," command replied.

*

Tristan was soaked to the bone, cold, and so tired she could barely keep her eyes open. However, when the helo touched down at their base, all she could think about was how Courtney ignored her and performed a dangerous extraction that could have resulted in a crash that killed them all.

She ushered her team inside the hangar and dismissed them for the rest of the night. Command had already told them they would debrief at 0800, which was about seven hours away. At least, they would be able to take a hot shower, get something to eat, and grab a couple hours of sleep. Instead of going with them, she remained in the hangar, still in her full gear and dripping water on the dry floor. The storm thankfully had continued moving south and never touched their base to the west of the mountains.

When Courtney and Maguire finally got out of the helo and walked towards the hangar, Tristan spoke up. "A word with you, Chief Hewitt," she said.

Courtney told Maguire to go on, then she turned back to Tristan. "Yes?"

"What the hell were you thinking?" Tristan spat.

"I was thinking, if I left you there, you'd die!"

"You disobeyed a direct order!"

"What are you talking about?"

"I told you to abort. I said it several times!"

"You might outrank me, but you are not flight command. When I'm in that helo, I am in command. My orders come from my CO, not you! I did what I was told to do!" Courtney growled.

"Are you serious, right now?" Tristan shook her head. "You could've crashed."

"You could have died out there, too. "

"I'm a green beret and a former Ranger. I would've gotten my team to shelter and easily survived to be extracted another time. That's what I'm trained to do."

"Yeah, well I'm trained to fly that helo into the armpit of Hell and back. In case you haven't noticed, I'm damn good at it or I wouldn't be flying with Special Forces. Think about that the next time you want to come at me for doing my job!" Courtney started walking away.

"What's really going on with you?" Tristan called to her back.

Courtney spun around and walked right up to her, leaving less than two feet between them. "First, you push me out of your life for no fucking reason, then jump down my throat when I do my actual job, and now you're questioning *me* and *my* actions?" She shook her head and turned to leave but looked back at Tristan. "Forgive me for caring enough to not leave you out there, because trust me, I certainly wanted to. I guess I'm a better soldier than an angry, spiteful ex-lover."

"What did you want me to do, tell you I loved you, then break it off? I did what I had to do. My life back home and my life here are day and night. I'm two very different people. I couldn't let this go on any longer because it would never work in the real world, and we'd both be left heartbroken and potentially careerless. There, you have it. Is that what you wanted?"

"You have no idea what I wanted because you never asked," Courtney replied, shaking her head before she left.

Tristan sighed as she watched her walk away.

Chapter 26

"I didn't think that would ever end," Fowler said, referring to their four-hour debrief as he rubbed his eyes and yawned. Tristan sat beside him in silence. They were all beat and had been given very little sleep before this morning's meeting.

"How many times do you have to beat a dead horse before you realize the mother fucker is dead?" Hoffman muttered.

Tristan chuckled but continued her silence. She honestly had nothing more to say about the mission and was over talking about it in general. "We have a team building exercise scheduled for 0700," she finally said as she got up from her chair.

"That sounds like code for PT," Perry replied with a fake smile.

"You all know me so well," Tristan laughed. "Get out of here. Take the rest of the day off. I'll see you all bright-eyed and bushy-tailed tomorrow morning."

"Are we seriously running a physical training exercise?" Fowler asked.

She simply smiled before leaving the room and heading straight down the hall to go check her email. She held her breath as she waited for the page to load. Then, exhaled nervously as she clicked on the email sent by Janice Brown.

Tristan C. Malloy,

The paperwork has been pushed through due to the extenuating circumstances. Obviously, the state prefers to get children out of foster care who have relatives willing to take legal guardianship, which is what we are dealing with in this case.

Your court date is set for November 4th at 9:00 AM with the Honorable Judge, James Gordon. We will meet in his chambers at the county courthouse to sign the papers.

Also, the Georges have hired an attorney and seek to move forward with adopting Loki. Don't let this worry you. The courts always lean towards placing the child with a family member first, especially in a case such as this.

If you have any questions, please do not hesitate to reach out.

Thank you,
Janice Brown

Tristan looked at the date in the corner of the computer. She'd been busy with her mission all week and had lost track of the days. She quickly printed the email and closed all her windows, then walked down to the major's office and knocked once on the door.

"Come in," he called.

Tristan stepped inside and popped to attention.

"At ease. What's going on?" he asked, leaning back in his chair.

"Sir, I just received the information for my court case. It arrived while I was out on mission."

He held his hand out, and she offered the paper she was holding.

"This is in two days."

"Yes, sir."

He rubbed his free hand over his freshly shaved jaw line while he held the paper with the other. "Women can't plan when they go into labor, just as you can't plan when the courts will set a date," he sighed. This wasn't the best time for her to abruptly leave for six weeks, but she'd just dumped a month's worth of intel into their laps that needed to be combed through and evaluated. "I'll get the papers signed today. You'll leave in the morning."

"Roger that, sir," she replied. "Also, I won't need the full six weeks. I'd like to just take five."

"Are you sure? By law, you get six, and you have to take them consecutively."

"Positive, sir."

"Okay."

"What will happen to my team while I'm gone?"

"They'll remain here under Fowler's command for a couple of weeks to answer any questions as we dig through the intel, and to help prepare for the next mission. They'll head back to garrison for two weeks, then return with you at the end of your parental leave. Are they aware of your situation?"

"No, sir. I'd plan to tell them as soon as I knew."

"Well, there's no time like the present. Tell Fowler to meet with me tomorrow afternoon."

"Yes, sir."

"Dismissed."

She popped to attention and saluted. He quickly returned the salute, then she opened the door to leave.

"Malloy, I expect a picture of this young man when you return."

"Roger that, sir," she replied with a smile.

*

Courtney saw Tristan come out of the major's office with a smile on her face but didn't bother talking to her. Instead, she ducked into the computer room and made a quick video call home to wish her mother a happy birthday. However, no one had answered. She assumed they were out at breakfast, until she realized it was Sunday. Every Sunday morning her mother volunteered at the activity center for the nursing home, something she'd done since her mother's parents were residents there during their final years; and her father played golf, a game she was sure he only played to get out of the house once a week since he'd retired.

With an audible sigh, she left the communications building and headed to the hangar. She wasn't scheduled to fly for the rest of the week, which meant she had a lot of time on her hands and not much to do with it.

"Chief," Howie said, noticing her walk out of the hangar.

"What are you doing?" she questioned. He had all the doors open and was busy cleaning the helo inside and out.

"Jezebel was looking rough. Blame it on my OCD," he said with a smile.

"Want some help?"

"Don't you have other things to do?"

"You mean more important?" she laughed as she climbed inside. "And no. I'm right where I need to be."

"But is it where you want to be?" he asked.

"Are we ever where we truly *want* to be?"

He shrugged.

"I heard your re-enlistment date is coming up. Are you hanging out with us another four years?"

"Or going where I truly want to go?" he laughed. "Yeah, I've already signed the papers. I figured why the hell not, you know?"

She nodded in agreement. "Okay, so tell me what we're doing, and show me what I can do to help."

He looked over at her to explain, but something in the distance caught his eye.

Courtney turned to follow his line of sight and saw Tristan and Fowler hugging. Then, he popped to attention and saluted her. Her head naturally turned to the side like a dog trying to understand something a human was saying.

*

Tristan walked along the flightline, kicking rocks with her boots as Fowler walked next to her.

"Are you serious?" he asked.

"Yes. It's not exactly ideal circumstances, but it's true. I can't let the same shit happen to him that happened to his mother. He needs me, and I'm going to do everything I can to give him a great life."

"Wow." He shook his head. "That's incredible." He gave her a half hug, then stared at her for a minute.

"You're still trying to picture me with a kid, aren't you?"

He grinned. "Maybe a little."

"Trust me, I'm still not used to it, and it's happening in 48hrs." She shook her head. "He's five; cusses like a sailor; has the grit of a soldier; the attitude of a wet cat; and trusts no one."

He grimaced. "Good luck with that."

228

"Yeah, thanks." She stopped walking and faced him. "Anyway, I'm only going to be gone five weeks. In fact, you guys will be sent back to garrison in three weeks, so we can rendezvous and come back as a team. You're welcome by the way. You'll all be home for Thanksgiving."

"That's great, but what's going to happen while you're gone?"

"You'll be the team leader. There won't be much going on from what I've been told, but you'll have to do what it takes to get the team ready for the next mission. Right now, there's nothing planned, but you never know. Be prepared for anything."

"Roger that," he replied.

"They trust you," she said. "And just think, if I really dig this parenting thing, maybe I'll retire, and you can permanently take my place."

He laughed. "I'll believe that when I see it. I'm pretty sure you bleed Army green."

"Damn right! Hooah!" she exclaimed.

"Hooah!" he replied, then popped to attention and saluted her. "I'll do my best to fill your shoes."

"I'm counting on it," she replied, returning his salute. "Now, go take the day off like I told you to do."

"What about the team?"

"I'm not ready to go into all of the details. We'll meet after late chow and tell them. As far as anyone on this base is concerned, I'm going home to handle a family matter and will return in a few weeks. That's really all anyone needs to know."

"Roger that."

When they parted ways, Tristan took a different path, hoping to avoid Courtney at all costs. *I wish I'd met you a year from now, or a year ago. Right now, the timing just isn't right. I can't navigate this thing between you and I while I go down an uncharted road. It's not fair to anyone. I can't risk getting lost, and I can't ask you to wait for me to cut a path.* She blew out a deep breath as she rubbed her thumbs around her temples. "Get it together, Malloy," she muttered to herself as she headed towards her barracks to pack her deployment bag.

Chapter 27

Tristan's eyes were closed, and her head was back against the wall of the C-12 transport plane as it touched down on the runway. She breathed in a long, slow breath. Then, let it out just the same. The plane had landed in two other places to pick up more soldiers on the flight back to North Carolina, then stopped in Georgia to drop off a group of them, making the commute that much longer. She'd spent the entire trip ignoring everyone around her. It wasn't until the wheels rolled to a stop on the airfield tarmac that they even knew she was awake. Polite pleasantries were avoided as she gathered her ruck and her deployment bag and filed out of the plane with the rest of the officers, leaving the enlisted men and women to follow behind them.

Tristan stood on the tarmac along with the rest of the returning soldiers as the garrison ceremony commenced. Families full of husbands, wives, and children waited patiently off to the side to hug their returning loved ones.

The base commander finished his welcome home speech, then dismissed everyone. Tristan pulled her ruck onto her back, grabbed her deployment bag, and began making her way through the crowd. There was no one there waiting to welcome her. There hadn't been for a long time. She was in and out so often, it had become less and less of a big deal over the years. She'd purposely stopped telling her mother when she was returning so she could avoid the huge spectacle. She tossed her deployment bag and ruck into her Jeep and drove off, leaving the base and the Army behind her for the next five weeks.

*

Being home usually made her stir crazy, but Tristan was happy with the quiet. She'd showered and unpacked. Then, she cleaned the spare room, leaving nothing in there except the bed, dresser, and nightstand. In the three years that she'd had the apartment, the room had only been used a handful of times.

With nothing left to do, she plopped down on the couch and pressed the call button on her phone. She thought about pouring a drink, but decided she needed to be stone cold sober for this call.

"Tristan?" Patty Malloy asked, answering the phone. "Are you home?"

"Hey. Yes, I landed this morning."

"Oh, my. Why didn't you tell me you were coming home again so soon? I'm out of town with my old sorority sisters until Thursday."

Tristan pinched the bridge of her nose. "It's fine, Mother. I'm actually back because I need to be in court tomorrow morning."

"What? What for?"

"I'm adopting Loki as my son. Surprise, you're going to be a grandma."

"Oh, Tristan!" her mother spat. "How could you do that?"

"How could I not?"

"I just...I can't believe—"

"Believe what? That I'm a decent human being? That I want him to have the life that was robbed from his mother? That I'm capable of raising a child? That I actually care about him? Which is it, Mother? What can't you believe?" she spat angrily. "He's an innocent little boy, and he is going to be my son whether you like it or not."

"Tristan—"

"No, I'm not done. Instead of acting like I've committed some horrible act, how about you grow up and own your mistake. This wouldn't have happened if my father had given two shits about his bastard child. Because if he had, and he was still alive, you would be this boy's grandmother anyhow," she growled. She hated yelling and disrespecting her mother. This was very unlike her, but she simply couldn't take it anymore.

"I understand what you are saying, but you have to see things from my point of view. None of this was ever easy. Not when you were little, and certainly not now."

"I get it, Mother. I really do. Dad made a colossal mistake, and it keeps coming back to haunt you, despite him being dead and gone. I know it isn't easy. I'm done dredging up dad's past. I want to focus on the future. This little boy is my blood. He was my father's blood, and my grandfather's. I'm going to be his mom and give him the best life that I possibly can. All I'm asking is that you consider being the grandmother you've always wanted to be because he's going to need it," she said with a deep sigh. "Mother? Are you still there?" she asked when she didn't hear anything.

"Yes," her mother sniffed and cleared her throat, obviously from crying.

"I didn't mean to upset you. I just want you to see it from a point of view other than your own."

"You are the most determined person I know. All your life you've achieved every goal you've set, and never backed down from anything that seemed too far out of reach. I'm very proud of you for so many reasons, and in so many ways. I know if you're doing this, you're going to give it your all. That little boy has no idea who he is getting for a mother, but I do." She paused to wipe a few tears. "I know it will take time to digest all of this, but I don't want to miss out on seeing my little girl as a mother...no matter how it came about."

"Thank you."

*

Tristan was up long before her alarm and had arrived early enough to drink a cup of coffee, then nearly throw it up from the ball of nerves wrenching in her belly. She adjusted the jacket of her dark gray pantsuit before going inside the building. It felt odd to be formally dressed in something other than her Army uniform

"Are you ready?" Janice asked, walking up to her.

"Absolutely," she replied, looking around for Loki. She finally found him with the security guard. He was dressed in a dark blue suit and tie. "Everything okay?" she questioned.

"Yeah. He wasn't too happy about wearing what he referred to as his 'church clothes.' Mr. Gary is explaining how dressing nice is for a lot more places than just church."

"I agree," Tristan muttered.

"We should get going. Our meeting is in a few minutes," she said, waving for the guard to send Loki back over to her.

"Is it true you're going to be my new mom?" Loki asked, looking at Tristan as they sat down at the table in the judges' chambers and waited for him to arrive.

"Yes, but you will always have your mom in heaven with your Gigi, just like I have my dad and grandpa there, too. It's okay to have more than one mom. And, you don't have to call me mom. We can work towards that, okay. I am your family Loki, and I always will be. I promise from this day forward to love you as my son and do my absolute best to be a good mother to you."

"Well," the judge cleared his throat from the doorway. "I don't need to hear any more testimony. Let's get these papers signed so the two of you can start your new life," he added, moving to take a seat.

"I object, your honor."

Everyone in the room looked up to see a slender, balding man with a combover, standing in the doorway. He pushed his glasses back up onto the bridge of his pencil thin nose.

"Who are you exactly?" the judge asked.

"Wilfred Abernathy, council for the George family, your honor."

"George family?"

"Your honor, if I may," Janice cut in. "The Georges were the foster family for Loki Adams."

"Yes," he mumbled, looking through the paperwork. "I have the adoption appeal right here." He thumbed through a couple of the pages, then lay them to the side. "Mr. Abernathy, your appeal is denied. I am invoking Tristan C. Malloy's right to change her legal guardianship to adoption of the minor child, Loki Adams."

"Your honor, you haven't heard our case."

"There's no need, Mr. Abernathy. Unless, of course, you have evidence proving Ms. Malloy is unfit to be the child's parent."

"Exhibit A, your honor," he said, handing over a piece of paper.

Tristan looked at Janice, who just shrugged. In her five years as a social worker, she'd never seen a foster family try to go against a birth family, to the point of hiring an attorney and showing up at the hearing.

"This is a military docket," the judge said.

"Yes, your honor. Ms. Malloy is on active duty in the Army, and she is single."

"Your point, Mr. Abernathy?"

"When she deploys, who will be the legal guardian of the child? The Georges will never have to leave the child with someone else for extended periods of time."

"Ms. Malloy, it's a fair question," the judge said, looking at her.

"Your honor, I'm special forces. I deploy all over the world. You won't find that in the fancy paperwork you have there because what I do is highly classified. However, my mother, who is Loki's grandmother, will be his legal guardian. She's prepared to take care of him when I deploy, as any grandmother would be."

"Mr. Abernathy, you have the answer to your question. Now, unless you have any further evidence, I'll kindly ask you to leave my chambers."

"She's a lesbian," the attorney blurted. "The Georges are a good, Christian family with values. The child would be raised properly."

Tristan balled her fists so tightly, she thought they would pop off her arms. Janice patted her on the arm and nodded. When she opened her mouth to speak, the judge held up his hand.

"Mr. Abernathy, there is nothing more I want to hear from you. I've made my ruling," he said, picking up the gavel. "Tristan C. Malloy, do you promise to take all responsibility for Loki Adams as his parent?"

"Yes, sir."

"I approve of this adoption and hereby grant you, Tristan C. Malloy, full legal custody of Loki Adams. I also grant the requested name change from Loki Adams to Loki Adams Malloy." He pounded the gavel, then signed the papers. Once he was finished, he shook Tristan's hand, then Loki's. "I have a feeling you're going to have a great life, young man."

"Thank you, your honor," Tristan said. Then, she got up from the chair and bent down in front of Loki. "Are you ready to go start our new life together, son?"

"I don't have to go back to the Georges?"

"Never ever again," she said.

"Yes!" he exclaimed.

Janice and the judge laughed.

Tristan grabbed his hand and walked out of the room. Mr. Abernathy was standing off to the side on his phone, obviously giving the Georges the bad news. She gave him the biggest shit-eating grin as she passed by, and Janice smiled as well. Once they were all outside, Janice went to her car and pulled out a small grocery bag.

"What's this?" Tristan asked.

"His personal belongings. The Georges kept anything they purchased for him. This is what he was sent with when he went to them."

"Wow." Tristan shook her head. "Doesn't surprise me. It's okay. We're going shopping right now, anyhow."

"Wonderful. Listen, Loki. You be good to her because I'm pretty sure she's going to be great to you."

"Thank you again, for everything," Tristan said, shaking her hand.

"No problem. I'm glad he's with you. This is where he belongs."

Tristan smiled.

"You have your copy of the signed documents from the judge. I'll send in the birth certificate adjustment request. Once that is changed, they'll send you a copy of his new birth certificate with the new name and you as his parent. In the meantime, your court documents will work in place of a birth certificate."

"Ok, great."

Tristan and Loki waved bye as they headed over to her Jeep.

"Can I take this stupid tie off?" he asked as she helped him get into the back passenger seat.

"First, can we make a few promises to each other?"

He nodded.

"I know you have a mom, but she is in heaven. I'm your mom here, and I plan to be here for a very long time. These are my promises to you as my son: I will never hurt you. I will always love you, no matter what. I will not say bad words to you, so you do not say them to me. I will not lie to you, so you do not lie to me. Okay?"

"Yes."

"I'm not going to make you say yes ma'am and all of that. I'm an officer in the Army. I've heard it enough to last a lifetime. However, I do want to hear you say please and thank you. Is that understood?"

"Yes."

"Great. Now, let's go take that tie off, remove these jackets, and roll our sleeves up. We have a lot of shopping to do. You need clothes and shoes, and toys for your room."

"I get toys?"

"Yes." She smiled, getting into the driver's seat, and starting the Jeep. She looked back over her right shoulder at him. "What theme do you think you want for your room?"

"What's a theme?"

"Decorations."

"What's that?"

"Stuff you put in your room, like the blankets and pictures on the walls. If you like baseball, then we would get you baseball stuff."

"Oh."

"What kinds of things do you like?" she asked as she pulled out into traffic and headed towards the mall.

"Um...I like those movies I saw at your house. The ones with my name."

"Oh, yeah. The Marvel movies. So, do you like just Loki, or Thor, too? What about Ironman and Captain America? Spiderman and Hulk?"

"Um...I like all of them."

"Great. We'll do your room in Marvel. That's easy." She changed lanes and rolled to a stop at the red light before looking back at him again. "What about toys? What kind of things do you like to play with?"

"I don't know."

"How about a bike? Did you ever have a bike?"

"No."

"Legos? Do you know what those are?"

"I've seen them."

Tristan pulled into a parking space and killed the engine. "How about this, let's start with clothes and shoes, then the stuff for your bedroom and bathroom. Then, we'll look at as many toys as we can find."

"Okay."

When they both got out of the vehicle, she grabbed his hand. "Loki, do you understand what happened today?"

"I think so."

"Can you tell me?"

"Um...I get to live with you."

"Yes. What else?"

"You are my family."

She smiled.

"Do you know we have the same name now?"

"We do? But my name is Loki."

She chuckled. "Yes, and my name is Tristan. But we have the same last name. Your new one is Loki Malloy, just like I am Tristan Malloy."

"But my name is Loki Adams."

"It was. The nice judge changed it for us so we can be the same. Is that okay?"

"I guess so."

"You still have Adams. We made it your middle name. So, you are Loki Adams Malloy."

"Do you have three names?"

"Yes. Tristan Cecile Malloy."

He laughed.

"Cecile was your great-great grandmother's name."

"She sounds old."

"Well, yeah. Now, she'd be well over a hundred."

"That's super old!"

Tristan laughed.

Tristan's bank account balance was proof they'd literally shopped until they dropped. Loki's closet and dresser drawers were full of clothes and a few pairs of shoes. His bedding now had Marvel characters on the comforter, sheets, and pillowcases, and matching pictures hung on the walls. The opposite side of the room had a bin full of new toys, including: a bunch of Marvel action figures and accessories, a remote-control car, and a magnetic building block set. A few books, games, and puzzles were up on a shelf, and drawing stuff was sitting in the corner of the new desk with a bike next to it.

She didn't want to overwhelm him, but at the same time, he was a small child who deserved a toy box full of his favorite toys. Their life together wasn't going to always be sunshine and roses, but at least they could have a couple of happy days before the dust settled and reality hit home. She still needed to set him up with a pediatrician and dentist, and then get him enrolled in school. Even more importantly, she needed to get him added to her records at the base, so he'd be on her insurance and listed as her child.

When she finally settled down for the night, she was exhausted, but thoughts of Courtney still found a way to sneak into her head before she succumbed to her sleepiness.

Chapter 28

Courtney lay in her rack, staring at the ceiling. As much as she tried to push the thoughts away, she kept remembering the way Tristan's body fit so perfectly with her own. She'd wanted to touch her and be touched by her the moment their eyes met. She'd only been in love once, or so she'd thought, but it had felt nothing like this. "It's my own damn fault," she muttered to the empty room. "*I* went after her."

When Tristan ended it, she was angry…and hurt. But she truly had no right to be either. It was over between them. She needed to let it go and move on.

"Damnit!" she cried.

*

The first week had come and gone quite easily for Tristan and Loki. They'd made homemade pizza, ate ice cream, played with toys, and watched movies. She wasn't sure which of them was going to gain the most weight during these five weeks as he seemed to eat as though he'd never been given food before. Loki's mind was blown when she'd taken him to the base to turn in a copy of the adoption records and get him added to her insurance. She'd felt completely out of sorts being on the base out of uniform, but he'd loved every minute of it.

"We need to get you enrolled in school today," she said as they sat together at the breakfast bar, eating pancakes.

"Okay," he replied, shoving bites into his mouth. "Is it at the church?" he sighed.

"Nope."

"Good."

"When you're finished, go brush your teeth and get dressed. I put your clothes on your bed."

"I hate brushing my teeth," he grumbled.

"Well, you can stop, but they'll just fall out. Remember the picture I showed you?"

"So."

"You won't be able to eat. Teeth are what chew our food. Besides, you'd look like a Muppet."

"What?" he laughed.

"I'm serious. Have you ever seen a Muppet with teeth?"

"What's a Muppet?" he chuckled.

"Boy, I have a lot to teach you." She shook her head. "Go brush your teeth."

"Okay," he said, sliding off the stool.

Tristan smiled as she watched him walk down the hall. *This parent stuff isn't so bad.*

*

Courtney was happy to get back in the air, even if it was just recon flights, checking the mountain roads. When she was in the air, all her attention was focused on flying and managing the controls. There was no space left in her head for anything else. In her mission briefing that morning, she was told Bravo Team would be tagging along, something she wasn't exactly thrilled about. She hadn't seen Tristan in five days, but it felt like yesterday.

243

"It's a glorious day to be flying. Is it not?" Maguire said as he walked out of the hangar with his checklist.

She glanced up at the clear, blue sky. "Yeah," she agreed. It was definitely better than the last mess they'd flown in. Thinking of that day only brought Tristan back to her mind.

"You've been pretty quiet lately," he said, sliding into his seat beside her to check his screens and gauges.

She shrugged. In truth, she'd been avoiding Tristan. "How's the new baby?" she asked, changing the subject.

"Good. I'm pretty sure Miranda has baby fever," he sighed.

She laughed.

"Speaking of children, here they come," he said, noticing Bravo Team coming out of the hangar in full gear.

"Are we missing someone?" Howie asked.

"Good to go," Fowler answered as he switched to the helo's channel on his radio.

"Nice of you guys to join us," Courtney radioed, then she worked the controls to lift them into the air.

"Wouldn't miss it," Fowler replied.

Courtney flipped over to the private channel. "Is Capt. Malloy with them?"

Maguire looked over his shoulder, then shrugged. "I don't see her. There's only five of them back there."

She switched back over and continued with the mission. They followed several man-made paths across the mountain that doubled as roads, but never saw so much as a stray animal. As soon as they turned around to head back to base, a warning alarm came on and one of the screens had a red box flashing in it.

"What the hell," Maguire said, checking all the gauges.

"There's an issue with engine one. I'm shutting it down," she replied. "Eagle, Outlaw One. We are en route to the nest. Advise, left engine is out. Over."

"Copy, Outlaw One."

"I'm going to do a manual restart," she said as she began flipping the switches to start it back up, but nothing happened.

"Eagle, Outlaw One. November Golf on manual restart."

"Copy, Outlaw One. Bring her in easy and set her down on pad 2."

"Roger that."

The helo was more than capable of flying on only one engine, but the mystery surrounding the second engine and why it shut down was puzzling. No one had messed with the engines since the last maintenance work up.

"Are we good, Chief?" Fowler asked.

"No worries. Ol' Jezzi can fly just as good with one engine as she does with two."

"Roger that," he said.

Courtney had no time to wonder where Tristan was or why she wasn't with her team. Her hands were full trying to fly and land the helo safely, along with worrying that whatever took out the first engine could potentially take out the second, causing them to literally fall out of the sky.

When the helo finally touched down, she said a silent prayer and flung her door open. She unbuckled her belts and hopped out.

"Fowler," she called when Bravo Team began walking into the hangar.

"Yeah," he asked, walking over to her.

"Where's Capt. Malloy?"

"On Leave."

Her brow scrunched in confusion. "The rest of the team didn't get leave?"

"Capt. Malloy took personal leave."

She nodded.

"She left right after we got back from the ORM."

"Oh."

"She'll be back in about four more weeks," he said, before heading off into the hangar.

Four weeks? What? Courtney's mind raced through different scenarios as she went into the locker room to remove her gear. Something was seriously wrong with the helo, but she couldn't get Tristan's mysterious absence out of her head. Was she sick? Had something happened to a family member? She slammed the locker door and buried her head in her hands.

"You good, Chief?"

Courtney turned around to see Capt. Warren standing in the doorway. She quickly popped to attention. "Squared away, sir."

"Carry on," he said, walking further into the room. "That was a mess up there. You have every right to take a second."

She softened her posture slightly. "I could use a lot more than a second," she said.

"You're actually going to get a few weeks. We're sending your helo stateside for a full maintenance overhaul. The colonel has authorized leave for your crew as well."

*

After touring the school and getting Loki enrolled, Tristan decided to take a drive with him. Her mother had asked to meet him, but she'd wanted to make sure the timing was right.

"We're going to take a little drive," she said, changing lanes on the interstate, already headed in her mother's direction.

"We're driving now."

"I mean we're going to another town. I have someone I want you to meet. She's excited to meet you, too."

"Okay."

"I know we haven't talked much about your Gigi. Was she nice?"

"Yeah. She gave good hugs."

"I think all grandmas do that." She smiled.

"Do you have a grandma?"

"I did. Actually, I had two of them. They're up in heaven now."

"A lot of people are in heaven," he sighed.

"Yes, but there are a lot of people down here with us, too."

He nodded in agreement.

"So, the woman we are going to see, she's my mom."

"She is?"

"Yes, and she is your grandma. Do you remember I said I had two grandmas?"

"Yeah."

"Well, now you have two. You have your Gigi in heaven, and this one down here."

He stared out the window at the passing cars.

"It's okay. You don't have to call her grandma. Her name is Patty."

He nodded.

"I know all of this is a lot," she sighed. "We are your family, too. Just like your mom and Gigi. You just didn't know about us until recently. We were always here though."

"Did my mom know you?"

"No." She shook her head. "I wish she had, because she was my sister."

"Really?"

"Yes. See, we are all the same family. Some of us are up in heaven, and some of us are down here."

"But you are my mom, now."

"Yes."

"I'm confused."

She laughed. "It's a tangled mess, I know. You have a mom and a Gigi in heaven, and you have a mom and a grandma down here. We are all family. How about we leave it at that?"

"Okay." He smiled, nodding his head. "What are all those drawings on you?" he asked, changing the subject as he looked at her arm.

"They're called tattoos."

"Do they wash off?"

"Nope. They are there forever. Each one has its own special meaning. I'll tell you about them one day."

He simply nodded.

*

Courtney walked into the *Canteen* a few hours later, freshly showered and feeling a little more pep in her step. Maguire and Howie were sitting at the bar, drinking a beer. A few Alpha Team members were playing darts. Two Bravo Team members were at the pool table.

"Gentlemen," she said, taking a seat on a stool. "I have some news."

"Oh, man. Jezebel's toast, isn't she?" Howie said.

Courtney laughed. "Yeah, she needs an overhaul. We're grounded for probably a month."

"Damn," Maguire muttered.

"On a good note, we are headed out of here on the next transport."

"What?" Howie questioned.

"Leave, boys. We're going on leave."

"Hooah!" They cheered, clinking their beer bottles together.

"When do we leave?" Maguire asked.

"The next transport going to the east coast is in three days. This gives us time to check in with family, and so on. Also, we'll be out for three weeks. Who knows when we'll get leave again, so enjoy it."

"Roger that."

*

Patty Malloy was nervous. Tristan heard it in her voice when she asked Loki simple questions. To save them all from the awkwardness, she grabbed the remote and turned the TV on. Loki waited almost impatiently for her to find the cartoons. Once she did, she nodded for her mother to join her. They left him in the den and walked into the kitchen.

"I know this a lot," she said.

"He looks a little bit like you did when you were his age. He definitely has the Malloy Irish eyes."

"Yeah." Tristan smiled.

"It's not the mess with your father. I've forced myself to bury all of that with him." She sighed. "He's five, Tristan. Most grandmother's get nine months to digest the idea of becoming a grandmother. Then, they get years of practice as the child grows. I've barely had two weeks."

"You'll get there. Our situation is different."

"I've told the sorority girls, and of course Gretchen. But I didn't mention your father and all of that. There's no sense in airing anymore dirty laundry. I simply said you'd adopted a little boy, and I now had a grandson."

"Well, that *is* the truth. No one needs to know how it came about."

"I don't know if Gretchen is smart enough to see the resemblance."

"We aren't the only family with green eyes," Tristan laughed.

"No, but it's distinct," she said, pursing her lips.

"Speaking of Aunt Gretchen, how are the wedding plans coming along?"

"The wedding is a week away. I would hope the planning was finished."

"Wow. I guess I didn't realize how much time has passed."

"It goes by fast. When do you leave again?"

"Two and a half weeks."

"I assume he'll be with me when you deploy?"

"Are you okay with that?"

"He is my grandson. I'll be there when you need me to."

"Thank you, Mother."

"Back to the wedding. Since you'll be in town, I need to get you added to the guest list and a reception table. There is plenty of room already at the kid's table. So, Loki will be fine."

Tristan nodded.

"Will you be bringing a date?"

"A date?" Tristan squeaked.

"Yes. Will someone be with you?"

She briefly thought about Courtney. "No," she sighed. "It'll just be me and Loki."

"Okay."

"Tristan, can I have a drink?"

"Sure," her mother said with a smile as she ushered him over to the refrigerator. "I have water, lemonade, milk, and sweet tea."

"Lemonade," he answered.

She helped him pour a small cup, which he eagerly drank before going back to his cartoons.

"He's very sweet."

"Yeah, he's come a long way in a short time. He was pretty broken when I first met him."

Patty hung her head.

Tristan's phone rang and she went into the other room to answer the call from the elementary school.

Patty went into the den where Loki was sitting, watching TV. "Do you want to see something neat?"

"Okay," he said, getting up.

She led him up the stairs to the room at the end of the hall. When the door opened, it was like stepping back into Tristan's high school days. "This is your mom's...uh, Tristan's old room."

"I know she's my mom now. You can call her that. I have a mom down here and one in heaven, too," he said.

She smiled and ushered him inside.

"Wow!" he exclaimed, looking around at the posters and medals hanging on the walls and the trophies on the shelf.

"Do you know what rugby is?" she asked.

"No."

"It's…a game. Anyway, she played it and was very good."

"Cool."

"It's like soccer and football together," Tristan said from the doorway. "I'll teach you when you get a little bigger."

"How much bigger?"

"Maybe ten?" She shrugged.

"Ten! That's in forever!"

Tristan laughed and looked at her mother. "We need to get going. The school wants an updated physical before he can start next week. I need to get home and look up the pediatricians who accept our insurance."

"I'll see you again soon," Patty said, patting him on the back as they walked towards the staircase. When they reached the door, she hugged Tristan. "I'm proud of you," she whispered.

"Thanks."

Chapter 29

Courtney looked at the soldiers who were sitting across from her on the transport plane. They had been picked up in Puerto Rico and were being shuffled from one base to the next. When she lulled her head to the right her eyes landed on Jezebel, tied down like a restless animal.

"Finally," Maguire said, bumping shoulders with her as the plane touched down.

"Yeah," she replied with a thin smile. "I'm sure Miranda is excited to see you."

"Don't jinx me."

She laughed.

"Do you have big plans while we're home?" he asked.

"Nah, just driving up to spend time with the family as usual," she said, gathering her ruck and her deployment bag as the plane taxied. Once it came to a stop, the rear door came down and the soldiers filed out in order of rank. Courtney ran her hand along the helo as she passed by it. "I'll see you soon, girl. Get well."

Family members were gathered on the side, waiting for each unit to get dismissed by their garrison CO. Courtney stood at attention with her bags at her feet. She was in her Army Combat Uniform like everyone else, except she and her crew members were wearing maroon berets, indicating they were airborne.

As soon as everyone was checked in and the short speech was over, she grabbed her bags and rushed over to the communications building.

"How may I help you, Chief?" the corporal behind the desk asked.

She set her deployment bag down at her feet. "I was hoping you could help me find someone. I was deployed overseas with a captain who…uh…gave me something personal to hold on to in case…uh…anything happened. Anyway, our deployment ended so quickly, I never could give it back."

"Oh, so you're trying to locate him?"

"Her, and yes. Yes, that's it."

"What's her name?" she asked.

"Capt. Tristan Malloy. She's with the 4th Special Forces Group, 2nd Battalion, I believe."

"Ah…here she is. We're not allowed to give out personal information for anyone in Charlie Company. I apologize."

Courtney sighed. "Not even for something as important as her grandmother's…wedding band?" she asked, seeing that corporal was wearing a ring on her left hand.

"Aww…" She bit her lower lip. "I'm really not supposed to do this."

"If it ever comes up, tell whoever that I ordered you to give me the information," Courtney said, knowing this could really backfire and land her in prison.

"Here's her address," she said, handing her a small sticky note.

"Thank you," Courtney replied, shoving the paper into her pocket before grabbing her deployment bag and rushing out of the building.

*

Courtney's small, one bedroom apartment on base smelled musty when she stepped inside. She tossed her deployment bag on the floor, then dropped her ruck next to it, before going over to turn the AC up and open the windows to get some air moving. Then, she pulled the piece of paper from her pocket and read the address for the first time. *Fort Bragg, North Carolina.* "This is just crazy," she muttered as she sat down on her bed. Her family was in Hope Mills, North Carolina, literally fifteen miles away. *Have we always been this close?* Her mind was slightly blown from finding out that Tristan was literally minutes away from where she'd grown up. She checked her watch. It was too late to do much of anything, except take a shower and bask in the comfort of her bed.

The next morning, Courtney dressed in jeans with rips in the thighs, a t-shirt, and flip flops. Then, she packed a bag and headed out the door to her midnight blue Camaro. She'd splurged a little when she bought it new a few years earlier, but she loved every minute of driving the muscle car, particularly with the windows down and the radio blaring.

She called her mother, letting her know that she was on the road, before pulling through the gates of the base. Once she was in the wind, she put the Army in her rearview mirror and mashed the gas pedal down. The drive from Savannah, which was where she was stationed, to Hope Mills, North Carolina was a little over four hours, putting her at home with her family in time for dinner. It had been a while since she'd been back, so she was sure her mother had pulled out all the stops and gathered the entire family. An eclectic mix of music played as she followed the interstate north.

A huge *Welcome Home* sign hung on the front of the Hewitt house on Walnut Lane, right next to the American flag that proudly waved year-round. She pulled into the driveway and got out of the car, trying her best to be quiet. Mrs. Clayborne, the older lady next door, waved and smiled. Courtney did the same. Then, she headed up the walkway and grabbed the knob, opening the unlocked door.

"She's here!" her mother exclaimed, rushing up to her.

"Welcome home, Kiddo," her father said, giving her a hug.

"Hi, everyone," Courtney said, hugging her parents. "Geema and Pop!" she cheered, scurrying over to her grandparents. Her grandfather stood on rickety feet to salute her.

"Welcome home, Kid."

"Thanks, Pop." She smiled and returned the gesture before wrapping him in a hug.

"You look like you need to eat, child," her grandmother said with a smile as she hugged her.

"I'm sure mom's been cooking all day."

"Of course. The ham is delicious, by the way. I may have snuck a piece earlier." She grinned.

Courtney laughed and shook her head.

"Welcome home, Court."

"Thanks Uncle Pete. Where's Aunt Viv?"

"In the kitchen helping with the food, as usual," he said, hugging her.

*

After an afternoon of eating food, talking, and laughing with family, and short visits from the neighbors who had watched her grow up, Courtney sat down on the couch next to her father and kicked her feet up on the coffee table.

"My twins," her mother said in passing as she looked over at them.

"Shelly, sit down and take a load off," Courtney's father said.

"I will. I just heard the dishwater finish."

"Oh, let the maid get it. She'll be here tomorrow," he said.

"Maid? Since when do you guys have a maid?"

"She's called a house-keeper," Shelly answered from the kitchen. "And your father hired her as my birthday present."

"It's the gift that keeps on giving," he exclaimed.

Courtney laughed.

"So, how are things really going, kiddo?" her father asked.

"Good."

"It's not like you to get leave in the middle of a deployment."

"Our bird needed an overhaul, so my crew came back for a couple of weeks." She shrugged. "Hey, speaking of my deployment, do you remember a guy named Curtis Powers from your time in the gulf?"

"Yeah," he said, nodding his head. "He was lieutenant, I believe."

"He's a lieutenant colonel now."

"Wow."

"He's the CO for my deployment operation."

"Really?"

"Yes, sir. I flew with him not long ago. He said he commanded the mission to retrieve your crew when you were shot down."

Her father nodded. "I never knew that."

"Small world, huh?"

"Yeah, I'd say so."

"Anyone up for a movie?" her mother asked, finally coming into the room.

"Nah. I'm actually going to go see a friend of mine," Courtney said, swinging her feet to the floor. "We were deployed together, and I found out recently she's stationed at Fort Bragg."

"I take it you still have lady friends?" her father said.

"Yes, sir. I'm still gay."

"There's nothing wrong with it. I'm just asking."

"Oh, Jimmy, leave her alone. I don't care if she comes home with a drag queen, as long as she's happy and loved in return," her mother said.

Courtney laughed. "I wouldn't go that far, Mom."

"Should we wait up?"

"No. I'll be fine. Thank you so much for the party today. It was nice seeing everyone."

"They all love you and wouldn't have missed seeing you," her mother said, walking over to take Courtney's seat next to her father. "Slide over, ol' man. There's a new Hallmark movie coming on."

Courtney shook her head and laughed before gathering her phone and keys.

*

Tristan was in the kitchen, with Loki on the floor watching the cartoons playing on the TV. They'd been discussing the animals they'd expected to see at the zoo the next day when she heard a knock at the door. *What the hell?* She wiped her hands on the dish towel and walked across the apartment. The blob she saw when she looked through the peephole didn't make sense. With an odd shake of her head, she started to walk away, but the person knocked again. This time, she turned the lock and pulled the door open enough to see who it was.

"What are you doing here?" she mumbled in shock.

"Look, I don't know what you're hiding. There's probably a wife in there who's about to come knock me on my ass, but you need to know I love you, Tristan. I'm in love with you. I know I went along when you said you didn't want a relationship. Hell, I didn't either," she paused running her hand through her long wavy hair as she pushed it out of her face and back over her shoulder.

"Courtney—"

Tristan went to say something, but Courtney cut her off. "I know I could be throwing away my career right now, but you had to know how I felt. I love you, and I'm pretty sure you're feeling this, as well. To hell with command. I'll go to Lt. Col. Powers when I get back and tell him it was all me. I fell in love with you, and I need my crew to be reassigned."

"Courtney, it's not that easy." Just seeing her made Tristan weak in the knees.

"Why? Why not?" Courtney asked, throwing her hands in the air.

"Because it's not just me," Tristan sighed, pushing the door open all the way.

Courtney looked around her, gasping when she saw the child on the floor. "Who is that?"

"My son."

"You have a son?"

Tristan nodded.

"I didn't…I had no idea."

"It's sort of a new development, and a long story."

"I'm sorry," Courtney murmured. "I shouldn't have—"

"It's a little too late for that. You're here now," Tristan said. "Would you like to meet him?"

"Are you sure?"

Tristan shrugged and waved her inside. "There's someone I want you to meet," she said, as they entered the living room. "This is my friend Courtney. She's in the Army, too. She flies helicopters."

His eyes grew large. "Cool!"

"This is my son, Loki Adams Malloy."

"Loki? Like in Marvel?"

Tristan smiled and nodded.

"I like it. It's nice to meet you," she said, noticing right away the child and mother shared the same sparkling eyes that were the color of fresh cut blades of grass. She cleared her throat. "How old are you, Loki?"

"Five," he said. "What's it like flying a helicopter?"

"Well…"

"Sit down," Tristan said, nodding towards the couch. "You want something to drink?"

"I'm good." She smiled.

God, you're gorgeous. Tristan thought as she swallowed the lump in her throat. Courtney was dressed in ripped jeans, a pastel pink t-shirt, and flip flops. She looked so relaxed with her hair down around her shoulders and a playful smile on her face as she explained flying in terms a five-year-old would understand. Loki hung on every word she said, so she must've been doing a good job.

Tristan finally sat down on the couch, leaving a good amount of space between herself and Courtney. "So, you didn't mention how you wound up on leave?"

"That's a long story, too," she said with a shake of her head.

"Courtney, are you going with us to the zoo tomorrow?" Loki asked.

"Uh…"

"I'm sure she has other things going on," Tristan said.

"Actually, I'm free. But…I wouldn't want to impose," Courtney replied.

"What's impose?" Loki asked.

"Uh…I guess it means go if you don't want me to." Courtney shrugged.

"I want you to. So, no impose."

Tristan smiled and shrugged. "You can join us if you want. We're leaving here at nine hundred."

"Okay." Courtney nodded. "I guess I'll see you in the morning."

"Awesome," Loki said before going back to his cartoon show.

"I should probably go," Courtney said, standing.

"Where are you staying?"

"With my parents."

"They live here?"

"Hope Mills," Courtney said as they started walking towards the door. "I actually grew up there."

"No shit?"

"Yeah. I guess we probably should've had those relationship conversations." She smiled.

261

Tristan shook her head and laughed. "I'm from Pinehurst."

"So, we grew up an hour from each other, but it took us going to South America to meet."

"I think I need a drink," Tristan mumbled.

Courtney laughed. "Yeah, I'm hoping my dad left the liquor cabinet open. I'm sure he'll be passed out on the couch when I get back."

"Well, I guess I'll see you in the morning. Have a safe drive and a good night."

"Goodnight," Courtney said with a bright smile that went straight to Tristan's core.

As soon as she closed the door, Tristan put her forehead against it. *I hope you know what you're getting yourself into.*

"I like her. She's pretty," Loki said when Tristan made her way back to the couch.

"Yeah, she is," she sighed.

Chapter 30

Courtney tossed and turned all night. Her mind kept racing through question after question. Did Tristan give birth to Loki? Was she married at one point? Is she divorced? Is she widowed? Did she have a relationship with a man? Nothing seemed to make sense. She'd finally dozed off two hours before the alarm buzzed.

"Son of a bitch," she grumbled, reaching out from under the blanket to silence it.

"Coffee is ready," her mother said, knocking on the door in passing.

Courtney tossed the covers back and swung her feet to the floor. The room she was sleeping in truly was a guest room. Her parents had knocked down the wall between her bedroom and theirs to give them a larger bedroom and a full bathroom with a tub, since they'd only had a walk-in shower for many years. The fourth room in the house was her father's office. The walls were littered with Army memorabilia from his time in the service.

She meandered down the hall to take a quick shower. Then, bounded down the stairs fresh and clean in a pair of jeans without the rips, sneakers, and a light blue Tar Heels t-shirt. She pulled her hair back in a ponytail as she entered the kitchen.

"You look ten years younger," her father said. "What's got all this pep in your step?"

"Must be that lady friend she went to see last night," her mother said with a wink.

"Oh, for crying out loud." She shook her head, then laughed at the thought of Tristan being called a lady with her tattooed arm sleeves and muscular build. "I'm going with her and her son to the zoo today."

"I see." Her mother sipped her coffee. "Is her husband in the service, too?"

"She doesn't have a husband." Courtney grabbed a mug and went to the pot. *I'm going to need coffee...a lot of coffee if I'm going to have this conversation.*

"Oh."

Courtney looked at her dad, but his nose was in the paper. He was old school and refused to read the news electronically, so the paper was still delivered every day. She took a long swig from her mug, noticing the difference in taste from the local Colombian coffee on the base, which was much stronger. She rubbed the fingers of one hand along her forehead.

"We dated...sort of. I found out she was stationed at Fort Bragg when I went on leave. I had no idea she had a kid until I showed up on her doorstep last night."

Her mother grimaced. "How'd that go?"

"They invited me to go with them to the zoo today." She shrugged.

"Your business is your business," her father said. "Just be careful with command."

"Roger that," she muttered, emptying her mug. "I gotta go, I'm running late. Love you, guys."

"Will you be home for dinner?" her mother asked. "Actually, why don't you invite her over?"

"Not the time for that, Mom. I'll call later," she said before going out the door.

*

After a brief conversation about their vehicles and how each matched the driver perfectly, they'd headed off to the zoo…in the Jeep. It was a weekday, so the parking lot was mostly open. Tristan pulled into a spot close to the front.

"Loki, have you ever been to the zoo?" Courtney asked as they got out and walked up.

"No."

"Do you like animals?"

"I think so."

"How about tigers, lions, monkeys, giraffes, zebras, and elephants?" she asked.

"They have those there?" he questioned as his green eyes lit up.

"Yeah, and a lot more, too," Tristan said.

"Cool!"

"You didn't have to pay for my ticket," Courtney said, bumping shoulders with Tristan.

"It's fine. We invited you." Tristan's eyes met Courtney's.

"Well, lunch is on me. If I recall, they have a pretty good pizza café."

"I love pizza!" Loki exclaimed.

Tristan pulled her attention back to the boy. "What should we see first?" she asked.

"The monkeys and birds are this way, and the tigers and lions are that way," Courtney stated, reading the sign in front of them.

"Lions," he said.

"Let's go." Tristan ushered him down the path. She was surprised to see how quickly he took to Courtney and vice versa. They walked together pointing out different animals to one another along the way.

"It looks like we're just in time for the feeding," Tristan said, glancing up at the small crowd. "Come on, we can stand on this side."

Courtney and Loki followed her around to get a better view of the animals.

"These ladies are African Lions. Amahle, the one right here closest to me, her name means beautiful one or prettiest one. Her sister over there, is Lesedi. Her name means ray of light. They are three-year-old litter mates who were born in captivity just like their parents. Their ancestors were born in the wild in West Africa, but they are heavily endangered. Now, who thinks I should feed them their breakfast?"

All the kids said, "Me!"

"In the wild, they hunt large animals like zebras and wildebeests. But, in the zoo they eat meaty bone carcasses with vitamin paste smeared on them." He opened the metal food cart and pulled out a meaty bone. Amahle patiently waited, watching his every move as he put the bone in the shoot. It dropped out the bottom onto the ground and she snatched it in the blink of an eye, then ran off. Lesedi paced back and forth, keeping him in her sights. When he pulled the bone from the cart, she growled, scaring Loki and startling everyone around them. He jumped off the ground and quickly grabbed Tristan's hand. She looked down to see if he was okay and he was glued to the scene in front of him as the keeper dropped the bone down the shoot. Lesedi raced to the bone, snatched it up, and ran off so quickly, she looked like a blur.

Everyone cheered.

"Wow!" Courtney said. "That was amazing."

"Yeah!" Loki added, still holding Tristan's hand. She'd expected him to let go, but he kept his palm firmly in hers as they headed off to see the monkeys.

*

Courtney watched Tristan and Loki walk hand in hand. She was still completely floored at the thought of Tristan being a mother. She had so many questions, but deep down wondered if she really wanted the answers. She hadn't been able to say no to Loki when he'd looked up at her with the same piercing eyes as Tristan. As scary as it was, she knew she needed to see this through. She'd purposely taken leave to find Tristan and tell her how she felt. She'd even stood in her doorway and told her she was in love with her. If Tristan felt at all similar, she owed Courtney the truth, no matter what it was. She was seeing Tristan in a completely different light in the civilian world, and she hadn't been wrong. She really did have two very different lives. Courtney wondered if she only fit into one, or if there was room for her in both...and did she truly want to be in both?

"Hey, slow poke," Tristan said as Courtney walked up behind them. Loki was close to the monkey habitat, watching them play with each other. "You okay?"

"Yeah. Just taking it all in." She smiled softly as the breeze blew a few locks of her brown hair.

Tristan's green eyes held hers as Courtney's familiar rosewater scent wafted through the air. "I know this is a lot," she muttered, shoving her hands into the pockets of her jeans.

"It is." Courtney nodded. "But I wouldn't be here if I didn't want to be."

Tristan's eyes watched her like a hawk, slowly zeroing in on its prey. She started to move forward, closing the gap between them when Loki rushed up.

"Did you see that one monkey swing on the rope? It was so cool!" he exclaimed, grabbing Tristan's hand, then Courtney's. "Come on. Let's go find the giraffes!"

Tristan's lips parted as if she were about to say something, but she simply smiled. Courtney held onto the smaller hand in hers and fell in step with them as they headed down the walkway.

*

The rest of the day was spent walking around the entire zoo, making sure to see every single exhibit, followed by spaghetti dinner at Tristan's afterwards where he talked about every animal until she put him to bed for the night.

"He loves animals," Courtney said with a smile as Tristan sat down beside her. "He seems like a good kid."

"Yeah." Tristan nodded. "Up until last week, he cussed like a sailor and acted like a wet cat. He's slowly coming out of his shell and starting to trust me a little more every day."

"Oh." Courtney gave her an odd look.

Tristan cleared her throat and walked into the kitchen. "Do you want a glass of wine? I'm pretty sure there's a bottle in here somewhere."

"Uh…sure," Courtney muttered, still confused.

After a minute or two of drawers opening and closing, Courtney heard Tristan curse. She got up and went into the kitchen to find her fumbling with the opener.

"Here, let me help," she said, smiling and grabbing the bottle from her. She opened the bottle easily and poured the rose´ into the two glasses on the counter. After setting the bottle down, she handed one glass to Tristan and picked up the other. "I didn't take you for a wine drinker." *Or a parent, for that matter.*

"I'm not…usually. Someone gave this to me as a gift. It's not bad though," she replied, taking a couple of sips as they walked into the living room and sat on the couch, facing each other.

Courtney took a long sip then blurted out, "Are you divorced?"

"Huh?" Tristan shook her head, nearly choking on the wine she'd just drank.

"You told me you weren't married. You have a son. I assume you're divorced."

"I've never been married."

"But…"

Tristan set her glass on the coffee table. "I don't know where to start," she sighed, rubbing her hands on her knees.

"The truth would be a good place."

"I've never lied to you, Courtney." Tristan shook her head. "Six weeks ago, I found out my father, who is deceased, had an affair on my mother when I was ten, and fathered another child."

"Oh, wow. I'm sorry."

"There's a lot more," Tristan said, meeting her eyes. "He basically wrote the child out of his life. She grew up mostly poor from what I've gathered and became a drug addict as a teen. She got pregnant in high school. Her mother took care of her child until she passed away in a car accident last year. Then, six months ago, my half-sister died of a drug overdose."

"Loki's her son, isn't he?"

Tristan nodded.

"Oh, Tristan. Why didn't you tell me?"

"What was I supposed to say?" She shrugged. "It all happened so fast. The social worker showed up when I was here on leave. I knew nothing about any of this. Until that moment, I'd spent my entire life worshiping my father. I took the DNA test, which proved everything. My mother wasn't much help. She'd known about the affair but had turned a blind eye when my father wrote his other child out of his life literally with a check."

"Oh, my God."

"I couldn't leave him in foster care or let some random family adopt him, so I adopted him and am raising him as my son."

Courtney reached over, placed her hand on Tristan's, and squeezed. "I wish you would've told me, but I see why you didn't. I'm sorry for showing up on your doorstep." She ran her thumb over her knuckles.

"I didn't know about Loki or any of this when we first got together." She shrugged. "I chose to push you away and move on when I found out. I'm sorry for that. At the time, it seemed easier than dumping all of this on someone I barely knew. Plus, we'd both said it was just sex…something to pass the time while on deployment."

"I'll admit, it's a lot to take in, and I know I agreed to not having a relationship or getting personal with each other, but it was so much more than that to me. Somewhere in the middle of South America, I fell in love with you," Courtney murmured.

Tristan flipped her hand over and held onto Courtney's. "I knew I was in love with you the night I found you in my rack," she said with a soft smile.

Courtney put her free hand on Tristan's cheek and slowly closed the distance between them. Her lips were soft and inviting, leaving Courtney wanting more. The sound of Loki's bedroom door brought Tristan back to reality. She quickly backed away, putting space between them just as he rounded the corner.

"Can I have a drink?" he asked, rubbing his sleepy eyes.

"Yeah. Here, let me get you some water." Tristan jumped up to help him, then put him to bed.

"I should probably go," Courtney muttered when she came back into the room.

Tristan nodded and walked her to the door. "Can I take you to dinner tomorrow?" she asked. "My mother is taking Loki for the night."

"Are you asking me on a date?" Courtney questioned with a grin.

Tristan cleared her throat. "Uh...yeah. Yes."

"Okay." Courtney smiled and nodded. "Put your number in my phone. I'll text you so that you have mine."

Tristan did as instructed, then she pulled the door open for Courtney to exit without so much as a hug goodbye.

"I had a great time today," Courtney said as she stepped out the door.

"Me too." Tristan smiled.

Chapter 31

Courtney wasn't sure how to dress. She wasn't sure how things would go and had only planned to be in town with her family less than a week, so she'd only packed jeans and a few shirts. Tristan hadn't given her much help by saying casual dress when she'd asked.

"She must be pretty special if you're up here pacing the floor," her mother said from the doorway.

"It's just dinner."

"Mmhmm."

Courtney ran her hand through her long hair, pushing it out of her face and over her shoulder. "I like her," she sighed. "Okay, more than like her."

"Is it mutual?"

She nodded. "On the base, everything was simple and easy. Here in the real world, I feel like a monkey fu—" She stopped speaking and looked over at her mother.

"You're not saying anything I haven't heard from your grandfather and father over the years," she laughed.

Courtney smiled. "The civilian side of life is hard," she said, exhaling heavily as she sat down on her bed.

Shelly sat down, patting her daughter's leg. "You like each other, and you both know it. That's a huge start. You mentioned she had a son, right?"

"Yeah."

"Okay. How did it go spending time with her *and* him?"

"Great."

"Is this what you want? A relationship with her? Because if you do, that includes her child. You have to be ready for that."

"Yes. I don't know. I think so," she sighed. "On the base it was just us and the moment. We never shared our personal lives."

Her mother nodded. "What made you seek her out when you went on leave?"

"She broke it off, then disappeared. I know why now, obviously."

"Ask yourself this. If you could turn back time knowing what you know now, would you do it?"

Courtney thought for a second, then smiled. "In a heartbeat."

"You love her, don't you?"

She nodded without saying a word.

"Does she feel the same way?"

"Yes, but it's complicated."

"Love is never easy, honey. And, neither is parenting, especially for a soldier who deploys quite a bit. I can see where she'd be hesitant. You have to put yourself in her shoes for a minute."

"I know."

"This dinner, I assume it's a real date...the first perhaps?"

"Yep."

"Don't put so much energy into what you wear or even where you go for that matter. Use this time to see each other for who you are outside of the uniform."

"Thanks, mom."

Shelly stood and bent down, kissing the top of her head. "I'd wear the jeans and that white top. It contrasts nicely against your dark hair and brown eyes."

Courtney laughed and shooed her out of the room.

*

Loki walked into the house and set his backpack down.

"Listen, you don't have to spend the night if you don't want to," Tristan said.

"I have fresh baked chocolate chip cookies and hot cocoa with marshmallows for later," her mother added.

"Do I have to call you grandma?" he asked.

"Of course not. You can call me whatever you like. I know we are still getting to know each other. That sort of stuff takes time."

"Okay." He nodded.

"I'm only a phone call away if you need anything," Tristan said.

"Can I sleep in your old room?"

Patty looked at her daughter and shrugged. "It's clean, so why not?"

"Cool."

"Don't forget your fitting tomorrow. I know it's last minute, but you and Loki are family and deserve to be in the wedding. Everyone will be happy to see you."

"Uh huh, I'm going to take off. Don't let him stay up too late," Tristan said.

Patty shooed her daughter out the door. "We'll stay up as late as we want. Grandmas always know more than moms." Tristan heard her say. She simply shook her head and got into her Jeep. She hated leaving him, but he had to get used to her mother and fast. She would be leaving soon, and Patty Malloy would become his guardian and caretaker while she was gone. They needed to have a good relationship with each other.

As she drove towards Hope Mills, she thought about Courtney. The shock of her showing up at the door had worn off, but she was still getting used to seeing her in the civilian world, where they were free to be themselves. She wondered if they would truly feel the same way about each other without the excitement of sneaking around. She never dated anyone in the Army. Her relationships always seemed to end at casual affairs. She had a lot more to think about now. She couldn't be parading people in and out of Loki's life. He deserved the stability and nurturing that came from a family, not a single mother with a history of casual dating and hookups.

A modest two-story house with a two-car garage came into view as the GPS announced she'd arrived at her destination on Walnut Lane. Tristan pulled into the wide driveway beside Courtney's Camaro and killed the engine. "There's no turning back now," she said to herself as she got out and walked up to the door.

"Hello, I'm Shelly Hewitt," the woman said when she answered the door.

"Tristan Malloy," she replied with a smile, extending her hand.

"It's nice to meet you. Come in, make yourself at home. Courtney is in the backyard helping her father fill the birdfeeder."

"I'm a little early. The drive took a little less time than expected."

"I believe they're almost finished. Would you like something to drink?"

"No thank you." Tristan smiled.

"The squirrels are going to be eating good for a while," a man said walking in from the kitchen. "Court spilled the food everywhere."

"No, I didn't!" Courtney laughed, coming in behind him. "That was you, old man!"

Tristan noticed the resemblance right away between Courtney and her father.

"Tristan, this is my husband Ji—"

"Chief Warrant Officer 5 James Hewitt," he said, extending his hand.

Tristan squeezed back just as hard when she returned his shake.

"Jimmy…stop trying to scare the woman," Shelly laughed.

"Daddy, you're not going to scare her. This is Captain Tristan Malloy. She's a former Ranger, and currently a Special Forces Operational Detachment Delta Team Leader," Courtney said, walking up to her with a big smile. The leather ankle boots she'd decided to wear, along with the jeans and white shirt, had a small heel that brought her to Tristan's eye level.

"Welcome to our home, Captain," he said.

"Thank you," Tristan replied.

"We should get going," Courtney said, ushering Tristan out the door before her father began asking her Army questions. The last thing she needed was a pissing contest between her father and her…whatever Tristan was.

"Should we wait up for you?" Shelley called as they went out the door.

"No!" Courtney replied, getting into the passenger side of the Jeep.

Tristan laughed and shook her head.

"I'm sorry. I'm an only child, and my dad is the epitome of an Army father, just like his father. They are retired, but you wouldn't know it."

"It's fine. You didn't have to pull my rank and MOS out on him though. It's his house. You're his daughter. I can be respectful."

"No, he would've grilled you like a private on the bottom of the food chain." Courtney shook her head.

"How many people have picked you up to go out on a date?" Tristan asked as she backed out of the driveway and shifted gears.

"Including you…two. The other was a sixteen-year-old boy and he scared him so badly, he dropped me off at the end of the street afterwards."

Tristan laughed. "Are you serious?"

"Yes. My parents are about as far removed from my love life as possible."

"They know you're a lesbian, right?"

"Well, they do now," Courtney teased.

Tristan brought the Jeep to a stop in a hurry. "Are you serious?"

"I'm kidding!" Courtney laughed, grabbing the dash. "I came out to them when I joined the Army. They've never seen me with another woman, but the whole don't ask, don't tell thing has worked well so far. They don't ask many questions, and I don't give them any reason to."

"They're going to eat you alive when you get back," Tristan chuckled as she started back down the road.

"My mom and I talk…a little. I mean she knows more about you than anyone I've ever dated. But my dad, he's fine with me being gay, as long as I'm happy. I think he'd be standoffish and protective of me no matter who I dated, male or female. That's just his nature."

"Daddy's little girl."

"Yep."

"That was me once."

"What happened to your father. You mentioned he was deceased."

"Car accident my senior year of high school."

"Oh, Tristan, I'm sorry."

"Don't be. It was a long time ago. But, yeah, we were very close. I was a rugby player for my high school, as well as the county club. When he passed so suddenly, it tore me apart. I turned down the scholarships to college and joined the Army."

"Wait, you didn't go to college? How did you get into OCS?"

"There's a lot we don't know about each other."

"True. We put off getting to know each other and went straight for the fun stuff." Courtney grinned. "That doesn't mean I don't want to know all about you. I mean, this is a date, right? That's what people do on dates. They talk."

Tristan sighed, knowing she was right. She'd asked her on a date to talk to her and see if this was actually going to work out between them. "I was enlisted for the first six years. I worked my way to sergeant in the Rangers. I'd taken classes at the community college, at the encouragement of my father, my junior year and over the summer before my senior year of high school. My grades began slipping after he passed, and I gave up the college courses. I did what I had to do to graduate high school, but other than that, I just wanted out. Anyway, I finished my degree online, taking courses when I could. As soon as I finished, I put in for OCS and was accepted. When I came out of there, I left the Rangers and moved to Special

Forces. I've been there for about seven years. I currently have a little over thirteen years in service total."

"Wow." Courtney shook her head. "That's quite an accomplishment."

"What about you. Did you go to college?"

"No," she said. "I told you, my grandfather and father were both Army pilots. Both warrant officers, too. My pops flew Hueys in Vietnam, and my old man flew Apaches in Desert Storm. I knew from an early age I wanted to fly, too. They tried to convince me to go to college, but being a third generation Hewitt, helped a lot when I dropped their names on my Warrant Officer Flight School application. I scored very high on all the tests and was accepted. I went through basic training, then WOCS. After that, it was aviation school. I actually just passed seven years in service."

"That's interesting. No one else in my family has served in any branch of the military, so it was quite a shock," Tristan said as they pulled into the Louie's parking lot.

"Oh, they were pissed. They kept telling me it was grueling work and not many women did it and so on. You know, the old school mentality."

"Yeah, I've faced that a lot over the years and continued to prove them wrong."

"Exactly," Courtney replied, looking around at the outside of the building.

Tristan gave her name when they walked inside, and they were shown to a candle lit table in the corner.

"I've never been here," Courtney said, taking her seat.

"I know it looks like a dump on the outside, but it's a pretty amazing place. My mother is a bit uppity, if you know what I mean, and she loves it. The first time we came here, she didn't even want to go inside, but once she realized it was more fine dining than fish and chips wrapped in paper, it became her favorite place."

"So, uppity, huh. What does she do?"

"She's retired now. But she started as a news caster, then went on to serve on the school board and city council. She was also deputy mayor and president of Tuftstown University. My father was an executive with the power company until he passed. Hence, how he knocked up his secretary."

Courtney grimaced. "How did she take to you adopting Loki?"

"When I found out in general, it was pretty bad. She'd hid it from me my whole life, so I blamed her just as much as my father, and she got the brunt of my anger because he's dead. She wasn't happy at me being involved at all, but I finally got her to see it from my point of view, and Loki's, to be honest. She's still getting used to it, but he would've been her grandson either way, whether I was in his life as his aunt or his mother. She doesn't see him as my father's love-child's child. She sees him as my son, and that's exactly how I want it, too."

"Does he know who you really are?"

"Yes. I'm very honest with him and have been from the very beginning."

Courtney nodded.

After giving their order, the waitress came over with their drinks. Courtney had settled on a glass of wine, while Tristan ordered a whisky on the rocks.

"I was surprised to see you drinking wine last night," Courtney said, holding her glass up.

"It was a gift." Tristan shrugged, touching her glass to Courtney's. "Here's to…"

"New beginnings?"

"I like that." Tristan smiled. "New beginnings."

Chapter 32

The rest of the evening was spent with small talk about their food and growing up an hour away from each other in two very different lives. After splitting a slice of decadent white chocolate cheesecake, Tristan paid the check and they headed outside to the Jeep.

"Thank you for dinner. I wish you would've let me get the check, though. You drove an hour to get me, then another half hour to dinner," Courtney said.

"I asked *you* out. It's customary to pick up your date and pay for the bill," Tristan said with a smile as she held the door open for her.

"And now, you're holding doors. Who knew you were so chivalrous?"

Tristan laughed. "It's a long walk back."

"I'm sure I could find someone to take me home." Courtney smirked with a raised brow.

"Where do you think we're going?" Tristan said when she got into the driver's side and started the engine.

"I really hope your apartment."

Tristan feigned surprise. "I have never taken someone back to my place on a first date."

"Good thing we've been there, done that," Courtney laughed.

"You're such a bad girl! What will your parents think of me if I keep you out all night and return you the next day in the same clothing, albeit a little wrinkled, and with messy hair?"

"My mom will think I had a great night. My dad's liable to make you marry me," she said matter-of-factly.

Tristan laughed so hard she nearly ran off the road. She quickly got into the turning lane.

"Where are you going?"

"I'm taking you back home!"

Courtney guffawed.

Meanwhile, Tristan took a back road that came out near her apartment complex. She pulled into her usual spot, killed the engine, and turned to face Courtney. "I don't know what I'm doing."

"What do you mean?"

"With you," she sighed. "What happens when we go back to Colombia?"

"What do you want?"

"I can't do casual, not anymore. I have Loki to think about. I also can't lose my career, either."

"I asked what you want, Tristan."

"You," she whispered, searching her eyes in the dim parking lot lighting. "I've wanted you since the second I laid eyes on you." She shook her head. "You make me crazy one minute and feel things I've never felt before in the next. I don't know how to do any of this."

Courtney reached out, placing her hand over Tristan's. "Do you know how much I've missed you? Our cheeky banter, the stolen moments, and late-night rendezvous,' me searching for you in every room I walked into, then feeling my heart skip a beat when my eyes finally landed on you," she sighed, looking into her emerald eyes.

Tristan squeezed the hand holding hers, then got out of the Jeep and walked around to open Courtney's door. Together, they walked hand in hand up to her apartment. When they stepped inside, they both took their shoes off at the door, and went into the living room where soft lights cast a warm glow through the room.

"You know...you haven't asked what I want," Courtney said, moving closer. "And maybe you're scared to find out the answer, but it's you, Tristan. You and everything that comes along with you, including Loki. When I said new beginnings, I meant it."

Tristan watched the sparkles from the light, play in her brown eyes as her knuckles and thumb softly grazed her cheek. The air in the space between them buzzed with electricity, making Tristan feel like lightning was going to strike at any moment. She'd never been nervous with a woman, especially when she was about to take her to bed, but Courtney was different. They'd slept together nearly half a dozen times, but this...was very new.

Courtney ran her hand up the center of Tristan's chest on the outside of her shirt, coming to rest above her breasts. Her body was hungry, craving Tristan's touch and urging her to tear her clothes off and have sex right there on the living room floor like wild animals, but the ache in her chest was telling her to take it slow and burn this night into her memory like the embers leftover from a hot fire. She couldn't remember ever truly making love with someone, and she wanted to feel every second of Tristan's body connecting with her own.

"You're so beautiful," Tristan whispered.

Courtney smiled, staring back at her with heavy lidded eyes as her lips began to part. Tristan leaned in, connecting with her mouth, stopping any words she was about to say. The kiss was delicate at first with her lips gently grazing Courtney's, but it was enough to make a heavy sigh full of longing, escape as Tristan's mouth left hers.

"Will you dance with me?" Tristan asked, pulling away from her and removing her phone from her pocket. Soft music began playing as she set it on the table and returned to Courtney with her hand out.

Courtney's lips curled into a smile as she stepped closer, running her hands up her arms to her shoulders, then connecting them behind her neck. Tristan reached out, brushing a strand of long brown hair from her face before wrapping her arms around her waist. Their hips slowly swayed together as their eyes stared longingly at each other.

Tristan's fingers played with the hem of her shirt, sliding under just enough to touch her smooth skin. Her own pulse raced with anticipation and wetness pooled between her legs. Courtney slid her hands down the front of Tristan's chest, then up under her shirt, where she gently swirled her fingers around her stomach.

As if on cue, they both began pulling the other's shirt up over her head, discarding it off to the side as they continued to sway together. Courtney's lacey bra was a nice contrast to the sports bras she always wore on the base. Tristan's gaze lingered on her, before reconnecting with Courtney's chocolate eyes once more. Her hands moved to her waist, just above her jeans, then slid up to unhook her bra and pull the straps from her shoulders, allowing it to fall. Courtney ran her hands up Tristan's back, releasing the clasp on her sports style bra. It landed atop the other garment on the floor.

Tristan's arms wrapped around Courtney once more with her palms sliding up under the long, wavy hair hanging nearly halfway down her back as she pulled her closer. Their bare torsos connected in a skin-to-skin embrace, while continuing to sway to the soft music.

Rosewater tickled her nose as she bent her head slightly, breathing Courtney in.

Courtney sighed and tightened her arms around Tristan's shoulders as she melded into the warm body against her. Her belly lit on fire with heat that rapidly spread lower as Tristan's lips grazed the delicate skin of her neck. She pressed her jean clad hips fully against Tristan's, gently rocking side to side with her.

Tristan leaned her head back, keeping their bodies fully connected as her eyes searched the pools of chocolate brown gazing back at her, before gradually leaning in just enough to touch her lips to Courtney's. Together, their mouths slowly opened and closed with their tongues lightly brushing against one another. Their swaying hips came to a stop as Tristan squatted slightly and lifted Courtney off the ground. She wrapped her legs around Tristan's waist as she began walking towards her bedroom, all while continuing their seductive kissing. Tristan lay Courtney on her back, with herself on top. She lifted her mouth from Courtney's, sighing heavily as she pulled her lower lip between her teeth and opened her eyes to Courtney. The desire she saw in the brown pools staring back at her was raw and completely intoxicating, fueling the fire burning deep inside of her. She bent her head once more and began sliding down her body, gliding a warm path with her mouth between her breasts as she continued along her torso until she came to rest just above the waistband of her jeans.

Courtney lay on her back, watching Tristan open her pants and grasp her lacy panties with a finger at each hip, before sliding the garments down her legs. The agonizingly slow pace they were going was both mind-blowing and excruciating, leaving her breathless and hungry. Her eyes roamed Tristan's bare torso, taking in the taut muscles and prismatic tattoos covering her arms and running down her sides as she began removing her own jeans.

Tristan was well aware of Courtney's pining eyes as she unclasped the button of her Levi's and opened the zipper. She took her time pushing her pants and subsequent underwear over her slim hips and down to the floor, before sliding back over her. Courtney's hand reached down, tugging her short hair as Tristan kissed her way back up Courtney's body. When their mouths connected in another salacious kiss, Courtney wrapped her arms around Tristan and rolled her to her back. She parted their lips as she sat back, straddling Tristan's hips. Tristan's eyes locked onto Courtney's as her hands slid up the front of her body, cupping and softly kneading her enticing breasts, before she sat up, bending her head, and replacing one hand with her mouth, licking, and sucking a hard nipple before moving up to claim her mouth once more. She spread the palm of her free hand at the small of Courtney's back, then ran it up under her hair while her other hand moved from her breast, tracing a lazy path down her stomach.

Ragged breath caught in Courtney's throat while her heart thundered wildly in her chest. Her belly fluttered as Tristan's hand inched lower, gently slipping her fingers through her wetness, drawing a soft moan from her lips when she began sliding her fingers back and forth through the silky-smooth folds. Courtney threw her head back, arching into Tristan as she moved her mouth from Courtney's breast to the base of her neck, licking a lazy path all the way up her throat.

The intensity in Tristan's eyes rocked Courtney to the core as she brought her head forward, connecting their lips in a sensuous kiss. Tristan's tongue touching her own made her hips rock involuntarily. Instinctively, Tristan pushed two fingers inside of her, causing Courtney to moan against her mouth.

The entire evening had been patiently slow, and Tristan had no plans to pick up the pace, despite the incredible feeling of Courtney enveloping her fingers. She gradually thrust shallow, then deep, keeping pace with their languid kissing as Courtney's hips began a gentle roll, matching the slow push and pull of her fingers.

Both of Courtney's hands moved from the back of Tristan's neck to the sides, resting partly against her cheeks. She pulled her head back just enough to separate their lips and look into Tristan's eyes. Her hips settled as her body began to pulsate around the fingers buried inside of her. She locked onto the green iris's staring back at her, desperate not to close her own eyes. Her body quivered and a guttural moan slipped from her mouth. It felt like a wild animal was inside of her, clawing to get out as the intense orgasm tore through her body.

Tristan had never seen anything more breathtaking than watching the fluctuation in Courtney's eyes as she climaxed. She quickly wrapped her arms around Courtney, kissing the side of her head as she collapsed against her, completely consumed and nearly breathless. The feeling of Courtney's heart pounding against her chest, was unexpected, but incredible just the same. "I love you," she whispered.

It took a second for Courtney's body to recover and the fog to lift from her brain. As Tristan's words began to register, she lifted her head, searching her eyes. The sincerity she found in them was more powerful than any physical connection she'd ever felt. She softly pushed

Tristan's shoulders until she was lying flat on her back. Then, she bent her head, claiming her lips in a slow, seductive kiss with light, teasing touches of her tongue and gentle nips of her lower lip as she carefully moved from straddling Tristan's hips, to lying on top of her.

Tristan ran her flat palms over the smooth skin of Courtney's back, from up under her hair, all the way down to her ass, reveling in the full skin to skin contact. Tristan chased in protest when Courtney pulled her mouth away to place delicate kisses and tantalizing traces of her tongue around her chest, teasing her pink, erect nipples. Tristan's heightened senses were already on overload from their passionate lovemaking. Her pounding heart and heaving chest gave way to quivering in her stomach and throbbing between her legs as Courtney's mouth and tongue drifted down her stomach, then veered off to her hip bones as she slid herself lower, skimming along the body underneath her until she settled between Tristan's legs.

She lifted her head, biting her lower lip between her teeth in a teasing smile as Tristan's heavy-lidded eyes landed on hers. She reached up, running her fingers up over Tristan's trembling abs from each side as her palms rested on her hip bones. The heady scent of her need made Courtney want to ravish her, but she moved agonizingly slow instead, keeping her eyes locked on Tristan's as she traced her tongue from the back of her knee, up the interior of her smooth thigh, stopping just outside of the inviting lips, glistening with wetness, and begging to be kissed, before starting over with the opposite leg. Tristan's hips lifted slightly, urging her mouth closer.

Gradually, Courtney flattened her tongue and passed it carefully over the top of her succulent lips. Tristan's entire body trembled, and her head snapped back against the mattress when Courtney's tongue licked down the center, then back up again, parting the silky folds. She reached down, running her hand through the long, wavy hair fanned out to the side as Courtney's mouth closed over her clit, gently sucking before her tongue swirled in lazy circles. Each pass of the velvety tongue where Tristan needed it, felt painstakingly slow.

Courtney's hands pressed down on her hips, keeping them from thrusting up to meet her mouth as warm wetness coated her tongue. Tristan moaned faintly in protest as she pulled back, removing her mouth completely. Their eyes met once more as she began crawling back up Tristan's body, caressing her lips over her stomach, then her breasts. One of Courtney's hands was on the outside of Tristan's shoulder while the other settled between their bodies at the opening of her legs. She leaned down, pressing their mouths together in a torrid kiss as her fingers slid through the wet folds and gently entered her.

The taste of herself on Courtney's tongue while feeling her inside, pushed Tristan over the edge of what felt like Niagara Falls. The waves of pleasure kept crashing over her, one after the other. Courtney pulled back from the kiss, and Tristan gazed up at her breathlessly while lifting her hips to meet each thrust of her fingers...until there was nothing left.

Courtney eased out of her gently and curled into her side as Tristan wrapped her arms around her and sighed. "I love you," she murmured, looking up at beautiful green eyes staring back at her.

Chapter 33

Courtney woke and stretched her sore muscles like a Cheshire cat, thinking about the night before as a grin spread across her face. She reached out, running her hand over the cool sheets next to her and realized: one, that she was alone, and two, someone was humming or singing. Having no idea where her clothes were, she pulled on a t-shirt and shorts from Tristan's dresser and left the room in search of coffee and Tristan, and in no particular order.

*

Tristan's hips swayed as she hummed along to the song in her head while rummaging through the refrigerator. She'd hated leaving Courtney asleep in the bed, but she looked peaceful with a thin smile on her lips, and her growling stomach was threatening to wake her. The soft sound of footsteps made her raise a brow. "Are you trying to sneak up on me?"

"I highly doubt that's even possible," Courtney chuckled.

"You are probably correct," Tristan replied, moving to the pot to pour steaming black coffee into two mugs. She added a spoonful of sugar to her mug and stirred it. Then, she smiled at the brown eyes looking back at her as she turned around, handing one of the cups to Courtney. "I don't have cream, but there's milk in the fridge, and the sugar is in that bowl."

Courtney stepped up next to her, also adding sugar to her mug. Then, she poured in a little bit of milk and twirled the spoon around, changing the color from black to a lighter brown shade.

"About last night…" Tristan started.

"It was magical. Do I wish every night could be like that? Absolutely, but I know they won't be, and that's okay. I meant everything I said."

"I was just going to say you snore." Tristan shrugged, then wrapped her arms around Courtney's waist and pulled her close. Courtney set her mug down and put her arms loosely around her neck as their lips came together in a soft kiss that relit the embers still smoldering from the night. "I meant everything I said as well," she murmured.

Courtney reveled in the feeling of being in her arms, before pulling away to go back to her coffee.

Tristan took a sip from her mug, then set it back on the counter behind her. "Nice clothes, by the way."

Courtney shrugged. "They'll do. I mean, I prefer Gucci, but…" She rolled her eyes and bit her lower lip between her teeth.

"Good luck with that," Tristan laughed, then asked on a more serious note, "When do you go back?"

"Middle of next week. You?"

"Not far behind you. My team is probably on the way home right now. We'll rendezvous and redeploy together."

"Do they know?"

"About Loki?" She shook her head. "Fowler does. I plan on telling the rest of them before we go back this time."

Courtney nodded.

"What about us?"

292

"We're going to have to go to the colonel and come clean with our relationship when we both get back," Tristan sighed.

"You're not my commanding officer, Tristan. I don't see where this is a problem."

"I know I'm not, but we're under the same command at the moment, and work with each very closely."

"Okay, but there's no conflict of interest. I don't have a say in what you do with your team, and vice versa. Plus, you can't recommend me for promotion, so that doesn't matter."

"You've thought this through, haven't you?" Tristan smiled softly and reached out, brushing her hand over Courtney's cheek.

"Yes, as a matter of fact, I thought about it my entire plane ride home. I love you, Tristan. This…us, it's what I want. It's why I came here to find you."

"I love you, too," Tristan said, grabbing her hands. "We'll deal with the Army when we get back to the Army. Okay?"

"Roger that." Courtney smiled.

"What are you doing this coming weekend? I know Thanksgiving is in a couple of days…" Tristan asked, changing the subject.

"Um…you, I hope," she teased, smiling brightly.

"That can definitely be arranged," Tristan replied, also smiling. "But first, I need a date to a wedding."

"Oh, really."

"My cousin is getting married Saturday. His mother and my mother are sisters. Anyhow, I wasn't even supposed to be here, but after the adoption and my leave, I'm actually going to be in town."

"That's good. We miss a lot of family things with deployment."

Tristan nodded.

"I'd love to go. I'll have to go back down to my place in Georgia for a dress, or are you going in uniform?"

"When I realized I was able to go, yes. My first thought was my dress blue uniform. However, my mother informed me yesterday morning, the bride's cousin who was supposed to be in the wedding with his son, had to back out at the last minute due to a death in his wife's family. So, she put Loki and I in their places. We actually have a tux fitting later this afternoon," she sighed. "I'm a groomsman, or groomswoman, whatever the hell it's called, and Loki is the ring bearer. Instead of a nice subtle by the way, this is my son...we're getting thrown into the middle of everything and will be on display."

"Aww. I'm sure your family will be thrilled." She smiled brightly. "So, I guess I'll have a lot of eyes on me, too."

"I didn't think about that," Tristan sighed.

"Are you ready to come out as a couple?"

"My family has known I was a lesbian for years, but you'll be the first person in my life they've ever met. So, yeah, we're going to stand out like two lesbians on a Hallmark card. Are you ready for that?"

Courtney laughed hysterically. "I guess I'll need to go get a dress!"

"It's formal, or semi-formal, if that's a thing."

"I'm sure I have something. What are the colors?"

Tristan shrugged.

Courtney chuckled. "Well, is it day or night?"

"Both, I think."

"For a Delta Force Team Leader, you sure are lousy at paying attention."

Tristan shrugged. "Why don't you come with us to the fitting? Unless you want to get back to your family. I completely understand. They probably think I've kidnapped you."

"I want to be wherever you are," Courtney said, wrapping her arms around her again.

"I hope you still feel that way after meeting my mother. We're picking Loki up from her on the way to the tux store."

"Can't wait." Courtney grinned, kissing her once more.

*

Tristan pulled the Jeep into the driveway of the two-story, colonial house and killed the engine. "Her bark is worse than her bite," she said, turning in her seat to face Courtney. "But she can cut you in half with her eyes."

"I'm sure I'll be fine." She smiled. "On another note, my mother was overly excited when I talked to her this morning. I'm pretty sure she's told the entire family about you."

Tristan nodded. "What about your father?"

"He'll warm up to you once he spends more time around you."

"Maybe we should introduce him to my mother."

Courtney laughed.

Tristan swung her door open and got out.

"Is this where you grew up?" Courtney asked as they headed up the walkway towards the door.

"Yeah. It sort of reminds me of the McAllister's house in Home Alone."

"They all do," Courtney replied, looking around.

Tristan squeezed her hand as she knocked on the door. A few seconds later, her mother pulled it open. The smile on her face thinned out as her eyes landed on Courtney and their linked hands.

"Mother, this is Courtney Hewitt."

"Patty Malloy," she said, holding her left hand out so that Courtney would have to let go of Tristan to return her shake. A sly move that didn't go unnoticed by Courtney, nor Tristan. "Please, come in. Loki is in the den, watching TV and playing Guess Who."

"Guess Who?" Tristan questioned as she closed the door.

"Yes. I still had it in the closet from when you were a kid," Patty replied as she led them through the house to the den off the kitchen.

Loki jumped up and ran over to Tristan, hugging her, then latching onto Courtney. "Look, I beat Pip three times! She taught me the right questions to ask!" he exclaimed, setting it up to show them.

"Pip?" Tristan questioned, raising a brow at her mother.

"We were trying to think of a name for him to call me. I told him my initials used to be P.I.P. before I was married to his grandfather many years ago. He decided it fit, so I'm Pip."

Loki paid them no attention as he set up the game. "Courtney, will you play with me?"

"Uh...yeah. Sure." She smiled and sat down on the couch, opposite of where he was on the floor.

When Patty nodded to her daughter, Tristan knew she was in for a talking to. "I'll be back in a minute. You two have fun," she said, then followed her mother down the hall to the study that used to be her father's home office. Patty closed the French doors when they stepped inside.

"Who is this woman?"

"My girlfriend. We met on deployment. She's in the Army also. Anyway, to make a long story short, we fell in love when neither of us expected it. I never told her about Loki, so when I went on leave without a word, she took leave too, and came to find me. She's actually from Hope Mills."

"I see. Obviously, he's met her."

"Yes. She went with us to the zoo recently."

"How does she feel about him? You have a lot more to think about now, other than yourself. That little boy has already been through so much in his short life."

"Really? Are you gonna go there?" Tristan shook her head and sighed. The last thing she wanted to do was argue with her mother, or disrespect her in her own home. "She was surprised, but that didn't stop her from trying to get to know him right away. She knows we are a package deal, and instead of running, she's here…in our lives."

Patty sighed. "I hope you know what you're getting into."

"If I told you I think I might wind up marrying her, would that be better?"

"Are you? You barely know each other, am I right?"

"I'm not proposing right now. But it's on the back of my mind. Loki needs the stability of a family. I'm not parading people in and out of his life. If things don't work out with her, I'll raise him alone. If they do, then he'll have

297

two loving parents." She put her hands on the sides of her face and rubbed her temples.

"You look tired."

"I'm stressed out."

"Maybe she should give you and Loki more time together before she joins the picture."

Tristan ignored her mother's statement. "Why didn't you ever remarry after dad? It wasn't because of me, I left home not long after."

Patty sighed. "I don't know. Your father was an outstanding man." She put her hand up when Tristan tried to speak. "I know he made some terrible mistakes, but he was the love of my life. We built a great life together. I just wasn't sure I could ever have that with anyone again, and part of me never wanted to find out."

Tristan nodded. "That's understandable, but if you don't give someone a chance, how will you ever know?"

Patty shrugged.

"I love you, mother, and I love Courtney. I'm asking you to give her a chance...for me, and for Loki. She's a great person, and she's good with him. You'd actually like her if you got to know her. She's charismatic and tenacious."

Patty nodded. "I take it she's coming to the wedding."

"Yes, she'll be there. Is that going to be a problem?"

"I'll find her a seat at the family table for the reception."

"I hate to change the subject," she lied. "But how was the overnight with Loki?"

"It went well. We spent some time in your old room. I think getting to know more about you, and our family, is helping him. He certainly had a lot of questions when I

298

pulled out the old photo albums of our family, plus the Malloy and Pratt families."

A small sense of relief washed over Tristan. Above everything else, she wanted to make sure Loki was comfortable and starting to feel like they were his family. "That's great," she replied.

"Rooms are blocked at the hotel for family who don't live in town for the night of the wedding. I'm planning to come home. Would you mind if I brought Loki back with me? Grace has a room saved for me; you should take it."

"Are you sure?"

"Yes. The last thing I want to do is sit around drinking cheap wine with Grace's friends."

Tristan laughed. "Okay. Thanks. We'll probably all go early and get ready there, then."

"That's fine. I believe most of the wedding party is doing the same," Patty replied. "I assume you and Loki will be here for Thanksgiving," she added.

"Yes. Although, we will probably go see Courtney and her family at some point."

"She's welcome to come with you."

Tristan was about make a snide comment but realized her mother may actually be extending an olive branch. "Thank you. I'll see what she has planned and let you know," she said as they walked out of the study.

"Yes! I win again!" Loki cheered from the den.

"Looks like you taught him well, Pip," Tristan chuckled.

Patty smiled. "He's a smart boy, but he could use some manners, and bathroom etiquette."

"We're working on that."

"He's in good hands."

"Are you ready to go?" Tristan asked as they stepped into the den. "We have to go try on clothes for a wedding."

"Pip told me," he said, cleaning up the game. "Courtney, are you coming, too?"

"Yes." She smiled.

"Cool!" he cheered.

"Take the game home with you, but bring it back next time you come over," Patty said.

"Okay."

Tristan grabbed the backpack with his overnight stuff and slid the game box inside before throwing it over her shoulder.

"Mrs. Malloy, it was nice to meet you," Courtney said. "You have a beautiful home."

"Thank you. Please, call me Patty."

Tristan smiled at her mother, then pulled the door open. Loki wrapped his arms around Patty's waist, tugging at Tristan's heartstrings before he took off out the door.

Chapter 34

"You look very happy," Courtney's mother said with a smile as she entered the house. "I was wondering if you were going to come back."

Courtney laughed and hugged her mom. "Truth be told, I needed a change of clothes."

They chuckled together as they went into the living room.

"Hey, kiddo. That captain treat you right last night?"

"Yes, sir. She's…" She tried to think of the right words to use. "Charming," she said with a smile as she gave him a hug and bounded back towards the staircase like a schoolgirl.

"I have a feeling we're going to be seeing a lot more of that captain, so be nice!" Shelly said to her husband. "Your daughter is head over heels in love."

"She breaks Court's heart, I'll break her," he muttered, reaching for the TV remote.

"Knock it off, you ol' fuddy duddy. She has a son. Maybe we'll finally get to be grandparents," Shelly said excitedly before leaving the room to go upstairs and get the details from her daughter.

*

Courtney lay flat on her back in the middle of the full-size bed she'd slept on all through high school, and every time she came back home. Her mind was reeling from the majestic night with Tristan, mixed with the chill in the air from meeting her mother, followed by the lousy idea of having to drive back down to her apartment in Georgia to get a dress.

"You look lost in thought," Shelly said, entering the room.

Courtney laughed. "I guess I am."

"I take it things went well on your date?"

Courtney nodded and sat up. "So well, I'm accompanying her to her cousin's wedding this weekend…as her girlfriend."

"Oh, my. That's a huge step."

"Not really. We've been together most of the last four months, but it's quite hard to date on a deployment base. Being stateside really puts things into perspective."

"What about her son?"

"He's adorable. It's really a tragic story. He's actually her nephew. She never knew her father had another child. Anyway, her sister died of a drug overdose and Loki was put in foster care until the state found Tristan. She adopted him as soon as she found out and is raising him as her own."

Shelly wiped the tear that slid down her cheek. "Wow. She's definitely something special."

"Yeah." Courtney nodded. "They both are."

"So, what has you sitting here racking your brain?"

"The wedding," Courtney sighed, flopping back down. "I don't know what to wear."

Shelly sat on the side of the bed. "Well, what would you normally wear?"

"My service dress uniform." She shrugged.

"Okay, what's wrong with that?"

"She and her son are in the wedding and wearing tuxes. It's formal dress. It would look tacky if I was in uniform."

"Okay, then wear a dress."

"I can't just go buy a dress off the rack in some store and go on her arm. Her hoity-toity mother would have a coronary."

"Oh, no. Don't tell me she's one of those snooty ladies without a hair out of place."

Courtney laughed. "Yes and no. She a mix between Diane Keaton and Jane Fonda. She's always well dressed, and very put together. Tristan calls her uppity. I mean, she seems nice, but she definitely gave Tristan a talking to about me."

"What's her problem? It's not like you're going to run off with the family fortune."

Courtney guffawed. "No, I actually think she's just protective of her daughter, and now her grandson."

"That's understandable."

"Okay, so you need to knock this lady out of her Louboutin's and make a statement on Tristan's arm. Am I right?"

"Something like that," she sighed.

"What color is Tristan's tux?"

"Charcoal grey with a matching vest and a burgundy wine-colored tie. The look is elegant and great for a fall wedding. What sucks is, I have the perfect dress…at my apartment. It's a Navy-blue Vera Wang with black Jimmy Choo lace up heels."

"That sounds pretty, and expensive."

Courtney chuckled. "I bought it two years ago for my co-pilot's wedding after the airline lost my luggage and his bougie sister took me to Saks. Then, after I spent my paycheck, his best man got sick, and I took his place…in uniform. So, my fancy dress and heels were never worn. But, because I bought everything on sale, I couldn't return any of it."

"Well, it sounds like you have the perfect opportunity to wear it. If his pompous mother turns her nose up at you in Vera Wang and Jimmy Choo's, you can tell her to pound sand."

"Thanks. You know what, my co-pilot's wife has a key to my apartment in case of emergency. Maybe I can get her to overnight everything to me. That'll cost as much as the gas to get there and back. The last thing I want to do is drive eight hours."

"Sounds like you have it all figured out," Shelly said, patting her on the shoulder.

As soon as her mother was gone, Courtney grabbed her phone.

*

Tristan was sitting on the couch, playing Guess Who with Loki for the hundredth time, when her phone rang. She quickly answered his question, then swiped to answer the call.

"Let me guess, my mother scared you and you're backing out of going to the wedding with me," she said.

"That's a bit presumptuous," Courtney said. "Although, I am terrified of your mother, I was calling to tell you Maguire's wife just overnighted my dress and shoes. They'll be here tomorrow."

"First, I told you she's all bark and no bite. Second, should I be worried his wife has a key to your place?"

Courtney laughed. "I didn't peg you for the jealous type."

"Do you have pierced ears?" Tristan asked, looking at Loki, who shook his head no.

"Uh…yeah, but I rarely wear earrings because I can't have them on under my helmet. Why? Are you surprising me with a pair?" Courtney said.

"Huh? What?" Tristan questioned.

"You asked me about my pierced ears."

Tristan laughed. "I was talking to Loki."

Courtney rolled her eyes. "Guess Who?"

"Yep. I've lost count of the number of games we've played."

Courtney chuckled. "I was calling to hear your voice, but also to invite you and Loki for Thanksgiving. My mother pretty much insisted. I promise to make my dad behave."

"Oh, I'm sure he can't wait to see me after picking you up and dropping you off twenty-four hours later," Tristan laughed. "Actually, my mother invited you to come to her house with us."

"Hmm…what time are you eating?"

"Dinner. I haven't been home for Thanksgiving in three years, so she usually goes to her sister's. I can tell she's happy I'm going to be here so she can cook. Don't get her started on how Aunt Grace dries out her turkey because she cooks it too long and serves cheap wine."

Courtney laughed. "We actually do more of a lunch thing. The whole family is here, and we sit around watching football. It's loud and hectic, but happy."

"We dress formal, eat off the fine China, and sip Chablis out of crystal glasses while a string quartet plays," Tristan teased.

"I hope you're not serious."

"Half and half," she replied. "My mother wouldn't be caught dead in a pair of jeans, but I get away with them as long as I have on a nice sweater or something that classes them up. We do eat off the fine China though, and all her nice glassware *is* crystal. My mother is the epitome of class. I'm sure I'm the cause of the grey mixed into her blond hair. I have never fit into her mold," she sighed. "Honestly, my father was just as crusty, rubbing noses with the elite of the town. He was a dashing, business executive who played golf as much as he worked. But he loved that I played rugby and would spend hours outside practicing with me and going to the gym to workout. A glass of Brandy and the occasional cigar were his vices, which my mother hated, but tolerated."

"My life was quite a bit different. My father was the typical Army dad. He deployed often, so it was just me and my mother most of the time. You've met her. She's very bubbly and upbeat. We've always had a great relationship. My father and I...we're very close, but in a different way. He's always been a leader, guiding my path, so to speak. His father did the same thing with him. It's no wonder I wound up an Army pilot, too. Although, I know I told you he was pissed about that at first. He was brought up thinking women couldn't be pilots and deploy to combat zones. Boy, was he wrong!"

"Yeah, no kidding," Tristan replied. "I remember seeing his face distort when you told him I was Delta Force."

"Completely blew his mind," Courtney laughed. "Anyway, I think we should do both. We can start with my family, then change clothes and go to yours. Would that be okay?"

Tristan looked at Loki. "Hey, how would you like to go to meet Courtney's family on Thanksgiving, then bring her with us to Pip's?"

He thought for a second, then shrugged. "Okay."

"It's a plan," Tristan said.

"Great. Can I bring anything?"

"I was about to ask the same thing," Tristan laughed. "My mother would never turn down a nice bottle of wine, but seriously, you don't need to bring anything."

"My family pretty much does everything. My mother is going to be over the moon when I tell her you and Loki are coming. She cannot wait to meet him. She's liable to jump right into grandma mode, which I'm apologizing for ahead of time."

"It's alright. I'll talk to Loki, so he understands and isn't overwhelmed. That's the only thing I worry about. He's only been with me three weeks."

"I'll have a conversation with my mom as well."

"Sounds good," Tristan said. "So, do I have to wait two more days to see you again?"

"Do you want to wait two more days?" Courtney teased.

"No, but I know your family doesn't get to see you often. I'm willing to share."

"That's so nice of you, but honestly they're making me crazy."

Tristan laughed. "I miss you."

"I miss you, too," Courtney sighed. "I have an idea, why don't we meet for lunch tomorrow? I need to pick up a few things anyway, so I can come closer to you guys."

"We can do that. Just let me know when and where."

"Will do. Have a good night. I love you."

"I don't think I'll ever get tired of hearing you say that."

"Uh, yeah. Me either," Courtney chuckled.

"I love you, too."

As she ended the call, Tristan sat on the edge of her bed and sighed. She wanted to believe their relationship would slide by command like it was nothing, but she had a strong feeling it would be the exact opposite, and that worried her. As much as she loved Courtney, could she give up the Army for her? And vice versa?

"It's your turn!" Loki called from the living room.

Tristan smiled. *Santa needs to bring you some new games!*

Chapter 35

"Are you ready to start school next week?" Tristan asked as they drove towards Hope Mills.

"Yeah, I guess," Loki replied, looking out the window in the backseat.

"It'll be very different from the church school. I think you'll like it, and I'm sure you'll make some new friends."

"Yeah."

"Are you excited to meet Mr. and Mrs. Hewitt?"

"Is that Courtney's mom and dad?"

"Yes. Remember we talked about them and how her mom is really going to like you?"

"Uh huh," he said, nodding his head as he watched the cars go by.

"I know we have been working on our manners. Let's try to say please and thank you, okay?"

"Okay."

Tristan turned down the street and noticed the driveway full of cars, with one parked on the street. "It looks like everyone is already here," she muttered, pulling up along the curb. "Listen, if you feel nervous or uncomfortable, just stay with me. I don't know any of these people either, okay? But I do know they are Courtney's family, and if they are anything like her, we'll like them a lot."

He nodded and grabbed her hand. They'd both chosen to wear tacky holiday sweaters that Courtney had helped pick out the day before, saying it was a family tradition, along with jeans. Tristan gave his hand a small squeeze and started up the walkway. The noise she heard as they reached the door, reminded her of the movie: National Lampoon's Christmas Vacation. *Here we go,* she thought, rapping her knuckles on the door. After nearly a minute with no answer, she pressed her finger on the doorbell…twice.

Suddenly, the door swung open, and Courtney appeared, also wearing a silly holiday sweater and jeans. "Come in!" she said with a big smile, ushering them into the house. When she closed the door behind them, she gave Tristan a brief kiss on the mouth, then bent down and hugged Loki.

"They're here, everyone!" Shelly exclaimed, rushing over. "Tristan, it's so good to see you again."

"You as well, Mrs. Hewitt."

"Please, call me Shelly."

"This is my son, Loki."

"Aren't you the cutest!"

"Okay, Mom. Let them come in and meet everyone," Courtney said.

"Come on, come on. The food is just about ready. The men are watching football in the den, and us ladies are watching the parade in the kitchen. Take your pick," she said, escorting them to the den like royalty. "Everyone!" she said, trying to get all their attention at once. "This is Courtney's girlfriend, Tristan, and her son, Loki."

"What's his name?"

"Loki, like pokey, Geema," Courtney answered with a chuckle.

"Captain Malloy," Courtney's father said sternly as he walked over.

"Thank you for inviting us," Tristan said, looking from Courtney's father to her mother.

"Hello, young man."

"Loki, this is Courtney's dad, Mr. Hewitt."

"Hi," he said, looking up at the man.

Courtney grabbed Tristan's free hand, while Loki held on tightly to her other one. "Let me introduce you to everyone. This is my Aunt Viv and Uncle Pete."

"We've heard a lot about you," Viv said with a big smile.

Tristan simply smiled cordially.

"This is my Geema, Gloria Hewitt."

"It's so nice to meet you," her grandmother said, squeezing Tristan's forearm with her frail hand. "He's a handsome boy."

"Thank you."

"And this man is the original Chief Warrant Officer Hewitt, but I call him Pop," Courtney said, introducing her grandfather.

"I hear you're a captain."

"Yes, sir."

"Weren't no women captains in my day."

"No, sir."

"Pop, she *was* a Ranger. Now, she's a Delta Force team leader," Courtney said.

"Court flies helicopters, just like her father and I did."

"Yes, sir. She's flown my team on several missions." Tristan smiled. "She's an outstanding pilot."

Courtney squeezed her hand.

"Loki, would you like to help me with the gingerbread house? I have it ready to decorate," Shelly said.

He looked up at Tristan.

"It's okay. Remember what we talked about."

Courtney let go of Tristan's hand and bent down, whispering, "She's a little loud, but that's because she was

311

very excited to meet you. She has hot chocolate with a ton of marshmallows waiting for you."

His face lit up and he let go of Tristan's hand. She felt a tug on her heart strings as he walked away. She'd never been to a house full of chaotic family before. It was overwhelming, but joyous.

"You look like a newborn deer, unsure of where to go or what to do," Courtney laughed and pulled on the 3D deer antlers in the middle of her sweater.

"I pretty much am. Holidays at my house were definitely not as loud."

"Or chaotic?" Courtney chuckled as they walked out the back door to the covered patio.

"No, not really. My parents had lavish, formal dinner parties, but when our family gathered for the holidays, it was more traditional and calmer. I was a bit of a raucous kid, so I wasn't at the parties until I was a teen. My cousins and I hung out in my room, usually playing with toys and what not during the holiday gatherings, only coming out to eat or open presents."

"When I was little, dad and pops were both deployed a lot, so we spent a lot of our holidays without them. Then, pops retired and went to work for the post office. Dad retired when I was in high school, so ever since then, it's been a big family party every holiday."

"What did you father do after the Army?"

"He was an air ambulance pilot at the hospital until he officially retired last year."

Tristan nodded.

"You mentioned your father passed in a car accident."

"Tristan nodded, looking out over the backyard. "He was coming back from a meeting with the governor in

Raleigh and was caught in a nasty pile up on the interstate. He died at the scene."

"Oh, my. I'm sorry."

"No, don't be. It was a long time ago," Tristan sighed. "But I was nervous driving for about a year after."

"It's interesting how that works. My dad was in a helicopter crash during Desert Storm. In fact, Lt. Col. Powers was a junior officer back then and commanded his retrieval."

"Really?"

She nodded. "He told me when he flew with me not long after you went on leave. Anyway, I feared it would happen to me when I first started flying, but my dad survived and went on to fly several more missions until he retired years later. I'm pretty sure his confidence is instilled in me, though. I certainly used it when Jezebel decided to take a dump on me midair."

"What? When was that?"

"It's actually why I'm on leave," she said, looking at Tristan's eyes. "I had your team with me when an engine went out. The other spit and sputtered, but I was able to get her back to the base and on the ground safely. The helo was sent back to my garrison for a complete overhaul. With no bird to fly, my crew was given leave."

"Why didn't you tell me?"

"It honestly slipped my mind until now. Once I saw you, and then found out about Loki...everything in my brain shifted."

"I'm glad you're okay, and my team." Tristan shook her head. "That could've been disastrous."

"But it wasn't," Courtney said, wrapping her arms around Tristan's neck, pulling her close for a kiss. "Do you know how much I love you?" she sighed, pulling away to look at her eyes once more.

"I have an idea, but I'm hoping you'll show me soon," Tristan replied, kissing her again.

"If you two love birds are hungry, we're about to serve the food," Shelly said, popping her head out the back door.

Tristan quickly pulled away from Courtney, making her laugh and shake her head. "Come on, if we let the men beat us to the kitchen, there will be scraps left."

"Don't worry. I know my way around a chow line." Tristan smiled.

*

Once lunch was eaten, along with a skinny slice of pie, Tristan and Loki spent another two hours at Courtney's parent's house, watching football and listening to stories about Courtney growing up while they helped decorate the Christmas tree. When it was time to go, they said their polite goodbyes, then headed outside together.

"Do you want to ride with us?" Tristan asked.

"Let me guess, your mother isn't going to like my car," Courtney replied with a grin as she bit her lower lip between her teeth and raised a brow when she hit the auto start button. The powerful engine of her newer model Camaro roared to life.

"You're such a badass." Tristan smiled, shaking her head. "She hates my Jeep," she added with a shrug.

"I'll drive myself to your place, then ride with you from there. Otherwise, you'll have to come all the way back out here tonight."

"Yeah, it's probably too soon for you to stay over," Tristan sighed. "I'm planning on telling him about us tomorrow. I'm not sure he'll understand, but he needs to know we are a lot more than friends."

"How do you think he's going to take it?"

"I'm pretty sure he has a little crush on you, so it might break his heart."

Courtney laughed. "He's five."

"Courtney, are you riding with us?" Loki asked.

Tristan raised her brows as if to say, 'I told you so.'

"No," Courtney replied, shaking her head at Tristan. "I'm driving my car."

"Can I ride with you?" he asked, getting out of the Jeep.

"Am I a bad driver?" Tristan asked.

"No," he laughed. "I ride with you all the time. I never get to ride with her."

"Okay." Tristan nodded.

"Yes!" he exclaimed. "Can I sit up front?"

"No. You have to wait a little bit."

"How long?" he asked.

"Ten years," Tristan said.

"Aw, man!" he pouted.

Courtney chuckled.

"I'll see you at my place," Tristan said, locking her fingers with Courtney's when Loki was wasn't looking, then she waited for her to get him situated in the backseat of the car with his seatbelt on, before jumping in her Jeep and leading the way.

*

After a quick change of clothes, Tristan and Loki were in trousers and sweaters, similar to the slacks and cable-knit Courtney had changed into before leaving her parent's house, except she was in heels while the other two were in lace up Oxfords.

The drive to Patty Malloy's house was quicker than usual with less people on the road. Tristan pulled into the empty driveway and killed the engine. *Here we go.* She took a deep breath and got out, along with Loki and Courtney. The warm white, outdoor lighting illuminated the house beautifully.

"Happy Thanksgiving," Patty said, pulling the door open after Tristan had knocked.

"Pip!" Loki said, hugging her tightly.

"There are sugar cookies in the kitchen," she whispered to him.

"Yes!" he ran off in search of them.

"Mother, he needs to eat dinner."

"Oh, he'll be fine. He's a growing boy."

Tristan eyed her suspiciously.

"Courtney, nice to see you again," Patty said with a smile.

"You as well. I brought you this," Courtney said, handing her the bottle of wine.

"Oh, how lovely. I'll put it in the chiller. I already have a bottle on the table for tonight," Patty said as she turned and headed towards the kitchen. "Dinner will be ready in five minutes," she called over her shoulder.

Tristan grabbed Courtney's hand and tugged as she led her up the staircase and into the first room on the right. "This was my old bedroom," she said, flipping on the light switch.

"Wow!" Courtney gasped, looking around at all the trophies and medals, and the vast number of posters. "This is so nostalgic."

"Yep, like stepping right back into high school," Tristan laughed.

"My parents added my room to theirs to make it bigger and give them a full bath. Now, I use the spare room when I come home."

"When I stay out here, this is where I sleep. She has two guest rooms, but this place just feels comfortable."

"Is that your father?" Courtney asked, walking over to a framed picture.

"Yeah. That's him, and I that day I won my first rugby championship."

"Gosh, you look a lot like him."

"Pretty much everything but the hair."

"I see a little bit of Loki in both of you."

Tristan smiled. "He's definitely a Malloy, that's for sure."

"Thank you for showing all of this to me."

Tristan grabbed her hands, then leaned in, kissing her softly. "Thanks for being here with me…with us. It means a lot."

"I love you, Tristan. I want to be anywhere you are…always."

"I love you, too." She let go of her hands. "Come on, I need to make sure Loki isn't overdosing on cookies. I have no idea what's gotten into my mother."

"It sounds like she's becoming a grandmother."

"I didn't think she even knew what that meant," Tristan muttered as they left her room and headed back down the stairs.

The table in the dining room was set with the fine China, crystal wine glasses, cloth napkins, and polished silverware. A juicy ham was in the center, with a few side dishes and a bowl of rolls. A bottle of wine was already open and breathing.

"This looks great, mother," Tristan said, walking from the dining room into the kitchen. Loki was sitting at one of the island stools with a half-eaten cookie in his hand. She shook her head no at him, causing him to pout as he set the cookie down on the napkin instead of putting it in his mouth. Her heart did a backflip inside, but she kept her cool. They'd come a long way in such a short amount of time.

"Thank you," Patty said. "I figured since you were having turkey earlier, ham would suffice. Loki, I poured you a glass of milk," she added, handing it to him.

"Don't spill that. Walk carefully," Tristan muttered as he passed by her on his way to the dining room.

"Come, let's eat." Patty ushered her daughter and Courtney to follow him. "Tristan, would you please do the honors?" she asked, nodding towards the wine bottle as she walked over to the head of the table.

"Sure," she replied, grabbing the bottle, and filling their three glasses halfway with buttery chardonnay.

Everyone took their seats and began passing the dishes and adding food to their plates. Courtney kept quiet, simply following along with everything Tristan did, all the way down to which fork and spoon to use.

Patty Malloy held her glass of wine up once each of them had a full plate of food. "Cheers to my daughter and having her home for Thanksgiving for the first time in three years. Cheers to my wonderful new grandson, who has torn my heart wide open. And cheers to you Courtney, for putting a light in my daughter's eyes that I've never seen before. Happy Thanksgiving, everyone."

"I'll drink to that," Tristan said with a smile as they all clinked their glasses, while Loki simply watched everyone, patiently waiting to dig into the food on his plate. Before she could cut his meat, her mother leaned in, slicing his ham perfectly.

"My daughter tells me you're also in the Army," Patty said, looking over at Courtney.

"Yes, ma'am."

"Do the two of you work together?"

"Yes and no," Courtney replied. "I'm a helicopter pilot and she's—" Courtney felt Tristan's knee smack into hers. She looked over to see her nonchalantly shake her head. "Um…" she cleared her throat. "I pretty much fly them to different missions."

"I see." Patty nodded. "Are you stationed at Fort Bragg as well?"

"I'm currently down in Georgia, but I'm from Hope Mills. My family is there."

"She's a third generation Army helicopter pilot," Tristan added. "Her father and grandfather both flew."

"Is that so?" Patty smiled. "Tristan is the only person in our family to serve in the military. So, it was quite a shock when she came home and told me she'd enlisted. My late husband and I always thought she would wind up in the corporate world with her strong leadership and organizational skills."

"I'd definitely say she utilizes those skills on a daily basis in the Army." Courtney smiled.

"Yes." Patty nodded. "So, do you have any siblings? I'm sorry to impose, but Tristan hasn't told me anything about you."

"No, ma'am." Courtney smiled. "It was always just me and my parents. They're still happily married."

"What does your mother do?"

"She's retired, but she was an elementary schoolteacher for close to thirty years. Both she and my father took early retirement at fifty-five."

"I retired at the end of last year when I turned sixty. I'd actually thought about taking a director position with the public library system, but now that I have Loki in my life, I couldn't possibly think of doing anything besides being a grandmother." She smiled.

"I didn't know that," Tristan said, swallowing the last sip of her wine.

"They offered, I said I'd think about it. Then, Loki came into our lives. I'm perfectly happy right where I am." She smiled and shifted her focus to Loki. "Are you excited about starting school next week?"

"Not really."

"Why not? You'll make new friends and learn new things."

"I didn't like my last school."

"Well, that's okay. I didn't like every school I attended either." She smiled.

"How many did you go to?" he asked.

"Oh…I don't know. Five, I believe."

"Wow. That's a lot!" he exclaimed.

"I'll tell you all about them next time you're here. I'm sure we can dig out my old yearbooks. Remember how I showed you Tristan's old books? Well, I have mine, too."

"Cool," he said, smiling brightly.

*

With the table cleared and the dishes in the dishwasher, Patty pulled a gift bag from her room and walked into the den where Loki was watching cartoons. "I figured you might be getting tired of guessing the same people over and over," she said, handing the gift to him.

Loki snatched the tissue paper from the bag, then pulled out a new game that was like the original Guess Who, except it was made by a different company. This one had panels that slid into the back of it, changing from people to food, land animals, and sea animals. "Wow!"

"That looks neat," Courtney said.

"Yeah. We definitely needed a change up," Tristan laughed. "What do you say?"

"Thank you, Pip!" He jumped up and gave her a big hug.

"You're welcome," she replied with a smile. "Come on, let's make some hot cocoa, then we can play it."

"Pip, why don't you have a Christmas tree? Courtney's family had one, and we helped decorate it when we were there," Loki said as they worked together adding chocolate and marshmallows to their mugs.

"I usually put my tree up the weekend after Thanksgiving, but with the wedding this weekend, I haven't thought much about it. Maybe you and I should put it up."

"Can we?" he asked excitedly.

Patty looked over at Tristan. "He can stay the night. We'll put the tree up, and I'll bring him with me to the rehearsal tomorrow."

Tristan shrugged. "Are you okay with that?" she asked, looking at Loki.

"Yes." He nodded enthusiastically.

"That's fine with me. Mother, do you want me to get both of the trees and decorations out for you?"

"Yes, but only one tree. I don't think I'm going to put the one in the living room this year."

"I'll help you," Courtney said, following her to the closet under the staircase where the tree box and plastic totes full of decorations were located.

"Since I'm rarely home for the holidays, she stores everything down here. It used to all be in the attic," Tristan said as they began pulling everything out. "This was my hideout when I was a kid. It was like my secret space. She never used it, so it was perfect for me."

Courtney smiled. "Yeah, I used to play in our closet under the stairs, too, until I accidentally got locked in there. After that, hell no."

Tristan laughed. "That had to be traumatic."

"Yep."

"This is the formal tree. Leave it to the side. She's only putting up the one in the den," Tristan said, sliding the box out of the closet.

"What's the difference in the two?"

"The formal one goes in the living room at the front of the house. It's white, with white lights and all white decorations. The other one is green and has colored lights. It's more traditional. She decorates it with colored balls and silver tinsel."

"I see."

"Looks like we have everything," Tristan said, pushing the stuff for the formal tree back inside the closet. "Come on before you get locked in there," she teased.

"Funny." Courtney shook her head and helped carry everything into the den where Patty and Loki were busy playing the new game.

Tristan opened the box and began putting the pre-lit tree together. Courtney helped spread out the branches as the eight-foot tree took shape.

"That's fine. I'll fluff it out myself. You two go on and have a wonderful evening. Courtney, it was nice seeing you again."

"Thank you, Mrs. Malloy. It was nice seeing you as well and thank you again for the invite. Dinner was excellent."

"That's our cue to hit the road," Tristan said. "Loki, you listen to Pip and be good, okay?"

"Okay," he said, giving her and Courtney hugs.

"He'll be fine. I have an extra toothbrush and clothes here, so we'll just meet you at the hotel."

"Sounds good." Tristan hugged her mother, then walked out the door with Courtney. "So, I wasn't expecting that," she said as they headed down the walkway towards the Jeep. "She's been very different lately. I guess being a grandmother has…I don't know, loosened her up a bit, maybe?"

"It looks like she really cares for Loki. Everyone says their parents change when they become grandparents." Courtney shrugged. "Maybe this is her new beginning."

"Yeah, you could be right. Whatever it is, I hope it stays that way," she said as she got into the Jeep.

"My mother is waiting for the moment she can call Loki her grandson," Courtney laughed.

"Really?"

"God, yes. She cannot wait to be a grandmother, and it doesn't matter how it happens, as long as it happens."

Tristan chuckled. "He really liked her."

"Yeah. Dad will come around. He's a stubborn old goat sometimes, but she keeps him in line."

323

Tristan laughed. "I'm pretty sure he's not a fan of me at all."

"He doesn't have to be. I'm the one in love with you, not him."

Tristan leaned over the console, kissing her softly before starting the Jeep. "Are you in a hurry to get home?"

"Since you'll be alone tonight, I was thinking of keeping you company." Courtney grinned.

"I like the sound of that." Tristan smiled.

Chapter 36

Courtney looked in the mirror at herself as she ran her hand down the front of her knee-length, navy blue dress. The front haltered up around one shoulder, then connected to the back near her waist on the opposite side, leaving half of her back and one of her shoulders exposed. It also had a slit from the knee up to mid-thigh on one side. The black lace up heels gave her an extra two inches of height. She wore her hair down in its natural loose waves, hanging mostly over one shoulder, and her jewelry was subtle with only a small pair of platinum hoop earrings and a matching bracelet.

"You look stunning," Tristan said, walking into their hotel room. "But I think you are beautiful no matter what, even in your ACU," she added, walking up and kissing her. She let her lips linger long enough to taste Courtney's tongue. Then, she bent and ran her hand up the thigh where the dress split.

"If you keep going, we're not going to make it down to the wedding," Courtney sighed.

Tristan removed her hand and kissed her again. "You are so gorgeous. I won't be able to take my eyes off you all night," she whispered as they parted.

Courtney smiled. "Will your mother approve?" she asked shyly.

"What my mother thinks doesn't matter. However, if it's designer, she'll love it."

Courtney laughed and shook her head.

"Speaking of her, I was just down there helping her get Loki ready."

"Does he look as dapper as you?" Courtney said, running her hand up the front of Tristan's rented tuxedo. "This is very sexy, by the way." It was a charcoal grey, three-piece suit, with a wing tip collared white shirt, a burgundy wine-colored necktie, and a matching pocket square. Her square-toed oxford shoes were black.

"As a matter of fact, he does. We're all dressed the same, except the groom has a bow tie and his vest isn't grey, it matches his tie."

"It's very regal. You're only missing a top hat and tails."

Tristan laughed. "If it were up to my mother, we'd probably be wearing them."

Courtney smiled. "I do love the fall colors though. They're very classy and traditional, but with a modern twist."

"Yeah," Tristan mumbled as she checked her watch. "We should get going. I'm escorting both you and my mother to your seats. You're sitting together, by the way."

"Okay." Courtney nodded. "Where will Loki be?"

"The wedding planners will be watching him and the flower girl until it's their turn to walk down. Then, he'll come over and sit between you and my mother."

"Sounds good." Courtney smiled, linking her hand with Tristan's when she held it out to her.

*

Patty Malloy was standing off to the side in a dark blue designer midi dress with a round neck and chiffon sleeves, and black pumps. A double strand pearl necklace hung down to the top of her breasts and dangling pearl and platinum earrings hung from her ears. She took one look at the woman walking hand in hand with her daughter and shook her head. "It seems we should've conferred," she said, taking in her dark blue dress, albeit with a lot of skin showing.

Courtney smiled awkwardly. *Fuck.*

"I think you both look amazing," Tristan said, holding a winged arm out to each of them. "Besides, great minds think alike." She smiled.

Courtney nodded and grabbed ahold of her arm.

"We're all walking down together?" Patty asked.

"You're sitting together, and I have to walk you both. We might as well all go at once," Tristan replied. Her mother lifted her chin and put her hand on her daughter's arm the same way Courtney had on the opposite side. Together, the three of them walked down the aisle to the groom's extended family seating in the second row. Tristan ushered them into their seats, then went back up the aisle to continue her groomswoman duties, as she liked to call it.

*

"Mrs. Malloy, I had no intentions—" Courtney started.

"It's fine, dear. Even the first lady occasionally hosts guests who arrive wearing the same dress. Of course, she must quickly change to keep from embarrassing the person who created the faux pas," she sighed. "We simply chose the same color, as did quite a few of the guests," she added, looking around. *At least she had the brains to wear something formal and fashionable, even if half the material is missing.*

Courtney nodded and smiled thinly as the music began playing; the groom walked down with his mother, taking his position up front. Her frayed nerves began to unravel when she saw Tristan appear at the end of the aisle, but they frazzled once more when she saw the bubbly blonde step up next to her and grab her arm. Slowly, they made their way down the aisle. Tristan glanced over, smiling at Courtney despite her mother returning the gesture as though it was meant for her.

Behind them, the second pair of groomsman and bridesmaid came down, followed by a third, then the best man and made of honor. Loki and the flower girl walked too fast but did what they were supposed to do, which was look cute and smile big. He escorted her to her seat like a little gentleman, then sat down between Patty and Courtney. The wedding song began playing right after, and everyone stood to watch the bride come down the aisle on her father's arm.

*

The ceremony itself lasted roughly fifteen minutes, then everyone went inside the elegantly decorated ballroom where round tables with assigned seating awaited the guests. The wedding party table was a long rectangle across the front of the room, with the large wooden dancefloor separating it from the rest of the tables in the room.

While the guests were inside making their way through the buffet line, the wedding party stood outside in the courtyard, taking photos with the photographer. Once they were finished, Tristan asked him to take a few pictures of her with Loki before bringing her mother in for a few shots with her daughter and grandson.

"The ceremony was beautiful," Patty said when her sister walked up once the photographer was finished.

"Thank you for all of your help," Gretchen replied. "I'm so glad you could be here and be a part of Caleb's big day," she added, hugging Tristan. "Maybe you'll be the next one. I saw that pretty girl you brought with you."

Tristan smiled.

"Anyway, the wedding party is going through the buffet line now, so you should probably catch up to them."

"Loki, come on. Let's go find your seat at the kid's table," Patty said, holding his hand. "I'll bring you a plate of food."

They all meandered inside together. Tristan scanned the room, spotting Courtney at one of the family tables, presumably next to her mother since the seat beside her was empty. Everyone at the table had a smile on their face as they ate, talked, and drank.

"I was wondering if you were going to join us," one of the bridesmaids said as Tristan entered the line. "I never did get your name when we met at the rehearsal."

"Tristan."

"I'm Diana, Vicky's friend. We were roommates in college," she said with a smile as her eyes raked over Tristan.

"Nice to meet you," Tristan replied, ignoring her eyes as she grabbed a plate and began making a side salad.

"Are you one of Caleb's friends?"

"He's my cousin."

"Oh, cool. Was the ring bearer your little boy?"

"Yes."

"Aww. He's super cute, just like his mom."

"Thanks," Tristan said as she continued through the line, filling up her dinner plate while carefully balancing her salad plate. Once she was finished, she went over to the table and set her plates down at the end of the groomsman side where her seat was located. Then, she made her way through the crowd towards the bar, stopping when she felt a hand on her back.

"Excuse me, are you single?"

Tristan spun around and lit up with a smile when her eyes landed on Courtney. "I can be for you."

"Nice," Courtney laughed. "I saw that young bridesmaid eyeing you like a lion watching a zebra."

"What? Who?" Tristan guffawed, shaking her head.

"The one coming this way."

"Tristan, I'm going to the bar. Would you like me to get you anything?" Diana asked.

"Uh, no thanks. I'm good."

She smiled and kept walking.

"She couldn't take her eyes off you for the entire ceremony," Courtney said.

"She actually tried to walk down the aisle with me when we were at the rehearsal, but we were put in order of our height and there was another girl shorter than her. Anyway, she was the bride's roommate in college."

"Oh, really?"

"Yeah, she talked the entire time we were in the food line."

"I'm pretty sure she waited for you to come inside so she could go through with you."

"I was actually looking for you to join us for the pictures, but you weren't around, and the photographer needed to get back inside."

"Oh, I definitely wasn't crashing that family photo. Your mother would've killed me with her Louboutin."

Tristan laughed.

"Did you see me walk down the middle, Courtney?" Loki asked, rushing up and giving her a hug.

"Yeah, you were great."

"Pip said I was a gentleman."

"That's right," Tristan said, hugging him. "What are you doing over here? I thought you kids had your own table."

"I wanted to say hi to Courtney and tell you both I made a new friend. His name is Trevor."

"Very cool," they both replied.

"Go eat all of your dinner so you can have a piece of cake later, okay?" Tristan said.

"Okay."

He ran off as quickly as he'd appeared.

"Your son is just adorable. I see where he gets it," Diane said, patting Tristan's forearm as she walked back by with a glass of wine.

"I'm going to pluck her eyeballs out with my Jimmy Choo's," Courtney grumbled.

"She's young and obviously clueless. Anyone in this room with half a brain can tell we're together. She'll figure it out eventually."

"Uh huh."

"I didn't think you were the jealous type."

"I'm not."

"Do you know how badly I want to kiss you right now?" Tristan sighed.

"That'll definitely get her attention."

"Yeah," Tristan laughed. "Along with everyone else in this room."

"I need a drink," Courtney sighed.

"Me too."

*

With nothing but empty plates on the tables and a small amount of food left at the buffet, the DJ called the bride and groom to the dance floor for their first dance. After that, he opened the floor up to everyone. Several people made their way to the front of the room and began moving to the music. Tristan went over to Loki.

"Are you ready?" she asked. "Everyone is dancing."

He thought for a second, then nodded his head.

"Do you remember the steps I taught you last night?"

"I think so."

"Remember, it's alright if you make a mistake."

"Okay."

"Let's go," she said, smiling and leading the way towards the family table where Courtney and Patty were both sitting, talking to other family members.

"Well, hello there," Patty said, hugging Loki. "Cindy, you remember my daughter, Tristan. This is her son, Loki," she added, talking to her cousin.

"Oh, my. The last time I saw her was probably Don's funeral."

"That was a decade ago. Surely, you've seen her since then?"

"She could be right. I'm deployed quite a bit," Tristan said. "Anyhow, it's nice to see you again."

"You too, sweetie," Cindy said, smiling.

"Courtney, will you dance with me?" Loki said, holding his hand out to her.

"Yes, I'd love to."

"Mother, would you like to dance?" Tristan asked when Loki and Courtney walked away.

"Oh, why not?" she smiled and stood up.

When they reached the dance floor, a medium tempo song was playing. Tristan held her mother's hand, then placed her free hand on her back. Together, they box stepped all over the floor.

"This reminds me of dancing with your father," Patty said, delighting in the joy of being on the dance floor with her daughter. "I'm really glad you're here."

"Me too."

"Look at him go!" Patty said, watching Loki lead Courtney around the dancefloor. "Your father would be so tickled with him. I'm sorry, Tristan. For everything."

"Thank you. It's all in the past now. I believe in new beginnings."

"Yeah, I like that. New beginnings."

"May I cut in?" Loki asked as the music slowed down.

"Why yes you may," Patty said, letting go of Tristan to dance with her grandson.

"May I have this dance?" Tristan asked, grabbing Courtney's hand, and pulling her close.

"I thought you'd never ask," Courtney said as they began to sway together. "You taught him well," she said, referring to Loki.

"I'm pretty sure he has a crush on you. It's going to break his heart when I tell him you're already taken."

"I thought you were going to do that yesterday."

"No. I decided to wait until he gets going with his new school. He's nervous as it is, so I don't want to upset him at the same time."

"That makes sense."

"Do you remember what happened last time we danced?" Tristan questioned, watching her eyes slowly glaze over.

"Vaguely. Maybe you can remind me later."

"I'd love to," Tristan said before spinning her around. "You do know all the men in here are watching you, right?"

"What?" Courtney rolled her eyes and shook her head.

"You're gorgeous, and this dress is very sexy, so I can't blame them. I'm sure they're wondering how in the hell I wound up with you on my arm, though."

"Then, they obviously don't know you."

Tristan smiled.

When the song was over, most of the people left the dance floor. Loki went back to the other kids, and Patty went over to talk with family friends she hadn't seen in a while. Tristan sat down in her mother's seat, next to Courtney, and sipped the fresh glass of bourbon she'd just gotten from the bar.

*

After the bouquet toss, which Courtney narrowly missed, and the garter toss, the dance floor lit up once more with fast music. The reception had been going for close to three hours and many of the guests were feeling the light buzz of happiness mixed with alcohol. Patty had already left with Loki, as well as some of the older guests. A handful of single men had come onto Courtney, asking her to dance, offering to get her a drink, and one even asked her to leave with him…all of which were turned down.

The bride had given up on her shoes and was wearing a pair of white, bedazzled sneakers. The groom and all his groomsmen, including Tristan, had removed their jackets, and were now sporting just their vests and ties. Tristan had rolled her sleeves back almost to her elbows, showing off her tattooed arms. Several of the other guests had removed their suit jackets as well.

"We're going to turn it up one time for the groom, who requested this song," the DJ said. Suddenly, a song called *U Gurl* by Walker Hayes, began thumping through the speakers. The country-pop tune had a lot of people heading to the dancefloor.

Tristan and Courtney were already on the dancefloor, so they stayed out there and started dancing playfully, flirting, and singing the catchy lyrics to each other. When that song ended, the DJ played a requested song by the bride, which was seductive and slow. A lot of people left the dancefloor, but those who were lovers, remained. Tristan pulled Courtney into her arms. Their bodies remained close while they swayed together. Courtney's arms were up around Tristan's neck with her hands linked together, and Tristan's hands were at the small of her back. The look in Tristan's tired eyes made Courtney want to kiss her.

"I'm ready to get out of here when you are," Tristan said when the song ended.

"Absolutely," Courtney replied, putting some space between them. Tristan locked hands with her as she led her over to the bride and groom to say goodbye. Then, they retrieved Tristan's jacket and began walking towards the exit doors in the back of the room. Courtney raised a brow and grinned at the young bridesmaid when they passed by her.

The elevator ride seemed to take forever. Courtney wrapped her arms loosely around Tristan's neck and kissed her. "God, I've been wanting to do that all night," she sighed when their lips parted.

"Me too." Tristan smiled, kissing her once more.

The bell dinged when they stopped at their floor, and the doors spread open. Tristan pulled the key card from her pocket when they reached their destination at the end of the hallway and swiped it in the automatic lock. The door swung open to the small living room space. Courtney immediately removed her shoes, and Tristan began peeling out of her suit.

"I still can't believe your mother and I were in the same colors," Courtney muttered, shaking her head.

"Several people were in blue." Tristan shrugged.

"Yes, but they weren't me."

"Why don't you take off this blue dress that happens to be the same color as my mother's, and get in the tub with me?" Tristan said, sliding the zipper down for her.

"That sounds like a great idea!"

Tristan started the hot water and poured some liquid bath soap in to make bubbles. Then, she finished getting undressed and packed her tuxedo into the bag to go back to the rental store in the morning. Courtney hung her dress in the closet, then twisted her hair up into a bun and clipped it in place on the top of her head to keep it from getting wet. She was way too tired to blow it dry. Tristan was already in the tub when Courtney walked into the room. She carefully stepped into the tub, leaning back against Tristan's chest once she was fully in the water.

"This is nice," Courtney murmured.

"Yeah," Tristan whispered, kissing the side of her bare neck as she ran her hands down her arms. "All day long I've thought of nothing but making love to you. I'm afraid this is as romantic and physical as it's going to get.

Who knew dancing for four hours would be so exhausting?"

Courtney chuckled. "Believe me, I understand. I barely had the energy to get in here, but I've thought about getting naked with you all day, too."

"Raincheck?"

"Deal."

Chapter 37

The throaty exhaust of Courtney's Camaro could be heard coming down the road as she turned into her parent's neighborhood. She had the windows down and the radio up when she pulled into their driveway.

"You look happy," her mother said, noticing the big smile on her face when she walked into the house with a backpack thrown over one shoulder and the garment bag holding her dress and shoes in her opposite hand.

"Yeah," she murmured, hugging her mother before heading up the stairs to deposit her stuff in her room.

"How was the wedding?" Shelly asked from the doorway as she tossed the backpack on the bed and hung the garment bag in the closet.

"Beautiful. Their ceremony was outside with strings of warm white lights illuminating the courtyard, and the reception was in the ballroom. The décor was very classic with a touch of modern chic. Honestly, it looked like the set of a wedding magazine photo shoot, which I'm sure was Tristan's mother's input."

"How was she?"

Courtney flopped down on the bed. "We were wearing the same color dress."

"Oh, geesh. Was it noticeable?"

"She sure as hell noticed," she sighed.

"What did she say?"

"I don't know. Some stupid comment about the first lady, then she pointed out how several people were also in dark blue."

"That doesn't sound like she had a problem with your dress."

"It's her delivery. She can make the nicest of words razor sharp."

"What does Tristan say about all of this?"

"She's thinks I'm reading too much into it. She knows how her mother is; that's who raised her."

"Maybe she's right." Shelly shrugged. "Anyway, Thanksgiving was nice. We really enjoyed having Tristan and Loki here."

"Yeah, they had a great time."

"Will we be seeing more of them?"

Courtney sat up and eyed her mother suspiciously.

"I thought I heard you coming down the road," her father said as he walked into the room. "That damn bird feeder is always empty," he muttered.

Courtney stood and gave him a hug.

"How was the wedding?"

"Great. I had a wonderful time."

"We were just talking about Thanksgiving," Shelly said.

"Ah." He nodded. "You're leaving in a couple days, right?"

"Yes, sir. I'm going back to Georgia tomorrow. Then, we fly out two days later."

"And the captain?"

"Dad, you can call her Tristan."

"I'm aware of that."

She sighed and said, "She leaves a week after, I believe."

He nodded and crossed his arms. "What are your intentions here?"

She stared at him like she was fifteen again, going out on her first date.

"There is a child involved. A child who needs stability in his life. It will be difficult enough with his mother in and out on deployment. He seems to be very attached to you already."

"I love her, and I love him…if that's what you're asking. We're together, and we're going to do everything we can to make this work."

"I just hope you know what you're doing. She's a captain who will continue advancing in her career."

"And I'm just a lowly Chief Warrant Officer pilot with nowhere else to go, right?" she snapped.

"Honey, we just want you to see clearly when you look at the future. We like Tristan, and her son, but there are a lot of variables to consider. That's all," her mother said.

"Don't you think Tristan and I have discussed all of this? We're not just sleeping together, we're in love. Who knows, maybe we'll get married one day," she said, throwing her arms up in the air while shrugging her shoulders. "Right now, we're happy and we're doing what we can to make this work. Is it easy? Hell no. We're both worried about command, and how that's going to go when we return because we're done hiding our relationship. For all we know, both of our careers could be over." She shook her head and began packing her bag. "I don't need this right now," she sighed in frustration. "I'm going to head back tonight and rejoin my crew. I have a deployment mission to get back to."

Shelly waved for her husband to leave the room when he opened his mouth to speak. She hated seeing her daughter like this, and knowing she and her husband were the cause, just made it worse.

"Damn them," Courtney murmured, sitting on the bed with her head in her hands after they left her alone.

*

"Yes!" Loki cheered after winning the new game for the third straight time.

Tristan shook her head and put the game to the side. "There's something we need to talk about," she said, patting the spot on the couch beside her.

"Okay," he said, getting up from the floor and sitting down next to her.

"So…" she cleared her throat nervously. "Courtney is very special to me. She's more than my friend. I care about her a lot."

"I like her, too."

"Um…do you know how some people love each other? Like a husband and wife who are married? Or a girlfriend and boyfriend?"

"I think so."

"Well, Courtney and I love each other like that. She's my girlfriend."

"She's not a boy, though."

"It's okay for boys to love boys and girls to love girls. Just like boys can love girls and girls can love boys."

He looked slightly confused.

"I know this is a lot."

He nodded.

"She's going to be in both of our lives, which means we will do a lot of things together, and she will spend the night here. Is that okay with you?"

"Yeah."

Thank God.

"Also, you know she and I are in the Army, and we have to go away to do our work?"

"Uh huh."

"Well, she's going away in a couple of days."

"Will she be coming back?"

"Yes, but not until sometime after Christmas."

He nodded. "What about you? Are you going away, too?"

She stayed silent for a second. She hadn't planned on telling him until he was situated in his new school. "As a matter of fact, I am," she finally said, grabbing his little hand. "I will be leaving next week."

"I don't want you to go."

"I know. I wish I didn't have to, but I'll be back. And you'll be with Pip while I'm gone."

"I will?"

"Yes. She loves you, and she's looking forward to you staying with her until I get back. I'll try to call you on the computer as much as I can, and Courtney will be with me, so we can call you together."

"I still don't want you to go."

She sighed.

"But I really like Pip. She's not my Gigi, but she's a good grandma."

Tristan smiled and wrapped him in a big hug. "I love you so much. I'm really glad you became my son," she said as she wiped a stray tear from her cheek.

"I'm glad, too," he said. "I like living here with you. I'm going to miss it when I'm with Pip."

"I'm going to miss you."

"I'll miss you, too, and Courtney."

"I promise we'll call you all the time. You're going to get tired of sitting in front of the computer talking to us."

"Not uh," he laughed when they parted.

"Come on. Let's go make some of the hot cocoa you and Pip are always drinking."

"Okay, but then can we play the game again?"

She pursed her lips in thought.

"Please?" he begged.

"Okay, but only if you promise to use your manners and be good for Pip while I'm gone."

"I promise."

A big smile spread across Tristan's face and her chest ached with a mixture of happiness, and sadness at having to leave him.

*

Courtney mashed the button for her phone to make a call over Bluetooth as she pulled out of her parent's driveway. They'd apologized, and she'd hugged them goodbye. She was no longer angry, but she was still offended by their actions. The only time they'd ever questioned her judgement was when she joined the Army...until now, and she'd hated it just as much back then.

"Hey, you," she said, wiping a tear from her cheek as she drove down the road.

"Loki and I were just talking about you," Tristan said.

"Oh, yeah? Good things, I hope."

"Yep. I told him you're my girlfriend, and I love you."

"Wow. How did that go?" she sniffled.

"Good..." Tristan replied. "Are you okay?"

"Yes and no. I'm on the road."

"Where are you headed?"

"Georgia."

"What? Wait! You're going back without saying goodbye?"

"I'll see you in a week."

"Not to me."

"I'm sorry, Tristan. I wasn't thinking."

"What happened?"

"My parents," she sighed, wiping another tear.

"Courtney, turn around. Come here."

"I'd thought about it, but you have a lot going on with Loki. Besides, I need to get back anyway. We're leaving Tuesday. I need to catch up to my crew before then."

"I hate this."

"I do, too. I'm sorry."

"Stop telling me you're sorry and start telling me what the hell happened."

"They're questioning our relationship, and everything that goes with it. I think they think you're going to hurt me. At least, my father, anyway. My mother is worried we're going to both break Loki's heart."

"Jesus," Tristan spat. "And you thought my mother was bad."

"They've never been like this before, except when I joined the Army. They were beyond pissed and did everything they could to talk me out of it and make the Army sound like a horrible thing to do with my life."

"I'm the first person you've ever brought home, right?"

"Pretty much, other than a boy I dated in high school."

"They're just worried about you. You're their only child, and you are very much daddy's little girl. I can see where they'd have questions."

"I'm almost twenty-seven years old. I'm pretty sure I can make my own decisions without them raking me over the coals with the consequences."

"I know. Trust me, my mother has tried to do that to me several times. You should've heard the shit she said when she found out I was going through with the DNA test about Loki. Not to mention when I'd decided to adopt him. I nearly told her to get out of my life, but she came around, and look at her now. She's become this amazing grandmother. I never knew she had it in her."

"They apologized as I was leaving, but it'll take a while for me to get over this. I love them both so much, but right now, I can't stand either of them."

"I'm sorry. I wish I'd been there with you."

"They wouldn't have said anything with you there."

"Exactly. I should've gone back with you, then brought you here to stay with us until you had to head back."

"You need this time with Loki. He's going to be lost when you leave next week."

"I know. We've already talked about it. He's excited to go stay with my mother though. He did say he was going to miss both of us. I promised we would video call him all the time."

"Absolutely. In fact, I'll call you both once I get back to Colombia."

"He'll get a kick out of seeing you in uniform. He's already seen pictures of me."

"I'm going to miss you," Courtney sighed. "Hell, I already do."

"I wish you'd have turned around, but I understand."

"I love you."

"I love you, too. I'll be there before you know it. Then, we'll have a whole different pile of shit to deal with."

"Yeah, but I think it'll be okay. At least, I'm staying positive, anyway."

"Good idea. I should let you go. Drive safely and call me when you get to your apartment, okay?"

"Will do."

Courtney pressed the end call button and turned the radio up. "Three and a half hours to go," she whispered, before singing along to *I Touch Myself* by Divinyls, which only made her want to turn around and go straight to Tristan.

Chapter 38

Tristan was up before the alarm on Monday morning. She wasn't sure who was going to be more nervous, her or Loki. She drank a cup of coffee as the sun rose, then made pancakes and bacon with a side of chocolate milk for breakfast. Loki woke without a problem when she went into his room. He got dressed and brushed his teeth without much hassle, then went into the kitchen to eat.

"Your backpack is by the door. I packed your lunch; a peanut butter and jelly sandwich and a chocolate pudding, as requested. Your thermos is full of water," Tristan said as she rinsed her cup. "Can you think of anything else?"

"Nope," he replied as he put his plate in the dishwasher.

"Alright then, let's hit the road," she said. "I talked to your teacher. She's very excited to meet you, and she loves your name. I think she likes Marvel, too."

"Cool," he said as he climbed into the Jeep.

*

The school wasn't far from her apartment, meaning it was close to the base and had a lot of military children attending. Tristan pulled through the drop off loop and came to a stop behind the car in front of her.

"Do you remember where to go?"

"Yes. Room six."

"Don't forget, I'll be right here when you get out this afternoon. If something happens, you demand that Mrs. Carter call me, okay?"

"Okay."

"I love you, and I hope you have a wonderful day."

He smiled.

"Can you do one thing for me?"

"What?" he asked.

"Try to make one new friend."

He nodded and grabbed his backpack from the floor when the safety patrol kid opened the door. She watched him go through the gate and enter the school. The impatient mother in a minivan behind her blew the horn as she wiped a tear from her face. "Oh, fuck off, lady!" she snapped, stopping shy of shooting her a bird through the open window. *Great first day,* she thought as she put the Jeep in gear and drove off.

*

Without Loki to care for, Tristan was lost in her apartment. The quiet was nearly unbearable, making her wonder what the hell she did before becoming a parent, because she couldn't remember. She'd spent the first two hours cleaning and doing laundry, then she took her uniforms to the cleaners on the base. After that, she literally had nothing to do. The silent calm brought back an itch she hadn't felt in weeks. Suddenly, she remembered her team was also back in garrison. She grabbed her phone and scrolled through the contacts, pressing the call symbol next to the one she'd been looking for.

"Captain!" Fowler answered.

"Hey, I'm just checking to make sure everyone made it back okay."

"Yeah, we arrived about a week ago. How are you doing? How's your son?"

"We're good. I dropped him off for his first day at his new school this morning. I honestly forgot what quiet was like."

He laughed. "We'll be back in the shit sandwich soon enough. Enjoy the quiet my friend."

"Yeah, no kidding," she chuckled.

"Hey, listen. The team has been asking a lot of questions. It's not every day your leader takes sudden leave for five weeks. A couple of them thought maybe your mother had passed but I assured everyone it was a happy reason, just bad timing with us being deployed."

"Thanks. I was actually planning on telling them on the flight back."

"Roger that."

"I'll see you in a week," she said. "Enjoy this time with your family."

As soon as she hung up, her phone rang in her hand and her mother's picture popped up on the screen.

"Hello," she answered.

"How was Loki this morning?"

"I'm pretty sure I was more nervous than he was."

Patty laughed. "I remember being a mess on your first day of school every year."

"Really?"

"Oh, yeah."

"I talked with him about my deployment."

"How did he take it?"

"He was sad at first, but he perked up when I told him he'd be staying with you. I made sure he knew I would video call as much as possible."

"I probably need to get some new games. I'm going to be stuck playing Guess Who fifty million ways for the next however many weeks," she laughed.

"I don't know how to thank you," Tristan said. "I know I forced you to let him into your life."

"Tristan, he's your son. How he came into this world is history. I love him every bit as much as if you'd given birth to him."

"I'm pretty sure you're his favorite person."

"I don't know about that. He seems smitten with Courtney. Does he know who she is to you?"

"Yes, I told him over the weekend. He was confused at first, but I'm pretty sure he understands. He was happy when I told him we would both video call him because we'd be together. She actually left already."

"I see," Patty said.

"What is it that you don't like about her?"

"I never said I didn't like her. I just want you to make sure without a doubt that you are doing the right thing. That boy doesn't need to lose anyone else that he cares about."

"I know. I thought about that quite a bit, which is why I broke things off with her at first. I knew I was in love with her, but I chose him. She fought hard to get me to see that she loved me, and the minute she met Loki, I knew she was going to love him, too. That's actually what brought us back together."

"I've seen the way you look at each other, and she's very good with Loki. I won't deny that. I only hope it lasts. That's all I'm saying."

Tristan shook her head. "I know."

After another couple of minutes, she made an excuse to get off the phone. She loved her mother, but she could be a righteous pain in the ass, especially with her incessant complaining about the wedding: from the DJ and what she referred to as booty music, to the dry chicken, mediocre cake, and cheap wine.

With nothing else to do except go stir crazy, Tristan went for a jog and wound up at the gym, where she spent the next thirty minutes lifting weights, before jogging back to her apartment to take a shower and get ready to finally go pick up Loki.

*

"Hey, sexy lady. I hope you're feeling better," Courtney whispered, running her hand along the metal on the side of the helo as she walked past it in the C-27 transport plane. Her crew was already in their seats, along with a dozen other soldiers who were being dropped off at a stop on the way.

"You look tired," Maguire said when she sat down next to him and pulled the straps down over her shoulders.

"That's because I am," she muttered, closing her eyes.

"Miranda said she had to overnight a dress and shoes to your parent's house."

"Yep."

"Hot date?"

"Last minute invitation to a wedding."

"Gotcha." He nodded. "Any word from Bravo Team, or their fearless leader?"

Courtney opened her eyes. "Are we really going to do this all the way to South America?"

"I was just making conversation."

"Then change the subject," she grumbled, closing her eyes once more. She *was* tired, but she was grumpy because she hated going back to Colombia without Tristan. The fact that she was arriving a week later didn't matter. "Did you meet your niece?"

"Yes. She's precious."

"Speaking of babies, did you have sex with your wife?"

"As a matter fact, we did it quite a bit, and unprotected, which was definitely something new."

Courtney shook her head. "I didn't need the details."

He laughed. "She did mention you a lot."

"Not during sex, I hope."

"Hell no."

"Good because I'm taken, and that would just be awkward," she teased.

"Taken? Since when?"

"Have we met? You know I don't kiss and tell."

He crossed his arms and pursed his lips like a pouting child, but her eyes remained closed.

"Did you get the repair report on Jezzi?" he asked after a few minutes of silence.

Courtney had just about nodded off when she heard his voice. "Nope. We're going to have to cross our fingers the first time we take her up," she muttered.

He shook his head and finally shoved his AirPods into his ears.

*

The safety patrol opened the door of the Jeep and Loki got in. He put his backpack on the floor, then put on his seatbelt. Tristan put the Jeep in gear and drove away before any of the crazy moms could honk at her.

"How was it?" she asked, although the teacher had emailed her at lunchtime to say he was fitting in with the other kids and making friends already.

"Thomas is my new friend. His mom is in the Army, too."

"Awesome. What about Mrs. Carter? Do you like her?"

"I think so."

"How was lunch?"

"One of the kids got in trouble."

"What? Why?"

"He put his finger in his nose."

Tristan nodded to keep from laughing. "Um...what about your food? Was your sandwich good?"

"Yeah. Thomas wanted to trade my pudding for his fruit snacks, but I said no way."

Tristan chuckled. "Good choice."

"I have homework."

"Oh, really? You're in kindergarten."

He shrugged.

"We'll check it out when we get home. How about an ice cream cone to celebrate your first day?"

"Yes!" he exclaimed as she pulled into the Dairy Queen line.

*

Courtney and Maguire walked into the *Canteen* together and plopped down on a pair of stools. Her thoughts were all over the place. She needed to go to command about her and Tristan but figured it would be better to do that together, which only made her miss Tristan even more. Plus, they still needed to test fly Jezebel, and that made her nervous. She needed to get in the air to clear her head, and she needed confidence in her bird to do so.

"Welcome back, Outlaws!" Judd said, raising his pool stick in the air.

"I really can't stand that prick," Maguire muttered, lifting his beer bottle.

"I'm pretty sure something happened between him and Tris...uh, Captain Malloy," she said, clearing her throat.

He glanced at her as she pulled her beer bottle to her lips. "Care to elaborate?"

"Nope."

He shook his head. "You know we're friends, uniform aside. You can talk to me. She's coming back at some point, and we all have to get along so we can end this shit and get out of here."

"Next week."

"Huh?"

"She's coming back with her team next week."

"I'd ask how you know, but you probably won't tell me," he muttered, shaking his head once more.

Courtney finished her beer and set the bottle down. "I was with her the entire time we were on leave. I love her with everything that I am, John."

"Does she feel the same way?"

"Yes." She smiled. "I don't know what command is going to do, but we're coming forward with our relationship when she gets back."

"Wow."

"I should've been upfront with you. You're right, we *are* friends. I'm sorry."

"It's fine," he said, smiling.

"Do you two want to join our game? Or are you going to make out all night?" Judd laughed.

"He's such a dickweed," Maguire muttered.

"I'll shut him up," Courtney said, spinning around on her stool. "I'll play. You and me. One game, winner take all."

"We're not playing for money," Judd replied.

"Bragging rights. Even better," she said, rubbing chalk on the end of a pool stick.

"She's feisty tonight. I like it," Judd laughed. "Okay, deal."

"Rack 'em," Courtney said.

Maguire sat back on his stool, shaking his head.

Courtney lined up for the break, then let her stick slam into the cue as hard as she could. Colored balls smashed together and scattered around the table, causing two solid ones to fall into pockets. She moved around and lined for a second, then a third shot, before missing her fourth. With four balls off the table, she moved to the side.

"You're good. I'll give you that," Judd said, setting up his first shot. A striped ball bounced off one side and rolled into the pocket on the other. He adjusted his position and quickly sunk two more, then looked up at her with a wide grin on his face as he proceeded with eliminating two more of the striped balls, before missing his next shot.

The squeaky door of the bar caught Courtney's attention, and she turned her head. For a split second her heart stopped as her eyes tried to focus. The person walking in was so similar to Tristan, she swore it was her. The pool stick fell from her hand, slapping the floor as she took a step. Suddenly, her vision cleared, and the person morphed from Tristan into one of the maintenance sergeants as he walked over to the bar and sat down.

"You okay?" Maguire asked.

"Uh...yeah," she muttered, clearing her throat. She turned back to the table where Judd and a couple of team members were watching her with odd expressions. "I must be tired," she said, patting Maguire on the arm, before walking out of the bar.

As soon as she was outside in the fresh air, she put her head in her hands and sighed as she leaned back against the wall. *Get it together.*

*

Tristan stared at her deployment bag and ruck sitting on the floor in her bedroom. In less than a week, she'd be on a plane, heading back to Colombia, and to Courtney. As much as she wanted to be wherever she was, it pained her to leave Loki behind. He'd just started his first week at his new school, and he was adjusting to his new family a little more every day. She feared he would regress with her deploying, so she set him up with a therapist Janice had recommended. She'd only taken him once. So far, he'd seemed okay with everything, but she knew her leaving could easily trigger memories of his mother and grandmother passing and leaving him. Her mother had agreed to take him to visit the therapist anytime she felt like he needed it, or if he asked to go.

Loki was already asleep for the night, and Tristan was sitting on her bed, staring at the screen of her laptop with the order for his Christmas presents. She clicked her mother's address, then reviewed everything one last time before hitting the order button. She hated not being home for their first Christmas as a family. This time of year was always her mother's favorite, so he'd at least be in good hands and have a nice holiday. She was about to turn the computer off when the video call screen popped up and began ringing. She smiled and clicked the green button to take the call. A few seconds later, a fuzzy picture of Courtney appeared.

"Hey you."

"I miss you so much," Courtney said.

"I miss you, too. Is everything okay?"

"Yeah. I just needed to see you and hear your voice," Courtney sighed. "How was Loki's first day of school?"

"It went well. He made a new friend and likes his teacher."

"That's great."

"Are you sure you're alright?" Tristan asked, sensing hesitation in her voice.

"I'm okay, just nervous about our test flight. I hate doing them, and we aren't even on the flight schedule," she sighed. "You know the Army, hurry up and wait."

Tristan laughed. "Yep. I'm sure we'll get back and be sitting around twiddling our thumbs, too."

"Yeah, but we'll be together."

Tristan smiled.

"I should probably get going. See you soon," Courtney said.

Tristan said her goodbye, then watched the screen go black. She'd loved before, to the point of caring whether that person was safe, but that connection had never transferred past the physical aspect. She had never truly been in love, and she'd certainly never felt the gut-wrenching ache she had when she and Courtney were apart. She never knew something was missing, that she wasn't whole, until Courtney came into her life. The desire to be both mentally and physically close to another person was thrilling and terrifying at the same time.

She finally closed the laptop and put it on the nightstand beside the bed. She wanted to close her eyes; needed to sleep. But she was too keyed up after seeing Courtney's smiling face and beautiful eyes. "Next week can't come soon enough," she sighed.

Chapter 39

"Hewitt," Judd said as he walked by the helo with his team. "You owe me a pool game."

"Pool must be your superpower," she laughed as she climbed into the pilot's seat.

"Funny, what's your superpower?" he shot back.

"Get in and I'll show you," she said, bumping fists with Maguire.

"Thanks, but no thanks."

"Scared?" she said, staring at him through her Rayban aviators.

"Radio the tower," he replied.

"Eagle, Outlaw One. Alpha One is requesting a ride along. Copy?"

"Outlaw One, Eagle. Alpha One is cleared for flight. Over."

"Roger that." She looked over at him. "Put your big boy pants on and get in."

He shook his head and waved his team off as he climbed in. Howie closed the door, then buckled his belt in the jump seat.

When the tower cleared them for takeoff, Courtney lifted the helo into the air and quickly banked left, flying at nearly a forty-five-degree angle over the base. Judd gripped the seat underneath him as the helo performed a slew of invasive maneuvers, stall and refire tactics, and other simulation as they tested the machine. By the time they landed, his knuckles were white, and his stomach was reeling. Courtney began shutting the engines down and he swung the door open, running away from the helo before tossing his lunch all over the flightline.

"I'm glad he got out first," Maguire laughed.

Courtney shook her head and chuckled as she filled out her flight log.

"Here comes a transport," he said, looking out at the runway.

She stopped writing as her eyes locked onto the C-27 touching down. Her pulse quickened as the plane taxied to the flightline and rolled to a stop. The aircrew chocked the wheels as the pilot powered the engines down.

"Let's join the welcome committee," he said, getting out of the helo and tossing his gear on the seat.

She followed suit, putting her maroon beret on her head when she pulled her helmet off. Together, they walked over to the waiting plane and stood on the flightline. She held her breath when the back door of the plane began lowering down.

*

As she boarded the plane, Tristan thought of Loki throwing his arms around her in a big hug when she drove him to school in her uniform on the way to the base. She'd promised to come back to him as soon as she could and call as much as possible, and he'd promised to be good for Pip and Mrs. Carter. Then, he ran into the school with his backpack flopping from side to side like the rest of the kids, and she wiped the tears from her cheeks as she got back into her Jeep.

As soon as she'd reached the base, her eyes were dry. She had a job to do, one that required a clear head if she was going to return to him. While they waited for their clearance paperwork, Tristan informed her team of the adoption. Everyone hugged and congratulated her.

Tristan stowed her deployment bag and ruck, then took her seat. Fowler sat down next to her on one side, with Nigel plopping down on the opposite side. She pulled the AirPods from her pocket, shoved them into her ears, and closed her eyes.

*

"Chief Hewitt, nice of you to join us," Maj. Irving said, returning her and Maguire's salutes as he walked past and took his position.

Courtney popped to attention as the group of green beret soldiers began walking down the ramp with rucksacks on their backs and deployment bags in their hands. Each of them dropped their gear and popped to attention while saluting. Her eyes immediately landed on Tristan.

"2nd Charlie, Bravo Team. Welcome back to Colombia," the major said, returning their salute.

"Hooah!" the team said.

"We'll rendezvous at 0700 in the ready room. Dismissed."

Tristan picked up her gear and huddled with her team as her eyes landed on the two soldiers in maroon berets. "Grab some chow and get some rack time. It sounds like we're heading out sooner rather than later," she said before dismissing them. "Did you miss me, Chief?" She smiled.

"Just a lil' bit," Courtney replied, holding her finger and thumb slightly apart before saluting.

Tristan laughed and returned the salute.

"You missed a good show earlier," Maguire said.

"Oh yeah?"

"I need to get back to my paperwork. I just wanted to come over and welcome you back," Courtney said.

"Thanks." Tristan nodded as her eyes locked onto Courtney's for half a second.

"She made Capt. Dewey lose his breakfast," Maguire said.

"Really?" Tristan laughed while watching her walk away. "I would've loved to have seen that."

"Don't hurt her."

"Excuse me?" Tristan said, stiffening as her eyes left Courtney and landed on him.

"I know you're together. I'm happy for you both. I'm just asking you not to hurt her."

"You have my word," she said before turning and walking away.

As soon as she reached her barracks room, Tristan tossed her bags on the rack and flung her beret against the wall. "Damnit," she growled. She and Courtney had decided not to say anything to anyone until they spoke with command. She'd purposely left their relationship out of the conversation when she'd told her team about her son. After snatching her beret off the floor, she left the room.

*

Courtney was standing in the hangar, talking with Howie about the helo maintenance schedule, when Tristan walked in. She quickly dismissed him.

"We need to talk," Tristan said as soon as they were alone.

"Okay? That's not the greeting I was expecting." Courtney eyed her suspiciously.

"You told Maguire about us?"

"Don't tell me you're mad about that."

"How can I not be?"

"Tristan, he and I have known each other for years. He's been by my side through thick and thin. I trust him with my life." She shook her head. "You're telling me Fowler doesn't know?"

Tristan sighed. "He knew after it was over. I haven't said anything about it recently."

"He still knew something happened between us."

"I'm sorry. I'm just on edge. I think we should go to command now and get it over with."

"I agree. It's been hard being here without you. I've felt like I was harboring a secret."

"You kind of were." Tristan smiled.

Courtney grabbed her hand and pulled her into the locker room. Their arms wrapped around each other, as their lips met in a heated kiss. Tristan's body melded to hers as they held each other.

"I've missed you so much," Tristan sighed against her mouth.

"If you knew how badly I wanted to peel you out of that uniform right now…" Courtney trailed off, kissing her again. "I love you," she whispered, pulling back to look in her eyes.

"I love you, too. Come on, let's get this over with," Tristan said. "Otherwise, someone's going to come in here and find us naked."

Courtney smiled and shook her head.

*

Tristan and Courtney started with Capt. Warren, who was her direct command. He wasn't sure what to say, so he accompanied them to Maj. Irving, who led them directly to Lt. Col. Powers.

"How long has this been going on?" the colonel asked.

Tristan and Courtney stood at attention in front of his desk, staring at the wall behind him.

"Sir, if I may," Tristan started. "We were attracted to each other for months. It wasn't until we saw each other while on leave, that we realized it was a lot more than that. I'm in love with her."

"Hewitt?"

"It was the same for me, Sir. I'm very much in love with her."

"I need to think on this," he sighed. "We'll meet in the morning before the briefing. Be in here at 0600. And stay away from each other until then. The last thing we need is this spreading around the base."

"Yes, sir," they said in unison, saluting.

"Dismissed."

"He's pissed," Tristan muttered as they left his office and walked down the hall.

"Oh well," Courtney said. "Life's too damn short. I love you, and I don't care anymore."

"I know. I love you, too," she sighed. "I'm going to be up all night."

"Me too."

"I'm going to tell my team. I suggest you talk to yours. They all need to know what is going on."

"I agree." Courtney squeezed her hand. "I'll see you in the morning."

*

Tristan didn't bother unpacking her gear when she went back to her barracks room. She had a feeling she was going to be on a plane right back out of there in the morning, heading home to face court martial or a forced retirement, either way it would be the end of her career. Above everything else, she thought of Courtney and hated being away from her. There was no point in separating them like feral animals. They'd already done the deed. All that was left was the consequence. It no longer mattered who knew. If they were headed out of there, the entire base would know why.

Chapter 40

After a nearly sleepless night, Tristan dressed in her ACU and pulled on her green beret as she headed out the door of the barracks building. She returned the salutes of a few soldiers who passed by as she walked across the base.

"Hey," Courtney said softly, meeting up with her at the door of the command office.

Tristan smiled when she saw the chocolate eyes staring back at her. She reached out, squeezing her hand. "I love you," she whispered before knocking on the door.

"Come in," Lt. Col. Powers called.

Tristan opened the door and nodded for Courtney to go in first. She walked in after, closing the door. They stood side by side at attention in front of his desk.

"It seems quite a bit of soldiers on this base already know about the two of you," he started. "Chief Hewitt, your aircrew says they've never seen you happier. Capt. Malloy, your team would lay dead at your feet if you needed them to. That's the embodiment of your leadership skills. You're both well respected amongst your peers, and those are the people who matter in this situation. Bad morale can kill a team faster than an array of bullets." He paused, folding his hands together. "You're both under my command overall, but you're not in the same direct command and have no promotional influence on each other. At this point, your relationship is technically not against the uniform code. However, I do have final discretion as you are both on a highly classified deployment and work very closely together." He pursed his lips. "I think you're both outstanding soldiers, and you're consenting adults. Do not let this relationship cloud your judgement in the field, and do not let it become a problem amongst your peers. You might love each other, but it's the same with the loved ones we leave behind when we deploy…the Army comes first. You're both here to do a job."

"Yes, sir," they said in unison.

"Dismissed."

They both saluted before leaving the room. Once they were on the other side of his closed door, they hugged each other as if their lives depended on it. Relief washed over Tristan like cleansing in holy water. She wasn't sure if she was going to pass out or throw up. She sighed and smiled brightly as they pulled apart.

Courtney blew out the breath she'd been holding and rubbed her fingers against her throbbing temples. She'd never been so nervous about anything in her life. A grin spread across her face when her eyes met Tristan's.

"Come on, let's get out of here before he changes his damn mind," Tristan said.

"I'm suddenly starving," Courtney muttered as they took the stairs two at a time.

"Me too."

"Join me for breakfast," Courtney said, still smiling.

"I thought you'd never ask."

*

Bravo team was gathered around a mess table, with Howie and Maguire sitting with them. Everyone had a tray of pancakes, scrambled eggs, and sausage in front of them. "Heads up," Fowler called, seeing Tristan and Courtney walk in together. Everyone at the table stood and clapped when they grabbed each other's hand.

"I feel like we just got married," Tristan muttered.

Courtney laughed and shook her head as they let go of each other.

Everyone else in the chow hall stared at their group in silence. The chow hall was the one place you didn't acknowledge an officer's presence when they walked into the room, so they were slightly confused.

Courtney hugged Howie and Maguire, and Tristan shook hands with everyone on her team. Then, the two of them headed over to the chow line while their peers sat down and went back to their breakfast. "I can't stop smiling," she whispered.

"Me either," Tristan said, locking eyes with her.

*

Tristan's team took up the front two rows on the left side of the ready room, while Alpha team took up the right. Courtney and her aircrew where behind Bravo team in the third row. The two-man pilot and co-pilot crew of an Apache attack helicopter were sitting on the opposite side.

"Welcome back to those of you who are returning from leave," Lt. Col. Powers said as he walked in and took a seat in the front of the room along the side wall.

"Over the past six months we have been two steps behind the cartel at every turn, but we've been collecting fragments of information left behind each time, while fishing through story after story and chasing leads from informants," Maj. Irving said from the podium. "All of these pieces came together to form two big chunks of information. Six weeks ago, Bravo team performed an

ORM on a waterfront warehouse in Venezuela. The images they returned proved all of our intel to be true."

Capt. Warren dimmed the lights, and the projector came on.

These are enhanced images from that mission," Maj. Irving said, using a red dot pointer pen. "This is Juan Ortega, Domingo Torres' right-hand. The man getting into this car is Armando Huerta, Domingo's driver. It is believed Domingo himself was in this car at the time the picture was taken." He switched the picture. "The warehouse is obviously moving product around as you can see here. When we turn around and pan out over the water behind the warehouse, you see the small dock." He pressed the button to zoom the picture. "The moonlight was just bright enough that night to catch the wake coming from the coning tower as the submarine slowly rose to the surface in the direct path of the dock."

"Holy shit," Fowler whispered, knocking his knee into Tristan's.

"Ladies and gentlemen, we have found Domingo Torres, the base to his entire organization, and the submarine he is using to transport drugs, guns, and other terrorist supplies undetected. We knew he was moving product over the mountain from Colombia to Venezuela. We've shut his trucking line down several times over the last year but could never find the final destination…until now."

"You are all here this morning because we are about to set the final act: Operation Hellraiser, in motion. Using a sub recon plane, we've been able to track the submarine and pinpoint the shipment schedule. We've also begun tracking Domingo Torres' movements back and forth across the border." He changed the picture once more.

"Ten days from now, the sub will dock at the warehouse in Venezuela to reload with a new shipment. At the same time, Domingo Torres will be crossing the border to catch a flight in Cucuta, Colombia at Camilo Daza International Airport. Bravo team, you'll be in place to take down the warehouse, and the sub. We need Juan Ortega alive if possible. Outlaws will fly you into position and hold for retrieval. Alpha, you're going after Torres. Colombian forces will be there to assist. We need to take him out before he gets into town. Night Stalkers, you're going in as back up in case he gets away. We need Torres and Ortega alive." He used yellow and red markers on the projector to mark the areas he was referring to. "This is it. Our one shot to end this shit once and for all."

"Hooah!" everyone shouted.

Lt. Col. Powers stood and walked to the podium. "We have zero cooperation from the Venezuelan government. They know we're coming in, but they're not helping. Also, Domingo Torres must be apprehended on Colombian soil, which is why we are prepared to take him at the airport, if need be, but we're hoping to snag him crossing the border at the mountain. If he runs, stop him at all costs. He cannot get away. That submarine cannot get away either. Put it on the bottom of the river in pieces. The warehouse needs to be purged and destroyed as well. Any questions?"

No one said anything.

"We'll brief several times between now and then. We'll also continue running recon surveillance on all subjects, as well as simulation drills," Maj. Irving said. "Each team will be brought up to speed on any changes as they happen. Team leaders, stay in contact with your CO's."

"Yes, sir," the group said in unison.

"Dismissed."

Everyone saluted. The colonel and major returned the salutes and left the room.

Tristan ran a hand through her short blonde, faux hawk styled hair.

"This is huge," Fowler said.

"Man, I thought for sure we fucked up that whole mission when the drone crashed," Nigel said, shaking his head.

"I guess we captured a lot more than we thought we did. It's a good thing we got the hell out of there without being seen," Tristan stated. She understood the need to do everything at the same time, but not having Alpha to back her up, or vice versa, was weighing on the back of her mind.

"He said ten days," Perry muttered. "That's Christmas."

"You have a minute?" Judd asked.

Tristan nodded and stepped to the side.

"Are you good with this?" he asked.

"Are you?" she questioned. "I don't think any of us have a choice."

He nodded and walked away.

"What was that about?" Courtney asked, stepping up next to her.

"Nothing." Tristan gave her a half smile and turned back to her team. "You all heard the plan. I'm sure we'll be running a lot of scenarios between now and then. Stay fresh and sharp. Dismissed."

Courtney had already dismissed her aircrew, which meant she and Tristan were alone in the ready room. "You're worried about this. I can see it on your face," she said.

"The lack of backup on the ground is a little unnerving, I won't lie. But my team has been here before. We'll be ready."

*

Tristan led her team as they jogged around the base in the early hours. It had been two days since they were informed of the new mission. The scenario ran through her head over and over, each time with a new variable. She'd read in the drone reports that at least ten men were visible on shipment days. And she knew from her time there, the building had two levels and was out in the open with little to no cover. They would have to cross the river in order to come undetected, but Courtney would land close to the warehouse to retrieve them once the job was done. Until that point, they'd be on their own.

"This is it. Cool down and grab some chow," she said, checking the mileage on her watch as they came up on the comms building. Courtney was walking out, dressed in her ACU, and heading towards the chow hall. "Good morning," she said with a big smile as soon as her team dispersed. Just seeing Courtney made the thoughts of the mission fly right out of her ears like a switch had set them free. "Do you have a minute?" she asked, nodding towards another building.

"Yeah. I was just talking to my parents," Courtney said, following her.

"I was hoping I'd see you last night," she said once they were inside an empty room in the supply building, used to house ammunitions.

"I was with Major Irving, going over the drone reports until my eyes were crossed, but I'm here now," she replied, leaning in to kiss her.

"Easy, tiger. You need a shower and I'm scheduled to be in the air in thirty minutes," Courtney laughed, putting her hand in the center of her chest, and pushing her away.

"Seeing you makes me forget about where we are and what we're doing."

"I know something I'd like to be doing," Courtney said, flashing a wicked grin.

Tristan raised a brow. "I thought I needed to shower," she whispered, moving in closer.

"You stink! And I really do need to be in the air soon," Courtney muttered just before their mouths crashed together in a zealous kiss.

Tristan's hands trembled, itching to touch Courtney. She shoved them into her pockets knowing if she started, she'd never stop.

"To be continued tonight?" Courtney asked, as they parted.

"Absolutely."

Courtney bit her lower lip between her teeth, releasing it as her mouth curved into a grin.

"Get out of here before I tear that uniform off you and make you miss the window for that flight you keep talking about."

"Roger that." Courtney kissed her once more, then left the room.

Tristan waited a minute, then walked out, heading in the opposite direction.

*

"You're running late. The smile plastered on your face makes me think Captain Malloy has something to do with it," Maguire said as he finished his pre-flight check and began buckling his belts.

"Yes, but it's not what you think. I ran into her on my way out to the flightline. She was jogging with her team," she replied, starting her own -pre-flight check. As soon as she was finished, she tugged her door closed and buckled her belts. Then, she pulled her helmet on. "Eagle, Outlaw One. You copy?"

"Lima Charlie, Outlaw."

"We are ready to rock and roll."

"You're cleared for wheels up."

"Roger that," she replied, then began manipulating the switches to start the engines.

The rotor blade began to spin above them. Once the blade reached the desired RPMs, she pulled the collective lever up, and the helo lifted off the ground. With her other hand, she pushed the cyclic between her legs, directing them to the south to follow the path of the GPS in front of her.

"It's a beautiful day to be in the air," Maguire said, adding, "On your birthday!"

She looked over at him and smiled, then put her eyes back on the terrain. "We're supposed to doing some touch and go dry runs near this empty outpost building up here. I'm going to come in from the north and set her down. Howie, you get on that gun. If I know Capt. Warren, he's going to have targets marked. Be ready."

"Roger," he replied.

Tristan set the bird down and Howie swung the door open. A red X was up in the far window. He quickly fired two shots through it as he got out of the helo. He ran out to a cover spot, then counted to ten before running and getting back in. Courtney quickly lifted the helo off the ground and flew off to the right.

"I'm going to circle around and come in from the south and hover," she said. "Howie, jump out and hit your targets. I'm going to come back around and get you."

"Copy that."

She took the helo down to a hover. Howie swung the door open and jumped out. As soon as he was clear, she lifted off and made a wide circle before coming back to get him, hovering once more. Howie jumped back inside, swung the door closed and strapped into his jump seat.

*

Tristan was walking along the flightline with Maj. Irving, discussing the readiness for the mission when the helo flew in overhead and landed on pad two.

"She knows what she's doing. You couldn't ask for a better pilot," he said. "She flew in and out of some hairy situations over in Afghanistan. Did she tell you about any of them?"

"No. I didn't detail my time in Bagdad either."

"Some things are better left in the past. We see some shit, doing what we do. I certainly don't go home and tell my wife. For all she knows, I'm commanding an air traffic control tower in Bermuda."

Tristan chuckled. "Sounds like me with my mother."

"The difference with you and Hewitt, you're both here in it together. Just make sure you two don't take it home when you leave."

"Roger that, sir."

"Let's regroup on Monday, 0800. We should have a new drone report by then. Enjoy the weekend."

He turned and walked away before she could say anything or salute him.

"Hey, what was that all about?" Courtney asked, walking up to her.

"More mission garb. How was your flight?"

"Monotonous, but good, nonetheless."

Tristan nodded. "I'm done until Monday morning."

"Really?"

"Yep. And I showered," she said, wiggling her brows as she grinned.

Courtney shook her and laughed.

"I was actually about to call Loki. Do you want to join me?"

"Wouldn't miss it. I need to turn in my flight log. I'll meet you in the comms room."

*

"Where are you?" Loki asked, staring at the two women in the fuzzy screen. Both were in their Army Combat Uniforms, and Courtney's hair was twisted back in a bun. They looked very different from what he was used to.

"We can't really say," Tristan replied. "But hopefully we'll be coming back soon. How is school going?"

"It's okay. The playground is my favorite part," he said.

"That was my favorite, too," Courtney added.

"Have you been flying?" he asked.

"Yes. I was in the air a little bit ago," she answered with a smile.

"Cool!"

"Me and Pip are working on a..." He paused. "Pip, what's it called again?"

"A care box," she replied.

"Yeah. We're making one for both of you."

"That's nice of you," Tristan said.

"I can't wait!" Courtney exclaimed.

"I thought you wanted it to be a surprise," Patty said.

"Oops." He frowned.

"That's okay. Everything in it will be a surprise," Tristan reassured. "I miss you guys."

"I miss you both," he said.

"So, I have a secret to share with you, Loki."

"What is it?"

"Today is Courtney's birthday!"

"It is?" he questioned.

"Yes," Courtney said, smiling as she looked at Tristan.

"How old are you?" Loki asked.

"Old enough," she laughed. When he stared at her, she answered, "Twenty-seven."

"That *is* old!"

"I must be ancient," Patty muttered, causing Tristan and Courtney to laugh. "Happy birthday, Courtney," she added.

"Thank you."

"Alright, guys. We need to go so other people can call home. We'll do this again soon, okay? I love you both."

Tristan ended the call, and they left the building, heading towards the barracks.

"I had no idea you knew," Courtney said.

"Of course, I did. I tried to celebrate with you this morning..."

"When you were covered in sweat and I needed to be on the flightline," Courtney laughed.

"Your loss." Tristan grinned and shrugged.

Courtney shook her head as her mouth curled into a smile. "I hate that we're in different buildings," she said, coming to a stop in front of hers.

"Captain Malloy," a guy called from across the way.

Tristan turned around.

"Who is that?" Courtney asked.

"I don't know," she muttered. "My team's going to the *Canteen* in a bit. Catch up with you there?" she said to Courtney as she walked away, heading in his direction.

Courtney shrugged and went inside. She was barely in her room when she removed the jacket and boots of her uniform, and pulled her hair free of the tight bun, shaking it out over her shoulders. "Happy birthday," she sighed, getting rid of the t-shirt and pants she was still wearing. She didn't exactly feel like going to the *Canteen*, but she wanted to see Tristan, so she pulled on a clean PT shirt and shorts and headed over.

Chapter 41

"Here she comes!" Howie said, quieting the bar. Everyone stopped what they were doing and faced the door. A minute later, Courtney walked in, and the place erupted in, "Happy Birthday!"

"What?" she stammered, covering her face with her hands in surprise. "Oh, my gosh!" She looked around, seeing Tristan and all of Bravo Team, all of Alpha Team, Howie, Maguire, the maintenance crew for her helo, and Capt. Warren.

"Happy birthday," each person said as she passed by them, walking further into the room.

"This is crazy." She shook her head, still smiling from ear to ear.

"It was all Capt. Malloy's idea," Maguire said.

"Yes, but Howie pulled it off," she replied, winking at Courtney.

"You still owe me a game, but since it's your birthday, I'll let it slide," Judd teased.

"He wants you," Tristan whispered, leaning closer to her as Courtney stepped up to the bar and ordered a beer.

"Too bad I'm all yours," she whispered back. "Thank you for this, by the way."

"You deserve so much more. I hate that we're here for your birthday and will still be here for Christmas."

"Maybe we'll get lucky and make it home for New Year's."

"Don't count on it. Not after the meeting I was in today, anyway," Tristan said.

"Great."

"We're here to celebrate," Fowler said. "The table is open," he added, nodding towards the pool table. Judd and his team occupied the other, nearest the dartboards, which they were also utilizing.

"I get first round," Howie said.

Courtney smiled and shook her head, accepting the pool stick from Fowler. Then, she proceeded to wipe the table in only a matter of minutes.

"Who's next?" Howie said defeatedly, holding the stick out.

"Nope. I'm not that stupid," Maguire said, shaking his head.

One of the maintenance sergeants stepped up, holding his hand out. As he chalked the end of the stick, Courtney waved her hand, seemingly giving him the break of the table. He sunk two balls, then missed his next shot. Courtney stepped up to the table, sinking three balls easily, before setting up a trick shot for her fourth ball, which rolled into the pocket effortlessly. She made her fifth shot, then missed her sixth. The sergeant missed again on his next turn, and Courtney finished the table. He shook his head and held the stick up for someone else to claim.

"I'm not that good, but I'll give it a shot," Fowler said, taking the stick.

Tristan shook her head when Courtney looked over at her and smiled.

He broke and sunk a ball, which he was proud of. Then, missed his next shot. Courtney took her turn, dropping three balls easily. She almost felt bad for him when he missed his next shot, then the one after that, as she proceeded to clear the table. By the time she'd sunk the eight ball, he'd only managed to drop two of his.

"You guys obviously don't play pool when you hang out in here," Capt. Warren laughed, grabbing the stick. He was better than the others, but still not good enough to give Courtney a run for her money. After she beat him, leaving three of his striped balls on the table, he shook his head. "Who's next?" he said, holding out the stick in defeat.

"I think I'll take that game you owe me," Judd said, smiling like a Cheshire cat as he stepped up to the table.

"Here's his chance," Tristan whispered. "He's been waiting all night for this."

"Keep dreaming," Courtney laughed, smacking her on the arm before re-chalking her stick and walking back to the table.

"All or nothing?" Judd said, holding his hand out.

"What?" she questioned.

"Bragging rights."

"Deal," she said, shaking his hand. He held on a little longer than she wanted, but she shrugged it off as she racked the balls. "You can break."

"That's a bad idea," he said through clenched teeth, shaking his head as he walked to the head of the table and began lining up his stick with the cue ball.

Courtney ignored him and stepped back against the wall. They'd played before. She knew he'd be a worthy opponent, but he was also cocky, and that was his downfall.

On the break, the balls scattered around the table, bouncing off each other and the sides, but nothing went into a pocket.

"Open table," he grumbled, stepping away.

Courtney's eyes scanned the table, always looking ahead to her second and third shot. Then, she bent down, lining up and shooting her stick into the cue ball. It slammed into the solid red ball, pushing it into the corner pocket. She quickly adjusted her position and sunk the yellow ball into the side pocket before moving once more and sending the blue one into the far corner pocket. The orange ball was locked behind a group of stripes, so she turned to the green one and took a shot on a whim, even though it wasn't alone in the opposite corner. It fell into the pocket after sliding against a stripe, but the cue ball went in behind it.

"Not bad," Judd muttered, nodding his head. "Now, pay attention. I usually charge for these lessons," he said, grinning at her.

"Does he always talk this much shit?" Capt. Warren laughed.

"Yep," all of Bravo Team answered.

"Quiet over there, Turd squad," Judd grumbled as he lined up his shot. The cue ball blasted through the group of stripes in the corner, sending two of them into the pocket. Then, he moved to the other side of the table, close to where Courtney was standing. She politely moved out of the way, and he turned towards her. "Come here. Watch closely," he said, calling her back over.

She rolled her eyes and shook her head.

"Is he trying to play pool or flirt with her?" Nigel whispered.

"Both," Fowler and Tristan said.

"He's not very good at either," Perry laughed.

"Damnit," Judd muttered when he missed the shot.

"Here, let me show you where you went wrong," Courtney said, serving him his own dish of bullshit. She set up her shot and quickly got rid of her three remaining balls, plus the eight ball, to end the game.

He leaned his stick against the wall and grumbled with his tail tucked as he went back over to his team at the dart boards.

"Next?" Courtney said, looking around the room with a big smile on her face.

"Captain Malloy!" someone shouted.

Tristan smiled and shook her head.

Courtney laughed.

"Come on, Captain..." one of the guys said.

"It's her birthday. Let her have fun," Tristan replied, sipping her beer.

Courtney raised a brow and a teasing grin spread across her face as she walked directly up to Tristan, then reached around her for her beer. "I'll go easy on you," she playfully whispered, setting it back down as she nodded towards the table.

Tristan sighed and set her beer bottle down before walking over to the table as the bar erupted in cheer.

"Let's go, Captain!" Nigel yelled.

"You can break," Courtney said.

Tristan shook her head from side to side as she began tightly racking the balls before putting them into position and removing the triangle. She began chalking her stick as Courtney bent down, lining up her break shot. *I hope you know what you started.* Their eyes met briefly before Courtney crushed the cue ball with her stick, sending the balls flying all around the table. The red striped one landed in the side pocket. Tristan nodded slightly, indicating her approval of the break.

Courtney set up her next shot, then quickly sunk the yellow striped ball into the corner pocket. She bit her bottom lip between her teeth masking her grin as she looked over at Tristan before sinking another ball, but out of nowhere, the cue ball rolled into the side pocket.

Tristan grimaced and shook her head. She walked around the table to retrieve the cue ball, sliding past Courtney close enough to feel her presence without touching her. She set the cue ball at the top of the table, then quickly shot her stick into it. The solid green ball went into the side pocket. She moved to the side, and took her next shot, sinking the solid red ball into the corner pocket. After that, she readjusted and sunk two more of her balls, before missing the next.

"Are you sure you want to keep going?" Tristan teased.

"Oh, look who has jokes," Courtney laughed as the crowd cheered them on. She locked eyes with Tristan as she flung her hair over one shoulder and bent across the table. The bottom of her t-shirt came untucked and slid up just enough to show a line of tanned skin above the waistband of the shorts hugging her tight ass.

Tristan swallowed hard.

Courtney carefully tapped the cue ball with her stick, sending another striped ball into the corner pocket, before straightening up and moving to the side of the table where Tristan was standing. She stood right beside her as she took her next shot, easily sinking the ball before missing again. "Are you sure *you* want to keep going?" she asked.

Tristan smiled and winked at her before moving to line up the cue ball with one of her last two balls. She made the shot effortlessly, leaving the table nearly empty, with only one striped ball, one solid ball, and the eight ball. Without hesitation, she adjusted her position and banked the cue ball off the side of the table. It slowly rolled across the green felt, barely tapping the solid ball as it came to a stop. Tristan shrugged, thinking she'd lost, but gravity pulled the teetering ball over the edge and into the pocket.

"Holy shit!" Hoffman exclaimed.

Tristan shrugged and lined up her shot for the eight ball. She pulled her stick back and fired away. The cue ball hit the eight ball, but it wasn't hard enough to roll it all the way to the pocket.

"Is it over?" one of the guys said.

"No," Tristan replied. "We've always played by the pro rules. It's a simple foul like any other missed ball."

Courtney knew this and had already lined up to sink her last striped ball, which she did easily, before sending the eight ball into the same corner pocket Tristan had missed on. Thus, winning the game.

"Happy birthday," Tristan whispered.

Courtney smiled and shook her head. She knew as soon as Tristan had taken her shot that she'd thrown the game. Everyone began cheering and singing happy birthday.

"She's your kryptonite," Fowler said as Tristan walked back over to the bar.

"Yeah, maybe," she replied.

*

Tristan looked down the hall as she knocked softly on the door. Despite command knowing about them, she and Courtney still needed to maintain a level of discretion around the base. She knocked again, wondering if maybe Courtney had fallen asleep. When their pool game ended, the soldiers in the *Canteen* began to disperse, including Courtney. Tristan had hung back, talking to Fowler and

Capt. Warren for a bit before calling it a night. Instead of going to her barracks, Tristan headed straight to Courtney.

"Hey," Courtney said softly as she opened the door wearing nothing but a white tank top and matching panties. The dark circles of her areolas were clearly visible, pressing into the thin material as she draped her arms loosely around Tristan's neck when she stepped inside.

Tristan reached around, grabbing her ass, and easily lifting her. Courtney's legs wrapped around her waist as she turned around, backing her up against the closed door. Her hands moved to Tristan's head, tugging on her short hair as their mouths crashed together fervently, each hungering for a taste of the other.

Tristan held Courtney tightly as she pulled her away from the door and placed her on the bed on her back. She broke the kiss as she rocked back on her knees and grabbed Courtney's hands, pulling her to a sitting position. She tugged the tank top over her head, revealing the beautiful breasts that had been teasing her. Their lips collided again as she pushed her back down while crawling on top of her. Courtney plucked at her t-shirt as she ran her hands over the muscled skin under it, but Tristan tore her lips from Courtney's instead, sliding lower down her body, licking, and sucking her peaked nipples before slinking lower, tracing a wet path down her torso with her tongue.

Courtney lifted her hips when Tristan's mouth reached the hem of her panties, while her fingers began dragging them down over her hips. Her eyes locked onto Tristan's as the garment disappeared. The unease of not knowing what was happening next thrilled her. She bit down on her lower lip, fighting to slow her racing heart as Tristan lowered her head, burying it between her thighs.

Her legs spread and her back arched as her breath hissed between clenched teeth.

Tristan's mouth and tongue worked together, devouring her with swirling licks and gentle suckles of her clit. Courtney's thighs trembled against her cheeks when she backed off, flattening her tongue, and lapping it up and down gently. Both of Courtney's hands reached down, searching for any part of Tristan to latch onto. She let out a throaty moan as Tristan pushed two fingers inside of her and began stroking as deeply as she could while ravaging her once more with her mouth.

Courtney's hips bucked against her face, begging for more. She tugged at Tristan's hair, her shirt, the bed sheets, anything she could grab ahold of as her body lost control. She desperately tried to keep her eyes open, wanting to watch Tristan feed on her, but they slammed shut with colors swirling psychedelically behind her closed lids like she was soaring through time in outer space. Blood rushed through her veins as her chest heaved and her heart hammered.

Suddenly, like an animal in the wild, she thrashed around, tearing at the sheets with both hands as the mind-blowing orgasm tore through her body. Tristan stilled her fingers and her mouth, simply feeling the throbbing pulse against her until it subsided. Carefully, she eased her fingers free wiping the glistening wetness from them and her mouth on the sheet, before sliding back up Courtney's naked body.

"Happy birthday," she whispered before kissing her lips softly and rolling to the side.

Courtney gazed at her eyes breathlessly as air finally began filling her lungs. She grabbed a handful of Tristan's shirt when she moved to get up. "Don't think this is over,

Captain," she rasped, pushing her to her back as she rolled on top of her.

Chapter 42

It had been two days since Courtney's birthday. The base had been busy hustling and bustling in preparation for the upcoming operation. Tristan hadn't seen her since the night they'd spent together. After running a training drill with her team, she'd spent the rest of the time reviewing drone updates of the traffic coming and going from the warehouse and tracking the coordinates of the sub alongside Maj. Irving.

When she finally ran into Courtney outside of the helo hangar, they were both in uniform and working, so she kept a little distance between them.

"I've missed you," she sighed, searching her chocolate eyes.

"Me too. This op has everyone on edge. I swear I've flown more in the last two days than I have the entire time I've been stationed here," Courtney said, grabbing the front of her uniform jacket and pulling her in for a quick kiss.

Tristan smiled as they parted. "Be safe up there."

"Always." Courtney smiled back before they parted ways. Courtney to the hangar for her final flight before the operation, and Tristan back to her team to inventory their gear and clean their guns in final preparation.

*

"Eagle, Outlaw One. We have company on the eastern pass," Courtney radioed as she cut back, following a truck that was traveling along the dirt road.

"Copy, Outlaw. Remain in recon."

"Roger that," she replied.

"Could just be a local traveler," Maguire said.

Courtney flew off, then swung out wide, coming back over the truck from the front to get a better view. As they grew closer, she saw the slender barrel of a gun coming out of the passenger window. She immediately pulled back the cyclic and up on the collective lever to lift the helo rapidly, then she pushed the cyclic to the right to fly them off the driver's side of the vehicle. She couldn't hear the popping sound of the gun firing and had no way to know if they actually were firing, unless their bullets struck the helo's fuselage.

"Eagle, Outlaw One. We have visual on a weapon. Permission to engage. Over," she radioed as she continued to maneuver the helo away from the truck.

"Negative, Outlaw. No engagement necessary. Return to the nest."

"What in the hell?" Maguire muttered.

"Roger that, Eagle," she radioed, turning the helo wide to head off in the opposite direction.

"What was the point of flying out here if it wasn't to stop more of their trucks?" he questioned, switching to the private pilot channel.

"No idea," she replied, moving her eyes from the horizon to the screens in front of her and back. "At least we know they're still trying to cross the mountain."

"What are your thoughts on this op?" he asked.

"Same as everyone else, hoping it works and praying it goes smoothly," she said before switching the radio channel back as she looked out the windows, waiting for the base to appear in the horizon. She was an excellent instrument pilot but preferred to fly by line of sight.

*

"We need three main provisions. First, ammo. As much as you can carry. This could be a hell of a fire fight. Second, food. If this goes south, we could be on foot and have to make camp. Third, full chicken plates. I know we all move better when we are lighter, but we have no idea what is in that warehouse. We're all coming back alive," Tristan said, addressing her team in the supply hangar. It was a beautiful day, and all the hangar doors were open to the flightline.

"Roger that," Bravo Team replied as each of them went through their tactical vest and ruck.

Tristan began checking her own gear as Alpha Team walked into the hangar.

"Look boys, it's the notorious Bravo Team and their flagrant leader," Judd grumbled.

"Is there a problem?" Tristan said.

"Outing you and your little play toy would be so gratifying." Judd grinned. "But I don't have time for this shit."

"What are you talking about?" Tristan questioned, moving closer.

"Oh, don't act like you don't know. You're not as fucking high and mighty as you think you are."

Tristan walked closer to him. "You've been carrying a chip on your shoulder for years." She shook her head. "It's history, Judd. Let it go."

"Let it go?" he yelled. "Are you serious right now?"

"You really want to do this?" she snapped.

Neither of them had noticed their audience had grown. Alpha and Bravo were joined by Capt. Warren and Maj. Irving, who overheard the raised voices as they walked along the flightline. Some of the maintenance crew guys were also outside, waiting for the incoming helo and a recon plane, and could easily hear everything.

"You're damn right I do!" Judd yelled.

"Don't do this," Fowler said, rushing over to Tristan.

"I'm sick of this son of a bitch disrespecting me," she spat.

"You want to talk about disrespect," he laughed. "You're the one sneaking around and screwing a subordinate on this base. How's that for respect?"

"What?"

"Oh, please. Spare me the questioning bullshit and own up to it!"

"She's not a subordinate. It would be the same if you were the one dating her, you dumbass." Tristan clenched her fist. She was plenty big enough to knock him on his ass. "Command is well aware, by the way. What's your real issue? Are you jealous? Is that what this is about?"

"Jealous? Fuck you! If you're what she wants, she can have you!" He stepped closer. "I'm sick of the Army kissing your ass like you're Captain America with tits!"

"Fuck you!" Tristan yelled as the two of them moved to lunge for each other.

"Enough!" Maj. Irving shouted, his voice echoing off the metal walls. Suddenly, the entire hangar became silent as everyone popped to attention. "Dewey, Malloy, in the colonel's office now!" he yelled.

"Yes, sir," they replied and took off, walking at a brisk pace with him right behind them.

"What the hell just happened?" Courtney asked, stepping up next to one of her maintenance crewmen.

"Capt. Malloy and Capt. Dewey just about came to blows. Maj. Irving had to get between them."

"Corporal, get back to your duty," Capt. Warren sighed. "They weren't fist fighting, and he didn't have to get in the middle, but it did get pretty ugly."

"What in the world?"

"I don't know. I'm pretty sure your relationship with her came up."

"They've had an issue with each other since before I ever got here, so it's a lot more than just us dating."

He shrugged. "They were shouting at one another like two kids in a school yard about to sucker punch each other."

She raised her brows and nodded. "Wow."

"Anyway, you were told not to engage because we need the cartel to think we've backed off. Did you actually take on fire?"

"Not that we can see. We just did a damage check. I honestly don't know if they were firing or not. We were in full sun and couldn't see the muzzle flash. But we all saw the automatic rifle pointed directly at us."

"Bastards," he grumbled. "Get out of your gear and grab some chow. I'm sure the major and colonel are going to have their hands full for the rest of the day. Let's regroup and debrief in the morning. We'll be going over the new weather report at the same time."

"Yes, sir." She saluted and went into the hangar when he returned the gesture, dismissing her.

*

"You've got to be kidding me!" Lt. Col. Powers smacked his hand on the wooden desk in front of him. "You are two Delta Special Forces team leaders! We're about to go into the mission this operation has been working towards for over a year! You're both captains in the Army, for god's sake. What in the hell has gotten into you?" He held his hand up. "Wait, let me clear a few things up, first. Capt. Malloy and Chief Hewitt are not under the same command here or in garrison. They are in two different units altogether. Yes, they're currently working together, but their relationship is not against uniform code," he sighed. "Now, is that all, or is there more?"

"Capt. Dewey, you were the aggressor," Maj. Irving said.

Judd stayed silent.

"Out with it," the colonel said. "You two were about to tear each other's head off. Tell me this was over more than a girl. You're both adults. There are plenty of fish in the sea! You're not even in the same dating pool!"

"Sir," Tristan said.

"Yes." He nodded.

"I believe this has nothing to do with Chief Hewitt and I dating."

"Go on," he said.

"I believe some old feelings resurfaced when we were both deployed here. Finding out the woman he liked, was dating me, was simply icing on the cake for him, and I'd finally had enough of his condescending attitude towards me and my team. Sir, I apologize immensely for my conduct."

"I apologize, too, sir," he muttered.

"Is she right, Dewey? Are you pissed because she's dating the girl you like, or is this deeper?"

"She's right, sir. I never should've let the past get in the way of my future."

"What I should do, is send you both back to garrison to be reprimanded and potentially dropped down in rank." He shook his head. "I'm heavily disappointed in both of you. I'm in the middle of a black operation. I don't have time to bring anyone else up to speed, and I can't leave your teams in the hands of Chief Fowler and Chief Johnson." He stood up and walked around the desk, standing close to them. "You're both green berets in the Army!" he yelled. "Grow the fuck up!"

They both stiffened.

"Whatever happened in the past, will be water under the bridge from this moment on. Otherwise, you'll both find yourselves out of the Army so fast, your goddamn heads will be spinning. Now, just so we're on the same page, shake hands."

Tristan held her hand out and Judd shook it, before going back to attention.

"Maj. Irving, go gather Alpha and Bravo teams, as well as Capt. Warren and his subordinates who witnessed the incident. Put everyone in the ready room." He looked back at the two captains in front of him. "You are both going to apologize to the entire room and promise not to do it again. You want to act like little kids, I'm going to treat you as such. You don't have to be best friends. In fact, you don't have to like each other, but you better damn well respect each other. I want you both waiting out in the hall for everyone. Maj. Irving will let you know when it's time. I suggest you take this time to have a heart to heart. Dismissed!"

"Yes, sir," they said in unison, before doing an about-face and leaving his office.

Tristan went around the corner and leaned her head back against the wall. "Jesus, Judd," she muttered, shaking her head. "I've given thirteen years of my life to the Army. Every rank I've had, every badge on my uniform and ribbon on my chest, I've earned with the same blood, sweat, and tears as every other soldier. Nothing has ever been handed to me. I was one of maybe a handful of female rangers, and now I'm one of only a few female green berets. I'm not some Army prized possession on a pedestal. I work, and have worked, just as hard as the *man* next to me my entire career."

"I know. I held a grudge for a long time. It was stupid. You're a damn good soldier. If I was smarter back then, I would've learned a lot from you, instead of trying to outdo you at every turn," he said.

"Thank you. And this thing with Hewitt…"

"I had a feeling she was into you, which only fueled my bitterness," he sighed. "She's obviously in love with you. I've seen the way she looks at you."

"Yeah, I don't know who loves *her* more, me or my son," she said, smiling thinly.

"You have a son?"

"Yes. He's five."

"Wow," he murmured, taken aback. "That's great."

"Dewey, Malloy, let's go," Maj. Irving commanded, still visibly pissed as he nodded towards the ready room.

"For what it's worth, I'm sorry," Judd said, sticking his hand out.

"I am, too. We should've talked and aired this out a long time ago. If we don't have each other's six, who will?" she replied, shaking his hand.

*

Tristan was lying in her rack, staring at the ceiling when she heard the soft knock. She got up and pulled the door open.

"Do you want to take a walk with me?" Courtney said, meeting her eyes and holding them.

"Sure." Tristan smiled thinly.

They walked out of her barracks building and headed towards the flightline, strolling slowly, side by side.

"I'm sure you heard about my shitty day," Tristan muttered.

"I did." Courtney nodded.

Tristan sighed and shook her head.

"Do you want to talk about it?" she asked softly.

Tristan stared up at the stars in the sky.

"I haven't known you that long, but I picked up on the hostility between you and Judd Dewey right away."

"We were both Rangers in the same platoon," Tristan started. "I was a sergeant and fire team leader in a Ranger platoon and had already been in the Army for six years. He was a first lieutenant who had led an infantry rifle platoon and a mortar platoon, before moving over to the Rangers." She shook her head. "He was a hotheaded, cocky bastard who pulled rank on me several times. I became the platoon sergeant not long after he joined us, and we mixed like oil and water. Instead of using me and my Ranger experience, he did things his own way. He made quite a bit of mistakes, and I was simply doing what I was trained to do. In my opinion, he wasn't ready to be a Ranger. It pissed me off. Anyhow, a few months later I finished my college degree and got accepted to OCS. I was put in his same position with a different platoon and never saw him. Fast forward three years later, we were the same rank and both going through SFAS to join special forces. I clearly had a lot more experience because I'd been in the Army for nine years at this point. I passed and moved on with my career. A year after that, I became a captain and joined Delta. I ran into him again in Bagdad. He was with an Alpha detachment. We barely spoke. Then, I ran into him here. He'd also joined Delta, and finally made captain. I guess I've been his nemesis his entire career. Everything he does, I do it better, and it pisses him off."

"Wow," Courtney muttered.

"He's been a condescending asshole to me...literally from the day I met him. So, after he jumped down my throat about you, I lost my shit." Tristan shrugged. "I'd just had enough."

"Wait, what? How was I involved?"

"He walked into the supply hangar and lit into me, saying I was sleeping with a subordinate and all kinds of crazy shit. I knew right away he was referring to you, although your name was never mentioned. I yelled back at him, telling him command knew about our relationship, and I may have called him jealous. That pissed him off even further. When he called me Captain America, basically the Army's poster child who had everything handed to me, I was done."

Courtney shook her head. "Petey in maintenance said you two were about to hit each other when Maj. Irving stepped in the middle."

"He's probably right. I don't know. All I saw was red."

"What happened with command?" Courtney asked as they began walking down the flightline, completely alone.

"We're both lucky to still be in the Army, let's put it that way," she sighed.

"Wow."

"It's all over with. Judd and I actually talked and apologized to each other."

"Really?"

"We were forced to shake hands and apologize to everyone who witnessed the argument, but outside of that, we had our own conversation. We're good now."

"I'm sorry you went through all of that. It was a crazy day all around." She shook her head. "We encountered one of the cartel trucks today out on the mountain road."

"Did they fire at you?"

"We saw the automatic rifle sticking out of the front passenger window, but I moved to a safe distance to confer with command, who told me to stand down."

"Really? They just let them go?"

"Yep." She shrugged. "We looked all around when we landed, but didn't see any strafing marks, so I have no idea if they actually took a shot."

Tristan stopped walking and pulled Courtney into her arms. They both leaned back to look in each other's eyes. "Can we stay like this forever?" she muttered.

"I wish," Courtney said, smiling at her.

"You make me forget everything running through my head, even if only for the few brief moments we get alone."

Courtney closed the distance between them, kissing her softly, allowing her lips to linger against Tristan's. "I love you so much," she whispered when they finally parted.

"I love you, too."

Chapter 43

"Merry Christmas," Maguire said, walking into the ready room at two in the morning. He took his seat next to Courtney. "Tough crowd," he whispered, looking around the room at Alpha Team, Bravo Team, and the Night Stalkers aircrew. Everyone was already geared up and ready to go.

Maj. Irving walked in with Capt. Warren, Tristan, and Judd, who quickly took their seats. "Good morning, folks," he started. "We're currently on the mission clock. The sub should be docking around four a.m., giving it time to get loaded and out into open water long before the sun comes up at seven. Domingo Torres has a flight scheduled for six a.m. out of Cucuta, which means he'll be crossing the border around five. Captains Warren, Malloy, and Dewey have all been briefed on the exact timeline of events. Bravo, the Outlaws will drop you off on the opposite side of the river, about two miles down...here," he said, pulling up the map on the projector and marking a yellow circle. "You're going to raft over and skirt along the bank on foot, attacking from the open, river side of the warehouse." He drew a red X. "This will give you full vantage point. Alpha, this is the road Torres will be using," he said, changing the picture to a different map and drawing a blue line along the road. "This is the cross point." He made a red X. "This is just an old, dirt mountain road with no thru traffic besides him. It'll be dark, and he'll be in a dark SUV. You and the Colombian forces will need to ambush him from these two directions. If Torres gets away, the

Night Stalkers will be high in the sky above you, ready to take him out," he said, drawing yellow arrows. "If there are no questions, let's move out. Bravo, you have an hour-long flight. Alpha, a two-hour drive through the mountains. Godspeed. Dismissed."

"Hooah!" everyone shouted.

"Lock and load, Alpha," Judd said as he began walking. He stopped next to Tristan. "Good luck out there."

"You, too," she replied, holding her hand out. He shook it, then led his team out of the room. She headed out behind him with her team, and both aircrews came out behind them.

"Kick the tires and light the fires," the lead pilot for the Night Stalkers said, high-fiving Courtney.

"Roger that!" she replied with a smile. Tristan was waiting outside the building when she exited. "Hey."

"I know you don't normally wear chicken plates," she said, referring to armor. "But I'm asking you to do it today. None of us know how this is going to go."

Courtney knocked on her flight vest, indicating they were in. Then, she smiled. "All good."

Tristan smiled back before walking side by side with her out to the flightline.

*

Tristan stayed with her as she walked around the helo, doing her pre-flight checklist. Maguire was already inside, as was the rest of Bravo Team. She'd spent the last evening, Christmas Eve, penning letters to her mother, her son, and Courtney. Over the years, the letter to her mother had gotten easier. However, the letters to her son and Courtney nearly did her in. She knew losing her life could be part of the job. A few months ago, that thought didn't bother her. Now, she had two lives depending on hers.

"Listen," she said once they were around the back of the helo.

Courtney signed her checklist and stopped walking.

"If something happens—"

"Tristan, don't."

"Courtney, listen to me, please. My letters are under the pillow in my rack."

Courtney shook her head but nodded in understanding. "I love you," she whispered.

"I love you, too," Tristan sighed, kissing her quickly.

They both took a deep breath and cleared their thoughts before climbing into the helo.

*

Courtney watched the instruments on the screens in front of her as she flew the helo over the mountain. It was a clear night with very little cloud coverage. Even with the halfmoon and sky littered with stars, it was still pitch-black outside. She glanced at the GPS, then switched the radio.

"Bravo One, we're ten mikes from the drop point."

"Roger that," Tristan replied, quickly giving the signal for everyone to get ready.

When they reached their destination, Courtney lowered the helo down to forty feet from the ground. Both side doors slid open, and Bravo Team jumped out, three on each side, fast roping to the ground in seconds. Howie shut the doors as they lifted away.

"Eagle, Outlaw One. Package has been delivered," Courtney radioed as she flew off. *Please be safe.*

"Copy. Proceed to the waiting zone."

"Roger that," she replied.

"Our waiting zone is thirty minutes away," Maguire said.

"Yep."

*

"Let's get the fuck outta here," Tristan said as they began hiking through the woods towards the river. She led the team with Nigel beside her, navigating their route. Hoffman and Tucker walked behind them, each carrying one end of the folded rubber raft. Fowler and Perry were directly behind them, keeping cover from both sides and the rear.

Once they reached the inky waterline, they unfolded the raft. Two of them worked on getting it inflated, two put the paddles together, and two stood back-to-back, covering them in a 360-degree view.

"Eagle, Bravo One. Ducklings are Oscar Mike," Tristan radioed once they were in the raft, quietly paddling across the river. Hoffman was in the front and Tucker was in the back, both with rifles on their shoulders, scanning the coastline through the scope while the rest of them paddled.

They pulled the raft from the water, sliding it up into the tall weeds, then placed their paddles inside and pulled their rifles to the shoulders. Using silent tactics with hand signals, Tristan led the group along the weeds and shadows of the shoreline. Everyone was crouched low, moving one behind the other. She quickly gave a signal for Perry and

Tucker to break off, taking cover behind one of the parked vehicles. Then, she signaled for Fowler and Hoffman to move. They both slid down into the water and swam along the shoreline, then around the back of the sub where they attached explosives, before carefully moving over to the other side of the dock. They came out of the water in the small, wooded area they'd hid in when they were retrieving the drone.

She checked the time on her watch. *3:58. Anytime time now.* The workers were all busy dollying crates outside and lining them up. Another, well-dressed man, held a clipboard and walked along the crates, before going back inside.

"Hostile approaching from the east," Hoffman whispered.

"Charlie Mike. Drop him if you have to," Tristan replied, telling him to continue the mission as she watched through her monocular. The man opened his pants and peed all over the bushes two feet away from Hoffman. *Don't breathe, kid.*

Suddenly, the water broke, and the submarine appeared, slowly making its way to the dock. The hostile quickly put his junk away and rushed inside the open warehouse.

"Shark is on the surface," Tristan said. "I count ten hostiles."

"Copy ten," Fowler replied.

"Bravo Four and Six, hold position," she said, telling Tucker and Perry to remain where they were. Then, she waited for the sub to tie up and open the conning tower. Four men climbed out. After what looked like a brief conversation, led by the well-dressed man, the workers proceeded to roll the dollied crates onto the dock. She zoomed in as far as she could on her monocular when the well-dressed guy paused and looked around. *Hello, son of a bitch.* She looked directly at him, almost as if they were staring each other down. "I have a visual on Juan Ortega," she radioed.

"Copy visual," Fowler replied, meaning he knew it was him, too.

"Bravo One, Eagle. You copy?" command radioed.

"Lima Charlie," she replied.

"Do we have confirmation on Juan Ortega?"

"Affirmative," she answered.

"Charlie Mike," command radioed.

"Roger that," she replied. "Bravo, we are a go for Hellraiser," she said to her team. "On my command." She watched the group load the first, then second crate into the sub, while eight more lay on the dock. She gave a quick hand signal to Nigel, then the two of them scurried past Perry and Tucker and flattened in the shadows against the building. "When Ortega comes back outside, toss smoke and light the assholes up. Fowler and Hoffman, you go inside. Nigel and I will go after Ortega and the sub. Perry and Tucker, you come in behind Fowler and Hoffman, but watch our six and yours. There will be at least two guys aboard the sub."

"Roger," everyone replied.

Tristan pulled two smoke grenades from her vest. As soon as Ortega walked out of the warehouse, seemingly checking the crates again, she flipped the switch and tossed them both at the back of the warehouse. Simultaneously, Fowler did the same as he and Hoffman rushed in. The pop, pop, pop, sound of their automatic rifles echoed.

"Sumergirnos! Sumergirnos!" Ortega began screaming, telling the sub to dive as he ran towards it.

Tristan rushed towards him as he pulled a handgun from the waistband of his pants. She dove into him, tackling him like a rugby player. They both went off the side of the dock just as he got a shot off, barely grazing the side of her Kevlar helmet. The two of them wrestled around in the water. The weight of her uniform and tactical vest was threatening to pull her under as she fought with him, trading blows, and pushing each other's head under until she finally pinned him in a headlock and squeezed long enough to render him unconscious.

Nigel had run out to the sub firing his gun, but the vessel pulled away from the dock, taking part of the wooden structure with it, leaving him nowhere to go.

"Blow it!" Tucker yelled.

"Capt. Malloy is in the water!"

"Damnit," he said, pulling out his infrared monocular to see if he could pick up her heat signature. "I don't see her," he said. The sub was about fifty yards from the shoreline and almost completely submerged. "We have to stop that sub. It's going to get out of range!"

Tristan swam backwards, keeping Ortega's head above water as the sub began going under. Gunfire continued inside the warehouse as Perry, Hoffman, and Fowler fought the hostiles. She finally felt the muddy bottom under her feet as she continued pulling him. Her radio started crackling. She looked out, unable to see the sub. "Blow the damn sub!" she yelled, but with her mic not working on the radio, no one heard her.

"Bravo One?" Nigel radioed, over and over, before finally saying, "Captain?"

"Blow it! Do it now! That's an order!" Fowler radioed back as he fired off shots at the last hostile in the warehouse.

A second later, Tristan's back slid against the shoreline as a loud boom sounded, followed by a huge splash of water. She sighed in relief and pulled Ortega up into the mud next to her. The popping noise of the gunfight ended, rendering everything silent. She took her earpiece out and shook it a bunch of times, then put it back in. "Eagle, Bravo One, do you copy?" she said, then repeated herself. *Please work.*

"Cap…uh, Bravo One!" Nigel yelled, hearing her.

"Bravo Three!" she exclaimed. "Call for the Outlaws, now! We have to get out of here!" She knew with her radio working intermittently, she couldn't switch channels to call for the helo. If she did, she could lose all contact with her team.

"Where are you?" he asked.

"Just make the call!"

"Outlaw One, Bravo Three. Do you copy?"

*

Courtney maintained a holding pattern twenty miles away, high in the sky. "I don't like this," she said.

"Me either," Maguire muttered. "We can't stay in enemy airspace for long, especially after they blow up that sub."

"I know," she sighed just as Nigel's voice came over the radio. "Lima Charlie. Oscar Mike!" she replied, quickly turning the helo and heading as fast as she could towards the extraction zone, which was literally the road in front of the warehouse.

"We're sure there are no power lines, right?" Maguire asked.

"Yes and no."

"What?" he squeaked.

"There are, but presumably, not where we are going. We have no choice. Put your big girl pants on and keep a lookout, so I can set this bird on the ground."

*

"Bravo One, you copy?" Fowler radioed, searching different channels until he found her.

"Lima Charlie," she replied.

"All the hostiles are down. We're setting the charges now."

"Copy that."

"Outlaws are inbound," Nigel said. "Bravo One, what's your location?"

Tristan looked around. "A hundred yards down river," she said, then her eyes landed on Ortega. She quickly checked for a pulse. It was faint, but it was there.

"Are you alone?" Fowler asked.

"Negative."

Fowler, Perry, and Nigel rushed to find her while Hoffman and Tucker finished.

"Holy shit," Fowler said, finding her and Ortega on the muddy bank. "Are you okay?"

"Yeah. He's not so good though," she replied, nodding towards Ortega.

Perry checked for a pulse, finding the same faint beat as Tristan. "He's barely alive, Captain. How long was he under?"

"Not long. We fought hard until I was able to put him a choke hold. I may have held on too long, but he nearly drowned me. I kept his head above water all the way to shore though."

"I hear the helo," Nigel said. "We need to get moving. Where's your rifle?"

Tristan looked out at the water.

Fowler helped Tristan to her feet and handed her his gun. Then, he ziptied Ortega's hands together in front of him and threw him over his shoulder, carrying him as Nigel led the way and Perry brought up the rear. Tristan walked alongside him. The helo was landing as they made their way to the warehouse.

"Charges are set," Hoffman said. "Whoa, Captain. What happened to you?"

"Ortega and I went for a swim," she muttered.

*

"It's going to be hard to do this without a vector call," Courtney said.

"We look clear. No power lines in site," Maguire said.

"Bravo One, are we clear to land?" she radioed. "If not, I'm going to need a vector. Over."

"You're clear straight down and up to three hundred yards to the south," Tucker radioed back.

Courtney looked at Maguire, who simply shrugged, as she set the helo on the ground.

"Here they come. Looks like they're carrying a body," he said, trailing off.

Courtney began unbuckling her belts and he reached over, grabbing her wrist. "Stop! We don't know who it is."

"She hasn't been on the radio at all," she yelled, jerking away from him.

"Look!" he shouted. "She's okay!"

Courtney lifted her eyes in time to see Tristan running with the rest of the team. *Oh, thank god!* She tightened her belts back down.

Howie swung the door open, and Fowler flopped Ortega on the floor. Tucker jumped in and helped pull him further inside and get him on the folding backboard as the rest of the crew climbed in.

"As soon as we are a hundred yards away, you hit it," Tristan said, looking at Hoffman. He was carrying the trigger device for the explosives they'd planted all throughout the warehouse and on top of the crates along what was left of the dock.

Once Fowler got into his seat next to Tristan, she reached for his radio, since hers was stuck on their team channel. "It's good to see you, Outlaw One," she said. "Our friend here is circling the drain, so it would be great if we could get out of here yesterday."

"Roger that. Good to hear your voice, Bravo One."

Courtney quickly lifted the helo off the ground and zoomed away. Once they were on the opposite side of the river, Hoffman squeezed the trigger. The warehouse went up in a huge fireball that went way up into the air. The crates on the dock had also exploded, blowing the wooden structure to pieces.

Tristan handed Fowler his earpiece and put hers back into her ear. "You copy?" she said, looking at him. He gave her a thumbs up. "Did we manage to get any intel out?" she asked.

"Nothing from the sub, but we took every notebook and laptop we could find," he said.

"Roger that."

"Captain, I lost his pulse," Perry said. "Starting CPR."

Tristan got out of her jump seat and helped Perry try to revive Ortega, who lay lifeless on the floor of the helo.

Chapter 44

The helo landed softly on pad two. Maj. Irving and Lt. Col. Powers were standing in the hangar, as well as two base MP's.

"We had to give him CPR in the air, but he's breathing on his own and has a pulse," Tristan said as they rushed up when the helo shut down. She jumped out, helping Fowler get Ortega out. Perry came out beside him, holding the IV bag for the line she'd put in his arm. They rushed him into the back of a van, then watched it drive away, heading towards the medical facility on the other side of the base.

"Everyone in the ready room in ten," Lt. Col. Powers snapped.

Tristan turned around and he was gone. "That didn't go so well," she muttered to herself as her team went into the locker room to remove their tactical gear. Courtney's aircrew followed, removing their flight gear.

"Captain, look at the side of your helmet," Tucker said.

Tristan turned her Kevlar head gear to the side as she removed it from her head. A large scratch ran down it, clearly where a bullet had struck and scraped. Her eyes locked onto Courtney's across from the room before she put the helmet on the shelf in her locker.

*

Lt. Col. Powers stood at the front of the room, pacing, and shaking his head. He paused and opened his mouth to speak, when the door swung open and Alpha entered, looking about as rough as Bravo.

"This morning's operation turned into quite a cluster fuck," he grumbled, smacking his hand on the podium. "Alpha, let's start with you. How in the hell is Domingo Torres dead?"

All of Bravo Team and Courtney's aircrew gasped.

Judd stood up at attention. "Sir, we believe Torres was driving the vehicle and had his driver, Armando, sitting in the passenger seat in his place as a decoy. If any sniper took a shot, they would be killing Armando as the passenger, not knowing Torres was really the driver. This is the only explanation we have."

"Who took the shot?"

"The Colombian forces, sir. We ambushed the vehicle together, but they shot the driver in the head. The vehicle swerved and rolled over. We immediately ran over to assess the occupants and found them both dead. The driver matched the photo of Domingo Torres. He had a bullet hole through his forehead. The passenger matched the photo of Armando Huerta. We got him out and began life saving procedures, but he had already succumbed to the injuries of the crash."

"Where is Domingo's body?"

"The Colombian forces took both of them, sir."

Lt. Col. Powers smacked the podium with his hand in frustration. "Bravo, please explain why you returned with Juan Ortega, soaking wet and unconscious."

Judd sat down, and Tristan stood up.

"When we moved in to ambush the warehouse and sub, Ortega pulled a handgun and began to shoot as he ran down the dock towards the sub. I grabbed him and we both went over the side. While we were physically fighting in the water, the rest of the team was attacking the warehouse. We retrieved quite a bit of intel from the warehouse before it was blasted. The sub was destroyed as it tried to make an escape with at least one cartel member at the helm. Ortega and I fought for several minutes before I was able to grapple and get him into a choke hold to render him unconscious. This was the only way to keep him from drowning me. I kept his head above water the entire time I swam him back to the riverbank. When my team found us, nearly a half mile down, our medic went to work checking his vitals. He had a weak pulse and was taking shallow breaths. We called for the evac and rushed back here as soon as we could. En route, we had to administer CPR to Ortega when we lost his pulse, but he came right back and seemed to be improving once we arrived, sir." Tristan sat back down.

Maj. Irving walked into the room and directly up to the colonel, talking low near his ear. The colonel nodded and left the room. Everyone talked quietly amongst themselves until he returned two minutes later. "Malloy, Dewey, and Warren, you stay here. The rest of you, head to DFAC and wait for your CO to find you. Dismissed."

"Yes, sir," everyone replied, saluting.

As soon as the room was clear, except for those who were asked to stay, Maj. Irving locked the door.

"I just got off the phone with General Singleton. Not only is Juan Ortega now dead, but the Colombian government has kindly asked us to pack up and go home. Apparently, they've got it from here," he sighed, shaking his head.

"What the hell?" Judd mumbled. "I'm sorry, sir," he quickly corrected.

"Those were my exact words as well," the colonel said. "Gen. Singleton has the C5 already en route to us. Our job here is done. Capt. Warren, ready the helos and drones to be loaded on the plane. Capt. Dewey, have your team ready the Humvees. Capt. Malloy, your team will ready the supplies and assist with loading. You all have one hour to clear this place out. Dismissed."

Tristan saluted and walked out of the room.

"Are you as confused as I am?" Judd asked.

"Yeah. I'm pretty sure there's a lot we aren't getting told, and by we, I mean the U.S. government."

"Yep."

Tristan checked her watch as they walked towards the chow hall. It was Christmas morning, and there was no time to call her son. Even if there was, all the Army's computers and hardware equipment was being torn out of the walls and loaded onto pallets.

"What's going on?" Fowler asked when she met up with her team.

"We're going home. The operation here is over," she said.

"What?" Hoffman mumbled.

"We all need to change into our full ACU, pack our personal belongings, then head over to the supply hangar and start getting the supplies and ordinance on pallets. The transport plane is already on the way," Tristan said. "Dismissed."

She wished she could go find Courtney, but Tristan headed to her barracks room instead, quickly removing her muddy, and still wet, tactical uniform before putting on her full regular ACU pants, t-shirt, and jacket. Then, she pulled on her spare pair of boots, and began packing the few personal items she had, along with her toiletries and uniforms, into her deployment bag and rucksack. She took one last look at the small room that had been her home for much of the last two years.

*

Courtney packed her uniforms, toiletries, and other personal items into her deployment bag. Then, she went to the locker room in the hangar and packed her flight gear into her rolling deployment bag. She hadn't seen Tristan since she'd left the ready room, and not being a higher rank, she wasn't privy to the closed-door conversations. All she'd been told by her CO was the operation was over and everyone was bugging out asap.

"Where's Captain Malloy?" she asked, seeing Fowler in the hangar.

"She should be here any minute," he said, tossing his bags to the side. The rest of the team followed suit before they began organizing the supplies to be packed up.

Courtney helped the maintenance crew move Jezebel outside so they could get her ready to transport, along with another Black Hawk and an Apache, plus three Humvees, and four drones. When she came back inside, Tristan was setting her gear bags down with the rest of her team's.

"Hey," she said, walking over to her. "I know I don't get to sit at the big kid's table, but this decision to make haste seems a little rash to me."

"It wasn't our decision," Tristan said. "But it's above all our paygrades, including Powers. That's how it usually is. We come in, do a job, then leave without ever knowing the outcome. We're used to it by now," she added, looking over at her team.

Courtney nodded. "Sort of like us flying everyone everywhere. We never know the full story."

"Exactly."

"I don't know when I'll see you again," Courtney sighed, searching Tristan's eyes.

"I'm sure it'll be a bit before any of us are deployed again, so we'll be able to find time to be together."

"Yeah." Courtney smiled. "I'm going to miss seeing you every day."

"Me too." Tristan smiled.

Chapter 45

The sun had set over the east coast of the United States, slowly bringing Christmas Day to a close. Tristan was exhausted and hungry, but she still managed to drop her stuff at her apartment, take a quick shower to wash off the grime from her mission earlier that morning, and pack one of her older rucks with overnight supplies before making the short drive over to her mother's house. She rang the bell and stood on the doorstep, leaning against a pillar to keep herself upright. The exterior light came on, blinding her with its brightness.

"Tristan?" her mother questioned, pulling the door open. "Loki!" she yelled, seeing her daughter standing in front of her.

"I made it," Tristan muttered. Then, she bent down, snatching Loki up into a tight hug when he ran to her. "Merry Christmas, son."

"Merry Christmas!" he exclaimed.

She set him back on the ground as she walked into the house. "Merry Christmas, Mother."

"It is now." Patty smiled.

"Where's Courtney?" Loki said, looking through the front window blinds.

"She's down in Georgia where she lives, but she'll be coming up soon to see you."

"Why didn't you tell me you were coming home?" Patty asked when the two adults went into the kitchen.

"Come see what Santa brought me! Look at all of this stuff!" Loki said excitedly.

"That's awesome. I'll come look at everything in a minute," she replied, then turned back to her mother. "Our operation ended. We packed up in haste and flew home. I've literally been up since about one this morning."

"Oh wow. Have you eaten?"

"Not since this morning, unless you count a protein bar on the plane."

"Honey, you look completely drained. Let me fix you a plate of dinner, then you can go up to bed in the spare room. There's no need for you to drive home now. It's already dark."

"Okay," Tristan said with a nod, before going into the den to see all the neat things Loki got for the holiday.

"There are presents for you over there," he said. "Me and Pip went shopping for you."

"You did, huh." She smiled and sat on the couch. He brought her gifts over to her and sat down beside her as she opened them.

"Yeah, and she let me get something for Courtney, too."

"That was nice of you," Tristan said, hugging him once more.

Tristan's phone rang in her pocket before she could open any of the gifts in her lap. She pulled it free, smiling when she saw Courtney's face.

"Hey," she said, answering the video call.

"Did you make it home okay?"

"Yeah, I'm at my mother's," Tristan replied, moving the phone so she and Loki were both in the picture.

"Hey!" Courtney said. "I miss you, little man. Wish I could give you a big hug right now."

"I miss you, too," he said, smiling from ear to ear. "There's a present for you under Pip's tree. She helped me pick it out."

"Aww, that's sweet. Thank you."

"Are you leaving again?" he asked, directing his question at both of them.

"Not anytime soon," Tristan said.

"Me neither. My aircrew is on leave for a week. Who knows what happens from there, but we're due a little time in garrison."

"So are we," Tristan replied.

"I can't wait until we're all together again," Loki said.

"Me too," Tristan and Courtney replied in unison.

"Tristan," Loki said, turning a little more to look directly at her.

"Yes," she answered with a smile.

"I think I'm ready to call you Mom. Is that okay?"

"Yeah." She smiled and nodded. "I think it's more than okay." She wrapped him in a hug to keep him from seeing the warm wet tears sliding down his cheeks.

"I love you both so much," Courtney said, wiping her own tears.

"I love you, too," Tristan said, holding the phone so she could see her.

*

Patty stood in the kitchen, wiping a small tear from her cheek. Her daughter's life had changed so drastically in only a few months, and she wouldn't change any of it. This really was a new beginning for all of them.

Epilogue

Courtney stepped out of the tent, inhaling the crisp, cool mountain air...and a very familiar coffee smell. She turned her head slightly, looking at the charred remains of the morning fire and the coffee kettle sitting on top of it, keeping warm. She moseyed over, carefully grabbing the kettle and filling her cup. She closed her eyes, taking a long whiff of the aroma before enjoying the first sip. Suddenly, she was right back in Colombia, standing on the flightline.

"It's good, isn't it?"

Tristan was standing a few feet away when she opened her eyes. "The coffee or the warmth?" She smiled.

"Are you cold?" Tristan asked, walking over to her.

"No. I was when I woke up alone. Where did you and Loki get off to?"

"We were both up early, so we went for a little hike. I taught him how to whittle a stick to spearfish for trout in case his fishing pole broke."

"Ah." Courtney nodded.

"It's nice being up here, teaching him the same things my grandfather taught me."

"It *is* beautiful here."

"*You're* beautiful," Tristan whispered, searching her eyes.

Courtney reached out with one hand while holding her mug in the other, and grabbed the front of Tristan's jacket, pulling her closer. Their lips met softly, lingering together.

"Mom!" Tristan yelled.

"Where is he?" Courtney questioned, suddenly worried.

"He's at the stream," Tristan said as she started walking around the other side of the tent. "Oh, geez," she muttered, slightly laughing.

"Please don't tell me we have to eat that for breakfast," Courtney said, seeing him standing at the edge holding a stick up with a fish flopping on it.

"I told you to wait until later."

"I'm sorry. I just wanted to try one time." Loki pulled his eyes to the ground as his chin dropped to his chest.

"I'm not mad, I just wish you would've listened better. We were going to catch fish for dinner, not breakfast."

"Oops."

"I'm proud of you for catching it though. Way to go! It only took one try?"

"Yep!" he exclaimed, back to being all smiles.

"Come on, let's skin it. You can have it for breakfast since you caught it."

"Count me out. I'll wait until dinner," Courtney said, sipping her coffee from a few feet away.

"Courtney, while you were sleeping, Mom showed me some bear tracks."

"What?" Courtney looked at Tristan with her brows raised.

"We saw a lot of different tracks. I was simply pointing each one out to him. Don't worry, they were nowhere near here."

"Uh huh."

Loki and Tristan went over to an old log they'd been using all weekend to skin and fillet their catch. At only five years old, he wasn't much help, but he was studying every move she made with the knife. When she was finished, he held out a piece of foil for her to put the fish meat in. Then, he sprinkled a little bit of lemon pepper seasoning on it and closed the foil up.

"Remember, poke the fire a few good times with a long stick to bring it back to life after you set the foil on the cooking grate."

"Okay." He smiled and took off to go cook his fish with his head held high and his chest puffed out.

"He's so cute," Courtney murmured as she walked back to the stream with Tristan, who was going to wash her hands.

"Yeah, I still can't believe he's been my son for almost four months."

"He's definitely right where he belongs. You are without a doubt two peas in a pod," Courtney laughed softly.

"There's room in that pod for a third," Tristan said, looking at her while she dried her hands on a rag.

"Funny you should say that," Courtney replied. "I put in a transfer request."

"What? Really?" Tristan muttered in surprise as her mouth curled into a smile. "Are you sure?"

Courtney nodded. "I spoke with my aircrew. I didn't want them to be blindsided, but it turns out they want to go with me. Maguire's wife found out recently that she's pregnant. She's from Raleigh, so she was very happy at the chance to be closer to her family. Howie pretty much goes with the flow."

"That's great, but it may not go through because we're not married," Tristan sighed.

"Are you getting married?" Loki said, confused as to what he'd overheard as he walked up, while putting them both on the spot.

423

"What do you think about that?" Tristan asked.

"Will that make you my mom, too?" he questioned, looking at Courtney.

"Uh...yes. Yes, it would," she said with a smile.

"Okay. I want you to get married."

Tristan looked at Loki, then at Courtney before bending down on one knee. "I don't have a ring, but this is something I've thought about a lot lately..." Loki tapped her on the shoulder, interrupting her. Tristan turned her head to see him handing her the circle he'd made from pine needles that he'd been twisting together all weekend. "Thanks," she whispered. Then, she held it out to Courtney as she continued. "What do you say to another new beginning? Will you marry me?"

"Yes!" Courtney said, dropping to her knees to kiss Tristan and pull her into a hug.

"This will have to do, until we have time to go shopping," Tristan said, sliding the pine needle ring onto her finger.

"I love it." She smiled brightly. They both reached out, pulling Loki into the hug with them.

"I love both of you," he said, wrapping his arms around them.

About the Author

Graysen Morgen is the bestselling author of several bestselling lesbian fiction titles. She was born and raised in North Florida with winding rivers and waterways at her back door, and white sandy beaches nearby. She has spent most of her lifetime in the sun and on the water. She enjoys reading, writing, fishing, watching her daughter play rugby, snowy vacations, and spending as much time as possible with her wife and their two children.

You can contact Graysen at graysenmorgen@aol.com; like her fan page on Facebook.com/graysenmorgen; follow her on Twitter: @graysenmorgen and Instagram: @graysenmorgen

Other Titles Available From
Triplicity Publishing

An Omega's Grief by Domina Alexandra. Bonnie's life is finally slowing down, but on a weekend getaway with her mate Rikki, things quickly turn sour when a human is killed right in front of them. Worse, Bonnie has a stalker with an unimaginable power, and if she doesn't confront this dangerous individual, it might cost her pack and friends their lives. With time against her, Bonnie will have to make her toughest decision yet.

Crossed Reins by Graysen Morgen. Barrel racing is Carly Rae Walsh's life, until it's ripped out from under her. With nothing to do and nothing to lose, she uses her years of horse whispering skills and intuition to train a troubled thoroughbred racehorse. Allison McKinley is a world class dressage rider who has stepped back from the spotlight to mourn the sudden death of her mother. The last thing she needs when she decides to start training again for competition, is her father's impulsive desire to own a racehorse, and his bizarre decision to choose a rodeo barrel racer as the trainer. The two women have nothing in common except horses, and even that's a stretch. Can they uncross the reins long enough to see what's happening between them?

Outside In by Breanna Hughes. Cali Evans is a survivor. Her life hasn't been easy, but her late father raised her to be smart, tough, and dependent only on herself and her wits. On the eve of her 21st birthday she meets Owen Bray - a beautiful and intriguing young doctor who equally frustrates and captivates Cali. That fateful meeting inspires Cali to make a better life for herself. The next day, hoping to make positive change, Cali hops a bus for the West Coast but never reaches her destination. Instead, she wakes up in an underground bunker with no recollection of how she got there. Upon her arrival, she learns that she's one of just forty survivors of a fast-spreading environmental toxin and that human life outside of the bunker has ceased to exist. Tired of the vague explanations and half-answers coming from the people in charge, Cali takes it upon herself to investigate the real reason why she's there and begins to uncover the sinister truth.

I Love You, Nora Whispered by Kathy L. Salt. Love in the time of horses and polio. England, 1948. Nora Lakes suffers from post Polio Syndrome and very low self-esteem. When her sister Martha manages to get her a job at Waterhouse Acre Stables, she can hardly believe it. She had never imagined that anyone would have employed her, damaged as she is. She also never imagined she would meet anybody like Katherine. Katherine Waterhouse was born with a silver spoon in her mouth. She has a mean streak and doesn't like people in general. What she does like, is horses. She wants to be a professional rider but growing up in a conservative house where her choices are limited by her sex, Katherine has always been trapped in her role as a woman. Nora and Katherine - two women with very different backgrounds, drawn to each other with an intensity neither of them is prepared for. Do they stand a chance?

Omega Rising by Domina Alexandra. A few months of peace. That was all Bonnie Collins was granted.

New trouble has surfaced and go figure, this trouble came with a new pair of claws. When an unknown pack comes to town, Bonnie is forced to make tough decisions that will influence her packs future. Things only get harder when her mate is taken, leaving Bonnie in charge of a pack who still doesn't trust her. With chaos all around, it will be exactly what Bonnie needs to finally embrace what she has become. An Omega Rising. Book 2 of the *Claimed Series*.

Loose Ends by Joan L. Anderson. After her estranged sister is killed when she falls onto the subway tracks in Paris just as a train arrives, Allison goes to Paris to deal with her sister's body and collect her things. But, after talking to the police about the accident and viewing the subway surveillance video, something seems odd about her death. When Allison's hotel room in Paris is broken into with only a few things taken, but not any money or credit cards, she begins to wonder if it really was an accident that killed her sister, or if it was murder. Once Allison returns to Washington, D.C. to handle her sister's affairs, she soon realizes that her sister had been living a secret life and wasn't the person she had always thought she was. As troubling things begin to happen to Allison in D.C., she starts wondering if she will be the next person to die.

Real Love by Graysen Morgen. Leigh Myer is a trauma nurse practitioner who is not happy going through the motions of her daily life. When a friend offers up her mountain cabin for a relaxing vacation, Leigh packs her bags. She's never been to the mountains and certainly never in heavy snow. A chance meeting with a fish and wildlife officer turns her idea of a quiet, relaxing vacation…upside down. Camden Gorely loves her job and loves the mountain she works and lives on even more. She's tired of having flings with vacationers who visit for days or weeks at a time, until she meets the elusive nurse from the city. Can Leigh stop running from her past and allow real love into her heart?

Enticed by Love by Lynn Lawler. Henrietta Bailey is a mysterious woman who has spent her entire life living in the town of Crescent, a sleepy beach community in central coastal California. She loves the beach, the ocean air, and the town itself. Her simple life fulfills her. However, she spends much of her time reminiscing about her long-lost love, a woman who left her devastated. Now, another woman awaits on the horizon; a wise, intelligent, and sexy lady who is sophisticated beyond her years. This woman yearns for her soul mate and lover. Will she be able to win Henrietta's heart, or will Henrietta be fated to live the rest of her days alone?

Love Undercover by Domina Alexandra. Remi Stone never expected to get the opportunity to work undercover for narcotics. But, when the chance arrives, she takes it. With drugs coursing through a high school, Remi has only until the end of the school year to find the suspects responsible. Undercover, Remi plays her role, moving one step further into the drug industry. She never thought she'd be moving one step closer to the woman who would change her life and take hold of her heart. There is just one issue. Remi Stone is undercover as an eighteen-year-old high school senior. And the woman she can't seem to ignore is her History teacher. There will be a lot of challenges along the way, including one that could cost Remi her life and her heart.

Playing the Game by Graysen Morgen. Randi Rojas is a professional soccer player who seemingly has it all, a successful career, a long-term girlfriend, a loving family, and a great group of friends...until a chance meeting with an attractive woman sends her way offside, and into a whole new game. Berkley Ward lives her life to the extreme, spending her days either in the gym or four-wheeling in the woods, and her nights patrolling the streets as an officer. Affairs with taken women are easy, but after years of playing games, she's finished...until she meets a beautiful woman and a game she can't resist. Both women play a dangerously seductive game of cat and mouse, teetering on the edge of friendship and affair.

Rebel Sweetheart by Sydney Canyon. When a headstrong, country music superstar starts getting threatening letters while on tour, her manager has no other choice but to hire someone to investigate the threats and keep her safe. Haley Nielsen is as stubborn as it gets. She does things her way, and her way only. The last thing she needs or wants is a babysitter following her every move and controlling everything she does. Shane Crowley isn't your typical private investigator, or bodyguard, for that matter. She's a former U.S. Deputy Marshal with a lot of experience, and an all or nothing attitude. Tempers flare and the energy burns red hot between the two women as they spend weeks together cooped up on Haley's tour bus, traveling the country. Will they stop resisting each other long enough to see eye to eye? Or will the letter writer make good on his threats?

A Tale of Spiders and Canned Soup by Kathy L. Salt. Living on your own can be hard, but even more so when you're dealing with haphephobia; the death of a twin sister; and a crush on your teacher. Mika is still in contact with her foster family who homes the loves of her life, three young children she would do anything for, when she begins attending University of Aberdeen and meets Pauline, an Australian that teaches Viking history. Neither woman is used to breaking the rules, and their way to each other is a hard one, especially when Mika vows to get custody of the children, whether she is ready to be a parent or not. *A story about growing up. A story about dealing with grief. A story about Mika and Pauline.*

A Night Claimed by Domina Alexandra. Bonnie Collins had plans. And being a werewolf wasn't one of them. Attacked by a rogue who was out to claim her and facing what she now has no choice of becoming, Bonnie can't let go of her human life as a Paramedic. The last thing Bonnie needs is more challenges. However, Rikki, the Alpha of Mill City will be just that. Finding her to be possessive and ruling, Bonnie begins challenging the Alpha's every breath. Finding out her attack was no accident only makes her more angry at the situation. A group of rogues are out to get her. With no clue why, Bonnie has no choice but to seek help from the alluring Alpha and her pack, accepting the new world she was forced into.

Stunted by Breanna Hughes. Professional stuntwoman Jessie Knight takes her job very seriously and although she works in the entertainment industry, she has zero desire for fame or notoriety. She also has a very strict no-dating policy when it comes to coworkers. That is, until she meets famous actress Elliot Chase on the set of her new film. The adrenaline rush of the stunts is nothing compared to the sparks that fly between them. After a passionate night together, a sex tape is leaked that sends Jessie and Elliot's private and professional lives into a spiral. Will the fallout be too much for them to last? Or will they find a way out of the mess together?

Mission Compromised by Graysen Morgen. Natalia Moreno is thrilled when she arrives in Fiji for a relaxing vacation. However, she soon discovers the overwater bungalow she's staying in has been double booked for the entire stay, and the resort is full. Annoyed and frustrated, she has no other choice but to share her hut with a stranger. Christian Garnier is sent to Fiji for what she refers to as a working vacation, until she finds out she has an ornery roommate for the next two weeks who is dead set on making her job twice as hard. Soon, all hell breaks loose, and the two women are sent around the world on a wild goose chase.

Stargazing by Kathy L. Salt. Lissa stared openmouthed at the GIF that played over and over on the screen in front of her. Heat flushed to her face, igniting her skin. Her heart started pounding in her chest. *Stupid internet, it should really come with a warning label.* She's never been interested in relationships or sex and as the years have gone by she has retreated more and more into her work. Everything changes when she meets Star, a porn actress with a heart of gold and a troubled childhood. *They say that opposites attract, but how much of that is true? What* *chance do they have when one of them is a virgin and the other one star in pornography?*

I Belong with Her by Domina Alexandra. Tajel Pierce loves the thrill of being a paramedic. Every call she goes on gives her a rush. She makes no time for a personal life. No one can ruin her love for her career. Then there is Arianna Castaldi, who just transferred to her new paramedic position in a whole new state. All she needs is a new start without any distractions. Arianna and Tajel's relationship doesn't start off perfect. Embarrassed of the one-night stand Arianna believes she had with Tajel, she wants to pretend they never met and make their relationship strictly business. The only choice they have to keep from strangling each other is to go from denying their feelings to accepting them as they work through intense 911 calls.

Awakened by Fate by Lynn Lawler. Jackie is a woman living life according to her own rules. She's married, but it's the unspoken, open kind. She can have as many female lovers as she likes; she just can't talk about them. After a bizarre encounter turns her world upside down, things slowly begin to change. She finds herself in desperation as she searches for answers. What she discovers is nothing is delivered in a neatly wrapped box. Now that everything has been brought out into the open, she finds she can't run away from her truth anymore. With her new life, comes new responsibilities and a different outcome than what she was expecting. Jackie isn't alone in the story. She meets several new people who help her along her journey.

Nautical Delights by S. L. Gape. Lady Elizabeth Barrington has spent her entire life trying to please her family; constantly opting for a quiet life, she utilises her profession as a doctor to keep out of her families' clutches; bar the annual two-week Caribbean private cruise, where there is simply no budge. Confined to two weeks on board the Iconica super yacht, she intends on keeping her head down and enjoying as much of the holiday as she can, whilst keeping her family at arm's length. Until a crew member catches her eye.

Worlds Apart by S.L. Gape. Hollywood A-lister Heidi Spencer-Brady is everything you'd expect of an Idol. Loved by all, the British Beauty is graceful, talented, humble and so far removed from the 'typical' LA scene. When her husband's infidelity with his new 'leading lady' is leaked, Dawn, Heidi's best friend and manager, goes all out to protect her. She arranges for Heidi to go back to the UK and stay on her cousins farm they had visited as children, much to the disappointment of the animal fearing Heidi.

Castor Valley (Law & Order Series Book 2) by Graysen Morgen. Jessie Henry is torn when she reads about the capture of the Doyle brothers, two young men who were part of her old gang. Unable to let them hang for a crime she's sure they didn't commit, Jessie leaves her wife and the Town of Boone Creek behind and sets out on a journey back to the one place she thought she'd never see again, *Castor Valley*. Ellie Henry watches the love of her life leave, not knowing if she will ever return. When she gets an odd telegram, nearly a week later, she fears Jessie is in trouble. With no other choice, she goes to the one person who can help her.

Fight to the Top by S. L. Gape. Georgia is a forty-year-old, single, Area Director from Manchester, UK who is all work and definitely no play. Having no time to socialise or spend time with her family she prides herself on being fit and well-polished. Erika is an Area Director for the same company, but in the United States. Whilst she is concentrating so heavily on the promotion she has been fighting for, she's starting to feel like her life outside of work is falling apart. The two women are exceptionally different, and worlds apart. Both of their lives are turned upside down when their jobs are snatched from under their noses, and they are suddenly faced with being thrown together by their bosses for one last major project...in Texas.

Boone Creek (Law & Order Series book 1) by Graysen Morgen. Jessie Henry is looking for a new life. She's unknown in the town of Boone Creek when she arrives and wants to keep it that way. When she's offered the job of Town Marshal, she takes it, believing that protecting others and upholding the law is the penance for her past. Ellie Fray is a widowed, shopkeeper. She generally keeps to herself, but the mysterious new Town Marshal both intrigues and infuriates her. She believes the last thing the town needs is someone stirring up trouble with the outlaws who have taken over.

Witness by Joan L. Anderson. Becca and Kate have lived together for eight years and have always spent their vacation in a tropical paradise, lying on a beach. This year,

Becca wanted to try something different: a seven day, 65-mile hike in the beautiful Cascade Mountains of Washington state. Their peaceful vacation turns to horror when they stumble upon a brutal murder taking place in the back country.

Too Soon by S.L. Gape. Brooke is a twenty-nine-year-old detective from Oxford, who has her life pretty much planned out until her boss and partner of nine years, Maria, tells her their relationship is over. When Brooke finds out the truth, that Maria cheated on her with their best friend Paula, she decides to get her life back on track by getting away for six weeks in Anglesey, North Wales. Chloe, a thirty-three-year-old artist and art director, owns a log cabin on Anglesey where she spends each weekend painting and surfing. After returning from a surf, she stumbles upon the somewhat uptight and enigmatic Brooke.

Never Quit (Never Series book 2) by Graysen Morgen. Two years after stepping away from the action as a Coast Guard Rescue Swimmer to become an instructor, Finley finds herself in charge of the most difficult class of cadets she's ever faced, while also juggling the taxing demands of having a home life with her partner Nicole, and their fifteen-year-old daughter. Jordy Ross gave up everything, dropping out of college, and leaving her family behind, to join the Coast Guard and become a rescue swimmer cadet. The extreme training tests her fitness level, pushing her mentally and physically further than she's ever been in her life, but it's the aggressive competition between her and another female cadet that proves to be the most challenging.

Never Let Go (Never Series book 1) by Graysen Morgen. For Coast Guard Rescue Swimmer, Finley Morris, life is good. She loves her job, is well respected by her peers, and has been given an opportunity to take her career to the next level. The only thing missing is the love of her life, who walked out, taking their daughter with her, seven years earlier. When Finley gets a call from her ex, saying their teenage daughter is coming to spend the summer with her, she's floored. While spending more time with her daughter, whom she doesn't get to see often, and learning to be a full-time parent, Finley quickly realizes she has not, and will never, let go of what is important.

Pursuit by Joan L. Anderson. Claire is a workaholic attorney who flies to Paris to lick her wounds after being dumped by her girlfriend of seventeen years. On the plane she chats with the young woman sitting next to her, and when they land the woman is inexplicably detained in Customs. Claire is surprised when she later runs into the woman in the city. They agree to meet for breakfast the next morning, but when the woman doesn't show up Claire goes to her hotel and makes a horrifying discovery. She soon finds herself ensnared in a web of intrigue and international terrorism, becoming the target of a high stakes game of cat and mouse through the streets of Paris.

Wrecked by Sydney Canyon. To most people, the *Duchess* is a myth formed by old pirate's tales, but to Reid Cavanaugh, a Caribbean island bum and one of the best divers and treasure hunters in the world, it's a real, seventeenth century pirate ship—the holy grail of underwater treasure hunting. Reid uses the same cunning tactics she always has before setting out to find the lost ship. However, she is forced to bring her business partner's daughter along as collateral this time because he doesn't trust her. Neither woman is thrilled but being cooped up on a small dive boat for days forces them to get know each other quickly.

Arson by Austen Thorne. Madison Drake is a detective for the Stetson Beach Police Department. The last thing she wants to do is show a new detective the ropes, especially when a fire investigation becomes arson to cover up a murder. Madison butts heads with Tara, her trainee, deals with sarcasm from Nic, her ex-girlfriend who is a patrol officer, and finds calm in the chaos of police work with Jamie, her best friend who is the county medical examiner. Arson is the first of many in a series of novella episodes surrounding the fictional Stetson Beach Police Department and Detective Madison Drake.

Mommies (Bridal Series book 3) by Graysen Morgen. Britton and her wife Daphne have been married for a year and a half and are happy with their life, until Britton's mother hounds her to find out why her sister Bridget hasn't decided to have children yet. This prompts Daphne to bring up the big subject of having kids of their own with Britton. Britton hadn't really thought much about having kids, but her love for Daphne makes her see life and their future together in a whole new way when they decide to become mommies.

Rapture & Rogue by Sydney Canyon. Taren Rauley is happy and in a good relationship, until the one person she thought she'd never see again comes back into her life. She struggles to keep the past from colliding with the present as old feelings she thought were dead and gone, begin to haunt her. In college, Gianna Revisi was a mastermind, ring-leading, crime boss. Now, she has a great life and spends her time running Rapture and Rogue, the two establishments she built from the ground up. The last person she ever expects to see walk into one of them, is the girl who walked out on her, breaking her heart five years ago.

Second Chance by Sydney Canyon. After an attack on her convoy, Marine Corps Staff Sergeant, Darien Hollister, must learn to live without her sight. When an experimental procedure allows her to see again, Darien is torn, knowing someone had to die in order for this to happen. She embarks on a journey to personally thank the donor's family but is too stunned to tell them the truth. Mixed emotions stir inside of her as she slowly gets to the know the people that feel like so much more than strangers to her. When the truth finally comes out, Darien walks away, taking the second chance that she's been given to go back to the only life she's ever known, but she's not the only one with a second chance at life.

Meant to Be by Graysen Morgen. Brandt is about to walk down the aisle with her girlfriend, when an unexpected chain of events turns her world upside down, causing her to question the last three years of her life. A chance encounter sparks a mix of rage and excitement that she has never felt before. Summer is living life and following her dreams, all the while, harboring a huge secret that could ruin her career. She believes that some things are better kept in the dark, until she has her third run-in with a woman she had hoped to never see again, and gives into temptation. Brandt and Summer start believing everything happens for a reason as they learn the true meaning of meant to be.

Coming Home by Graysen Morgen. After tragedy derails TJ Abernathy's life, she packs up her three-year-old son and heads back to Pennsylvania to live with her grandmother on the family farm. TJ picks back up where she left off eight years earlier, tending to the fruit and nut tree orchard, while learning her grandmother's secret trade. Soon, TJ's high school sweetheart and the same girl who broke her heart, comes back into her life, threatening to steal it away once again. As the weeks turn into months and tragedy strikes again, TJ realizes coming home was the best thing she could've ever done.

Special Assignment by Austen Thorne. Secret Service Agent Parker Meeks has her hands full when she gets her new assignment, protecting a Congressman's teenage daughter, who has had threats made on her life and been whisked away to a Christian boarding school under an alias to finish out her senior year. Parker is fine with the assignment, until she finds out she has to go undercover as a Canon Priest. The last thing Parker expects to find is a beautiful, art history teacher, who is intrigued by her in more ways than one.

Miracle at Christmas by Sydney Canyon. A Modern Twist on the Classic Scrooge Story. Dylan is a power-hungry lawyer who pushed away everything good in her life to become the best defense attorney in the, often winning the worst cases and keeping anyone with enough money out of jail. She's visited on Christmas Eve by her deceased law partner, who threatens her with a life in hell like his own, if she doesn't change her path. During the course of the night, she is taken on a journey through her past, present, and future with three very different spirits.

Bella Vita by Sydney Canyon. Brady is the First Officer of the crew on the Bella Vita, a luxury charter yacht in the Caribbean. She enjoys the laidback island lifestyle, and is accustomed to high profile guests, but when a U.S. Senator charters the yacht as a gift to his beautiful twin daughters who have just graduated from college and a few of their friends, she literally has her hands full.

Brides (Bridal Series book 2) by Graysen Morgen. Britton Prescott is dating the love of her life, Daphne Attwood, after a few tumultuous events that happened to unravel at her sister's wedding reception, seven months earlier. She's happy with the way things are, but immense pressure from her family and friends to take the next step, nearly sends her back to the single life. The idea of a long engagement and simple wedding are thrown out the window, as both families take over, rushing Britton and Daphne to the altar in a matter of weeks.

Cypress Lake by Graysen Morgen. The small town of Cypress Lake is rocked when one murder after another happens. Dani Ricketts, the Chief Deputy for the Cypress Lake Sheriff's Office, realizes the murders are linked. She's surprised when the girl that broke her heart in high school has not only returned home, but she's also Dani's only suspect. Kristen Malone has come back to Cypress Lake to put the past behind her so that she can move on with her life. Seeing Dani Ricketts again throws her off-guard, nearly derailing her plans to finally rid herself and her family of Cypress Lake.

Crashing Waves by Graysen Morgen. After a tragic accident, Pro Surfer, Rory Eden, spends her days hiding in the surf and snowboard manufacturing company that she built from the ground up, while living her life as a shell of the person that she once was. Rory's world is turned upside when a young surfer pursues her, asking for the one thing she can't do. Adler Troy and Dr. Cason Macauley from Graysen Morgen's bestselling novel: *Falling Snow*, make an appearance in this romantic adventure about life, love, and letting go.

Bridesmaid of Honor (Bridal Series book 1) by Graysen Morgen. Britton Prescott's best friend is getting married and she's the maid of honor. As if that isn't enough to deal with, Britton's sister announces she's getting married in the same month and her maid of honor is her best friend Daphne, the same woman who has tormented Britton for years. Britton has to suck it up and play nice, instead of scratching her eyes out, because she and Daphne are in both weddings. Everyone is counting on them to behave like adults.

Falling Snow by Graysen Morgen. Dr. Cason Macauley, a high-speed trauma surgeon from Denver meets Adler Troy, a professional snowboarder, and sparks fly. The last thing Cason wants is a relationship and Adler doesn't realize what's right in front of her until it's gone, but will it be too late?

Fate vs. Destiny by Graysen Morgen. Logan Greer devotes her life to investigating plane crashes for the National Transportation Safety Board. Brooke McCabe is an investigator with the Federal Aviation Association who literally flies by the seat of her pants. When Logan gets tangled in head games with both women will she choose fate or destiny?

Just Me by Graysen Morgen. Wild child Ian Wiley has to grow up and take the reins of the hundred-year-old family business when tragedy strikes. Cassidy Harland is a little surprised that she came within an inch of picking up a gorgeous stranger in a bar and is shocked to find out that stranger is the new head of her company.

Love Loss Revenge by Graysen Morgen. Rian Casey is an FBI Agent working the biggest case of her career and madly in love with her girlfriend. Her world is turned upside when tragedy strikes. Heartbroken, she tries to rebuild her life. When she discovers the truth behind what really happened that awful night, she decides justice isn't good enough, and vows revenge on everyone involved.

Natural Instinct by Graysen Morgen. Chandler Scott is a Marine Biologist who keeps her private life private. Corey Joslen is intrigued by Chandler from the moment she meets her. Chandler is forced to finally open her life up to Corey. It backfires in Corey's face and sends her running. Will either woman learn to trust her natural instinct?

Secluded Heart by Graysen Morgen. Chase Leery is an overworked cardiac surgeon with a group of best friends that have an opinion and a reason for everything. When she meets a new artist named Remy Sheridan at her best friend's art gallery she is captivated by the reclusive woman. When Chase finds out why Remy is so sheltered will she put her career on the line to help her or is it too difficult to love someone with a secluded heart?

In Love, at War by Graysen Morgen. Charley Hayes is in the Army Air Force and stationed at Ford Island in Pearl Harbor. She is the commanding officer of her own female-only service squadron and doing the one thing she loves most, repairing airplanes. Life is good for Charley, until the day she finds herself falling in love while fighting for her life as her country is thrown haphazardly into World War II. Can she survive being in love and at war?

Fast Pitch by Graysen Morgen. Graham Cahill is a senior in college and the catcher and captain of the softball team. Despite being an all-star pitcher, Bailey Michaels is young and arrogant. Graham and Bailey are forced to get to know each other off the field in order to learn to work together on the field. Will the extra time pay off or will it drive a nail through the team?

Submerged by Graysen Morgen. Assistant District Attorney Layne Carmichael had no idea that the sexy woman she took home from a local bar for a one-night stand would turn out to be someone she would be prosecuting months later. Scooter is a Naval Officer on a submarine who changes women like she changes uniforms. When she is accused of a heinous crime, she is shocked to see her latest conquest sitting across from her as the prosecuting attorney.

Vow of Solitude by Austen Thorne. Detective Jordan Denali is in a fight for her life against the ghosts from her past and a Serial Killer taunting her with his every move. She lives a life of solitude and plans to keep it that way. When Callie Marceau, a curious Medical Examiner, decides she wants in on the biggest case of her career, as well as Jordan's life, Jordan is powerless to stop her.

Igniting Temptation by Sydney Canyon. Mackenzie Trotter is the Head of Pediatrics at the local hospital. Her life takes a rather unexpected turn when she meets a flirtatious, beautiful fire fighter. Both women soon discover it doesn't take much to ignite temptation.

One Night by Sydney Canyon. While on a business trip, Caylen Jarrett spends an amazing night with a beautiful stripper. Months later, she is shocked and confused when that same woman re-enters her life. The fact that this stranger could destroy her career doesn't bother her. C.J. is more terrified of the feelings this woman stirs in her. Could she have fallen in love in one night and not even known it?

Fine by Sydney Canyon. Collin Anderson hides behind a façade, pretending everything is fine. Her workaholic wife and best friend are both oblivious as she goes on an emotional journey, battling a potentially hereditary disease that her mother has been diagnosed with. The only person who knows what is really going on, is Collin's doctor. The same doctor, who is an acquaintance that she's always been attracted to, and who has a partner of her own.

Shadow's Eyes by Sydney Canyon. Tyler McCain is the owner of a large ranch that breeds and sells different types of horses. She isn't exactly thrilled when a Hollywood movie producer shows up wanting to film his latest movie on her property. Reegan Delsol is an up-and-coming actress who has everything going for her when she lands the lead role in a new film, but there one small problem that could blow the entire picture.

Light Reading: A Collection of Novellas by Sydney Canyon. Four of Sydney Canyon's novellas together in one book, including the bestsellers Shadow's Eyes and One Night.

Visit us at www.tri-pub.com

Made in the USA
Columbia, SC
14 July 2022

63464562R00271